AUG   2006

The Bird Woman

Also by Kerry Hardie

FICTION

A Winter Marriage

POETRY

A Furious Place
Cry for the Hot Belly
The Sky Didn't Fall
The Silence Came Close

The Bird Woman

A Novel

Kerry Hardie

Little, Brown and Company

NEW YORK   BOSTON

Copyright © 2006 by Kerry Hardie

All rights reserved. No part of this book may be reproduced in any form or
by any electronic or mechanical means, including information storage
and retrieval systems, without permission in writing from the publisher,
except by a reviewer who may quote brief passages in a review.

Little, Brown and Company
Hachette Book Group USA
1271 Avenue of the Americas
New York, NY 10020

Visit our Web site at www.HachetteBookGroupUSA.com

FIRST EDITION: August 2006

The characters and events in this book are fictitious. Any similarity to real persons,
living or dead, is coincidental and not intended by the author.

The author is grateful for permission to include the excerpt from the following
previously copyrighted material: *The Gift Healers*. Reprinted by permission of
Anne Walsh and Clodagh Gleeson. First published by Brandon Press in 1995.

Library of Congress Cataloging-in-Publication Data
Hardie, Kerry.
    The bird woman : a novel / Kerry Hardie. — 1st. ed.
        p.   cm.
    ISBN-10: 0-316-07623-6
    ISBN-13: 978-0-316-07623-4
    1. Clairvoyants — Fiction.   2. Women healers — Fiction.   3. Presbyterian
women — Fiction.   4. Mothers and daughters — Fiction.   5. Terminally ill
parents — Fiction.   6. Parent and adult child — Fiction.   7. Northern
Ireland — Fiction.   8. Ireland — Fiction.   I. Title.
PR6058.A622B57   2006
823'.914 — dc22   2005026605

10 9 8 7 6 5 4 3 2 1

Q-MART

Interior design by Nancy Singer Olaguera, ISPN Publishing Services

Printed in the United States of America

For Sean, who walked with me
every step of the way

—⦿⦿⦿—

Every year in Ireland about twenty thousand people go to healers . . . looking for cures for an extraordinary range of things: burns, brucellosis, skin cancer, bleeding. And many claim to be cured.

[These healers are not] chiropractors or homeopaths or that whole section of alternative medicine: those who have developed unorthodox skills and knowledge to put at the service of the sick. . . . They claim neither special training, knowledge, nor skills, but a gift passed from God. Or from nature. Or from inheritance. Or passed on from someone else. Ultimately they do not know whence the gift comes. . . .

They are not faith healers either. An infant who heals can hardly be said to have faith. . . . Faith healers rely . . . on prayer and faith: these do not. The phenomenon of these healers is comparable to water diviners in that they use a gift that nobody can begin to understand, yet many avail of. . . .

The more you know of these gift healers the more baffled you become. No one seems able to offer an explanation for their extraordinary abilities. . . . The more baffling this mystery grows, the more fascinating it becomes. "There are more things in heaven and earth, Horatio, than are dreamt of in your philosophy."

—FROM *The Gift Healers* BY REBECCA MILLANE,
BRANDON PRESS 1995

The Bird Woman

Prologue

*S*ometimes life goes on at an even pace for months, years, the rhythm the same, one step following after the step before, so you get to thinking that it's always going to be this way, and maybe part of you even longs for something to change.

Then all of a sudden it does. And when it does, it doesn't change only the once. The first change comes, then the next, and before you know it the changes are at you so thick and fast that you're running as hard as you can and still you're not keeping up.

The phone call came from Derry, and everything changed. My brother, Brian, rang, only he didn't — he got his wife, Anne, to phone for him. I listened until I'd got the gist; then I made her go and get Brian.

"I'm not being uncivil," I told Anne. "But it's his mother we're talking about, not yours. Some things even Brian has to do for himself."

I heard Anne put down the phone; then I heard footsteps and voices off, then footsteps again and the phone being lifted.

"Yes, Ellen," Brian's voice said down the line.

It was strange hearing Brian. If you'd asked me I'd have said I'd forgotten what his voice even sounded like, but the minute I heard it I knew every nuance and inflection — I even knew what his face looked like as he talked.

Only I didn't. It was more than ten years since I'd laid eyes on Brian; he might be fat and bald for all I knew, he might have grey hair and reading glasses, he might have three toes missing from his right foot or no right foot at all.

But if he did, all that was in the future. For the moment I spoke to the brother who lived in my mind.

"Cancer," I said to Liam, the word sounding strange, as though I was being needlessly melodramatic. "It seems she had a mastectomy two years ago, but she wouldn't let them tell me. This is a secondary — something called 'metastatic liver cancer.' They're talking containment, not cure."

Liam stirred in his chair, but he didn't speak; he waited for me to go on.

"Brian said she's been living with them for the last two months. Anne's off work, and the Macmillan nurse has been calling in. She took bad four nights ago, and now she's in the hospital. They told him she might have as much as two months, but more likely it'll be weeks. . . . No one's mentioned sending her home."

We had ordered the children next door to do their homework, had banished them, unfed, and with no explanation. They were too surprised to object. Now Liam was searching my face, but I kept it blank and calm. Liam had never been to Derry, had never met any of my family; my life up there predated him and belonged entirely to me.

There was power in that and also safety: I could dispense information as I felt inclined, could tell him or withhold from him, I didn't have to let him see what I didn't want seen.

So I talked on, my voice as flat and dead as my face, and I knew as clear as I knew anything that keeping him shut out like this was dangerous and wrong. But I was a long way off from myself, and I couldn't get back. I didn't want to get back; I was too afraid of what might be there waiting for me if I did.

4

"How many hours' drive to Derry?" Liam asked. "Five? Six? We'll bring the children. When do you want us to leave?"

"I don't."

"Wait till she's nearer the end? You'd be taking a bit of a chance, wouldn't you? But if you want to be there when she dies. . . ?"

"You're not listening to me, Liam," I said. "I'm not going. Not now, not next week, not next month, never. And neither are they."

"Ellen, she's your mother, you have to go —"

"Have to? Who says? Why do I have to?" So much for flat and dead — I could hear the hysteria rise in my voice.

"Because you'll regret it for the rest of your life if you don't."

Liam's mother had died of a stroke when Andrew was not quite two and I was heavy with Suzanna. It was a long vigil, and they were all there — her husband, children, grandchildren; her brothers and her only sister. I wasn't. Liam had said I was better off at home; he said everyone would understand. But I hadn't stayed away on my own account, I'd stayed away for Maura herself. I'd liked Maura; she was a big-boned, overweight countrywoman, red-faced and dowdy, with wonderful deep, warm eyes. She was devout, too — Liam was anxious when he brought me there first, for all that he swore to me he wasn't. But she'd never said a word about my not being Catholic, or our not being married, or Andrew not being christened, not a word. Maybe she'd felt for me because I was a stranger, or maybe she'd liked me as I'd liked her. Whatever it was, she'd always taken my part.

Liam had thought it the best of deaths, but I hadn't. I wouldn't want to die like that myself, everyone pressing and watching, I'd want a bit of privacy and peace. So I'd cast around for something to do for her, and staying away was all I'd been able to think of.

But that was Maura. It wasn't why I wouldn't go North to see my own mother.

"It's the last chance we'll have to set things right," he told me now. "She'll see her grandchildren before she dies."

5

I sat there, my belly full of this cold emptiness, waiting for the surge of anger that would protect me from despair. It didn't come. Instead I felt tears rising up in me, and I pushed them down. I looked for the thing that comes through me and into my hands, but it wasn't there; my body felt only numbness and exhaustion. I stood up and crossed to the sink, ran cold water into it, fetched potatoes from the larder, the tears running soundlessly down my face. Liam got up from his seat and tried to hold me, but I pushed him away.

"I have to make the dinner," I said.

"Dinner can wait. Leave that, Ellen. Sit down; we have to talk."

"Talk? What for? What's there to say? She's my mother, this is my business, not yours. But I can't stop you going if that's what you want. Do what you want — you will, anyway — but I'm not going and neither are they, and that's flat." I dumped the potatoes into the water and covered my face with my hands. My whole body shook with those great gulping sobs I thought I'd left behind me in some childhood drawer with the ankle socks.

Liam had the wit to sit himself down again and wait. Gradually the heaving died down, but the tears still came; they slid under my hands and ran down my wrists and soaked themselves into my sleeves. At last I wiped my eyes with the back of my hand, blew my nose in a tea towel, and turned to face him.

"I know she's my mother, you don't have to keep saying it," I said. "But I don't want to see her again. And I never want to forgive her. Never, ever, ever, Liam. That's what I'm saying, and that's what I mean."

"Why?"

I stared.

He stared back, waiting.

"You know well why," I said slowly.

"No," he said, "you're wrong, I don't know. I know you don't like her. But I don't know what she did to you to deserve the way you feel."

I couldn't speak.

"What did she do to you that's so bad, Ellen, tell me that? Not come to our wedding? I wrote to ask her — you didn't. It was obvious you didn't want her there."

"She never came to see the children —"

"You'd have shut the door in her face if she had —"

I put my hands over my ears like a child.

"She made me what I am."

That silenced him. It silenced me as well. I turned my back and started in on the potatoes, the tears running down my face again — yet again — and dripping into the muddy water. Sometimes I don't know what I'd do without domestic tasks. The simple, ancient rhythm of them. I'd no idea I felt like this, no idea it ran this deep.

I heard the door open, but I kept my head well down, I was bent over the sink, scraping away, the tears still dripping.

"Daddy," came Suzanna's voice, cool as you please, from somewhere to the left of me. "Daddy, why is Mammy crying again?"

"O where hae ye been, Lord Randal, my son
   O where hae ye been, my handsome young man?"

"I hae been to the Wildwood; mother, make my bed soon,
   For I'm weary wi' hunting, and fain wald lie down."

I sit at the table and say it aloud. It's a poem I learned at school — years and years ago in Derry, when I still called it Londonderry, when I still knew who I was.

It's a ballad, very old, about a young, strong man who goes out hunting with his hounds and comes home sick and dying. His mother keeps tormenting him — where's he been, what's he eaten, where's his hounds? All these questions.

 Addison Public Library
Addison, Illinois 60101

"O they swell'd and they died; mother, make my bed soon. . . ."

His true love has poisoned him, see. His hounds have died, and you know rightly that's what's about to happen to him too. His mother can't save him, no one can, for he's been to the Wildwood, a place I know well.

Liam found me in the Wildwood. He picked me up, lifted me onto his horse, carried me clean away. In the early years, whenever I was so homesick for the North that I was certain sure I couldn't thole it down here for another minute, I'd hear the words in my head and something would change. It always worked.

And later on, whenever I was fed up with Liam, or out of sorts with my life, I'd think of the Wildwood and how he saved me from it, and I'd calm down.

Missing somewhere may not only be about wanting to be there, it may be a bone-deep need for the voices and the ways you were reared to, even when you know well how lonely they'd make you now. Lonely with that special, sharp loneliness that comes when you've got what you longed for and it isn't enough anymore — it isn't ever going to be enough again.

And that's what's ahead of me now. The bag's packed, the alarm's set, but I'm walking the night house, sleepless. And when I'm not walking I'm sitting here all alone.

All alone, and trying to frighten myself into remembering how Liam saved me, to frighten myself into being so grateful again that I'll forgive him for what he's done. I try, but it doesn't work. The kitchen doesn't work either, though I love the kitchen at night — its lit quietness, the floor washed, the work done, everything red up and put away. But the kitchen is different; everything's different and so far away from itself it might not ever get back.

I go upstairs again, past our shut door, with Liam sleeping behind it. I want to shake him awake, but what's the use? Liam awake won't

Addison Public Library
Addison, Illinois 60101

bring me sleep, and I'm sick of hearing my own voice saying the same things over and over.

Suzanna's door's next. I go in and watch her, flat on her back, her duvet pulled into a scrumpled nest all around her. You could dance a jig on Suzanna and she'd only stretch and maybe smile and wriggle back down into sleep. She's eight years old, full up with herself, her own child. She has Liam's soft brown curls all round her head, and it's her will against mine.

I stand at the half-open door of Andrew's room, but I don't go in, for the slightest movement wakes him. Andrew is different — so different you'd nearly think him Robbie's child and nothing to do with Liam at all. But Robbie's child was a girl, and she slid from out of me way before her time. I held her in my hand — all the size of her — and I called her Barbara Allen, after the song. Then the ambulance came and they put me on a stretcher and one of the ambulance men took her, he said he would mind her for me, but he lied, for I never saw poor wee Barbara Allen again. That was the day I saw Jacko Brennan die in a bomb a full month before it happened. Then they put me into the hospital and they filled me up with drugs to keep the Wildwood away.

Chapter 1

The first time ever I saw Liam he was standing at the bar of Hartley's in Belfast. I was married to Robbie then — I'd been married to Robbie for near on four years for all I was only twenty-three. I was married and that was that; I'd no more thought of going off with anyone else than of dandering down to the travel agents and booking myself a nice wee holiday on the moon.

I was to meet Robbie around eight, along with a bunch of his drinking friends that he'd known from way back. I walked in, and the minute I saw Robbie I knew from the cut of him that he hadn't just strolled through the door. Stan and Rita were there, they were sitting at a table along with a couple more of our crowd, plus a black-haired girl with a widow's peak whom I'd never laid eyes on before. She was wearing jeans and a sweater, and she hadn't a scrap of makeup on her, though it was Friday night and there wasn't another woman in the place without heels and lipstick and mascara. She wasn't talking to anyone, and no one was talking to her.

Robbie was up at the bar buying a round, and he called me over.

"Mike phoned," he told me. "Christine started early. He's away up to the hospital to hold her hand —"

"I thought she wasn't due for another month?"

"So did she. But she got ahead of herself, and nothing would do her but she had to have Mike. I told them a bit of a story at work, and they're not expecting me back till sometime next week. I'm covering for Mike while he's otherwise occupied, I've been round at the gallery all afternoon.

"This is Liam," he added. I looked up at this tall, thickset man with brown curly hair and grey eyes. "He's from Dublin, so he is. He's up here about a show in the Arts Council Gallery."

Robbie was an electrician with a firm on the Lisburn Road, but he did nixers on the side whenever they came his way. His mate Mike did the lighting for the Arts Council Gallery, and he made sure to always ask Robbie when he needed an extra hand.

"Robbie's been great," Liam said. "We've been sorting out what we'll need for the show —"

Robbie nodded, but he didn't say anything. I knew right away he didn't like this Liam. Then the drinks came and more chairs were fetched across, and when everyone finally settled down again, there I was, beside Liam.

Liam was introduced all round and so was the black-haired one in the jeans, whose name, it seemed, was Noreen. Liam told us he was a sculptor, and your woman Noreen was a potter from Cork and something called the Crafts Council of Ireland was organising a group exhibition in the North in November. They were up here in Belfast, he said, to look at the "space."

No one was listening; none of us cared. I saw Stan look at Robbie, and his eyes closed down from inside, plus that wicked wee pulse that means he's up to something was showing beside his mouth. After that, I knew not to bother my head with them; that look of Stan's meant Liam and Noreen wouldn't be with us for long.

Stan wouldn't be one for socialising with those from the other persuasion. Especially not when they came from the South.

Liam gave me a cigarette. I was only a few weeks out of the hospital and still smoking like a chimney. He brought out a lighter and stuck it under my nose and flicked it. It didn't light. He looked at it, surprised, then shook it and tried it again, but still it didn't light. I remember being surprised that he was surprised by his lighter not lighting; I mean, it isn't exactly unusual — lighters are always playing up or running out or just not working. I was watching him and thinking all this in an idle, distant sort of a way; then I glanced down at his other hand, laid flat on the table, and I got this terrible shock. It was a big hand, broad, with a thatch of brown hairs on the back and nails that weren't that clean. I looked, and the noise of the bar dropped away and I couldn't look anywhere else, for I knew for certain sure that I had some business with this Liam that I didn't want.

Business? Ah, tell the truth, Ellen. You knew this "business" of yours was bed, and maybe a whole lot more.

I dropped my cigarette, and it rolled onto the floor. I bent down and started fishing around for it, the sweat springing out on my skin. *I'm going crazy again,* I thought, though I wasn't seeing anything and nothing was happening that definitely shouldn't be happening; there was only this weird knowing-something-ahead-of-its-time that always frightens me stupid.

I didn't want to come up, I'd have stayed right there, safe among the chair legs, but Robbie was watching me like a hawk since the hospital, so I didn't dare.

I found the cigarette, wet through in a puddle of beer, then I unbent myself and lifted my head up over the edge of the table. My eyes met Robbie's.

For fuck's sake, woman, Robbie's eyes said, *for fuck's sake get ahold of yourself —*

Implacable, his eyes. No softness, nowhere to hide. So I knocked back the vodka, straightened my backbone, and turned to this Liam and talked.

I drank a lot that night, and I wasn't the only one.

I was waiting for Stan — it was always Stan who made the moves — but he didn't; he let them sit on.

He'd glance across at Liam, who was labouring away, trying to get the conversation up and running; then he'd sneak a wee look at Noreen, but she'd given up and was staring into her glass.

Sound move. She wanted to go — any fool could tell you that — but she couldn't catch Liam's eye, he was way too busy with me.

I began to wonder what game Stan was playing. Stan could be cruel — a cat-and-mouse streak a mile wide. Was he waiting for Robbie to catch on that someone was trying too hard with his wife?

The paranoia was fairly setting in when Stan starts reminding Robbie we're meeting up with Suds Drennan and Josie at ten. Then he turns round to Liam, his face dead serious, and he tells him he's sorry but the place we've fixed to meet Suds and Josie in wouldn't be anything like the bar we're in now.

Liam nods and smiles warily. He knows he's being told something; he just hasn't figured out what.

Stan says what he means is the bar we're going to wouldn't be that mixed.

They're all attention, even Noreen. This is Belfast after all, this is what they're here for. Stan says "hard line," he mentions their accents, he mentions the fact that Liam's called Liam, which is a Catholic name. . . . He lets his voice trail off regretfully. They understand.

Northerners love frightening Southerners — telling them what not to say, where not to go, where not to leave their Southern-registered cars — seeing their eyes grow large and round. The Southerners love it too, you can nearly hear them telling themselves what they'll tell their friends when they go back home down South.

Everyone loves it: the drama, the bomb blasts, the kick of danger in the air. So who's suffering, tell me that? No one at all, till some unreasonable woman starts into grieving over the daughter blown to bits, the son sitting rotting in jail, the husband shot through the head, his body thrown down an entry or dumped on waste ground.

Some woman, or maybe some man. For men grieve too, and even your hardest hard-man is not as hard as he likes to let on when it comes to next of kin. And children are soft; children cry easily and long.

It's a sorry business alright, we humans are a sorry business, the way it's all mixed up inside us, the ghoulish bits that come alive watching the horror, the soft, gentle bits that will go thinking the sky's fallen in when we find out that someone's not coming home to us ever, ever again.

Where was I? In Hartley's, 1988.

So we left them sitting there, the two of them, and went dandering off up the road to the Lancaster, which is a mixed bar, safe as houses, where you'll get served till two in the morning, no bother at all. And I was drunk, and frightened even through the drink. I thought if I could only get clear of Liam that awful feeling that he was my fate would vanish away.

At the Lancaster we fell in with the crowd we still knocked around with from student days, so we sat down and set about getting much drunker. And somewhere along the way Robbie began collecting money. He was organising a carry-out to drink back in the flat.

It had got so late it had turned into early. There was no drink left, half the crowd had gone home, and the rest were mostly passed out in their seats or they'd slithered down onto the floor. Suds was still hanging in there, but wee Peter Caulfield was out for the count and so was Suds's girlfriend, Josie.

Time for bed. Robbie made it up onto his feet, shook Stan awake, pulled out the spare blankets, and dumped them onto the floor. Stan was all for bedding down there and then, but Rita was soberer — she found their coats and somehow got him downstairs. Then she heaved his arm over her shoulders and staggered him off up the road.

Suds had given up; he was curled on the floor like a baby, and there was no way Josie was about to wake him up and take him home. I shook out a blanket and covered her up, then I threw another one over the foetal Suds. He stirred, tucked the edge of it in under his chin, smiled, and snuggled down deeper into the manky old carpet without once opening his eyes.

I thought I'd start lifting the glasses and bottles out into the kitchen, but I couldn't seem to aim my hand straight, so I sat and smoked a cigarette instead. I could drink for ages without passing out or vomiting in those days. I thought I was great and Robbie was proud of me; I never once stopped to ask myself did I like it or what was the point or was it worth the crucifying awfulness of the hangover the next day.

I was desperate for bed, but I held off joining Robbie; I wanted to be certain sure that he wouldn't wake up. I didn't like sex with Robbie when he was really drunk, I could have been anyone or no one for all he cared, he was clumsy and rough and only thought of himself.

I'd have bedded down with the rest on the floor, but I knew there'd be no holding Robbie if he woke in the morning and I wasn't there alongside him where I belonged. He'd accuse me of doing I-don't-know-what with I-don't-know-who — then he'd take me by the shoulders and shake the teeth near out of my head while the rest of them scuttled off-side as fast as they could like so many crabs with the runs. And it was all in his head. There wasn't a sinner who wasn't way too afraid of him to look sideways at me, much less try to get a leg over Robbie's wife.

But if I hated Robbie in bed when he'd drunk too much, I hated him worse when we were out together and the drink took him in that twisted way it sometimes did. There were times he got so jealous I couldn't even take a light off someone. I'd be grabbed by the wrist, pulled from a room, pushed into a corner of some landing or hallway, and fucked against the wall. That was Robbie with the drink on him: not caring how I felt, not caring if anyone saw, not caring about anything except himself and whatever it was that was eating him alive.

I've seen me walk home holding my skirt closed to keep it up, torn knickers stuffed into my pocket, dead tear trails running down my face.

And in the morning he'd be all over me: how sorry he was, how he knew I didn't look at other men, how it was only the drink —

If he remembered at all, that is.

And I learned fast; I'd forgive him fast — at the start because I was shocked and ashamed, later because I knew if I didn't he'd stop being sorry and start into listing the things he'd seen me do with his own two eyes. What I'd said to this one, how I'd flirted with that one —

It was a funny time, I can see that now, and I know what Liam means when he says he can't understand why I stood for it. But it wasn't like that — it wasn't a question of standing for things.

I was young, I didn't know much, I thought if he was that jealous it meant he was dying about me.

And I was dying about him — I really was — he was that good-looking and streetwise and together. Sometimes I'd be waiting for him and I'd see him coming up the street before he'd spotted me. Then I'd stand there, watching him, and I couldn't believe my luck.

Chapter 2

When I met Robbie I was a good girl trying hard to be a bad one. I was at Queens, studying Russian and living in a flat with four girls from Lurgan who were all doing geography and knew each other from school. I'd got talking to one of them in the coffee bar at the end of the first week: they'd rented this flat, she said, and there was a room going spare if I didn't mind it being a wee bit poky.

"How poky's a wee bit poky?" I asked.

"There's space for a single bed. And a window as well, but it's too high up to see out."

I said yes right away. It was cheap, and already I hated my landlady. Besides, if there'd been enough room they'd have stuck in another bed and I'd have had to share. But they didn't really want me, nor I them. They were into country and western and the Scripture Union and cocoa in their pyjamas and studying hard. I wasn't, but I might as well have been. I was stuck with them, knowing there was more to this student-thing than I was getting, not knowing how I was going to lay hands on it. Until I met Robbie, that is, and everything changed.

It was in the canteen of the Students Union. I mostly didn't go there because it was cheaper to eat at the flat, but I was going to see a Russian film at the University Film Theatre and there wasn't time to go back before it began. There I was, a plateful of food on a tray in one hand, cutlery from the plastic bins in the other, when what happened only Robbie knocked into my elbow and near sent the whole lot flying.

"Sorry," he said.

"That's alright," I said, though my fried egg had a wet, orange look to it and the chips and sausages were afloat in spilled Fanta. Then he was trying to give me his plate and I was refusing and he was insisting, and the end of it was we were sitting at the same table sharing his chips and his fry and I never did get to *The Battleship Potemkin* and the girl I was supposed to see it with never spoke to me again.

After that I was Robbie's girl.

I thought it had all been a providential accident, but a week hadn't passed before he was telling me he'd had me picked out, he was only waiting his chance.

"What d'you mean by that?" I asked him.

"I fancied you, stupid," he said, sliding his hand between my thighs. But I wasn't having that, or not right away, so I made him spell it out.

He'd fancied me, he said. He'd seen me around, but somehow I always vanished before he got near enough to speak. Then there I was, right under his nose, so he'd knocked into me, just to get talking like, and look how we'd ended up.

Robbie wasn't a student, but he lived two streets up and he shared a flat with students. He used the university canteen because it was a good place to pick up girls. He looked at me hard when he said the last bit, but I wasn't going to rise to that one; I knew it was sort of a test to see would I make a fuss.

I didn't rise, but I did take my courage in both hands and I asked him why he fancied me. I wasn't fishing for lies, or for compliments either — I badly needed to know.

He said it was my hair, but he wouldn't say anything more.

Later, when we'd been to bed a few dozen times in about two days, he said he'd been right, so he had, I looked so repressed, a volcano waiting to blow.

I didn't say anything. Part of me was offended, and part of me was the opposite. *Repressed* at least held potential. And I sort of liked the volcano bit. But maybe he'd meant *frustrated?*

A couple of weeks later I moved into Robbie's flat. His flat-mates smoked dope and drank way too much and never went near the Scripture Union. I was shy with them, but I liked them as well, and soon I knew loads of the wrong sort of people and felt I was halfway alive.

Just the same, it wasn't that long before we started looking around for a place of our own. It was Robbie's idea, but I was into it too. We wanted to be by ourselves.

We found a place and moved in, and Robbie began to talk about getting married. I'd say I was nearly flattered to begin with, but then it dawned on me that he meant it and I panicked.

I couldn't, I told him, I hadn't even finished first year. Besides, I was too young, and everyone would think I was pregnant.

He gave me a funny look.

It was a shock that look, I can tell you.

"Hold on now," I said to him, hardly knowing what I was saying. "Marriage is one thing — I could maybe even get used to it. But not pregnancy. Pregnancy is definitely, definitely out."

He laughed and said he could always get a rise out of me, and when did I want to get married, what about early July? He'd take extra time, and we could go off somewhere over the Twelfth Holiday and I could start into my second year with a ring on my finger, then everyone would know who owned me.

You'd think, wouldn't you, that I'd have had the wit to hear that, but I didn't. I never had sense — my mother was never tired telling me that — I never had any idea of what I was doing till it was done.

Before we were married I took Robbie home to Derry for the weekend. Londonderry, I should say, for I was a proper Protestant then, a paid-up member of the tribe. It only turned into Derry after I'd moved down South.

We went to Londonderry on the bus. Separate rooms and best behaviour. Robbie's idea. I could have told him for nothing we weren't about to get anyone's blessing.

My brother, Brian, took me aside about half an hour after the introductions.

"You're not *serious*, are you?" He didn't expect an answer.

I phoned my mother from Belfast for her verdict, though it was plain as the nose on her face what she'd thought. But I couldn't ever leave her be, I always had to force her hand, to make her spell things out in black and white.

There was a small, deep silence down the phone line. Then, in that neutral, damning voice of hers, she told me he was common.

And I laughed aloud, for he *was*, he was all the things she had reared me against — he was working-class, sectarian, he drank too much, he neither knew nor cared what people thought.

And there was I, the teacher's daughter.

I laughed, but she'd hurt me and she'd meant to.

Poor Robbie, he wanted me to have my family's blessing; he was trying in his own way to do right by me.

Dream on. The only thing in his favour was that he wasn't a Catholic, but even I couldn't make her say that out loud, for being sectarian was part of being common.

So that was that. My father was dead, and I'd no other siblings, which meant there was no one else to object except for

Robbie's family. And they did, by Christ they did. If they said I was the wrong girl for him then that was far and away the kindest thing they said.

None of them liked me. His brother Billy said four years, five at the most — it would take that long for the bed to cool. And there'd be no children — not unless I got caught — there'd be nothing to hold us together, so we'd part.

His sister Avril said my mother's unsayable: *at least she's a Protestant*. Which shocked his sister Rita, for it had never once occurred to her that anyone belonging to her would even think of marrying out.

They said all this to Robbie behind my back, knowing full well he'd repeat every word to my face. He wouldn't listen any more than I would. He booked the Registry Office, and he put the notice in the paper; then he told them they could come if they wanted or stay away, it was all the same to him.

We didn't even ask my family.

In the end they all came, but Billy was right, it was four years and only half a child, and yes, he was right again, I was taking no chances, I hadn't been on the Pill that first night with Robbie, but I was round at the family planning clinic first thing the next morning.

The baby — what there was of her — was only because I got drunk and slipped up.

You'll think me hard, but I wasn't hard, only very young. And you weren't reared there, you don't know what it is to grow up in a place where everything seems normal enough on the surface but underneath it's all distorted and wrong. And the worst part is that you don't even know it's distorted because for you it *is* normal, and if you don't leave it behind and live somewhere *truly* normal, you'll never find out.

I suppose the Catholics were right when they called it a war, though our lot denied it. It was a war, but it wasn't like a normal war; there weren't any uniforms or fronts or advancing-and-retreating armies, and when the peace finally came there wasn't any going back home to your own place and learning how to forget. A civil war.

A few years back, Liam showed me a catalogue someone had sent him, the work of a German painter called Otto Dix. These were portraits Dix had done in Germany between the two World Wars, Liam said, when Germany was all busted up and the streets were full of profiteers and prostitutes and starving young soldiers minus their arms or legs.

But it wasn't despair that Otto Dix had painted; it was people who'd made money fast and were getting through the pain of the world by living as hard as they could. Black-marketers, pimps, club owners, satirists. The paintings were normal, but at the same time they were distorted, they fairly glittered with rage and hopelessness, they hurt you as you looked. I glanced through the first few pages then shut the catalogue fast and put a big pile of ironed clothes down on top of it to cover it up. I wanted to be by myself with it, to turn the pages slowly and stare at the pictures, which frightened me yet somehow brought me home.

Robbie only ever struck me the once, and that was on account of his sister Rita leaving her husband and my not being home all night.

Rita was fifteen years older than Robbie, she had more than half-reared him, so his feelings were softer for her than for Avril or any of the brothers. Rita was married to a man by the name of Larry Hughes, who had strong paramilitary connections. Larry was UDA and no picnic to live with, but he'd got himself a longish stretch for aiding and abetting on a murder charge, so it was a good while since she'd had to.

Well, Rita buckled down, she went out to work, reared the two young ones, never looked at another man nor missed out on a prison visit. Not for Larry's sake, mind, but to keep Larry's comrades in the Organisation off her back — or that's what she told Robbie. And she told him she'd be gone the minute Larry was out, but he never really believed her. He thought it was only talk.

Larry did five years then got early release, and home he came. The key was in the lock, the fridge was stuffed with food, the whole place was spotless. But when Larry lifted his voice and yelled for Rita he knew from the feel of the silence that the house was empty.

He went mad. He went straight to the mother — no joy — then he went and got Robbie out of his work, for if anyone knew where she'd gone it would be Robbie.

But Robbie didn't know. He told Larry over and over till Larry had no choice but to believe him.

Larry started coming on heavy. He wanted her found or he'd know where to lay the blame, he told Robbie. Robbie was soft for his sister, he said, and every bit as bad as she was. He wasn't rational. Robbie was sorry for Rita, but in his book she shouldn't have left no matter what, so he let himself be worked on and shamed by Larry, and the end of it was that Robbie said he would find her, and off he went with Larry to leave no stone unturned.

They asked everyone, they looked everywhere, they even sent Avril to the women's refuge to check if she was there. But Rita wasn't in Belfast at all; she was on the boat with the kids and heading for London, where the cousin of an aunt-by-marriage had promised to make room for them till they got a start. The mother knew alright, but she wasn't saying. If Larry found Rita, the mood he was in, Rita wouldn't be walking for months.

So, no joy all over again, and off they went to a bar to make a few further enquiries. Larry started running Rita down. He said she was a fat, idle, good-for-nothing bitch, a toe rag, not fit to lick the corns on his feet, and a whole lot more besides. Robbie took it for a bit then he said that was his sister Larry was slagging off, but Larry didn't care whose sister she was, he got worse and worse, till the filth fairly rolled off his tongue. So Robbie hit him — which took some courage — and soon they were rolling around on the floor among the chair legs, half the bar either joining in or trying to pull them apart.

Robbie made it home in the early hours. He was battered and bruised, his tail between his legs; he was looking for comfort, but I wasn't there.

No way was I there, I wasn't stupid. I was afraid of Larry, and there was a girl I was friendly with just round the corner who owned a passable sofa. I left no note, in case they came looking.

The next day I took my time. I went to a lecture then sat on in the coffee bar, and when I got home I let myself in very quietly and stood in the hallway, listening. Silence. The flat was empty, Robbie away back out to work. But he wasn't away back out to work. He was there, in the kitchen, waiting.

"Where were you?" he asked, but I didn't answer. He lifted his hand, and the black eye he gave me took weeks to lose its colour.

That was back in the early days, we weren't long married, and I suppose I bought into the hard-man myth along with near everyone else in Belfast at that time. And he was sorry, really sorry — he promised he'd never do it again, and he didn't.

But not doing it again was killing him — even I could see that — it was the reason he shook me till my teeth rattled; it was why he couldn't let me be when we were out together.

And he was a nice lad when he let himself off the hook. That's all he was, just a lad who thought he had to be a hard-man, take no shit, drink till he couldn't stand up, and look out for his own. He was bright too — every bit as clever as I was. He'd grown up on the streets, education was crap, but a part of him hungered after it. That's why he hung round with students — it wasn't only to pick up girls, the way he let on. And he wasn't a hard-man either, he was a soft man with a hard-man's training. His own man as well, for he'd feinted and ducked and somehow stayed clear of the paramilitaries. Not so many — reared as he was — managed that at all.

So that was Robbie, poor Robbie that never did anything on me but what he'd been programmed to do: find a girl, stick a ring on her finger, get some kids on her, feed them and clothe them, and keep the whole show on the road whatever the cost. Well, we'll leave Robbie out of this now, I've nothing to hold against him — not the torn knickers, nor Barbara Allen, nor the hospital for the mind that came after the hospital that saw the last of Barbara Allen. He couldn't help himself. He was near as much a victim of himself as I was.

And those were strange times, and people found strange ways of coping. Sometimes down here I remember those times and hardly believe myself that some of the things that happened happened at all. And I couldn't ever talk about them to folk here. They'd think I was mad or I'd made them up.

Chapter 3

I cried a lot after Jacko died, so the doctor put me on antidepressants. He said they might do the trick.

I took the tablets and felt even worse, so I cried *all* the time, and the more I cried the more I couldn't stop. Robbie kicked up, so I kept going back, but nothing the doctor did seemed to make any difference.

Robbie said he'd come with me the next time, and I was glad. He talked to the doctor, the doctor talked back, then the doctor sighed and said that a week or two in Purdysburn might be worth a try. Robbie looked at me, I nodded my head, and the doctor filled in the forms.

What you can't see doesn't exist. If you start into seeing things that aren't there at all you have to be schizophrenic or mad. Purdysburn is Belfast's mental hospital, so my going there made sense to me as well as to Robbie. And it wasn't so bad, once I was used to it. Plus it was such a relief not to have to try to be normal that the crying stopped a few hours in, and I hardly noticed.

The dining room frightened the wits out of me that first night. All those mad people, eyes down, eating away; I was terrified someone would take it into their heads to speak to me.

Then when no one did I started wishing they would.

"D'you not want that?" It was the fella sitting across from me, leaning forward, staring at the potato bread I'd been pushing around my plate. I didn't answer.

"Give it to Annie," he said. "Annie's mad for potato bread." He still hadn't looked at me, but I was looking at him and what I saw was a pasty-faced lad hardly older than I was, with hoody owl eyes that looked out from behind those round National Health glasses, the same as John Lennon wore.

"You're a picky eater," he said to what was left of my Ulster fry. He had little slim wrists and brown tufty hair that stuck out round his head as though he'd just woken up.

"I've a tapeworm," I told him. "That's why I'm thin."

"You have not. If you had one of them you'd have cleared the plate."

"It's asleep," I said. "On account of the medication." He lifted his eyes slowly and looked at me and didn't look away. His eyes were light blue, and the lids were large and his gaze seemed to come from a long way off.

"Which one's Annie?" I asked, just for something to say.

"The auld doll at the end of the next table."

His name was Michael. After that, I always sat beside him in the dining room. He was the first person I'd spoken to, and that gave him stability in my uncertain world. That, and the impermeable distance in his half-closed eyes. He was in because he'd tried to drown himself. He didn't tell me this right away, he waited till he was used to me, then he sprang it on me one afternoon, the two of us sitting in the dayroom, smoking.

"It takes all sorts," I said when I'd heard his news. "The Lagan's a dirty old river, I wouldn't go jumping in it myself."

"Who said anything about the Lagan?" He stared into the middle distance. "I built a raft, so I did. Pushed off from Ballyholme Bay."

"Where's Ballyholme Bay?"

"Bangor, County Down."

"Rafts are so you can float, not so you can drown."

"Fair point," he said. "I had a bike, a Harley."

I stared. For a moment I wondered if he was *really* mad.

"It's a hard world, so it is," he said carefully. "I couldn't just go off and leave her now, could I?"

It took me a minute to get it. "You put the *bike* on the raft?"

He nodded and lit another cigarette. "I put the bike on the raft and chained my leg to the wheel. That way we'd both go down together —"

"Sounds like a cry for help to me," I said firmly.

"Don't be negative."

"I'm not being negative. *Oh look, there's a man and a bike on a raft. Looks like they're floating out to sea* — Did it not cross your mind that someone might try their hand at a rescue?"

"It was four o'clock in the morning. I'd have been home and dry — or more to the point, wet — but for this wee lad running away from home." He was staring at me as he spoke, with that blank owl gaze that told nothing. "He takes one look, sets down his red plastic suitcase, and scuttles off to raise the alarm —"

"You could have jumped in right away," I said stubbornly. "You didn't have to wait around."

"I got the tides wrong. It wasn't deep enough to drown."

He was serious. I wanted to laugh, but I stopped myself. Either the story was true or it wasn't. Either way, he was mad. I wasn't prepared for his question.

"And you?" he asked.

"Me?"

"There's no one else in the room, is there?"

"I had a miscarriage," I said. "Then something else happened. And after it happened I couldn't stop crying."

A raised eyebrow and that look again.

"It's true," I said. (Why was I sounding defensive?)

"There's more."

"No, there isn't."

"Yes, there is."

"I see things that don't happen. Sometimes they happen, but not always. And not till a good while after."

Then I told about walking down the street and seeing the bomb going sailing over the security fence and onto the roof of the bar. How I was somehow inside the bar at the same time as being outside, watching. And then about seeing Jacko Brennan being blown to smithereens.

"And I'm screaming and screaming," I said. "And people are coming running and they're taking me to the hospital and I'm losing Barbara Allen, which is what I call the baby." I could hear my voice, and it was going high and shaky. He held out his cigarettes, and I took one and he lit it and I saw that my hand was shaking as well as my voice.

"Only it didn't happen," I said. "I mean, Jacko dying didn't happen. Losing Barbara Allen happened alright. But six months later Jacko died, and it was all the way I saw." He waited. I took a long drag at the cigarette and went on. "It was evening. I was ironing, and the window was open and I heard the blast and I knew exactly where it came from and I knew that Jacko was dead. But this time I didn't see a thing. I went on ironing. But the shaking started in my hands, and it went up my arms and wouldn't stop. I sat down and waited for Robbie. Robbie came in, and he said it was true; there'd been a bomb and Jacko was dead, but that was all hours and hours ago. Funny, wasn't it? Jacko, dead like that? And why hadn't I turned the light on, why was I shaking?

"That's all he said. He never once mentioned me seeing it all six months before it ever happened. Maybe he didn't want to think about that or maybe he saw the state I was in and he didn't want to make things worse. . . . But he took me over to the hospital, and they gave me sedatives. They said it was shock. The next day I started this crying-thing, and it wouldn't stop."

"Who's this Jacko Brennan?"

"No one special. I only knew him to nod to, say hello —"

"That's not mad, it's clairvoyant."

"There's no such thing, stupid. People who see things are mad."

"You're mad if you think that. You should be in Purdysburn."

"I *am* in Purdysburn, and so are *you*." I glared at him. "Anyway, what's so great about what you did? What's so great about trying to drown yourself?"

He looked back at me, unblinking. For a moment I wanted to kill him; then I started to laugh and I couldn't stop. I laughed and I laughed, and when I came up for air, he was looking at me still, his expression completely unchanged.

"That's more like it," he said.

After that I had company. Michael and me, a twosome. It was June, and the trees in the grounds were green and thick in the summer night. The dayrooms were all on the ground floor, and it wasn't a heavy-duty part of the hospital, most of the windows weren't locked. After dark people flitted about like moths. The staff must have known, but nothing was said. Perhaps they were sorry for us; or perhaps it kept us quiet, and they didn't care. I'd climb with Michael through a window of the empty dining hall, and we'd walk about under the trees and lie on our backs spotting stars through the darker darkness of leaves. We told each other stories, sometimes from books, sometimes incidents that had happened in the past. It was lovely, so it was. Words spoken into the night. Small, soft words, far off and glimmery like the summer stars. Sometimes we climbed into the trees and sat in the forks of their branches, swinging our heels. I was better at climbing than he was, more agile, more sure-footed; I'd join my hands into a stirrup to give him a start then I'd scramble up behind him.

After the first week I asked Michael if he fancied having sex with me, but he turned me down.

"Sorry," he said. "Nothing doing."

"Why not? Are you gay?"

He gave me his sniffy look. "I don't fancy you," he said. "Besides, I'm married."

"What's that got to do with it? Anyway, I don't believe you."

"That I'm married? Or that I don't fancy you?"

"Both," I said. "I don't think you're married. I think you fancy me but you can't get it up." (It was wonderful, that hospital. All your inhibitions went sailing off down the river.)

"Correct," he said. "On both counts. It's the drugs. Why don't you try Catriona?"

"Do I look like a dyke?"

"Silly girl — ugly word. Catriona's so beautiful. Those red lipstick circles she draws on her cheeks. I'd try for her myself if I was able."

"Is she a dyke?"

"Who knows? She might feel like giving it a go if you asked her nicely. Lots of people have a bit of both."

"Speak for yourself," I said. "I certainly don't." I was shocked. Besides, I was afraid of Catriona, though I didn't say that to Michael. She saw blood coming out of the taps, which was worse than seeing people being blown to bits.

Michael stared at me, a long, slow, speculative look from

those hooded eyes. "You're very narrow-minded for a redhead," he said.

I wanted to ask him what he meant, but I didn't. I was afraid of my hair, even then.

Michael never touched me, never as much as took my hand walking back through the dark. And I was glad enough, for it kept things light and simple. My forwardness was really only bravado.

Robbie came, and when he did Michael vanished from sight.

"Hubby alright?" he'd ask me afterwards. "Not pining?"

"Robbie," I'd say. "His name's Robbie."

But he went on stubbornly calling him Hubby. I wouldn't answer him when he did. I sulked, but he wouldn't shift; it was Hubby this and Hubby that till I lost my temper.

"Lay off, would you? You've never even set eyes on him."

But he had. He'd seen Robbie from a window.

"I wouldn't want to meet him on a dark night down a back entry," he said. "He's the sort kicks the shite out of people like me —"

He had a point, though I didn't say so.

Robbie hated coming to the hospital. Shame made him narrow his shoulders and kick out sparks with his steel-shod boots. His wife in that place, labelled forever, was more than he could handle. And no Barbara Allen. He'd wanted Barbara Allen as I never had, and now she was flushed down some hospital sluice, gone when she'd hardly started.

My mother came on the bus from Derry. I told her the doctor had said I could ask for a transfer to the hospital there. That way she could visit more often.

She gave me a long, straight look and told me I had a husband. Then she said Londonderry was just a wee village for talk, and folk said these things ran in families, and what about my two wee nieces? Had I no thought for Brian and Anne at all?

"Oh, folk know alright," she added. "I don't try to hide what can't be hid, that's not my way. But some things are best not advertised."

Hard words, but there was a tenderness in that hospital, a looking-out-for-one-another that nearly made me not mind them. We were all raw with our own failure, and as well as that our minds were turned down low with drugs so we weren't so keen on judging. That was a kind of liberation, for what could you do at the bottom but laugh — the laughter of gentleness, not of derision? Derision was for out there. Derision and fear-of-derision had landed us in here. We had broken ourselves on our own wheels, trying to be what we thought was required of us, trying to be "normal." Failing. In here we moved slowly, taking care, as wounded things take care. Oh, there were dislikes and resentments alright, but only because we were human. Mostly we were as careful of each other's sore places as of our own, or nearly so. And in a funny way there was no one out there as real for us as the ones inside that we lived with every day. Perhaps what bound us together was pity more than love. I don't know; I don't know where the one stops and the other starts.

I was discharged before Michael was. I wrote out my address and I said good-bye, and it never once crossed my mind that I might not see him again. I'd accepted the gifts he'd given me — gifts that were given freely, as you give when you are young. I took them without thought or gratitude; took them in the fullness of youth, when life is opening and everything seems natural and yours by right.

I sent him a postcard. Later on I scribbled half a letter, but I lost it on a bus. I never rewrote it. I was living my life, I forgot about Michael. When at last I remembered, my letter came back with "unknown at this address" scrawled over the envelope. Perhaps he's alright, perhaps he's alive, but I get no sense that he's out there still. The depression was very bad with him; it never let him alone.

I am thirty-six and already so much left undone and regretted. What will I do when I'm old?

Chapter 4

Where was I? The day after the night I first met Liam. Saturday. I met him again in the street late that morning. He was walking towards me, his head down, his eyes on the pavement, no sign of Noreen. I was dying with the hangover and the lack of sleep, but I wanted to be out of the flat and away from Robbie, away from Robbie's foul words, away from the misery in his eyes when he came out with them.

I'd told him I'd messages to do. I was out the door almost before he knew I was going.

When I saw Liam my first thought was to turn on my heel and run, but I didn't. I'd be past him in a flash, I told myself, there was no call to be drawing attention to myself, running off like an eejit. So I went on ahead, my eyes on the ground, the same as his were. Then the next thing I felt a hand gripping my arm and a voice saying my name out as if it was news to me.

"You can leave go of my arm," I said. "I'm not about to run off with your wallet."

He let go. He said he hadn't seen me till I was nearly past, he hadn't meant to hurt me.

"How about a cup of coffee?" he added. "Wouldn't you let me buy you a coffee or a drink or something? Would you fancy a bite of lunch?"

No, I said, I didn't want a drink, or not yet, and where was Noreen, wouldn't she be wanting her lunch any minute now?

"That should keep you busy and out of trouble," I added nastily.

"Noreen got the early train to Dublin. Said she couldn't be doing with Northerners. Always arguing and complaining and telling the rest of us what to do. Said *she* knows when she isn't welcome, even if *I* don't."

"And don't you?"

"Oh, I do. It's coming through loud and clear, I just don't want to admit it's what I'm hearing —"

My head hurt, and I wanted to get away from him. By now I was well on my way to forgetting all about the business with him the night before. It seemed like a dream, a stupid dream, and I was sick of myself and the way I let my imagination lead me up garden paths. Then he put out his hand and took mine. Straightaway I was back there, ready to drop with the knowing of what I had known last night. And with the fear of it.

He didn't let go of my hand. Instead he put his other one under my elbow and drew me round to face him. I kept my head down, my eyes well away from his. But I let him move his hands to my upper arms and hold them there to steady me. After a while his hands dropped.

"Right," he said. "Lunch," he said, and steered me into the Sceptre and sat me down in a snug. Then off he went to the bar and came back with sandwiches and pints of Guinness.

"I don't like Guinness," I said.

"You could do with building up."

I don't remember any more than that, I don't remember what I said next or what he said next or whether I drank the Guinness or left it sitting or poured it over his head. But I remember how I pressed back into the chair, how I tried to get small and still inside my clothes to get away from him. He never touched me, and I never touched him, but when I got back to the flat two hours later, I had a story ready for Robbie and I wasn't slow running it past him. I told him I'd rung my mother from a pay phone while I was out. Brian and Anne and the babies had been there with her.

"They're away off to the West for a week's holiday," I said. "They've rented a house — a place off the coast of Mayo called Achill Island. Brian came on to ask did we want to come with them?"

Robbie was looking at me, but I was busy taking the dishes off the drainer and stacking them into tidy piles by the sink.

"*We?*" Robbie said, so I knew he'd bought the rest of the lie.

"Well, not exactly," I said, still not looking at him. "He asked were you working, and I said you were. Then he said did I want to come?"

———— ❦ ————

A new cottage had been built hard behind the old one, its front door facing across to the other one's back door. For the old couple or maybe the young couple — family, anyway — a natural proximity. Sometime later someone had added a joining arm so the two had become the one, with a bit of a yard in the space between. Hardly even a yard. Just a rough place for hens to pick over and washing to hang, sheltered from wind and weather.

Achill. We'd been there four days. I had carried a kitchen chair out and was sitting doing nothing at all, the gnats rising, the shirts I'd washed in the kitchen sink just stirring in the quiet air. Liam had gone off after groceries and a mechanic to look at his car. There was a noise he didn't much care for in the engine, he said, and maybe he wanted some time off from me as well, maybe he'd bitten off more than he could easily chew. For myself, I was glad to be on my own. My thoughts went wandering about in the whitish sea light that you get off that western coast.

The yard was three sides cottage, with the fourth side closed off by a big thick dark fuchsia hedge, red now with hanging blooms that were starting to drop. It was early September, a bare two months since they'd let me out of the hospital, a bare four since the bomb had gone off that killed Jacko and left me not able to stop crying. The yard had been covered over with a scrape of rough concrete, breaking up now so the weeds and the moss had taken hold, the whole place littered with things that were most likely never going to be used again but just might come in handy one day: broken boards and odd stones and shells carried up from the beach, floats for a fishing net in a tangled heap, a black plastic bucket half filled up with rainwater over by the wall. A shallow brick drain was clogged up with silt and leaves and drained nothing.

If I lived here I might learn to do less, I thought. To wash less, to go on wearing things that were soiled. Even in the few days we had been here the urge to clean it all up had died in me. I no longer itched to chuck out the junk, to unblock the drain, to sweep it all down; I no longer wanted to do anything much except sit on the straight-backed chair in the soft bloom of light and stretch out a hand to check the shirts on the line.

On the first day I'd washed all the windows in the kitchen. I'd intended doing the whole house, there wasn't a clean window anywhere; they were splattered with rain marks and mud and had deep layers of ancient cobwebs veiling the corners. Liam laughed when he saw what I was at. I asked him why, and he went red and shook his head, but I pressed him and finally he said he thought it strange to be starting in on cleaning on your holidays.

But that wasn't why he'd laughed, and I knew it. I kept on at him, and he went redder, but still he wouldn't say. In the end he gave in and told me about being on the sites in London and working alongside an old Cockney who thought Liam was way too innocent and needed wising up. He had a dirty old tongue in his head, Liam said, but he meant well — he was forever passing on bits of tips and information. It seems he'd told Liam to look out for women who were workers because women who were workers were always on for sex.

I rinsed out the cloth in the water, then turned and washed down the last pane. But I didn't give them a shine with newspaper as I'd intended, and I didn't wash any more. I was angry. I didn't laugh and brush it aside; my mind closed like a trap round his words. I remembered Robbie — what he'd said about knowing as soon as he saw me that I was repressed, a volcano ready to blow.

I'd made a mistake with Robbie, I thought, and I was surprised at myself, for this was the first time I'd let myself think such a thing.

Now it looked like I might well be on the way to making another one with Liam. I took my coat from the peg without a word.

"Where are you off to?" Liam wanted to know.

I didn't reply. I shrugged on my coat and was gone through the door without looking back.

Out on the road I went steaming along, the wind on my face, my hair ripping out, the bog stretching red-brown to either side. The sky was flying above me; the wind keened in the telephone wires; my ears sang with the lovely fresh running noise of water going pelting down the ditches. With every step I took I was freer, the anger draining away.

"What ails ye?" Liam was asking me, coming up from behind.

"You know rightly," I said, without slowing down. He started to say he was sorry, but I wasn't having it, I turned around to his face.

"Why shouldn't women like sex?" I demanded. "And why do men have to sneer and joke if we do? Wouldn't you think men would be pleased that we like it? Wouldn't you think it would make life easier all round?"

He started to try to say something, but I only laughed in his face. I threw my arms round his neck and pulled him to me; then I undid my arms and pushed him away and went striding off over the bog, all the anger gone from me.

It's a wonderful place, Achill; there never were such skies. I was used to skies from Derry, but still it wasn't like Achill. Achill had the best skies that ever I saw in all Ireland. It could be ink black up ahead, but away to the left you'd see light breaking through in a shaft like a floodlight, while off to the right there'd be rain, a grey curtain, and behind that again you'd see where the rain had passed over and the land was shouldering its way back up through the gloom.

So we went striding along together, all thought of regret vanished clean away and Robbie only a flicker of guilt at the back of my mind.

Night came, and we sat by the smoking fire with a bottle of whiskey that I was throwing into me but Liam had hardly touched. It was awkward as hell, but I didn't care. We'd ease up in bed and no need for talk — our bodies would say it all. Or that's what I thought, but I'd reckoned without Liam: when I put my hand on his leg, you'd think he'd been stung by a wasp.

He hadn't brought me here, he said, for *that*.

"Why not?" I asked him. "What's wrong with *that*?"

It seemed Liam thought we should learn to talk first.

"If we can't talk," he said, "there isn't a future —"

I gaped at him. No future was fine by me. A bit on the surface of me was playing with the notion of leaving Robbie, but deeper down that wasn't what I meant to do at all. Deeper down I wasn't leaving Robbie, I was having a bit of a fling with Liam and while I was at it destroying whatever shared future I'd glimpsed that night in the bar. I was trying to avoid my fate, you see; I thought I could go with him to Achill and then sneak back home again to Robbie. Outwit my fate, give it the slip.

So I sat there, not believing what I was hearing, thinking it all some game on his part that would resolve itself in an hour or so's time in the bed. Only it didn't. He'd taken himself off to a different bed the first night, and the next and the next. And for all I knew he would do the same tonight.

In the day we'd walked long, long walks, together but alone. And now we were both so miserable we were relieved to be apart.

I sat on, thinking these thoughts, glad of his absence, wondering should I cut my losses, find a bus, and head back to Belfast, but knowing I wasn't yet able for Robbie or the city. Beside me on the windowsill were two oval stones, very white, and the skull of some long-dead ewe. Or some long-dead ram — how would I know? What did I know about sexing live sheep, much less something like this, stripped of its flesh and blood?

It was ugly, the bone grey and pitted, the horns broken off at the tips. A row of hefty grey teeth stuck out from the upper jaw, but the lower one had long since vanished away, and round holes, empty and dark, stared out where the eyes should have been. Once it was its own sheep, I thought, with some sort of life of its own and some sort of consciousness. Idly, I looked down at my hand in my lap, imagining the bones lurking under the flesh, wondering would they stay linked in the grave or fall away, like the sheep skull's lower jaw.

I should have kept a tighter hold on my thoughts, for I got more than I'd bargained for. I watched, and my skin turned yellowy-blue, as though it was badly bruised, then puffed and swelled, and the yellowy-blueness darkened into black. A foul stench hung on the air, and I saw my flesh breaking open, heaving with maggots and pus. I screamed and jumped up. I tried to throw my hand off from me, but it stayed joined onto my arm. It was like trying to throw your own child away; you can't do it even if you want to, you can't rid yourself of a part of yourself just because you don't like what it does or says or because it's manky with maggots.

I don't know how long it lasted: it might have been half an hour or only seconds. But I watched, and it all changed back. My hand was my hand, the flesh clean and regrown, and not a maggot in sight. I reached for my cigarettes, but the same hand shook so hard I couldn't get one out of the packet.

Sweet Jesus, I thought. Not that again, don't let it be that again. How am I going to live if I can't even think a thought without seeing it act itself out before my eyes?

But it was — I knew well that it was. I was seeing things again. Barbara Allen and Jacko Brennan came flooding back, and my little bit of quiet and kind idleness in the broken yard was gone.

I sometimes wonder now, could I have left Robbie if Barbara Allen had lived? There are times when I think I could, but more often I think I couldn't. He wouldn't have let me take her, that's certain sure, and I don't think I could have defied the whole world and myself and gone off without her, but I don't know. It's no good thinking and saying to yourself "I'd do this" or "I'd do that." You don't know till it happens; you don't know what you will find in yourself till it's found.

What I do know is that I couldn't have gone to Liam half as easily as I did if something of what had been between Robbie and me hadn't died along with Barbara Allen.

43

But all that was ahead, and nothing to do with my standing there, shaking from head to foot, my eyes on the sheep's skull, full up with fear. It wasn't that I thought it foretold anything. It was it happening at all that scared me stupid. The bruising, the maggots, the pus — they had come and gone in a flash — but the speed of it all somehow only made the thing worse. It was as though my life were a bicycle I'd been riding happily down the road: one minute I was up there, the wind on my face, and the next I was sprawled on the tarmac, broken-boned and with all the wind knocked from me.

I didn't hear the car; I didn't hear Liam getting out or shutting the door or walking around the house. The first thing I knew he was standing in front of me, and I moved forward without knowing what I was doing and threw myself against him. His arms went around me and held me, and I never wanted him to let go. He held me without words, but small, soothing noises were coming from low in his throat, the same sounds you make to comfort a hurt dog.

I don't know how long we stood like that, and I don't know how we moved from being like that to sitting together there in the yard, his hand holding mine, me telling him in a big jumbled rush about what had just happened, about Barbara Allen and Jacko's death, about the hospital and its drugs which had stopped me seeing things.

The empty eyes of the sheep's skull stared from the sill.

"Is this the first time you're after seeing anything since the hospital?"

I shook my head. "The night I met you — there was something then."

He just nodded; he didn't ask what. I put my hands over my face, and I started to weep. I felt the tears running through my fingers and down my wrists. He stroked my head, then he shifted a bit and put his arms round me again, and I wept into the warm place under his chin. After a while I stopped. I drew away from him. I patted my pockets, looking for something to blow my nose in, and I found a scrumpled bit of tissue and blew. I felt better. The weeping was a release, it had got me past the fear to a place where what was happening to me was simply what was happening, it wasn't any longer something I was desperate to shut out.

"D'you think have I a screw loose?" I said when I'd finished blowing.

He shook his head. "I do not. You see things. Sometimes just things. Sometimes things that are going to happen but haven't happened yet. That's not the same as having a screw loose."

I looked at him then. He was so serious and so innocent, his grey eyes very round and wide open, his brown curls lifting in the strengthening breeze. I started to laugh. He looked surprised, then a bit offended.

"What're you laughing at?" he asked.

"You," I said. "Is there nowhere you'd draw the line?"

"What d'you mean by that?"

"If I told you there was a wee man dancing a hornpipe on your left shoulder I think maybe you'd believe me."

He smiled. "Why not?" he asked. "Because I don't see something doesn't mean it isn't there. It just means I don't see it."

Fear hit me in the belly with the force of a man's fist.

"You don't see it because it isn't there," I shouted at him. "It's a chemical in my brain, making me think I see things, that's all. But they're not there, they're not there, they're not there —"

Everything crumpled, and I started to sob again. "Easy now, easy," he was saying, holding me tight in his arms and stroking my hair. "Easy, girl, easy."

⸺∞⸺

The wind had risen in the night. Storm waves rolled in, and the damp sands blew with flocks of shiny bubbles like tiny hermit crabs scurrying off sideways as fast as they could go. Further down there were big curvy swathes of pale foam, and I took off my shoes and walked in them, kicking the empty white fizz with my bare, bony feet, making it fly. The wind blew, and the clouds raced over the big, clean sky and the air snapped and rushed about my head like a flag. Where the beach curved out of the wind there were stranded castles of dark-cream foam like the tipped-out froth from hundreds of pints of Guinness.

A lone dog was trotting about, some sort of a collie cross, black and white with splashes of tan. When he came to a castle he'd crouch down and bark, his tail would lash back and forth, then he'd pounce. Nothing. The castle had disappeared, leaving only splatters of foam and claw marks deep in the sand. He couldn't work it out. He'd stand there with such a puzzled, affronted expression on his face that I laughed aloud.

I was happy as a lark. We both were. Happy with the happiness of two people who have just found each other's bodies and are amazed by them. Liam hadn't moved away off from me after the time in the yard. It showed in a touch to my hair, a hand on my arm. Later, when I'd sat in beside him on the sofa, his arm had gone around my shoulders and stayed there. After that it was only a short step to bed and the pleasures of bed.

And pleasures they were. We had bodies that matched on a deeper, surer level than anything I'd known with Robbie, though Robbie was more athletic and knew better what he was doing. But Liam made me laugh, which Robbie never had. He talked to me, where Robbie was all silent concentration. And Liam got hungry — he was forever jumping out of bed and bringing back half the fridge and spreading it out on the coverlet. Then he'd feed me from his hand till I felt like a bird or a horse. Soon the sheets were greasy with buttery prints, and I slept with tiny islands of discomfort on my bare skin, never giving it a thought.

I should have known from that. I'm too fastidious by nature not to mind, and I didn't. I thought I was only in ankle deep, when I'd waded in up to my neck.

But that day we were just beginning, and it seemed all the weight of the last hard months had fallen away and nothing but ease remained. We went strolling along the strand, the dog trotting behind us, the tide pulling out and out till you felt you might walk to America. Liam asked me why I feared it so — this habit I had of seeing things. Was it on account of not knowing if it would stop?

I didn't answer him. I picked up a length of stick that the sea had laid down, and at once the dog was lepping and yapping for me to throw it. I didn't. Instead I wrote my name in big broad strokes on the sand. Then I looked at Liam out of the corner of my eye and I wrote his name under mine. Then I wrote "Dandy the dog" under his. I took another peek at him to be sure he was watching me, and I lifted the stick and drew a big wide circle around the three names, linking us all together. He was disappointed, and I knew he would be. When I went to circle the names he had thought it would be with a heart. And it almost was, for it seemed a small thing to do for him when he'd made me so happy. But I held back, I wanted to stay in the happiness; I didn't want to move on into hearts and love and all the trouble they'd bring. I dropped the stick and fell into step beside him.

"Sometimes, after Barbara Allen, when it started to happen," I said, not answering his question, "I could make it not happen if I tried hard enough, but I had to shut myself down so tight it sometimes felt like I'd die. My head ached from keeping from thinking things, and my jaws ached from keeping my mouth clamped shut. That was the best thing about that place. The hospital, I mean. Having the drugs to stop it from happening, not having to do it myself."

"What makes you so sure it was the drugs?"

I turned round to face him.

"You saw what happened in the yard." I made my voice hard and cold so he'd know not to push. "It's only started again because I'm off them."

"Have you got those pills with you now?"

I shook my head. If you ask my mother she'll tell you I'm a bad liar. I wondered would he see through me as easily.

"You wouldn't go back on them, would you?" he asked.

"Just watch me. I've a prescription. I will if it's going to start again."

"How long between stopping the drugs and it starting again?"

I thought for a minute. I didn't want to tell him the truth, but my mouth seemed to open and speak of its own accord. "The night I met you. But I was out of my head, things happen when you're drunk. Yesterday was different — I was stone-cold sober."

"The first time was when you were pregnant? It never happened before?"

"No." I stopped and poked at a beached jellyfish with my toe. It was one of those clear ones with pale mauve marks in its centre. They don't sting, or not from the outside anyway. It's like putting your foot on a jelly cube warmed in the sun. Liam was watching me, waiting. "W-e-ll," I said.

"Well?"

"I had kind of flashes before. Once or twice. Nothing much."

He didn't ask, he just looked at me with the question in his round grey eyes. He was good at that — just looking, not asking. I almost always fell for it at the start. This time I hadn't meant to tell any more, but I did.

"We were over seeing my granny one Sunday," I said slowly.

"She lived outside Derry, a place called Dunnamanagh. It's where my mother was born, there's a farm. We'd had our dinner, we were only waiting for them to send us out so they could talk. *Little pitchers have long ears*, that's what they'd say." I wobbled the jelly-fish with my toe. "It was spring, a beautiful day. I thought I'd go mad, stuck inside, behaving." I sneaked a glance at him, but he wasn't watching my face, he was watching my toe on the jellyfish. "Being thrown out was the best thing about those visits. The hay barn; looking for stray eggs; dandering about in the fields. There were four of us — me and Brian and my cousins, Heather and John. Heather was only nine, she was messing about, showing off, turning cartwheels over and over in the sun. It was lovely, so it was, the meadow all yellow with dandelions —"

I picked up a stone and threw it into the sea. The dog rushed after it and stuck his nose in where the stone had gone under. He brought his face up, and it streamed water. He looked at me reproachfully.

"I was watching Heather. One minute she was hands down in yellow flowers and the next there weren't any flowers, just wee silver balls in the sun as far as the eye could see."

"Silver balls?"

"Dandelion clocks. The flowers had all died and turned into clocks. I opened my mouth to call out, but the next thing they'd turned themselves back into yellow flowers. And it wasn't like it is in a film when you go backwards or forwards, there wasn't that wee blurry bit that comes up and says to you '*watch out now, here comes fast-forward.*'"

I threw another stone. The dog did his thing.

"And no one else saw what I saw," I said. "I looked at them, and I knew for certain sure they hadn't seen."

"Did you tell Brian?"

"You're joking me. Brian would have said I was mental."

"What age were you?"

"Fourteen, maybe fifteen."

"That was the first time?"

I shrugged. "The first time I remember." I paused. "But I didn't remember. I forgot on purpose; I never wanted to think about it again. . . . I was only young, I thought I was going mad, it was really scary."

He must have heard in my voice that that was it, I'd gone as far as I'd go, for he didn't press me. Looking back, I can't believe I talked to him the way I did. I could have lived with Robbie a thousand years and I never could have said to him half of what I said to Liam right from the start.

Chapter 5

It's in you and that's fine; I don't think there's anything to be frightened of. I think you should learn to handle it, not go back on the drugs."

We were looking down on the heave of a big dark sea, the waves coming in short and strong to smack up hard on the great bank of stones where we sat. They were sea stones, heavy and round, knotted and veined like wood, rattled and rolled by the crash of each breaking wave.

The beach curved off to the right, where it ran into dunes and sheep-grazed sea turf. The low dunes were sunlit, the grass brilliant green, the sand a rich gold, but above, the sky was slate black and the gulls rose into it, shining like chips of quartz in the stormy light. There were cormorants coming in off the sea in small, straggly bands, and half a mile back a big grey seal had stuck its head up out of the water and stared its fill.

Liam was telling me what to do but pretending not to. He'd held off a good while, but he was comfortable with me now so he let himself. Men seem to think that's what women want of them, and maybe we do, or maybe a part of us does. I did with Robbie; I didn't know what I was doing in Robbie's world, so I thought it was great to have someone to ask who'd know the answers. Then slowly it dawned on me that Robbie didn't know either. I wasn't supposed to notice, but I couldn't help myself, so after a while I stopped asking. He went on telling me anyway, and I'd stand there looking at him, the rage rising up in me, spilling over into my face in judgment. He must have seen it, but it didn't stop him; it only made him worse.

"There's no way you're mad, Ellen, only clairvoyant," Liam said. "This thing is a gift; you shouldn't be trying to blank it out with drugs."

At first I couldn't believe what he was saying. In my book hearing and seeing things that aren't there is schizophrenia. Go back a hundred years or so and it's possession. No part of me could accept, as Liam did, a world full of beings and things that were real as day but we couldn't see. Even thinking a thing like that outside in the wind and the air with Liam beside me scared the living daylights out of me. Letting it creep in when I woke at night gave me the screaming abdabs. I'd grab hold of him and scurry into his body looking for refuge, only I didn't go telling him that, I let on it was all appetite. The way I was reared, you didn't say if something scared you — that was weakness. You didn't let others see weakness, even your nearest relations. Weakness was a secret between you and God, who knew anyway, who wrote it all down in a big black book and judged you and found you wanting.

There was another thing about the way I was reared that kept smacking me in the face with Liam, and the more I tried to wriggle my way around it, the more it stood in front of me blocking my path. My mother was a woman with very strong views on what you did or did not do, and one of them was that it was just plain ignorant to remind a Catholic that he or she was a Catholic. Especially if you had time for them. It was something you left unmentioned, out of good manners.

And now here was Liam, as Southern and as Catholic as they come, and for the life of me I couldn't turn round and say that believing there were things in the world you couldn't see was Catholic, and seeing things that weren't there was even more Catholic, which he was, but I wasn't. More to the point, letting go and seeing what might happen would have been like deliberately stepping off from a narrow ledge to fall into bottomless darkness.

Suddenly all the comfort I'd had from Liam flew out the window. He was ignorant and superstitious, and that was the reason he'd listened so patiently to all my talk. I was better off with Robbie — Robbie didn't live in a whole moither of strange half-notions; Robbie had his two feet on the ground.

But thinking of Robbie was as dangerous as walking into the heaving sea. I hadn't phoned or sent a postcard, and today was the very last day of the time I'd said I'd be here with Brian and Anne. If I didn't come home now he'd ring up my mother. No, he'd leave it a day or so longer because he wouldn't want to admit that he didn't know where I was. You'd think I'd have lifted a phone even then just to cover my back, but I didn't. I'd got into a strange mood of fatalism and I didn't seem able to act or make up my mind — all I could do was let things drift.

So I sat there on that wall of stones with my face turned into the wind and my hair flying back behind me, caught between the devil and the deep and not sure which was which. I kept my eyes fixed on the sea. The dog stuck his head under my arm and butted at it. He wanted sticks thrown, but it was too rough, and anyway I wasn't in the mood.

After a bit the dog left off nudging and threw himself down on the stones in disgust. Still I didn't speak, though I knew that Liam was waiting. I didn't speak because I couldn't; it was as if my whole body was caught between these two men and what they were trying to make me be, and all it could do was freeze and refuse. Then the seal we had seen before came back and stuck its head up out of the water and stared at us. I looked straight into its eyes, and it looked straight back into mine. They were huge and soft, like liquid filling a glass right up to the brim and ready to spill over. The dog sat up beside me and started to mew; then he let a yap out of him, and the seal gave us this sorrowful pitying look and slid slowly down under the water. It must have gone motoring about under there because after a while it broke the surface again, only this time it was further over and closer in.

It's the strangest thing, a big grey seal in a strong running sea, for it isn't like anything that should be in the sea at all, it isn't fishy or birdlike or scuttling, but a warm-blooded mammal with eyes more human than a dog's. More human than most humans, if by human you mean full of speech and feeling. Yet it lives in the endlessness of the unbounded seas, and you can see that it can handle all that, even the loneliness. It can live down there where the pull and slide of deep water changes all colours and rubs out all edges; it can handle the fish world of swayings and scuttlings, then poke up its head and look with over-water eyes at our oxygen world, which is fixed and flashing with daylight.

And when it comes in close and swims around, staring, you can't help feeling that it is like searching for like, searching for warm, milky creatures that know the beat of hot blood and suckle their young. If you speak or sing it draws nearer, and its kingdom looks out through its eyes and enters us through ours.

When I saw that seal I wanted to weep for myself, for I knew with a strange, strong knowledge that if I did as Liam said I might learn to be easy out there, I might even come to love the slide and suck of great moving masses of water far out in frontierless seas. But I knew as well that for any ease and joy I might have in that other kingdom, I'd always fear it, and I'd never stop wanting to be one thing only and undivided — I would never, ever get over the awful loneliness of being *other*. I didn't want to see things or hear things or live under the sea; I didn't want to be different or special like that, only to be special to some man who wasn't broken and hard like Robbie and maybe have another Barbara Allen to hold in my arms.

But at that time I couldn't seem to stay out of the other world nor find the courage to fully enter it either. I still can't, I still live caught between the two, though at least when the underworld claims me now I know to hold my breath so I don't come up near drowned. But back then, I sat on the stones with Liam knowing nothing beyond what I was reared to. I was the child who has only ever seen what is revealed by day, who hasn't known that in darkness you lose what is near but you see beyond into galaxies.

I remember looking up at Liam from a long way off, and he got to his feet and stretched down and pulled me onto mine and we tramped off over the short, springy grass, which he said was called machair, with Dandy dancing alongside and the sheep getting up and moving off at sight of him, sheep with curling horns like my skull on the windowsill, and arses dyed indigo blue.

Boredom and fear belong to the mind, and pain and exhaustion belong to the body, but the spirit knows none of these things — the spirit knows only light. So we moved off, and the movement must have jogged me out of the mind and its fear and into the body — home of pleasure as well as pain — which still glowed with its discovery of Liam's.

And maybe into the spirit as well, for it is amazing, looking back, how easily I sloughed off the seal and its dark warnings, and went skipping and dancing like Dandy into Achill's shifting light.

Chapter 6

"Marie and Dermot will be here on Thursday," Liam said. "We're welcome — for as long as we like — but I'd need to be thinking of getting back."

Dermot was Liam's friend, the one who'd lent him the cottage, which belonged to Dermot's family on account of his mother being from Achill. He'd told me that much, but nothing at all about anyone coming.

"What day's today?" I asked, blank as I could manage.

"Tuesday."

I got up from the table and made a fresh pot of tea. I took my time, heating the pot, and then sliding the lid in carefully under the rim, making sure there was no rattle from the tremor in my hand.

I carried the teapot to the table.

"There's an architect looking for me for some work," Liam said, "and I've put him off twice already. It's a good job, and there's others will jump at the chance if I don't turn up and show willing."

Liam went on talking about this architect, enthusiasm in his voice. I poured the tea, schooling my face to say nothing.

"A new house, no expense spared," Liam said. "The client's rich — seriously rich — wants the fireplaces hand-carved in Kilkenny marble, plus balustrades and fountains and garden ornaments as well. God only knows what it'll look like, but I'm not about to argue. With luck it'll pay for my own work for at least a year."

I hardly listened. I'd thought there was no time limit, no end, that it was only me that had anything to decide or go back to. And I wanted him to ask would I come home with him to Kilkenny. Ask — so I could turn him down.

I buttered more toast and slathered it in marmalade and ate it without speaking or looking at him. He said later he was watching for the slightest sign, but I didn't let on.

Why would I? His body told me I was the world to him, yet here he was, chatting away, fireplaces and features and to hell with me.

When we'd finished breakfast we left the dishes in the sink and went out. Dandy wasn't at the door, but we weren't five minutes down the road and there he was, trotting along, business as usual. He'd adopted us, waited outside the door most mornings, and when we came back he'd go off home up the hill. I wanted to feed him, but Liam said no, somebody owned the dog. He only came with us for company and a walk.

It was a perfect day, the first we'd had, the sun shining down on the blue sea and everything looking subtly wrong in the calm, clear light. The sounds were different too, fine-weather sounds — the *cack, cack* of a leisurely gull, the fizzle and pop of seaweed drying, the drone of a bee in the lazy air. Strangest of all was Slievemore, no longer a black looming mountain half lost in the shifting cloud, but a big bony hill against sky that was far too blue.

I took my shoes off and made for the water. The tide was out; little low waves ran over my feet, and off to the left three cormorants sat on a rock and held their wings out to dry in the sunny air. A big curlew was strolling about at the sea's edge, but Dandy bounced and danced along beside me, ignoring the curlew, the curlew ignoring him, both of them too much at ease for the effort of chase and flight.

Ease. And I in my turmoil.

I glanced back. Liam was squatting down, staring at something — a crab or a bit of old wood, I couldn't see. Liam was always stopping and looking; he'd get excited at things no one else would bother their heads with — a heap of old stones or a rope of brown seaweed laid out on the sand. It was all new to me, this standing and looking. *The devil and idle hands*, that would have been the way I was reared. My family went to Portrush for a week every summer when I was young, but then Daddy died and she said that was that, there was no more money for holidays and going away. She took us on day trips to Donegal instead, but they were all action: pulling and squirming, strictly no dawdling, the freezing plunge, the scrape of the towel, wet sand in your knickers and socks. I didn't know grown-ups ever just stood around and gawped at things; I didn't know they were *allowed*. Not that I thought myself grown up, but Liam was four years older than me, and that made him nearly ancient beside my twenty-three.

But now I'd discovered I liked doing this looking; sometimes I'd find myself getting near as excited as Liam did himself. Sometimes. Not that day. Liam called out to me, but I didn't stop or let on that I'd heard him; I was too busy putting space between us. I glanced back once, but by then I was round the headland and Liam had dropped out of sight and sound.

It was different round there, rougher and stonier, with long piers of rock that marched out into the sea. The sun still beat down steadily, but it was much more exposed and the water was ruffled with hundreds of tiny blue ripples all running in fast from the west. Oyster catchers picked around among the weed, ringed plovers scuttled in the stones, winds pulled at the pools so they shivered and shone, and there wasn't a sinner in sight. My feet were soft from city shoes, so I hopped from rock to rock, watching my step and thinking of yesterday and the seal.

And today it was Liam and leaving here that were twisting me over and under like string in a cat's cradle. The confusion of it all. One minute I couldn't stand the sight of him, and the next I wanted to be here with him forever, standing about and looking at things, never far from his side. This new confusion was nearly worse than the seal confusion, and the two falling so close together was a whole lot worse than either on its own. Try as I might, I couldn't seem to get anything sorted or straight.

Bird sounds, wind sounds, the lapping of water. It was all so quiet and far away it felt as though there was no one left on the face of the earth but me. But for all the absence of people, I wasn't alone. The cracks in the rocks beside me were crammed with whelks and winkles; further down they were spiky with blue-black mussels and clogged with drying seaweed that shifted before my eyes. The more I looked, the more I couldn't stop looking. There were limpets everywhere, and between the limpets, barnacles, and crawling over them glistening flies as big as the nail on my thumb. Huge blue-grey sea slaters scuttled the rocks, sand fleas hopped on my feet, and the seaweed laid down by the tide in heaps was heaving with questing birds. Everywhere you looked everything was jam-packed with life, doing nothing at all with itself except living.

And the more I saw how alive it all was, the more I got this creepy feeling that it was way *too* alive, it was all too busy and strong for me, and if I went on looking another minute it might do like the skull had done and turn into something else.

So I stopped looking. I scuttled across the rocks like one of the slaters, and when I found Liam, I flung myself at him, demanding a bus.

"A bus?" he said, his hands on my shoulders, pushing me off and holding me there. "Where to?"

"Belfast," I said.

"Back to Robbie?" he asked, the anger showing in his eyes and tightening his mouth.

"None of your business."

"What if I think it is?"

It's nearly three in the morning, very dark, for the cloud has thickened and crowded out stars and moon. I've been a long time remembering Achill; it's been strange to see it so close up in my mind when I haven't really thought of it for years. I suppose I was already deep in love with Liam, but I didn't know it, I thought it was only my body responding to his. And I thought I could live rationally, could make that body give up what it wanted and do whatever I told it to do.

But I didn't go back to Robbie. Liam was angry enough to say what he thought of him, and somehow after that I couldn't make him big enough in my mind to submit again to that life.

Instead I went running home to my mother in Derry. Did I say that? Here am I, sleepless with dread at the thought of the morning and what it will bring, when back then Derry was home and my mother and refuge of sorts.

A delusion that even then was short-lived. After a week of her I was so beside myself I walked into the town and had all my mass of flame-red hair cut short in some sort of crazed, inarticulate protest. I came home near bald and wild with dread that I'd driven Liam off from me for good. Which was what I wanted and what I couldn't bear.

I looked in the mirror. This poky white face like a rat's with tufts of red all around it looked straight back out at me. I got out the antidepressants and sedatives they'd given me in the hospital and shook a whole load of tablets into my hand. That felt good; it felt painful and dramatic. Then I caught myself on. There were neighbours of ours, RUC men, who'd been shot at their own front doors. I knew what death looked like — I didn't want to be dead.

I picked up the nail scissors and eased the sharp points in under the flesh of my palm till the blood began to come. It hurt, but at first I liked that because it made me forget how I was hurting over Liam. Then I stopped liking it; I looked at myself and what I was doing and filled up with self-disgust. I set down the scissors and sat at the window reading the graffiti on the walls of the houses across the way. IRA SCUM and DEATH TO ALL TAIGS. I felt sorry for myself and martyrish — Romeo-and-Julietish — as though by falling in love with a Catholic I'd gained some sort of special status. I wept till my eyes were swollen and red, and I felt much better. I knew I wanted to go on living, I just couldn't work out how.

My mother gave out when she saw my hair, which got up my nose because she was never done telling me to tie it back and stop it from flying away out like a flag. I said there was no pleasing her. She said to keep a civil tongue or I wasn't welcome in her home.

"It's my home too," I said.

"It is not," she said. "You've a home of your own in Belfast, in case you'd forgotten. A husband as well, and it's time you were thinking of going back to him."

So there it was, out on the table. She wasn't blind — no phone calls, no sign of Robbie, no talk of me going away.

I saw the stiff line of her shoulders, and my heart sank inside me, for I'd backed myself into a corner and I knew that I'd have to tell her the truth or go.

Not right away though. Instead I got the bus to the Waterside, tramped up the hill to Brian and Anne's, and stood ringing their bell in the pouring rain, desperate for someone to talk to.

"Merciful God, Ellen," Anne said when she opened the door, "whatever have you done to yourself? You look like a scalded fox with a dose of the flu."

That was better than a rat, but only marginally. I decided there was no way I was going to tell her anything, not even the amended version I'd worked out on the way over. In this version I'd thought I might say I was *maybe* thinking of leaving Robbie, and Liam wasn't going to appear at all. Anne was no fool though — I knew she might spot that there was someone else lurking — so I had a contingency plan prepared with Liam's name changed to Fred. That way I'd only have to deal with the leaving-Robbie issue; I could leave the Southern Catholic bit till later or not at all.

But Anne knew more than I thought. She took me in to the fire and brought me a glass of wine and a towel to dry what was left of my hair.

"Brian's away out at a meeting, and the weans are in their beds," she said. "We'll have a nice wee talk, so we will, you can tell me all about it."

She was friendly and sister-in-lawish and fishing for information, but the harder she tried the more I shut tight as a clam. In the end she told me out straight that my mother had phoned while I was on my way over. It seemed Robbie had rung up looking for me. He'd asked her if we were back from Achill.

"I needed to get away from Robbie," I said, "so I told him I'd gone with you and Brian and the weans to Achill. He knows you can't stand him. I knew if I said I was going with you he wouldn't want to come."

That stopped her in her tracks. In Anne's world the more you disliked someone related to you the more they weren't supposed to know that was the way you felt.

You'd think, wouldn't you, that in a city the size of Derry there'd have been somebody I could have talked to, but there wasn't. I was always too awkward and shy, could never join in the way I saw other girls do, couldn't whisper and confide. So I'd kept myself to myself and spent my time waiting for when I might leave.

It was the same now. I sat there, saying less and less, getting lower as each minute passed. And the longer I sat on Anne's good settee in her clean and tidy living room with her clean and tidy life all around me, the surer I was that I had to find the courage in me to walk through the door and out into the storm. And the surer I was that I had to, the surer I was that I couldn't. Suddenly I understood that the life I had with Robbie was all about getting away from this. Then I knew that I hadn't gone far enough, that I had to leave the life I was living and travel further and make another one over again. I saw the seal heading down into black water, and I knew I had to learn how to drown.

And fear of it stopped my throat, so I choked on the glass of wine Anne had poured for me, sending it flying all over her sofa, and me flying out of the door.

When I got home I apologised to my mother for giving her lip. She nodded her head without looking at me, but I saw her mouth tighten with satisfaction and I had to clamp my own shut or I'd have been out on my ear.

I lasted another three days with her then I took the deepest breath of my life, phoned the number Liam had given me, left a message for him, then got on a bus that was headed down South.

Chapter 7

*I*t was dark when the bus pulled into Kilkenny city. There were people waiting on the pavement, but I kept my eyes in front. I'd been worrying myself sick all the way down. Would Liam meet me when I got there? Would I still want to see him if he did? Could I even remember what he looked like? I closed my eyes tight and pictured as hard as I could, but all I got was Robbie. I stared out at the lights and the darkness because it was better than staring in at Robbie's face, which wouldn't go away. I tried again for Liam, but the harder I tried the more completely I'd forgotten. Kilkenny was coming up on every signpost, so I knew we were near. By the time we'd swung off the ring road, I was wound up tight as a scream.

The bus drove into the station yard and stopped. I reached up and took my things from the rack, then walked slowly, slowly down the centre aisle. I climbed down the steps, my eyes on my feet. I lifted my head and there he was, and I knew him right away.

He took my bag and pulled me to the side so the girl behind me could get past. Then he stood there, looking down at me, smiling like an idiot.

"You've no hair."

"Not much. Anne says I look like a scalded fox with a dose of the flu."

"Who's Anne?"

"Brian's wife."

"Ah. The sister-in-law. Is this all the luggage you have?"

"There's another one in the hold."

We went round to the side of the bus where the driver was unloading. I pointed to a small blue suitcase.

Liam lifted it out, set it down on the pavement, folded me into his arms, and that was that. Or it was till we reached the house and we had a row over nothing at all on account of the state of our nerves. Then we went to bed and that was that again.

Liam is a stonemason and a sculptor. He went to art college in Dublin, spent a couple of years in a stonemason's yard in Cork, then moved himself here because he'd had about enough of cities. Liam comes from Tipperary — that's the next county — a place called Graigmoyla, forty-odd miles to the west of here.

"Kilkenny seemed a good compromise," he'd told me on Achill. "Close enough to home but not too close. People I knew around the place to give me a start."

By that he meant near enough to see his family when he wanted to, but not so near that they're forever dropping in. Liam is one of five, and he's slap in the middle. Connor's the oldest; he lives in the home-place with Kathleen, his wife, and they work the family farm. His father still lives there, and he keeps his hand in, though these days he does less and less. Then there's Eileen and Liam, and after him, Carmel and Tom. Liam thinks a lot of his family, especially Connor and Kathleen, but he has to have a bit of a distance from them or he feels like he needs to come up for air.

Which suits me as well. I like the Kielys now that I'm used to them, I do my bit in the family-thing, but I wouldn't want to live in the midst of the nest. Liam comes and goes, and they're tactful enough to keep their distance and give us a bit of space. We have his mother to thank for that. She laid down the rules in the early days — without her, it might not have entered their heads to hold back.

We're not one of these couples you never see apart. Not now, anyway, though we were to begin with, when I was new and everything was strange. I was glad enough of it back then, but it's different now and I wouldn't want to be always tagging along in Liam's wake. It passes, the twined-fingers stage. You don't see it going till it's gone.

I'm getting ahead of myself again. When first he came to Kilkenny, Liam stayed with Dermot Power and his wife, Marie, the same two who'd lent him the house on Achill. Dermot was a painter, his oldest friend, so Liam wasn't shy about cluttering up their living-room floor while he looked around for a house he liked at a rent he could scrape together. He was in no hurry, so he stretched his welcome. It's a good story now — they laugh in the telling — but by all accounts he wore their patience thin.

Liam knew what he wanted, you see, and he wasn't about to compromise just to have somewhere to live. He wasn't like Robbie, saying yes to the first place we saw that wasn't a total dump. Liam watched and waited, taking his time. At last he found a stone-built farmhouse with outbuildings and an owner willing to rent at a price he could afford. There was even talk of a lease, but it was only talk, the documents never appeared. Liam said quietly that he might be interested should Mr. Fitzgerald ever be thinking of selling. Mr. Fitzgerald let on not to have heard, but Liam knew well that he had. They understood each other. He would live there, and if it worked out to their mutual satisfaction it might come to a sale.

Back then that was part of buying a house — goodwill and

compatibility were valid currency, to be taken into account. Not now. These days no one cares who you are so long as there's a bank to come up with the mortgage. And neighbours don't matter the way they used to now that everyone has a car.

For two years Liam had rented, but by the time I stepped off the bus he was already mired in the long, slow business of buying. It all took forever. Mortgages were hard to come by, and he'd no fixed income to show. His family helped: his father stood guarantor with the bank, and Connor and Kathleen lent him money for the deposit. The worst part was getting permission from Pat Fitzgerald's five siblings. Pat (he'd long ceased being "Mr. Fitzgerald") was the oldest son, so he had the farm, but the house had passed to them all when the old people died and emigration had scattered the rest to England or America. Two of them were hard to find but easy enough to persuade. The other three had done well for themselves, they'd no urgent need, so they couldn't quite make up their minds to the sale.

"It's only natural," Pat said. "It's where they were reared, so they'll take their time. Push, and they'll dig in their heels; we have only to leave them be and they'll come round."

So they were let be, and they came round. I wasn't surprised, I'd been watching Liam, and I knew well he'd have his way. Robbie could want something and there'd be hell on if he didn't get it. Then he'd spot something else and away he'd go, the first thing entirely forgotten and left behind. Not Liam. Liam knew when to push, and he knew when to wait, it was nearly sinister, this relentless patience. It shocked me a bit. I had thought him all ease and good nature, but it seemed there was a whole lot more to him than I'd let myself notice.

It's a narrow house, two stories high, tucked sideways into a steep treed hillside with a muddy half-cobbled yard at the back and a mesh of fields at the front. A lovely place, secret and domestic, the small, ambling meadows like thrown-down cloths scattered over with horses and sheep.

There's a few other houses around the place, but nothing too close, I can hear Haydn's dogs at night, and a voice if it's raised to a shout. In winter there's the shine of Fitzgeralds' lights through the empty trees when I'm bringing in fuel from the yard. Quiet. That's how it was when I came here, that's how it is still in spite of the cars drawing up to bring folk for my hands. A quiet green place of spring wells and stone walls studded with white thorn and ash. About as far from Derry as the moon.

Around the yard there are outbuildings in different stages of dilapidation. There's a gate at the side that leads to a bit of an orchard with old, twisty trees climbing the slope, and behind them the land rising steeply up to the ridge. Below the house the land slopes gently down, and off in the distance the Blackstairs Mountains walk the horizon. The main gate from the yard opens into our boreen, which gives onto a single-track road, which gives onto another road where two cars can pass if you're careful.

There are more houses now. Coady's empty dwelling-house by the spring well has been renovated, and there are new bungalows here and there on the road that leads up to the ridge. I don't mind it, though at first I did. I'd got used to solitude; I didn't want neighbours.

When first I came here the place was more like a barn than a house. The roof leaked, the plaster walls blossomed with damp, the windows rattled at every breeze. Liam saw none of its defects. He showed me around like a man showing off a mansion; I might have been looking at antique rugs stretched on polished wood floors, at traceried ceilings, at mahogany sideboards laden with fine bone china. He had all sorts of plans for the house — its potential had long since changed in his mind into fact.

The front door opened directly into what had once been a traditional farm kitchen, with a flight of stairs climbing up the back wall, and two small rooms opening off it at either end. But time passed, Pat married, his new wife had set about making changes as new wives do. When she'd finished, the old range had gone and the big room had been divided. In the poky, wee kitchen an electric stove stood on rickety legs, and a miserable one-bar heater burned pound notes if you turned it on, which we rarely did, for we'd no pound notes to burn. Somewhere along the line Pat and his wife had built themselves a new bungalow three fields away and put the house up for rent. The bungalow was double glazed with fitted everything. Liam was planning to undo most of the changes and bring the house back to what it had been.

Upstairs there were three bedrooms and a makeshift bathroom that took up part of the landing. It had a sink, a toilet, a rust-stained bath, and a paraffin stove that took the edge from the cold. The bedrooms were small and low-ceilinged, their rectangular windows set low down near the floor so you had to kneel on the boards to look out. In the biggest bedroom was a double iron bedstead with an old feather mattress, the sort with a hollow in the middle that you both fall into no matter how far apart you've started out. Not that I minded until I was pregnant. I liked sleeping sprawled over Liam.

So it was no palace, but that didn't bother me. The flat in Belfast hadn't exactly been *Ideal Home* country either, and there I'd opened my eyes every morning on Robbie's bony shoulders, which never quite lost their tension, even in sleep. Here I would open my eyes and there would be Liam, flat on his back and snoring his head off, his brown curls rising and falling with every breath. I'd wriggle and squirm myself closer into his arms, then lie there smiling like an idiot until I grew bored with contentment and kicked him awake.

There was an ash tree outside the window and on windy nights in summer it swished and tapped on the glass, and on windy nights in winter it rattled and banged, and there was nothing I loved more than its lonely, companionable sound. Liam loved it too, he would never have cut it down, but when Andrew was four he was plagued with dark dreams and he'd wake in fear at the sound and the shadows moving across the wall. So the ash tree went, and I had to content myself with the one further round to the side of the house, which kept a civil distance and was never intimate with us. I'm sorry now that I let Liam cut it down, I should have taken time with Andrew and brought him back to loving the tree, for from that day he wanted everything that frightened him removed from him and there's no peace in living like that.

But all that was a long way off. It was autumn when I came here, and I was stunned by this bosomy, treed land with the blue hills rising up from its plains and the march of bluer mountains away to the east. I had never been to "the South" that was south, I thought it would all look like Achill or Donegal — acid land, wild and empty, all wind and sky and that haunted light. Nothing had prepared me for the ease of this place, its soft skies and luxuriant growth, its wide meadows and its loose brown rivers.

Settled weather. There never was an autumn like it. Day followed day, week followed week, we would wake to mist like a wraith at the window, breath-thin, a wash of moisture drifting about the house, the sheds, the trees. The fields were heavy with dew; the horses and sheep stood up to their hoofs in vapour, grey as the sea. Even as I watched, the meadows brightened. By eleven the mist had burned clear.

Then sunlight, silence. Each day, the air higher and thinner. Leaves dropping down in the stillness, knocking against the layered branches, a hollow, papery sound. And the cheep of birds, small flurries of song, the chestnuts fiery, the ash going lemon yellow in the soft, clear light. At evening the sky all around the horizon laid out with layered white cloud, like fresh, folded linen. Above this, a pure, thin blue, with combings of fine cirrus, the wisps of an old woman's hair.

I'd no idea what I was doing there, only kept from panicking by squashing down all thought. Derry, Belfast — they seemed like stories I'd invented, black-and-white photos, a long way away and in another time. I would wake in the early morning and lie in the breathing stillness, so happy I dared not move.

I should do this remembering more; it might bring me contentment. What's happiness? Nothing at all. Wind in the trees. You only notice when it dies away.

We hid ourselves from Liam's family, but with his friends it was different.

"This is Ellen," he'd say. No explanation, no word of where he'd got me from. It must have seemed strange to them — one day I hadn't existed, the next I was part of his life. A few of them asked about Noreen, but he only shook his head and smiled. Maybe they saw the way we were together and that stilled their tongues.

They seemed an odd lot, scruffy and garrulous, into music but indifferent to fashion. That was strange to me. There was more money in the North in spite of the unemployment, and if you were young you were mad for style. Here it was the opposite.

Most of Liam's friends seemed to live in jeans, and the girls my age hardly bothered with makeup at all. Everything was borrowed, thrown together, improvised. They thumbed lifts or rode around the place on antique bicycles; the few cars they had access to were clapped-out wrecks that no one ever serviced, much less washed.

But it didn't stop them enjoying themselves. Any excuse was a good excuse, and what money they had disappeared right away on a good night out with plenty of drink. Just the same, the talk was all of America and emigration and getting your hands on a green card.

That was then; it's all completely different now. The banks are lending, the emigrants are coming back home, and everyone's learned about possessions with the speed of light. But then was when I came, and it was so unlike what I was used to, it fairly made my hair stand up on end.

But Liam looked out for me, he knew I was frightened still, alert for any hint of the things I saw that weren't there. We'd be in company, and something would shift on the edge of my vision; I'd tense, but before I'd had time to panic, there he'd be, at my side. And it wasn't like it had been with Robbie, I didn't feel hunted down by his eyes, just less always the stranger in the crowd. Which was odd, when you think about it, because for the first time in my life I truly was.

I knew I ought to write to Robbie, but I couldn't put pen to paper and I couldn't bear to ring him up and hear his voice. You think with a new love you'll leave off loving the old one, but it doesn't always work like that, or it didn't for me. I knew I'd never go back to Robbie no matter what happened with Liam, but I cared for him still and I knew I'd hurt him sore. And I was his lawful wife, and Robbie set store by such things; if I wasn't going back I should tell him so he could get himself a divorce. Robbie needed a wife — and children, too — that way lay his only chance. But I didn't write or phone, I sent no word.

I signed on in the nearest town. There were no jobs anyway — half the country was signing on, they asked about qualifications, and when I said a degree in Russian they shoved the forms across at me, the same as in the North.

Liam was standing beside me, one hand on the counter, the other one dropped to my leg, which he planned to squeeze if I needed help.

"Different country, different ways," he said. "One squeeze for yes, two for no."

I was nervous as a kitten, for I'd got it into my head that they'd turn me down flat if they found out I was a Prod. But they didn't. I answered their questions and filled in their forms, and I didn't need help from Liam. Then they said it all had to be processed and told me when to come back.

The minute we were outside the door, Liam asked me about the Russian.

"Did I not tell you?" I said, all surprise, though I knew very well that I hadn't. Robbie had used it against me — he'd liked going on about fancy degrees and a fast track to the dole, while he was only City and Guilds but it paid the bills. I'm being hard on Robbie, I know that. Robbie was a grafter, never out of work, and he measured himself by the wage packet he brought home. I took any job that came up — unskilled and low-paid, I wasn't fussy — but they never lasted that long, and I felt inadequate when I wasn't working, so Robbie's sneers got to me.

At that time, with glasnost and the crumbling of the Soviet Union, I felt worse about the Russian than ever. As though I'd just put my shirt on the favourite and watched him come limping in last.

"They told us at school there'd always be a need for Russian translators," I said lamely.

But Liam liked having a girlfriend with Russian, he didn't care if it didn't get me a job. He started asking me words, and then he'd repeat them back and laugh at the way he had to make shapes with his mouth that it definitely didn't want to make. In no time at all he knew basic words, and it was only a skip and a jump before he could mispronounce whole phrases in pidgin Russian. We'd use it in company to say private things, and when people asked he'd say he had this personal tutor who was teaching him Russian in bed.

The weather changed. Transparent rain fell from a whitish sky that sat low on the hills and wiped out the line of the mountains. A soft trickling sound. Gentle. Our life turned inwards, enclosed by the falling rain. We'd go to bed in the afternoon, and afterwards I would lie with my head on Liam's belly; the house, our lives, ourselves, cocooned in the quiet rain.

I woke one night and got out of bed and went to kneel at the window. The rain had stopped, and the sky, wiped clean, was black and pierced with stars. In the morning the sunlight was different. Sharper, more defined. And a nip in the thinning air that pinched at your fingers and made you remember gloves. The sky was blue and intense, and the ash held its last yellow leaves to the radiant light. Light caught the filaments woven by spiders; it shone the wet grass and burnished the late gnats afloat in the air like sparks. From the ditches and fields came the dense gleam of light on water.

And there was I, uneasy, out of place, yet hardly caring so long as there was Liam.

Where was I from, what was I doing here, when was I going home?

Alone with Liam, I forgot the questions.

And Liam, never once asking me, letting the reins hang loose. Feeding me apples, feeling my breath on his hand.

Chapter 8

The sale of the house came through. The papers were signed in March, and the new roof went on in the dry spell before Easter. Everyone helped. Connor brought us the slates from a ruined house on the farm, and one of Liam's brothers-in-law had sawmill connections and got us a deal on the rafters. The insulation was a cobbling together of leftover stuff from a job on a schoolhouse, while tools and ladders and nails and the like were borrowed or scrounged. It was like that down here — you never just went to a shop and bought something; it all worked on who you knew and what way they'd find to help out.

Liam's friends were handy enough — artists often are — and they'd have a crack at most jobs provided you weren't too fussy about the look of the finished item. We weren't too fussy; we wanted a roof on the house that would stand the wind and the weather and that's what we got. I enjoyed it — a crowd of us up there, swarming about on the roof in the sunshine, busy as honey-bees. I worked hard alongside the men, and by the end of it I was stronger and fitter than I'd been for years. They accepted me, or they appeared to. I have good hands — always had. They were that way long before the Healing started.

By this time Liam's family was well aware of my existence. I hadn't meant them to be — Liam had promised me he'd say nothing — but you can't hide anything down here, and anyway Connor had caught us. He'd called in one morning early, and there was I, in the kitchen making tea, with nothing on me but Liam's old woolen dressing gown that I'd washed on him and shrunk down to half its size. I don't know which of the two of us was the more embarrassed. The only one who wasn't was Liam, who came in through the back, three eggs from the laying hens in his hand, and introduced us, cool as you please. I turned pure red, and I couldn't look at Connor; then I scuttled off up the stairs and pulled on my jeans and a sweater. But I didn't go back down; I stood at the door and listened till the voices ceased and Connor had gone.

When Connor came next he told Liam we were both expected for dinner on Sunday.

I wouldn't go, though Liam said I was only making things worse for myself.

"They won't stop asking, you might as well get it over and done with."

But he went alone. The afternoon was fine, and I meant to go out for a walk but I hung around waiting instead. It was well after six when the car pulled up, and I heard Liam whistling to himself as he closed the yard gate. He came in carrying a pile of bed linen that his mother had sent, and apples and pears from Kathleen.

"Did they ask about me?"

"They did," he said, dumping the fruit on the table.

"Well?"

"I told them you didn't like Catholics."

I stared at him, not believing my ears. He laughed. I shot out of my chair and pummelled him, hard as I could, but he only grabbed me and held my arms pinned to my sides. I swore I'd stay quiet if he let go.

He let go, and I went for him again.

He was wise to me, was Liam; he never once tried to persuade me, but off he would go, and when he came back I was always out of sorts.

"What is it you think they're going to do to you, Ellen? Invite you to Sunday lunch and call you a whore?"

I was offended; I shook my head stubbornly and wouldn't answer. At that time living together here was still something that was talked about. Besides, they were Catholics — under the thumb of the Church — their disapproval wasn't negotiable in my mind. That I was unsure and embarrassed didn't come into it at all.

Then I ran into Connor one Saturday in Kilkenny when I was shopping, and he said he was due to meet Kathleen outside Dunnes and she would want tea, and why didn't I come along?

So I did, and Kathleen was plump with short brown hair and warm, direct eyes. We had tea, then we had a drink, and the end of it was that I promised her I'd come over with Liam the following Sunday. At that time Liam's mother was still alive, and Connor and Kathleen were living in a house down the road from the farm. Kathleen said we should call with them first and she'd show me the house, then we'd all go over together, and that way it wouldn't be so bad.

And it wasn't. I liked them, especially the parents. And they made me welcome, for all I was a Protestant, living in sin with their son.

Fixing a house can be a habit you get yourself into. Once you are in it you go on doing it — you barely notice the months turning into years. And you get used to there always being some room you can't use, some wall being ripped down, some passageway piled with rubble that your foot knows to step over. I never minded in the early days, when the nesting thing was strong on us, but there came a time when I wanted to call a halt. Enough was enough, I said, but Liam couldn't listen. He loved that house, he never grew tired of planning, and he didn't mind dirt or mess.

He couldn't listen, and I couldn't leave it alone. But then the commissions began to come in, so he had to go into the workshop full-time and let the house be. Liam's work was beginning to sell, there were new demands on his time, he even began to turn down the building work that he'd always done to bring in some ready money.

Liam was strong and able. People employed him and found that they liked him, so the next time they needed a hand they came looking. Sometimes they didn't come to the house, instead they'd run into me in the supermarket and ask me if Liam was free. At first the answer was always yes, but slowly it got to be no. I'd been proud of saying yes, but I was prouder still of saying no, and I liked them knowing to ask me for Liam, it didn't make me feel awkward — it made me feel almost accepted.

It was hard for me here to begin with, and it made no difference that the hardship was mostly of my own making. I couldn't help myself; I felt I had *Protestant* written in neon lights across my back. Liam was never done telling me that it was the opposite. He said once folk heard the North in my voice they assumed I was Catholic, for Northern Protestants never came this far south, or not to live. He told me, but I couldn't listen, I was too used to scanning everyone and everything, too deeply tuned to the fact or conviction that difference meant threat.

As well as that, I missed the North. There was a gritty excitement about it, especially if you were young and not worn down, not paying the price in grief or in prison visits. There, violence was the stamp of reality — at the very least it was the yardstick by which you measured reality — and once you're used to the hit of danger it's hard to wind down and adjust to a seamless flow of days. That's the way of violence — it drowns out the subtle, despises the ordinary, barges straight to the head of the queue. Here everything was always the same, and how could you know you were even alive if mayhem and chaos didn't lep from the radio every time you turned it on? Sometimes I thought I'd fallen through time and landed facedown in a featherbed to smother in its softness.

With me, it was "in the North this or in the North that" — I was always on about it, always bringing it up. Mostly folk changed the subject, as if what I'd said was foolishness or bad taste. Or that's what I thought then; now I think they were just bewildered. And on the whole they were amazingly patient with me. Patient and polite.

As for the Wildwood, it kept its distance. I had odd flashes — a blur and change at the edge of my vision — but nothing that stayed around or turned into anything else. And these shadowy "sightings" (for want of a better word) were always easy to deal with. I'd only to shake my head as you'd see off a fly, and they'd vanish away.

"You're learning to handle yourself," Liam had said when I told him.

I wasn't at all, though I didn't say that, and I soon learned to keep my own counsel. I was avoiding even thinking about it, just forgetting as fast and as hard as I could and leaving well alone.

We still had a permanent cash-flow problem, so I'd do a few evenings in one of the pubs if there were any hours going begging. There never were at the start, but once people knew my face and who I was they'd ask from time to time. I always liked bar work — I'd done it in Belfast, after Queens, when I couldn't get what my mother called "a proper job."

By then you would never have thought our house was the same place I'd first stepped into. It was snug and dry, the windows were sound, and it was painted white inside from one end to the other. We'd knocked the middle room into the kitchen so it wasn't poky and wee anymore, and we'd fired out the cooker and put in a range that we had off one of Liam's sisters, who was busy updating. It had its drawbacks, that range: it was solid fuel, so you had to be there to fill it, and you couldn't run radiators off it the way you can with the newer models. Just the same the kitchen was always warm, and the water was spanking hot. I love the kitchen — it's mine and I keep it scrubbed clean as the dairy at Gran's, and mostly it smells of baking. I like the rest of the house as well. It's home, I don't care if Liam still thinks it isn't finished, I don't care if it isn't perfect.

We applied for a phone, but back then you had to wait months, so when we finally got it in I sent my mother the number. I'd sent the address, but not right away, I'd taken my time to let her get over the shock of my leaving Robbie. I hadn't told her about Liam; I thought I'd let her draw her own conclusions, which wouldn't exactly be hard, for she'd know I wouldn't have moved down South except for a reason, and if I didn't so much as mention a name then the reason must be Catholic. I knew she wouldn't like me leaving Robbie, for all she thought he wasn't good enough. I'd married him, hadn't I? I'd made my bed so I should lie on it. She was very strong on lying on your bed, was my mother, though the Presbyterian Church allows divorce. I waited, but she didn't write back. I might as well have tossed a bottle into the sea.

About two months after I'd sent the phone number, a letter came with a Derry postmark. I knew the handwriting. I turned it over and over, then I put it on the dresser, and it looked at me for a couple of hours, till I lifted it down and opened it. A single sheet, the writing on one side only. She had written telling me not to be expecting any phone calls. I'd moved to a different country, she wrote, it was too expensive to phone.

I sat with the letter laid out on the table. Liam came in and asked who the letter was from, and I handed it to him. He read it through, which didn't exactly take him all afternoon. I laughed, but he didn't. Then he took my two hands in his, and the next thing I knew I was crying.

"She can say what she likes, I don't care — it's nothing to me," I said. I was shaking my head from side to side, the tears flying off my face, which I couldn't mop with Liam holding on to both my hands.

Liam didn't speak, but he let go my hands and he put his arms round me and held me and stroked my hair.

"You're a long way from home," he said. So I cried and cried.

It wasn't all like that. We had the usual rows — nothing spectacular, just run-of-the-mill complaints as we each of us discovered that neither one was as perfect as we'd let on. I thought when he said he'd do it tomorrow, he meant that he'd do it tomorrow; it took me a while to grasp that tomorrow meant sometime in the not-completely-distant future. For his part, he thought when I said tomorrow I meant sometime in the not-completely-distant future.

There were other things — I could make a list, but it wouldn't be a long one. All couples have one — ours was shorter than most, and bit by bit we were learning each other's ways. It's this thing in me that comes between us, always has, always will. Yet that was what brought us together, for Liam understood it before ever I did, and more than that, he didn't mind the way I was.

I changed down here. You change anyway, but I think the

physical place that you live in makes for more difference than we sometimes allow. The buildings and streets of the city bring a particular alertness; the hard greyness sharpens the wits and the tongue, it hastens the feet. But the soft, dense colour of this place did its work on a sensual, physical level, sending me down from the mind and into the body, as rain finds the hollows and low places after long drought, filling them so that they lose shape and turn into mud.

So it was for me. I lost shape, inwards and outwards. My feet pulled through mud and forgot to resist it.

Chapter 9

There was a young one working in the supermarket in the town, a girl of maybe nineteen or twenty years of age. The first time I saw her I couldn't get over her; I had to force myself not to stand and gawp, for she was the living, breathing spit of Robbie poured into a female form. After a while I got more used to seeing her, didn't get the same shock. All the same, I could never entirely just shrug and pass her by.

One morning I was over at the fruit and veg picking out onions, and there she was, up ahead of me, lifting bunches of bananas from a box on a trolley and setting them out on the shelf. She turned and glanced in my direction. Her face was a Pierrot's — a dead-white, painted-on, chalky mask. I looked around, but no one else was staring. Maybe there was something going on that I hadn't heard about, some children's thing in the town to do with face painting or mime. She was a bit old for face painting, but it could be she was the face painter and she'd used some on herself as well. . . .

I went back to the onions, keeping my eyes to myself, concentrating, for I knew there was something up and I was growing afraid. When I'd finished with the onions I moved on to the carrots, then the mushrooms, then I started in on the fruit. The hairs on the back of my neck had risen, so I let myself sneak another wee look to find out what she was at. The thick white paint had entirely gone; her face was back to being pink and normal.

I knew right away that it was Robbie, but I tried to pretend to myself that it wasn't, for I didn't want what I knew. All day I was jumpy and tense with waiting, but nothing happened. When I found I was sticking close to the phone, I took myself out to the garden and made myself dig and rake.

Liam came home and found me out there, and he was delighted with all the work I'd done.

"You must have a few farm genes in you after all," he said. "From that crowd up in Dunnamanagh, your mother's people."

The phone rang at nine. I picked it up, and it was my mother, telling me Robbie was dead. It seems he was driving someone else's car — too fast and too full of drink most likely — and he'd smacked it into a wall and killed himself and the girl who was sitting beside him. My mother said that his sister Rita had phoned her; she'd said to be sure to let me know the funeral was in two days' time.

"Why would she want you to let me know?" I asked her. "I'd left him, hadn't I? They surely don't want me there at the grave?"

"You're not thinking of going?" Her question came sudden and fierce down the line.

"Why are you telling me if you don't want me to go?"

She didn't answer, and I didn't expect her to. She was phoning because I was Robbie's wife still. Phoning me so I'd know she'd been right all along.

But she needn't have worried, I didn't want to see them bury Robbie, I didn't want to go back to the North. But I sent flowers, yellow freesias, which have the sweetest scent I know and a shape like a promise if promises had shapes. I wept for him then, and I wept for Barbara Allen, and if I'd known how I'd grieve for him in the weeks to come I'd have gone to the funeral as well. I didn't regret him, you see, and I thought that because there was no regret I wouldn't have to remember.

I was wrong. The minute his coffin was safe in the ground some wall came crashing down inside me and my body was filled with a longing so physical and intense that it felt like pain. I thought of Robbie, his brown eyes and his brown hair and his strong, whippy body so different from Liam's, and my heart fairly broke. I wanted to see him one more time, to be in his company one more time; I wanted things to be as they'd been back then, when he was my song and I was his, and the song that we sang together was who we were when we sang it.

It had taken me a year to do it, but I'd written at last to Robbie. I'd told him where I was and that I would sign any papers he cared to send my way. I never had an answer — I didn't expect one — I knew that my letter would make him angry and remind him when he wanted to forget. But when I heard of his death, I was glad that I'd sent it. Sometimes silence can be every bit as bad as the worst of words.

When the grieving came on me I had to endure it. I couldn't stop it or change it by act of will. No more could Liam. At the start he had moved to comfort me, but I'd turned away from him, for I couldn't bear his touch.

Then when it had passed I tried to reach him, but he wouldn't let me back. At first I thought that his distance would go once I'd drawn him into sex, but it didn't. I couldn't understand that: how could he make love with his body while his mind stayed cold and apart? Making love for me was all of myself. We went together into the Garden, we lost ourselves and remade ourselves, and afterwards everything started afresh.

When he stayed so closed off from me I was deeply unhappy. I knew that my grieving for Robbie had hurt him, but I knew it had nothing to do with the way I was with him. As well as that, I was starting at shadows — afraid of these deaths that sent signs my way before they rightly happened. Liam went about his life steadily. If you hadn't known what had been between us, you mightn't have thought there was much wrong now. But I was edgy and lonely inside myself. I walked about in the night, and often I didn't go back up to bed but fell asleep at last in a chair in the kitchen. I'd begun to consider going back to the North, but I couldn't think of anywhere to go. I'd lost touch with my friends when I moved down here. Besides, they'd been Robbie's friends more than mine. I sat in the kitchen and thought of the past.

I hadn't lied to Liam when I'd told him the seeing began with the dandelion clocks in Dunnamanagh. It had. So I hadn't lied, but there were a couple more things from around that time that I'd just sort of passed over. Fiona Clarke was one of them.

The Clarkes lived a few streets away from us. There were three children: Trevor, who was Brian's friend; Susan, just a few years older; then Fiona, who'd gone off to London before ever we'd moved to the Glen.

It happened like this. There was a great-uncle of mine, a single man all his life, who took a heart attack and died there suddenly in Dunnamanagh. I think my mother liked funerals — the baking and talking and sandwich cutting, all the women in the kitchen together. Whatever the way of it was, she had us out there the minute she heard the news.

I was in the kitchen with the women. She said I was old enough now, so there was no getting out of it, that was me stuck. But I was keeping my head down, buttering soda bread like there was no tomorrow, staying out of things if I could. The women behind me were pawing over another death, a suicide by the sound of it, and only a few weeks past. I was all ears, for suicide has a strange, strong glamour about it when you are young and you've little enough idea of the suffering it causes. I heard the name Clarke, and then someone said something else and mentioned "the brother, Trevor." In a flash I realised the suicide must be Susan Clarke. And I knew Susan Clarke on account of Brian and Trevor; she'd gone off to Belfast to nurse just the summer before.

I was fifteen at the time, old enough to know what they were saying but not old enough to be told things straight out in my own right. And suicide was a scandal with us. Not as bad as it was for Catholics, but still bad enough for lowered voices and phrases that slid across truth. So I bided my time till after the great-uncle's funeral, then I got Brian off by himself and I asked him what way Trevor's sister had died and how had they managed to keep it so quiet?

Brian looked at me strangely, then he said I was off my head. "Susan Clarke's not dead, she's alive and kicking. You don't have to believe me; she's home next week — you'll see her with your own two eyes."

Then he asked who'd told me. I said I'd heard it in the kitchen.

"Who from?"

I thought hard. I heard the voices behind me again, but I couldn't work out exactly which voice had said what.

By now Brian had had enough. "You're off your head," he said again, "or you dreamt it." And that was the end of that.

A week later word came that one of the Clarke girls had overdosed on alcohol and antidepressants alone in a bedsit in London. But it wasn't Susan at all, it was the older girl, Fiona. By law there had to be an autopsy, so the Clarkes could do nothing but sit by the phone and wait for the authorities to finish their business and sign the release form for the body. It was terrible, so it was. The strain of waiting, not knowing when they could bury her. Brian spent a lot of time with Trevor, and I was that busy avoiding being left alone with Brian that it took me a while to notice that he was doing the exact same thing with me.

At first I thought those women had named the wrong sister, but when I went over it carefully in my mind I couldn't precisely remember hearing a name. I decided I must have thought it was Susan because I'd forgotten Fiona existed. And I realised in a way I didn't care to think about that I'd "heard" the news of Fiona's death a full ten days before she'd died. I never spoke of it to Brian. He was already courting Anne — maybe he talked it over with her, but I doubt it. Brian was always secretive and private, the same as I am. And he didn't like things he didn't understand.

As for me, I couldn't work it out, and I still can't. All I can clearly say is I ended up knowing something ahead of when it happened. And it wasn't like Jacko Brennan, for I'd never met Fiona Clarke. I'd barely even known her name when she died.

But it started me into thinking back, and I hit on one or two things that might have been premonitions or might have been just a slanty sort of coincidence. I was frightening myself, so I pushed it all to the back of my mind and tried hard to keep it there, well out of sight. Over time I mostly succeeded, or maybe I mostly forgot. But I got so I didn't like overhearing things; if someone had something to say to me they could stand themselves in front of me and look me straight in the eye.

Then we lost a hardly there baby, and everything changed again. But this time it wasn't like Barbara Allen; I didn't even know this baby was there till it wasn't.

It happened like this. We'd gone to the River Barrow one Sunday morning in early summer. Liam wanted to fish, so we walked till he'd chosen his spot; then I'd left him to it and wan-

dered off by myself. The Barrow's a lovely river, broad and generous, running through meadow and woodland and small, quiet
towns. It's good walking too, for it used to take barges, so there's
an old tow path hugging one of the banks.

That day there wasn't a sinner around, and I'd thoughts to
think so I'd walked a long way — to one of the eel weirs —
before I'd even noticed how far I'd gone. It was a dry May, so the
level had dropped, and when I saw the smooth pool of the weir in
that leafy place I took it into my head to wade out and take off my
clothes and swim where the water was deep.

I knew nothing of eel weirs back then or I'd never have ventured near it. I know now. The weir is formed by two walls of
stones that rise out of the bed of the river and meet in a V, not
quite closed at the join, which is where the nets are set when the
eels are running. The eels come through when the floodwaters
rise, are guided into the weir by the walls, then sucked to the net-
ted gap on the fast-flowing water deep in the pool. But as I've
said, I knew nothing of this, saw only the smooth green surface
between the walls and the shallow race to each side, where the
water plunged past the weir. And I love being naked in the river,
the water so soft and murky; I wanted to float about in it watching my white limbs wavering down there in the silty silk.

But there was to be no floating. I slipped crossing over the
race and never gained the pool at all.

It happened in a flash. One minute, up there in the sunny air,
and the next, I was under the water, a great blind current rolling
me over and over. Then a hand reached in and caught hold of my
hair and up I came, spluttering and choking, my lungs full of
water, the hair near ripped from my head.

Liam's hand.

The feel of my wet cotton dress on my skin in the chilly May
sunshine, the huge force under the water that had me then let me

go. The cold bite of my flesh, the young green of the leaves, the empty smell of the water under the flowering thorn —

And another force starting a wrenching inside me that wouldn't let up until it had done its work and the baby was gone.

———

Robbie's death changed things for both of us, but losing the baby just at that moment changed them again. Why? I don't rightly know, I suppose it shook Liam out of brooding about my past with Robbie and smacked him in the face with the truth: that I might have been grieving for Robbie, but this baby was of the two of us and nothing to do with Robbie at all. Whatever it was, it made him tender towards me, and once I felt him close again I lost all wish to leave.

A bare six weeks after the miscarriage we were married in the Registry Office in Dublin. Dublin had been Liam's idea, he had wanted to ask my family down and he thought it might be a sort of a halfway house.

I said not to waste the stamps.

He didn't believe me; he thought the right letters would bring them, but he was wrong. My mother wrote. A brief, formal letter, wishing us well, offering no gift or excuse.

Anne sent a set of boxed linen, a long red formal tablecloth with matching everything. There was a letter in with it, short and embarrassed. She wrote that she was sorry, but they couldn't come. I sat with the letter in my hands, the sticker on the cellophane wrapping looking up at me: Ulster Weavers by appointment to Her Majesty, the Queen.

I put the whole lot on the fire. Not on account of the Queen — I was no Nationalist. On account of the insult, for that was the way that I saw it. Liam came in as I was turning the blackened box with the fire tongs, letting the flames to the heart of it, watching them eat at it till it fell apart. He didn't say anything, but after that he didn't ask his family either. That was for my sake, to even things up.

There's another thing about Robbie's death. That was the one and only time that she's rung me in all the years I've been here.

Not long after our marriage, I started another baby. Liam watched me like a hawk, but he'd no need to, I left off mending roofs and clambering about in the river and lifting stones for whatever wall we happened to be rebuilding. Losing two was enough for me, I'd no wish for another Barbara Allen.

When Andrew was born I couldn't get over his maleness, his genitals, his little spout of a penis. I had made this body inside my body, yet mine was a female body and this, beyond doubt, was a male. It was pure strange. Stranger still to look into his eyes and have no idea at all who it was lived in there.

We called him Andrew after my dead father, and Liam wanted his second name to be Daniel after his own. I was happy with that, for his parents were good to me and it softened it for them that there was to be no christening. Just the same, I was glad that Daniel came out of the Bible and wasn't some saint's name, like Eugene, though I kept that thought to myself. Prejudice runs a whole lot deeper than logic. Feelings are feelings — they don't always match with the things you tell yourself in your head.

It wasn't only on my account that there was to be no christening. Liam isn't completely set against God as I am, it's just he has scant respect for the Church when it comes to the overwhelming sinfulness of sex. Yet for all his talk he's every inch a Catholic. Deep down, I'm certain sure he still thinks it's the One True Faith. And he's naturally religious in a way that I never was, nor could be — I don't think it's ever even crossed his mind to doubt.

The Church didn't care for people like Liam in those days. À la carte Catholics, that's what they were called — people who hung in there yet wouldn't buckle down. But that was back then, now is completely different, now you nearly have a search on to find a Catholic who isn't à la carte.

Everything blossomed for us after Andrew was born. There was all the usual: my body's soreness, the broken nights, the problems I had at the start with breast-feeding. I was always tired, though Liam helped and Andrew fed alright and he wasn't that bad when it came to sleeping. Tired, but oddly happy. It was a bit like those snowstorm-things we had when we were children: the bubble of glass with Mary and Joseph and the donkey, or sometimes an Austrian-looking village, deep in the snow. You picked up the bubble and shook it about, and the snowflakes danced in the crystal air and fell down quietly, quietly, covering the earth.

For a while we lived like that, inside the bubble, though no one picked it up and shook it. May came and I carried him into the fields and showed him the whitethorn blossom that lay on the trees like snow. Day followed day.

Suzanna was born almost two years later. This time there was no glass bubble, or if there was, I hardly noticed, for we were still grieving for Liam's mother, and anyway, two is a whole lot different from one.

Chapter 10

There'd been nothing for ages and ages, and I was that busy with babies I'd hardly given it a thought. Then one summer afternoon I was lying out in the orchard, Suzanna beside me, and I felt a spiralling movement start in my feet and move slowly up through my body till it passed itself out through the top of my head. Useless to try to describe it in words. I can say it like that — so matter of fact — but once it started there was nothing I could do to stop it, and it was definite to the point of violence in its force. And I say "movement," but it was more as though an autonomous entity had got inside me and was following its own course — completely within the body yet moving the body as your sleeve will move if your outstretched arm traces circles onto the air.

As soon as it passed I sat up and looked around me. In the whole of my life I had never felt anything like it, yet Suzanna still lay there, gurgling beside me, Andrew still searched out snails in the grass, everything looked the same. I was so astonished I nearly forgot to be frightened.

I got to my feet, brushed myself down, gathered my babies to me, and headed off to find Liam. I meant to tell him, truly I did, but he wasn't in the workshop, where I looked first, he was in the kitchen with Dermot, planning the show that was coming up soon for them both in Cork. By then Suzanna was crying,

Andrew was wanting his tea, and Liam was that busy listening to Dermot he hardly noticed me at all. He says now that I seemed alright, and maybe I did, for I had Suzanna on one arm, sucking away, and Andrew's mouth was open like a baby bird's for the egg I was spooning in with the other hand. Children don't wait around for attention until you're in the mood. Anyway, how would Liam or Dermot have noticed anything? They were head-down-and-hard-at-it, sketching out plans on the backs of the unpaid bills.

When Dermot left, Liam was hyper. It was Dermot this and Dermot that, and he'd eat now because he had to go off to see Tommy Quinn about getting stands made for the work. He ate standing up, talking away, then put on his jacket and off he went out the door.

After that something got stuck in my throat, and I couldn't tell him at all.

I'd never heard of any such thing, nor read of it either, and whatever it was I knew that it wasn't normal. Yet I didn't think I was mad this time, for it wasn't to do with my mind, it was all in the body. I set myself to endure it until it went away.

But it didn't go away, it came back and came back, though at first it wasn't for long and it always chose a time when Liam wasn't there. It was always the same. It started in my feet then moved itself up through my body and on out through my head. Often it came at night when I'd just gone up to bed and Liam would still be downstairs, reading or watching television or talking with someone who'd called. As soon as he came up it stopped of its own accord.

Then it got more unpredictable in its timing. Sometimes I'd be in the kitchen, baking or cleaning, and something would move in my feet and they'd start into flexing and stretching themselves before I'd rightly noticed in my mind what was going

on. The next thing I knew this energy-thing would come spiralling up with such force that I had to hold on to the table till it
passed. Sometimes Liam opened the door only seconds after, and
I couldn't believe he saw nothing, for its presence had been so
strong I'd have sworn it left stains on the air.

I feared it by then — I thought it must be some evil thing, too
bad to be spoken of or written down.

⸺ ⧞ ⸺

The first time the Healing came it was for Whiskey, the golden
retriever that Liam's brother Tom had given us soon after
Andrew was born. She was six weeks old when Tom got her — a
bundle of trembling fluff — and he'd trained her himself for
hunting, which meant months of patient work. By the end of it
she was good, very good, but only when it suited her. That was
the problem. It wasn't that she didn't understand what he wanted
her to do, she understood alright, and she might just do it, or she
might not. It drove Tom wild — right to the edge of mistreating
her — so he caught himself on just in time and gave her to Liam,
who didn't hunt and wouldn't mind her ways.

She was a lovely creature, tall and elegant and the warm,
deep-golden colour of sand. All the same, you could see what
Tom meant, for she did what she wanted when she wanted to,
and no one was going to tell her otherwise. That was okay by me,
for she was good around the house and gentle with the children.
Andrew loved her; he'd lie curled in beside her telling her his
secrets from the minute he learned to talk. Suzanna loved her
too, but she was rougher. At eight months of age she grabbed
hold of a fistful of Whiskey's fur, hauled herself onto her feet, and
set off on her own personal walking frame.

Then Whiskey cut her paw, a long incision, deep between the
pads, and no matter what we tried on it, it wouldn't close. It

wasn't only home remedies out of the first-aid box either. Liam was tired taking her to the vet, who was tired thinking up new ways to strap it so she couldn't lick off whatever he'd just put on. We even tried an upturned lampshade round her neck so she couldn't get at her paw in the night, but by morning she had it pulled off and torn into pieces and we never found out how. The only thing left was to muzzle her, so Liam did, but she whimpered and fretted and got herself into such a state that he had to take it off.

So I bathed her paw in a soda-bicarbonate solution, which was better than nothing at all, and then when I'd finished I knelt on the floor and took the sore foot in my hand. That's when it happened. A tingling started in my head, and the spiral-thing began in my feet and my hand let go of the paw of its own accord. I was afraid; I thought I was going to see something, so I stayed down there, waiting, this strange, empty feeling inside me. Then my hand moved, and I watched it as though it belonged to some-one else. It stiffened and spread itself out and held itself over the paw.

The next morning the cut had closed and was almost knitted together. Liam said maybe that vet wasn't altogether useless, and I said nothing. I'm close by nature, but this thing makes me worse — I'll hug a secret like a coat wrapped tight against freez-ing weather.

Two months after that Andrew fell on the path. He'd a stick in his hand, which drove into his mouth and ripped the soft gum where the upper jaw joins the soft, fleshy skin of the lip. Liam car-ried him in. He was hysterical, his mouth streaming blood, his eyes on me, desperate.

I don't know what happened next, for the thing had started and this time it came from someplace where I'm not divided so there was no one to stand around and watch.

Liam says that I took the child, laid him down on the couch, and held my hand, the fingers splayed out, a few inches over his mouth. I didn't speak, not even to comfort, but Andrew's shrieks turned into sobs and then his eyes closed over and the bleeding slowed and stopped.

Afterwards Liam still wanted to take him to the surgery, but at the word *doctor* Andrew opened his eyes and started to whinge. Liam said no more, and I sat holding Andrew's hand till he fell deep asleep. Then I picked him up and carried him to his bed. When I came down Liam wanted an explanation.

"Mouths are easy cut," I told him. "Easy cut and easier healed — it's the saliva."

"What were you doing with your hand?"

"Nothing. Calming him, that's all. Sometimes I do it with the children. It soothes them, I don't know why."

I turned away from him, for Liam knows me well and I was shaken. I started taking things out of the fridge, ready for making the dinner. Liam sat with Suzanna on his knee, watching me, drawing his own conclusions.

The next day I had Andrew on the sofa in the kitchen. He was sorry for himself — his mouth was still very tender — but he wasn't feverish and he was hungry. The day after that he was run-ning round.

Liam wanted to talk, but I wouldn't have it. I closed the door in his face and shot home the bolts.

"Andrew always heals up well," I told him. "It mustn't have been as bad as it looked — we just panicked because of the blood."

I went to the Cork opening with Liam and Dermot and Marie. Liam was pleased. At that time I was always saying I'd do things, and then when it came to the point, I backed off. It was February. Suzanna was only thirteen months old. We'd left them with Kathleen and Connor, but still I was anxious, for it was the first time and what if they woke and wanted me and I wasn't there?

"They'll live," Marie told me, when I said I might just go and phone. Her grey eyes looked straight into mine and refused to waver. "It's your life as well as theirs, Ellen. It's hard the first time, but after that it gets easier fast. Before you know it, you'll jump at the chance of a night away."

Liam nodded and said she was right. Marie knocked back her drink and handed it to Dermot for a refill. I smiled, pretending to agree.

I'd rather be home with them, I thought. Not having to stand here and smile and pretend and think of things to say.

We were in a pub with half an hour to go before the opening, standing up at the bar because Liam and Dermot were so tight with nerves that they couldn't sit down. Marie was wearing black — a black shirt, buttoned low and tucked into a skintight skirt, with see-through black tights and high heels. I was wearing a dark-green dress that I'd bought in Belfast and still thought of as almost new because it was hardly worn.

Marie's naturally pretty, she has wavy brown hair, good skin, and a lovely mouth. But that night she didn't look pretty — she looked so sexy it fairly smacked you in the eye.

I made some remark.

She nodded, satisfied. "I wanted to look like a vamp, not a wife."

I gaped at her. Once I'd have been excited if a girlfriend had said that. I'd have reached for my drink, thrown it into myself, then got up to buy us more to be sure of a good night out. Now I caught myself in the mirrors behind the optics. I looked as if I'd just swallowed a lemon. It stopped me in my tracks.

More than that, when I'd come here first I'd thought these women were dowdy and didn't know the score. Now I felt incompetent at being female in their company. In five years. And I never saw it happen.

"Don't worry about it." Marie was standing beside me, watching me watching myself in the mirror. "It doesn't last, you'll get yourself back. It's only what happens while you're having the children —"

I saw myself flinch. Marie stared out from just behind my shoulder, and I couldn't read her face and then I could. Suddenly I knew that she'd had about enough of Dermot and was getting ready to move on. Still watching ourselves in the mirror, I saw that she meant me to know. She nodded and twisted her mouth, a wry little smile at one corner. All this was nothing to do with "the Seeing"; it was two women telling each other, in the way that women do.

I was glad when she dropped her eyes and turned back to Liam and Dermot. Marie was too much for me. Too female, too old, too knowing. And somewhere, down in the depths of herself, she was suffering and alone.

After the show we went in a crowd to a restaurant to eat, and later again we moved to the hotel bar to go on drinking after hours. By then we'd thinned down — the gallery staff, two journalists, and a handful of fellow artists. Liam and Dermot were already blootered, but so adrenalined and euphoric that it hardly showed.

The place was packed, so we stood in a bunch at the bar. A man who might have been at the show came up to Liam and got into conversation. Wants to meet the artist, I thought, looking around for Marie, who was busy with one of the journalists and not to be distracted. Then I felt a hand on my arm, and Liam's fan was asking me what I was having and would I go over with Liam and meet his wife?

He got the drinks, and we made our way through the crowded room to a table at the back. "I'm Philip," he said, putting down his drink, "and this is Paula, my wife." A pretty brunette with hairdresser-hair looked up and smiled through immaculate makeup and patted the seat beside her.

We shook hands, introduced ourselves, and sat down. Right away Philip went silent and looked straight at Paula. I knew she had something to say, but I thought it was Liam, not me, that she wanted to speak to.

"It's no good you fighting it, petal," she said, hardly glancing at Liam.

I thought I hadn't heard her right.

"I saw you come in," she told me. "That little lady's making life very difficult for herself, I said to Philip. She's got it, but she's making herself very busy pretending she hasn't. She seems to think she can wish it away, but she can't."

Liam went still as a setter marking a scent. He stared at me and so did Philip, but I sat frozen, waiting for what might come next.

"I'm a healer," she said so casually she might have been telling us that she ran a boutique. "We're from Sheffield, I've been working here. We come over every few months for a week."

I didn't take my eyes off her.

"Group-healing sessions in Cork, then readings with private clients in the evenings," she went on. "We've been here a week; we're going home tomorrow."

"A faith healer?" The sound of my own voice surprised me.

She shook her head. "No, faith's got nothing to do with it," she said lightly. "A gift healer. And I'm a clairvoyant as well." I stared some more. She was in her late thirties and wearing a light-blue dress that made her skin look translucent. Philip was in a grey suit, very smart, his hair groomed, his manner bouncy and brimming over with good humour.

"We like coming to Ireland," he told us. "People know what you're talking about here — they don't just think you're a quack." There was suddenly an edge of bitterness in his voice, and his mouth turned down at the corners. Paula laughed, and straightaway he perked up and was chirpy as a sparrow again. They were the oddest couple. Guileless, somehow. Transparent as children, and nothing remotely bad or devious about them, nothing even I could reconstruct as evil.

She went prattling on about some man from the other side that she thought a lot of. She was telling us how excited he'd got when he saw me come into the bar.

"He made me send Philip off to bring you over."

I was like a rabbit watching a weasel — horrified and fascinated — hating what she was saying, unable to look away. And what she said was completely mad, and I knew it was mad, yet she was so down-to-earth in herself that she nearly sounded sane.

"Ellen doesn't want to see things," Liam said. "It frightens her. She says she doesn't want to know what she shouldn't know —"

"Oh, but she's right, absolutely right. So many people wandering around and they all want to talk, and most of them can't be trusted. You have to be selective. You have to be able to put your foot down when you need to and say no."

There was a silence.

"If they're all out there, wandering around, talking away," Liam said slowly, "then how d'you get any peace to talk with the ones you want?"

"It's like being in a restaurant. Conversations go on all

around, but you aren't listening to all of them, are you? You're focusing in on the person you're with, shutting out all the rest."

I screwed up my courage. "Who are 'they'?" I asked her.

"Spirits," she said, completely matter-of-fact.

"Are they dead?"

"Not always. Sometimes they're just wanderers — people who're asleep or in comas. They won't do you any harm unless you let them. Mostly they keep to themselves, but sometimes they don't. Sometimes it's like a drunk at another table who tries to start up a conversation."

"What do you do then?" Liam asked.

"The same as you'd do in a restaurant — tell them to go away. If I want to talk to someone, *I* start the conversation. I don't speak to just anyone."

I gaped at her. She was a tough one alright, yet she seemed such an airhead, pretty and twittery and vague. Her lot was harder than mine — it's no joke having people no one else can see drifting in and out of your field of vision. What she had to live with would have driven most people round the bend.

Then suddenly all the life seemed to leak from her. She said she was tired and needed her bed, so they wished us good night and they went.

And I thought we were only waiting to get away from them. I thought we would crease up laughing the minute they were gone —

We didn't. We sat there, saying nothing. I was tombstone-cold, though the packed room was hot with life.

After a bit we collected ourselves and headed back to the bar. It wasn't the same. I was knocked nearly sober by the encounter, but Liam was stumbling drunk and still he wouldn't quit. He wanted more drink and more company, and when at last he could take no more we went up the stairs to our room and he stretched himself on the bed and passed out cold.

I took off his shoes, his trousers and shirt, then I crawled in beside him and lay there, thinking of Paula, till the light grew.

When we were up I asked for them at the desk, but I only knew their Christian names. The receptionist looked down the list, then said she was sorry but they'd already left and she couldn't give out an address without permission.

It changed me, that meeting, for it's a strange thing to be recognised, even honoured, for something in you which you'd thought was shameful and must be hidden away. It changed Liam too, for out of it came his idea that I should be at this healing game, and once it was in his head he gave me no rest.

Chapter 11

The first time Catherine came to the house it was to see Liam about an artists cooperative she was busy trying to set up. Liam wasn't around so I brought her into the kitchen and gave her a cup of tea. She wouldn't sit down. Instead she leaned herself against a press, her hands hidden in the stretched sleeve ends of her sweater, her tea mug nestling in the woolly cup of her hands.

Whiskey got up from her mat in the corner and sauntered across to inspect her. Catherine glanced down absently, then nuzzled Whiskey's nose with one sleeved hand. After a bit she forgot about the dog and stopped nuzzling, but Whiskey put her nose under Catherine's elbow and nudged, then waited for more. Catherine rubbed the dog's nose again. When she stopped Whiskey looked at her consideringly, then took herself back to her mat.

Catherine's a potter, but she makes nothing useful. She throws giant teapots, then covers them over with tangles of leaves and flowers and insects in strange-coloured glazes that look as wet as water. There's nothing delicate or beautiful about these flowers; they have stems as thick as a man's wrist, dark-red protruding stamens, giant insects crawling about in their depths. All very sexual and unnatural, so it's not just that her teapots are huge, they're very disturbing, which attracts attention and buyers.

She's also elegant, really elegant, and it's not to do with clothes but the way her bones hang together. She has white skin, a crooked smile, and a mass of thick dark hair that falls to her shoulders but is cut to different lengths to take out some of the weight. In fact, she looks a bit like Whiskey — not golden but dark, with the same long legs and narrow nose, the same languid poise. She's as odd as two left feet, but either she doesn't know or she doesn't care, she isn't one bit interested in what people think of her, so she's free to do as she likes.

The day was cold, but the kitchen was far too warm to be wearing gloves to drink your tea. As I was thinking this she set down her mug and folded the stretched sleeves back on themselves. Her fingers were red and swollen and sore.

"Chilblains," I said.

She nodded. "Bad circulation. And working with water and clay. My studio's so cold the tea cools nearly as soon as it's poured."

I said nothing.

"All my sweaters have stretched sleeves," she told me. "That way I kill two birds with the one stone — the tea stays halfway hot and my hands thaw out a bit. The trick is to finish the tea before it's got cold or your hands have warmed up enough to itch, which drives you mental."

I've had chilblains. They're not much to look at, but the level of quiet torment is powerful. So I nodded and sat there, sipping and listening. I like tea so hot that it burns the back of your throat, but to drink it like that you have to concentrate, you have to sip and not talk. Anyway, I liked watching her. That elegant, angular grace. And she was so sure in herself, so unapologetic. I felt I could leave it all to her, I didn't have to think up words to fill the silence.

When she'd finished with chilblains she began on a piece she was making for a commission. I hadn't seen her work then, so I couldn't properly follow her talk of insects and spouts and petals. It all sounded weird and unlikely.

"The idea at the start was definitely more than a little bit flaky," she said. "I thought most likely it wouldn't come off, but I had to give it a try. . . . And now I have it almost there and it's nothing only brilliant." She laughed aloud with pleasure at the thought of its brilliance. Her nose was running from coming in out of the cold, and she rubbed it on the folded-back bit of her sweater. Her eyes shone, and half her hair had come loose from its clip and I sat there thinking her work mustn't be any good or she wouldn't be boasting about it the way she was.

"You don't talk much, do you?" she said abruptly.

"I used to," I said slowly. "But then I sort of stopped."

It was a peculiar thing to say, but I didn't mind because it was what I wanted to say. Those days I mostly opened my mouth and the words that came out were about as close to what I meant as an ice cream is to a glacier. So I didn't talk much, or not out loud, I talked inside in my head. Maybe that's why I would get closer to Catherine than to anyone else I've known. Because with her I could say what I meant to say, and though it was clumsy it didn't sound too stupid with her listening. People were always surprised at our friendship because Catherine's successful and sought-after and social and I'm not. Seeing us together made them stop and look at me twice. Which I liked. I liked seeing people stopped short, and I liked it that Catherine sought me out.

She nodded and set down her empty mug on the draining

board and asked when would be a good time for her to come back.

"I'll tell him you called," I said. "Why don't you ring before you come over the next time and then you'll be sure of catching him in?"

I told Liam that Catherine Casey had called in about some co-op thing for buying materials, and would call back another time.

He was interested right away. He said it was time they got themselves organised and what did I make of Catherine? Had I liked her, did I think she was strange?

"She's beautiful," I said. Somehow it was all I could think of to say.

"Is she? Well, yes, I suppose she is, I hadn't thought of her like that. Just that she's easy on the eye."

"She went on about teapots and flowers. Told me how brilliant her work is."

Liam laughed. "That would be Catherine alright. She gets a bit carried away with herself. She doesn't mean it the way it sounds; she just gets overexcited."

Liam says I have a judgmental face. I think he's right. Too many Covenanters in my lineage, my mother from a long line of Ulster-Scots Presbyterians, my father a Presbyterian out of Glasgow, moved to Derry for his job in Her Majesty's Customs and Excise Service. My face is narrow, the nose too long, the skin too white, the eyes too light, the hair too red and wild. Not carrot red but blazing fire–flame red; it springs round my head like burning wire, crackles with all the life that's somehow not in my face. You'd think it would ease my face of some of its judgment, hair like that, but it doesn't. In an odd, demented way it adds to the effect.

Sometimes I leave my hair loose, and it tickles like spiders crawling my face, but I'm not about to go for the rat look again, so mostly I pull it back hard and tie it tight on my neck. I like it like that. I like economy and plainness.

Liam doesn't. Back then he'd take the bands from my hair and shake it loose, and when I protested he'd tell me I should have been a nun. I'd tell him Presbyterians don't approve of nuns, Presbyterians don't renounce the world, they live in it instead. He'd look at me then; he'd call me his Wee Puritan, but sometimes — even in those days — he'd call me his Wee Black Bigot instead. On Puritan days he'd offer to show me how to live in the world. I'd tell him I already knew, but to go on ahead and show me again, if that was what he wanted —

Afterwards, he'd tell me he liked corrupting Puritans.

That was okay by me — I liked being corrupted — but on Wee Black Bigot days I'd get thick with him, and wouldn't be shown.

"To hell with you, Ellen," he'd say, "you've a Presbyterian soul."

It would be my turn to look at him then. Liam isn't sectarian — he doesn't think Presbyterians are heretics, and he doesn't much like pious Catholics or the Church.

He thinks that means he's free from bias.

But you don't see your own ways unless you're with someone who wasn't reared as you were; you don't notice the things you do without question unless you're standing alongside someone not bred to those ways. And there I was, reminding him with my every gesture, and it wasn't comfortable. And Liam likes comfort, so in his heart he doesn't like Presbyterians, even lapsed ones like me, who don't like us either.

It's no different for me. "I'm not a bigot," I'd tell him. "I'm only how I was reared."

Liam has one of those fleshy, almost hairless bodies, very strong, very full of health and good humour and well-being, so he doesn't dwell up in his mind, he lives a warm, sensual life through his flesh. And there's something lovely about a man like that, especially when he's young; he gives off a sort of vitality, you feel you could warm your hands on him, and I did — I still do.

But because he loves life and the body's life, there's a part of him that's threatened by economy and plainness. So he wanted me to be me and not me — the two things at the one time — and I couldn't. I still can't, I can't loosen up, I can't ever just give in and do what he wants, no matter how badly he wants it. If I did that I'd lose myself, and I'll never, ever do that again, or never willingly. One Purdysburn was enough for me, I've no wish to learn my way around another.

Sometimes I'd undo the bands and take out the clips and let my hair down for him myself. Those times he'd say that if he didn't know me for a Presbyterian he'd think I was a witch. But he knew there was no part of me was a witch no matter how he might yearn for it. Witches are too slack, too earthy, for a woman of my temperament — witches don't mind dirt. And somewhere he was relieved, for he liked the transparency of me; he didn't want to have to deal with all that underworld of twisty darkness, though he thought he longed for it.

So I'm perfect for him, the combination that makes life impossible for me and safe for him. I'm a living, breathing contradiction, a travesty of nature, a Puritan with second sight.

———

Catherine came back without phoning first, and Liam wasn't there so she hummed and hawed then asked could she leave him a note? I invited her in.

Tea again and that business with her hands in her sleeves

around the mug till she'd warmed them enough, then the mug set down and the sleeves folded back.

Suzanna was in her highchair eating mashed-up banana and making a mess. For something to say, I asked Catherine had she finished her teapot.

"I went on about it, didn't I? I do that. I know I should hold back and be cool, but I forget. I suppose now you think me the most unmerciful show-off?"

I'd nodded before I could stop myself, but she only laughed. I couldn't work her out, but I didn't seem to be offending her, which was somehow relaxing and caught me off my guard.

"I'm onto a new one, completely different from all the others so far. I'd tell you it's going to be great, but you'll only think I'm too full of myself again —"

"Don't you get tired of teapots?"

"I do, oh, I do, I get so I've totally had it with teapots — I never want to see another as long as I live. . . . Then I'm lying in bed, thinking of nothing at all, and a new one floats into my head."

She was off again. When they came floating into her mind, she said, she didn't just see the teapot, she saw it where it should be, saw the setting that showed off its true potential.

"Like where?"

"Oh, you know, somewhere grimy. A student flat or an attic, or one of those cloakrooms you see in old Georgian houses, all broken floor tiles and elephant-foot umbrella stands and jumbles of boot-jacks and Wellies. But they never end up in places like that — they're too expensive. It's my own fault. Well, not entirely — the gallery's pretty strict on pricing. But the end of it is they cost so much that normal people can't afford to buy them." She stretched out a hand and helped herself to a piece of shortbread from the cooling tray. "So I set them up in places where they look the way they *should* look and I have them photographed. Then someone rich comes along and takes them home to live on a blond wooden floor or a Persian rug." She shrugged and poured herself more tea from the pot. "I shouldn't complain. I do what I like doing most, it pays the bills, and at least there's no danger of anyone taking me remotely seriously —"

"Don't you want to be taken seriously?"

She shook her head. "I'd hate to be taken seriously —"

Out went the hand for more shortbread. She ate it, then licked the crumbs off her swollen fingers.

"Are you from a big family?" she asked abruptly.

"No, why?"

"Because both times I've come here you've been baking."

"Suzanna's birthday cake," I said. "She's two on Sunday. You don't have to be from a big family to bake."

"No, but it helps. Mind, I'm from a big family and I don't bake at all. Reaction. That's what the teapots are about. I mean, teapots must be *the* symbol of rural Irish hospitality, and here I am, making them into oversized grotesques with strong sexual undertones — and they'd even pour if you could lift them."

"How many of you are there?" I'd had enough of teapots.

"Seven. And you?"

"Two. Only me and an older brother. My father died when I was eight."

"That's tough. Did your mother remarry?"

"Indeed she did not." I must have spoken more bitterly than I'd intended, for I saw the startled look on her face. "It would've been against her principles," I said, to explain.

"You make her sound fierce."

"She was. Is, I should say, she isn't dead. It was a stiff upbringing, alright, I could resent it if I let myself, but what's the point? That's the way she was, and I daresay it was hard enough, being left with two young children to rear. That's what everyone told us anyway. We were Millstones around her Neck."

"Does she visit often?"

I shook my head and wiped banana sludge from Suzanna's face.

"Not since I came to live down here. Which is six years now."

"But she's seen the children?"

"No. She's never set eyes on Liam either. He phoned her when Andrew was born, and she sent a stuffed donkey. He phoned again for Suzanna, and she got a babygrow from Marks and Spencers." Why was I telling her all this stuff? I rubbed at Suzanna's mouth again, and she gave me a glare. "My mother's not a maternal sort of woman," I added.

"Are you a Catholic?"

For a minute I thought I hadn't heard her right. I'll never get used to being asked that straight out, in the way that people do down here; in the North you'd never ask — it wouldn't be civil — you work it out from clues and intuition.

"Presbyterian," I said, cold as I could. "But I don't like religion, I'm not religious."

"I am," she said, finishing off another piece of shortbread.

I was startled. She didn't look one bit that way, and in my book being religious didn't go with being an artist, or making sexual teapots, or having the sort of looks that Catherine has.

Just the same I was careful not to say anything, for I didn't want to encourage her. I hate it when people start telling you what they believe in. It's boring and embarrassing and none of my business anyway. So I wiped away, getting the last stray blobs of banana off of Suzanna's chin.

Suddenly Catherine's hands pushed themselves into my line of vision. She held them out to me, palms down, the redness and swelling right there in my face. I knew what she wanted.

"No," I said, without looking up.

She withdrew her hands.

"There you go," she said lightly and turned away. When she turned back she'd folded her arms, and the sweater sleeves covered her hands.

I got up and started stacking the cups and the plates that were scattered about on the table.

"There's creams you can get from the chemist," I said, turning my back on her, carrying them across to the sink. "And you might think of buying yourself another heater."

No answer. I glanced round, but she was already half out the door. I'd no desire to stop her.

Chapter 12

Catherine would never have asked me about her hands if it hadn't been for Martin Foley and his second wake. Martin Foley had been a close friend of Liam's at college, but he was gay, so after they'd finished he'd gone off to London to live a more open life. For a while there were great reports of his doings, then the first flush wore off, and word came less frequently. Which was only as you'd expect — lives change, the focus shifts. They still phoned each other, but less and less often, and both times when Liam was over in London, Marty had been away. A couple of years later a mutual friend had run into Marty and came home saying he'd gone very thin and didn't seem to want to know him anymore.

You'd think, wouldn't you, that Liam would have known from that? But he didn't; he wasn't used to disaster.

After the funeral he'd gone to see Marty's parents to ask if he could do a headstone for the grave. They were dead pleased, they said he could do what he liked, for Marty had thought so much of him. They wanted to pay but he'd told them not to insult him.

It had taken Liam a long time to complete the headstone because it was so emotional for him. He'd been terrible fond of Marty, and it grieved him that he hadn't been trusted enough to be told about his sickness. But Marty had kept it from everyone —

even the parents hadn't known till almost the end. He'd told them he'd wanted to spare them the shame.

When the headstone was finally ready, Liam got it into his head that he wanted to hold a celebration for Marty — a kind of a second wake. So he set a date and invited along his closest friends from the time that they were all students together.

We held it in the workshop because Liam said Marty was most alive when he was working and that was where it should be. There were six asked — five men and one woman — plus various partners of both genders.

It was late in October when they all assembled, only a few nights away from Halloween. I'd suggested Halloween night itself, but that was too much even for Liam, though he couldn't rightly tell me why. He seemed to have this idea that Marty's soul would be wandering around on that night and the wake would draw it close, as a lamp when it's lit draws a moth.

I'll never get over being amazed at them down here; they hold the modern world firm in one hand, but all the time they have the old world grasped tight in the other. You think they are rational beings, and they are, but all the lost centuries are in them too — and sometimes closer than they care to think of or acknowledge.

It had been all hustle and bustle and preparation. We'd been busy as the blackbirds that flew back and forth all through the short day, stripping the pyracantha by the workshop door of its tangles of bright berries. By nightfall the table groaned with food, a big fire was lit, there were candles set in the windows, and Liam had the headstone up on a plinth in the place of honour. It was a beautiful thing, a granite slab with the name and the dates, and down at the bottom a single sentence.

Only that which cannot be lost in a shipwreck is yours.

"He always said it when he was nicking something he wanted

from one of his friends," Liam told me. "We said it ourselves — taking the piss — but we nicked far more off him than ever he did off us, and it was always, always ideas. He had more than all the rest of us put together; they'd come flying out of him like sparks from a Catherine wheel."

Liam didn't know where the quotation came from, but he put it there anyway, and up at the top he carved a deep frieze of thrushes and twining leaves. There were thrushes all around the place as the winter drew in — shy birds, with speckledy dun-coloured plumage, hopping about, watching our comings and goings with bright, clean eyes. Liam said they reminded him of Marty. He said it wasn't right that he'd had to go and live among strangers.

We were shy enough ourselves at the start, but soon the drink did its work and the food warmed our bellies. When I was through with the feeding and bustling about I went and sat myself down beside Liam. He smiled at me, and his arm went around my shoulders and his hand took mine. I sat there listening, and as often as not when a story was finished it wasn't only the speaker's eyes that were bright with tears.

We might as well have had it on All Saints' Eve, I thought, for I'd never met this Marty but I knew him now, and I'm certain I wasn't the only one who felt him near. I am telling all this so you'll better understand what happened next.

There's a painter from Waterford by the name of John Ryan, and it seems he has psoriasis, a painful, itchy skin condition, so unsightly that when he was at college he always wore long-sleeved shirts buttoned tight at the wrists. He told of a hot, bright day when he and his friends were sitting outside and Marty had talked him into rolling his shirtsleeves up and shaming the devil.

"Then what happens next only this girl I'd been sidling up to for ages and ages comes over and sits herself down on the grass right beside me," he said. "Well, one look was enough, she took herself off, and we both knew that she wasn't coming back. Marty did his best. He called her a shallow piece, unworthy of my affections, and a whole lot more besides. It made no difference. That was the old heart broken for at least a month."

We laughed then, but not without awareness that John Ryan had come alone and his shirtsleeves were still buttoned tight.

I was drunk; I don't remember the details except that Liam asked me would I try. It was the occasion as well as the drink — there was an innocence about the night and also a sweetness that's hard to explain. I don't think I'd have tried it at any other time, no matter who it was did the asking.

Well, I woke in the morning and couldn't believe what I'd done. I lay there remembering, flushed with shame, and more than I ever wanted anything I wanted Liam to wake and tell me that what I thought had happened hadn't happened at all.

Liam woke. I asked him had I put my hands on John Ryan or was it a dream? I had, Liam said. He spoke of it almost casually, he seemed pleased with me and surprised at the state I was in.

A few days later John Ryan phoned. He said his skin was falling off in flakes, but new stuff was forming underneath, as pink and smooth as a baby's bottom. Liam talked to him, I didn't. He said the excitement in John's voice was wonderful to hear. Liam was excited just telling me this, and fool that I was, I began to feel a bit pleased with myself as well.

Of course, John Ryan told the story to anyone who would listen to him, and Waterford's only the next county. It was after that that word got out and they started to come to the door.

—⚬⚬⚬—

Liam was there when Catherine came next, so they talked in the workshop. After she'd gone he said he was thinking of helping to run this collective, especially since they were extending their brief to venues and shows. That was fine by me. Liam's sociable, and his work is solitary; I'd always encourage him when outside things come up.

So Catherine started dropping over with information and plans. Mostly it was too cold for paperwork in the workshop, so they'd closet themselves in the little back room that Liam used as an office; then afterwards they'd come to the kitchen looking for tea. Sometimes she came and Liam wasn't there, so she'd call in with me to leave papers for him and she always had a spare half hour for talk. Neither of us mentioned her hands or my refusing her. I was a bit uncomfortable with her at first, for I thought she would bring it up again, but she didn't. After a while I began to notice I wasn't exactly discouraging when she put her head round the kitchen door.

It was around this time I started looking out for a job. Not much of a job — a few hours was all I was after. But not bar work, something regular and local and only in the mornings.

I wanted money, you see. Money to send Andrew to play school, which Liam was against.

"Aren't there trees and fields and animals all about us?" he said. "Let the child run; there'll be time enough later for shutting him up indoors with a pile of books."

But it wasn't for learning I wanted it. Andrew had always been quiet and self-absorbed; happy to play alone for hours, he never strayed far from my side. I hadn't thought anything of it at first. He'd want other children as he grew older, so what harm till then if he was my wee boy?

But he didn't want other children. Suzanna did: at two years old she had the run of any house around that held young children, and when I called to pick her up she wasn't ever ready to come home. Not like Andrew. Even when with his cousins he'd want to know before we left what time we'd be back to collect him. And when we did, there he would be at the gate, watching out for us, waiting.

He was uncertain with other children, suspicious and wary.

"He's just shy," Kathleen said, "don't be worrying about him. He'll ease up once he starts school."

But I was afraid it would be the opposite. I thought if he didn't learn now how to be in company, he'd be forced off by himself at school.

I don't know how it was that I came to tell Catherine my fears, but I did, and somehow once I'd started I couldn't stop. She listened, and when I paused or halted, she waited, so I told her the next bit and then the next.

"What age is he?"

"Three. He'll be four in April; they'll let him start school in September, but if he does he'll be on the young side. There's a play school in Hubertstown. He could go there for a year, and then he'd be five when he starts into proper school. He'd be that bit older, more used to the rough-and-tumble. But Liam's against it. If I want it I'll have to find the money for it myself —"

So it was Catherine who showed me the ad in the paper for part-time work in the library in Hubertstown, and it was Catherine who met me there and took the children off while I went for the interview. She helped me and encouraged me; she seemed to think it was alright to be doing what I was doing, she seemed to find it quite natural that two women should be conniving together against the will of a man.

When all the details were sorted, I told Liam about the job in the library. We were outside, the wind cold but the morning bright, the daffodils opening, the buds on the ash tree darkening and swelling, the children just through the gate, splashing about in the puddles with Whiskey beside them. We did this every dry morning now that the spring was breaking. It was one of our pleasures, and a good time to talk.

"I want Andrew to go to play school," I said to Liam, looking hard at the ground. "Suzanna can go to Kate's house; I've fixed it with Teresa. She doesn't want any money, just to have Kate stay over with us when they're going out, which she does anyway." I was babbling now, falling over myself to get all the arrangements in place before he could think of a reason to stop me taking the job. "But I'll need the car — only in the mornings; it's yours for the rest of the day —"

Liam drained his mug and set it down on the wall. Then he turned to me, put his hands on my arms, waited for me to lift my head and look him in the face.

"Why the library, Ellen?"

I didn't understand. "What's wrong with the library?" I said defensively. "I know the pay's not great, but it's only mornings. You'll have the car back in the afternoons —"

"It's not the car; we can work that out. And I can see you might want a break from the children — I've no problem with that either. But, Ellen, why the library when you could be at the Healing?"

"The Healing?" I felt myself go rigid under his hands.

"Like you did for John Ryan. You've a gift, Ellen. Gifts are supposed to be used, not hidden."

"That was a fluke, a one-off. It wasn't me, it should never have happened —"

"Not you? Christ, Ellen, who else was it?"

"Marty," I said, believing it, yet amazed to hear myself say it.

Liam gave me a funny look. "What about Andrew then? I suppose that was Marty as well?"

I wouldn't speak. I looked at the ground. The fear was twisting me up, my stomach felt like a nest of snakes, writhing.

Liam pressed on, stubborn, relentless. "Remember the woman in Cork, Ellen? Don't try pushing it down and suppressing it, that's what she said. And that's exactly what you're doing now."

"That's my business —"

"Your business? End of story?" His voice was tight. "It's got nothing to do with me or the children? And what about the people who come to the door?"

"One or two. Now and again. You make it sound like a queue —"

"Ellen, they come for help and you turn them away —"

It was true. There'd been people calling, and mostly I turned them away. Not always. There'd been a knock on the kitchen door one evening last week when Liam was over with Dermot. I'd got up and opened the door myself, I hadn't just called out the way they do down here, I want to know who it is that I'm asking into my house. There was a woman standing there — in her early forties by the look of her — a big loose-boned woman with an outdoor face all tight and drawn with pain.

I hadn't asked her what ailed her — I hadn't needed to, for I'd known it was the raw burn on her right arm under her white cotton sleeve. I'd taken her hand, drawn it towards me, and held my left hand over the place. She'd cried out and pulled away as the heat from my hand found its way through the fabric and met the skinned flesh beneath. I'd held her fast. When I'd seen her face ease out, I'd dropped her hand.

"Come in," I'd said then, for I knew well her arm would heal and I had to make sure she would keep it to herself. I'd acted all in one action, no thought edging its way in, but the minute it was done I'd cursed myself, for I should have dressed it before I used my hands at all. That way I could have told her it was the herbs in the cream that would do the trick.

Stacia, she'd said her name was. She'd wanted to pay me, but I'd hushed her and told her I didn't want it known. She'd given me a quick, hard look, but she'd seemed to understand. She'd said it didn't hurt her anymore, and it was hard to keep your mouth shut when something good happened to you, but she'd tell her bees when she got home and that might be enough.

That'd made sense to me. I'd made tea, and we'd sat there, talking about her bees and how she had sixty jars a year from her two hives. Then she'd told me about these bee tribes in Nepal, how their bees live in their attics and are as much a part of their households as a cat or a dog would be in ours.

"There are holes in the roof so the bees can come and go," she'd said. "An opening into the house as well, so they've only to stick in a spoon and scoop when they're looking for honey."

I'd liked that. Mostly I get angry when strangers come knocking and asking, I shake my head and shut the door fast and leave them to think what they like. But this one was different. After she'd gone I kept hearing the drone of the bees and seeing a golden darkness of massed bees and sweetness. For days I listened, and I didn't like the silence of our house; it seemed a poor, thin thing, and the house not alive.

But I didn't tell Liam about her, for I knew he'd only use it against me the next time I turned someone away. Liam was reared with softness, you see, he was taught it so he expects it back, and he has an ease about him that means it often comes. He can draw it from people — even from me — and he never even knows he's doing it.

I'm not like that, nor ever was. It was always all suspicion with me, the expectation of hardship. Anger comes easy — I'll blaze up, and the life will blaze up in me and I don't have to feel the fear. But Liam can wait through the anger till it burns off and I get to the fear underneath. Then he'll sneak up on me, offering me comfort, and I can't defend myself against him.

Chapter 13

$\mathcal{I}$ took the job in the library, and it paid for Andrew to go to play school. He cried at the start, then got used to it; he liked the stories and bringing home paintings, and when he saw the nature table he thought he'd died and gone to heaven. As for Suzanna, she was happy as a sandboy at Kate's house, and Kate's mother, Teresa, brushed away my thanks. Life was easier with Suzanna; the children were company for each other, and wasn't she always leaving Kate over with us anyway?

"It's great, knowing you're there for the asking," she said. "Not having to go looking for babysitters, not having to worry."

And I liked the work. Books, quiet voices, speaking only when I was asked something, not having to think up things to say like in the pub. It was a small library, open only for limited hours, and after the first week of instruction I was mostly by myself. I liked that too. Having a world that was all my own, that Liam wasn't part of, nor the children.

The spiralling held back in the library. I'd feel it in my feet alright, but it was only a shadow of itself that started up then died away. I knew what it was saying. *I'm here and don't you forget it.*

I wasn't about to forget it. At work it was only reminding me, but at home there was no such restraint. As the months passed it gathered itself, growing stronger and more intrusive till I was finding myself near as hard to live with as Liam was. It did what it liked, when it liked; sometimes it started just when the dinner was ready, or as I was on my way out through the door. I stopped it then — I closed myself down — which worked if I acted fast and made sure that it knew that I wasn't messing. I know that sounds odd and vague, but it's hard to find words to explain something that isn't visible or rational.

And closing myself didn't solve the problem. When I put it on hold it stayed inside waiting, and all the time it was waiting it was punishing me till I let it out to run its course. It was as if I was filled with this weird electricity. It crackled inside me and fizzled my nerves so I started nearly out of my skin at a sudden touch or a noise.

I couldn't help myself; I was so used up with bearing it all that I'd nothing left over for anything else. And soon I was so used up that I even left off fearing the currents themselves. Which is not to say that I grew unafraid or lost the conviction that something fierce and alien was using me as a path. But I grew used to it, like the pain of an arthritic knee or the kick of a baby inside you. Never comfortable, but something you thole because you have no choice.

But if it's a knee or a baby you know why.

In a mixed marriage schools are potholes. You see them ahead, but somehow the steering pulls and before you know it you're into them anyway.

Liam wanted them to go first to the national school, which is local and Catholic, then at second level to Kilkenny College, which is Protestant and fee-paying.

"If we do that they'll have both traditions," he told me. "We just put their names down now for Kilkenny College, and have it all settled. That way there'll be no fighting between us, no last-minute scrambling to get them in —"

I thought it was all my worrying about Andrew that had brought this on, but I think now he knew there was stuff coming up that I'd find hard to swallow. First Communions, for starters. I was so ignorant back then that I hardly knew what a First Communion was. I know now, for Andrew keeps me informed.

"What's the point in putting them down for a fee-paying school when we couldn't afford it?" I asked him. The truth was I didn't want to plan; I didn't want to have to think or decide till nearer the time.

"There are grants if one of the parent's a Prod," Liam said. "Anyway, I'll be famous by then, we'll have money coming out of our ears."

"I'm not sure I'd want that," I told him.

"Not want money coming out of our ears? Why ever not?"

I shook my head. "Not the money, the school. I'm not sure I'd want them taught fear the way I was," I said.

As soon as the words were out I was wondering. Was it true, what I'd said? Did they teach me fear, or did I bring fear to what they taught me? I don't know, nothing stays the same anymore, everything shifts and changes. I only know that the squat dark church on the Northlands Road comes into my dreams, and the flavour of those dreams is dread.

But Liam was off like a horse when the starter flag drops. No one taught fear like the Church taught fear, end of story, no competition. Which is what I can't stand about Catholics — it always has to have been worse for them than for anyone else. But I didn't argue because I didn't want to — I didn't want to talk about religion at all, it made me too afraid. And I couldn't say that because it wasn't rational, and being irrational made me afraid as well.

It was different at the start. Back then we could say what we liked; we liked saying what we liked, it was so freeing. I remember the early days, the things I came out with, the way Liam laughed till I blushed with shame.

"My mother would never allow us to call Catholics Taigs," I'd told him once happily, out of my happiness. "She said plenty of Catholics were decent, good-living people. It wasn't their fault that their church taught them ignorance and superstition."

Liam's eyes had opened wide. He'd stared at me, then he'd cracked up — you'd have thought what I'd said was funnier than *Cheers* and *Fawlty Towers* wrapped up together. I stared in my turn. Why was he laughing? What was the joke?

Then I'd heard myself, and I'd understood. Something had shifted inside me; a hairline crack had opened up on a smooth-plastered wall, a fine fall of dust, and I'd laughed along with him. It was like one of those dreams where you go to a party and look down and find you've no clothes on. Then you wake, sick with relief because no one has seen you, no one at all, it was only a dream.

After that I could say what I liked. He'd look at me, amazed and bemused, but he took no offence nor ever held my words against me. I know now that that was easy enough for Liam, who hasn't a paranoid bone in his body and has never been hurt for being Catholic. But it seemed to me wonderful after the North, where everyone's always offended at everything all the time.

I said the wrong things because I knew no different. Up there we were too afraid to talk face to face, so silence seemed the only way. We talked among ourselves of course, told one another what *they* thought, what *they* were after, we stoked our own fears till they blazed up and licked at the rafters. For the rest, we left it to the politicians who defended and accused from the safety of the television studios. We listened to our own and turned away from theirs, unable to hear, deafened by the anger that rose in our blood and beat in our eyes before they were through the first sentence.

But at least that "ignorance and superstition" stuff I'd said only to Liam. Far worse was the time when his brother Tom was setting me straight on what the South thought of the North.

Southerners, Tom maintained, were evenhanded. "We might not like Northern Protestants much, but we wouldn't be pushed about Northern Catholics either. They'll never forgive us the Treaty. Seventy years on and they're still saying we sold them out, still accusing us of leaving them stranded under British rule."

I was astonished. "Sure, what way could you have stopped it?"

"Gone on fighting. Or that's what they come down here telling us."

"What business of yours was it anyway?" I was all indignation on his behalf. "You'd got down here, hadn't you? You'd no call to go interfering up North; we didn't want any part of an Irish state."

There was a small, deep pause. "Protestants didn't want it, Ellen," Tom said gently, "Catholics did." Another silence. "'Tis the one island, Ellen. Some would say *our* island. And by that, I mean all of us."

For the first time I saw the border as he did: a red line wriggling the map, following no logic of landscape, dividing where there should be no division. And Liam's family wouldn't be hard line at all; they don't like the IRA going blowing people up, and they wouldn't be slow to say so.

After a while down here I began to hear myself, and I didn't always like what I heard, but also I began to notice my aloneness. You only find out who you are when you live among strangers, when there's no one else the same as you to agree and tell you you're right. And you're different when you're reared the other way — it's a different tribe, you learn different habits, there's different things expected of you. I began to unlearn the different ways, but who was I going to be instead? I couldn't just turn myself into someone I wasn't.

The more I heard myself, the more I fell silent; if I hadn't had Catherine to talk to I'd have turned mute as a swan. Her being my friend was her decision, not mine. She made the running, all I did was leave the door open when she came. And perhaps she's so odd in herself that she didn't notice the oddness in me or in what I was saying. But she's odd in a social, extroverted way — she isn't gauche as I am.

I tried to talk to Catherine because I wanted to make the words in my head come out of my mouth and not stay stuck inside going round and round. But it was hard. I couldn't tell her about the Healing and I couldn't talk about my old life with Robbie, so all that was left was Liam and the children, and local things that happened nearby. One time I began on some story about Robbie, but when I said the words out loud they sounded so strange and unreal that I hardly believed it myself. These people here lived in a different world — so soft — how could they know?

This thing in me didn't help either. It made me different a second time over, and that was hard too.

So Catherine started coming to the house as Liam's friend, but nearly before I noticed it I was treating her as mine. Then Liam told me she used to be a nun.

I couldn't believe what I was hearing. Nuns are sort of taboo in my world, they're *them* not *us*, seen but not spoken to — you wouldn't want to, their very existence makes you nearly more uncomfortable than priests. Anyway, nuns are all ancient and plain, any fool knows that, there was no way that Catherine could ever have been a nun.

So I thought he was joking, I didn't believe him, but he went on insisting and after a bit it dawned on me that it might be true. I was really upset, but Liam was pleased with himself, he knew he'd tipped over my neat little applecart, and he couldn't bring himself to hold back from making it worse. He swung back his chair, laced his fingers together behind his head, and told me she'd been a Cistercian.

"Oh, yes," I said, tipping carrots out of a saucepan, knowing there was more coming. "And what's so great about that?"

"Cistercians are contemplatives."

"You mean they don't talk?"

"Only when they really need to. They pray for the world instead."

"What, *all* the time?" I was shocked again. "Whatever use is that?"

Liam laughed. "Nothing exists unless you can see it and touch it, isn't that right, Ellen? And you with the invisible running through you —"

I glared at him. "Would you ever fuck off and stop patronising me?"

Whiskey got up from her mat and stood there, regarding me steadily. She doesn't like it when I swear at Liam. It's the tone of my voice; she knows that we're close to a fight.

"Liam says you don't like it that I used to be a nun."

"Why should I care what you used to be? It's got nothing to do with me."

"He said you think I should have told you."

"Liam's very full of my opinions all of a sudden. What else did he say?"

"That you think that if I had to be a nun I could at least have stayed a nun. Not go giving it up and pretending to be normal."

Liam's big mouth. Alright, that's what I'd said, but he didn't have to repeat it to her face. I was taking the dishes from the rack. Carefully, so they didn't chink on account of the shake in my hands. They'd been laughing at me, I was sure of it. And I don't like being laughed at, it makes me go stubborn inside.

"I can't imagine wanting to be a nun," I said at last. "Even if I was a Catholic."

"Would it help at all if I talked about it?"

"No. Definitely not."

She stood there, not saying anything.

"I didn't mean to offend you."

I was suddenly contrite, God knows why — she was the one who'd deliberately misled me. "You haven't offended me."

I waited for more, but none came. I wished she'd say something or go away, but she did neither.

I went to the hooks by the door and took down my jacket.

"I have to get the children," I said. She didn't move. I put on the jacket and picked up the keys.

"It's not the nun-thing I mind," I said suddenly. "It's you not telling me."

"I thought I had — indirectly — I forgot that you wouldn't understand. If you'd been Catholic, you would have. Most people are, so you don't think about it, and you just make assumptions."

I didn't say anything.

"Ellen, speak to me."

I just looked at her. I wanted to speak, but I couldn't because I knew I wasn't allowed to say what I wanted to say. I shook my head.

"Ellen, say it."

"Did it never occur to you that your assumptions might be a wee bit arrogant?"

She flushed. I'd never seen her do that before. "Perhaps they are," she said slowly. "I'm sorry I didn't make myself clearer. It's not such an easy thing to drop into a conversation."

I nodded and walked through the door and away from her across the yard. I wanted to run back and say I was sorry; I hadn't wanted to be ignorant and rude, it was just that I was confused because she wasn't who I thought she was and everything was changing and going wrong. And I was so tired from what Liam calls the-invisible-running-through-me. So tired and angry and frightened. And it kept getting more all the time, it wouldn't stop.

I wanted to say all that but I didn't, and she was my last chance. It was no good talking to Liam anymore, all he did was tell me what I should do — he'd long since made up his mind.

I opened the door of the Renault, repositioned the cushion so it covered the hole in the seat, climbed in, and turned the ignition. It started first time, but I hardly noticed, I felt so deadened and hopeless. Then there was a knock on the window and it was Catherine, so I wound it down the two inches it goes before it jams. She didn't speak. She put her hand flat through the window, the fingers splayed out, and I put my hand up and touched her fingers with mine. I looked at her, and she made a face and shrugged her shoulders. I knew she meant it was all a fuck-up and what-the-hell, and we'd gone too far together to turn back now.

———— ❧ ————

A magpie has tail feathers set in a fan that spreads out from under the two at the centre, making twelve in all. These feathers are black-dipped-in-petrol — they shine with greens and purples and peacock blues. The head is black, and the wings are white with blue side feathers and black-and-white primaries. The bird is mostly head, though it doesn't seem so when it's on the move on account of the tail being so long. The beak is very strong and sharply undershot.

How do I know this? From lifting a dead magpie, spreading its wings and its tail, taking a good, long look. Where did I get this magpie? From the heap of birds that Connor took from his trap and threw on the ground, their necks wrung, one Sunday when we were over visiting.

Connor had a contraption set up in the garden. He was proud of it, so it had to be inspected. It was like a cage, but semi-detached, the one half closed with a live magpie in it, the other half with the tunnel-like entrance you'll find in a lobster pot.

"The magpie in the trap's called a lure," Connor said. "He's in there, calling out, so the magpies up in the trees fly down and find their way into the other half and can't get out. Beautiful, so it is."

He had four of them trapped in there. He reached in, pulled out the birds one by one, and wrung their necks. But he left the first bird — the one called "the lure" — to go on calling out.

"'Tis cruel," I told Connor. "Getting them down to aid him, wringing their necks like that."

"'Tis not to aid him they come, girl, 'tis to kill him," Connor said. "He's a stranger, and he's trespassing inside their territory. 'Tis murder they have on their minds, not aid."

I didn't believe him. The place is full of magpies; they're too busy raiding the songbirds' nests and tearing at rabbits squashed on the road to bother with killing each other. But aid or murder, it made no difference to Connor. He's a hunter, he liked his trap, liked wringing their necks and throwing the feathery corpses down in a heap. And magpies are vermin, everyone knows that, who cares if they're killed?

"Well, don't be lending it to Liam," I told him. "I won't have it. And don't either of you start thinking you can set it up and I'll get used to it because I won't."

"'Tisn't cruel, girl," Connor said. "'Tis the magpie that's cruel, not the trap." But he didn't push it. He likes me, and I like him, and I like the way he calls me *girl*.

I picked one up from the pile. I could feel how warm its flesh was; I could feel its life around it still, like a shroud. It was September, the air growing thinner, the haws on the whitethorns blooding, the crows and the magpies gathering, ready to take back their own. The trees were still full, the grass still green, yet everything waited, everything knew. I loved this moment: the swallows gathering on the lines, the cold lick under the warm autumn air, the feeling that something ancient and fierce was crouched down, waiting its time. I walked off a little way from Connor and Liam, the dead magpie in my hands.

Sometimes I think all of the body is holy and all that the body does is holy. All the bad things it does as well as the good things — everything — lusting, drinking, stealing, even murder. But I can't explain that or understand it. It isn't all good, any fool knows that. But somehow it's all holy.

What I think I mean is that everything is one. It's not that good and evil don't exist — they exist alright, and good is still good, and evil is still evil — but they both belong to God, are of God, and God must be everything or He wouldn't be God at all.

I don't say this to anyone except myself. But no one can stop me thinking it. Even I can't stop me thinking it, though God knows, I try hard enough.

This isn't the sort of thinking I was reared with. Back then there was Right and Wrong, and in the middle was God, just and exacting, silent and clean, clothed in unending light. Right stood to one side — solitary and upright — his back forever turned on sinful Wrong. And no shady in-between place, no way these two could ever be associated; they were worse than neighbours whose grandfathers had disputed a boundary years before, the ill feeling going down through the generations, growing fiercer as time passed.

But I don't believe in God, and if I did I'd hate Him. Yet I know that everything is holy, and I know it from that time I was holding the magpie, while Liam and Connor stood there together and talked. And it wasn't a strange or frightening experience; it was calm and quiet as morning and brought me great peace.

Everything. Not some things only — not life only, or the universe only, but *everything*. Holy and praising God. Even though God doesn't exist, has never existed, and never will.

So I think this, and then I think, *I can't be thinking this, can I be thinking this?* And I know that I am. But I don't get afraid. It comforts me, though I don't want to think it at all.

And mostly I don't. I cook, mind the children, do the housework, go to work. I'm a proper wife and mother. I don't believe in God.

Magpies are cruel, everyone knows that. And they're valiant, territorial, beautiful, rapacious, fearless. Nothing is simple; everything is part of everything else.

———◦◦◦———

"It's making you sick, Ellen, holding it back, turning people away, pretending you haven't the gift. You have to let people come, you've no choice."

I stared at him. Was it really Liam who was saying these things, trying to make me do what he knew I couldn't?

I should be less secretive, he said. I should be grateful.

If you do not bring forth that which is in you, that which is in you will destroy you.

That's from the Gnostic Gospels. Or so Liam said. He stood in the kitchen, stubbornly saying such things, while I sat at the table, stubbornly hating him. I didn't know where he got this stuff from. I'd had the Bible stuffed down my throat from the time I could walk, and I never once heard of the Gnostic Gospels. Maybe they're Catholic. More likely he had the quote off Dermot's Marie. He used to crack up when Marie first got into this stuff, started reading those New Age books, talking that way that they talk. Then he started doing the same himself.

He went from me; I didn't know who he was anymore.

If I'd let it out, my life would be easier, he said. So would his, so would the children's. I was making everyone suffer. The Gospel According to Liam.

"I have a job," I told him, "I haven't time for another. I work in the library, remember?"

"Give it up. Do this instead."

"I can't."

"Can't give it up, or can't do this?"

I stared at him again. He knew what I meant.

"Ellen, why can't you?"

"I just can't."

It was true. He could see what it did to me even to speak of it, even to sneak a look at it sideways and indirectly.

So he left off badgering me for a bit, but we both knew he'd get back to it.

Who was this stranger, where had he gone to, my Liam who held the gate open and waited beside it, who never set dogs to my heels?

Chapter 14

Catherine had been hanging about the kitchen since Christmas, dropping the odd hint, giving me the chance to talk.

It screwed me up, for I wanted to talk, but even more than I wanted to, I didn't. We were outside — Catherine's idea — she said she'd smelled the spring on her way over and now she wanted to find its first stirrings. What she had smelt I don't know, for the rain had eased but the wind prowled the yard, sinking sharp little teeth into any bit of flesh exposed. Catherine squatted on her hunkers, poking around in the muddy grass, pulling it back from the spikes of dark leaves that were going to make snowdrops. Catherine can't ever just look, she has to be touching things, feeling them, getting her fingers dirty. The wind blew her hair round her face and pulled at the long, coarse manes of the horses beyond in the field where the shadows were taking over. The crows moved about on the sodden grass, their untidy black feathers poking up like fingers.

It was five o'clock. I pushed my hands further down into the sleeves of my coat and waited for her to tire of her nature studies.

"Do you get pleasure from it?" she asked me out of nowhere.

"From what?" I asked, sharp as the wind. As soon as she'd opened her mouth I'd smelled Liam. Well, I thought, she'd have to work hard if she wanted information.

"From the Healing."

"What healing?"

She swivelled her gaze from the snowdrops and stared up at me.

"The thing you do that makes people better."

"That people *think* makes them better."

"Okay. The thing you do that people *think* makes them better. Do you get pleasure from it?"

"Pleasure?" I gave a sort of a laugh. "You must be joking."

"Why d'you say that?" She poked at the snowdrop leaves again, pretending she'd never seen them before.

"Because it's horrible."

This time there was real surprise in her face. "Horrible? Oh, Ellen, I'm sorry, I never thought it might be like that. What way horrible?"

"Just horrible." I shrugged and stopped, but she went on looking up at me, waiting. "All tight and tense with something huge running through the tightness and tenseness," I said. "I feel like a seed that's being burst open from inside, whether it likes it or not." I didn't know where the words came from or why I was trying to explain. "Pleasure is soft. Pleasure has nothing to do with this."

"What a medieval face you have, Ellen." She was holding her muddy hand up to her brow, straining against the dusk that was closing us in.

"You mean what Liam calls my Reformation Look?"

"You sound as if you've had about enough of Liam?"

It was a question, but I chose not to answer it. What was the use? She'd made up her mind, just as he had. She got to her feet and wiped her muddy hands down her muddy jeans. "It's freezing out here, let's go inside. When do you have to collect the children?"

"I don't. Liam's picking them up from the party on his way home."

The kitchen table again. Sometimes I resent how much of my life has already been used up sitting at that kitchen table. Catherine's too. I looked at her.

I'll have to let her have her say, I thought. So it might as well be now, when I'm nearly past caring.

"Turning your back on life is pointless," she said. "I've tried it myself, so I know."

"That's all right then, I'll take your word for it. In fact, I wasn't thinking of joining a convent, or not right now."

"Jesus, Ellen, why d'you have to make everything so difficult? For *me* the convent was pointless — meaning *totally beside the point*. For others, it's not. But there are more ways of turning your back on life than entering a convent."

I waited.

"Turning your back on life is pointless because life doesn't just pack up and go away. And it's not about going off somewhere else and finding a different door either. The door is here; it's the one we see every day, the one with the dirty finger marks, the one that sticks in the damp. Our own door is the door we have to walk through."

She set her mug down on the table, took out a cigarette, and lit up. Catherine is strict with herself, she wouldn't normally smoke in the kitchen. I'm tired telling her Liam does so she might as well, she only smiles and shakes her head and takes her unlit fag outside, whatever the weather.

"Maybe the thing about living is simply the living itself," she said. "I mean, I think it's the living itself that connects us with something deeper."

"You sound like one of Marie Power's self-help books. What's all this got to do with me?"

"Nothing. All this is for me, not you; I'm working things out." She inhaled deeply and breathed out a long jet of smoke. I waited again.

"Ellen, I'm not trying to make you walk through any door if you don't want to, truly I'm not. But I'd say that it's time you tried opening your eyes and taking a quick peek at where it is you're standing. If you don't like what you see, you can always shut them again."

"I don't want to look," I said. "Once you've seen, you've seen, it's inside your head and you can't get it out."

"What is it that you're so afraid of?"

"I don't know, I'm just afraid. If you're afraid of the dark, you're afraid of the dark, you don't hang around working out what there is in there that makes you afraid."

"Would you let me try to talk about it a little?"

"No. I've had it with talking. I don't want to talk, and that's that."

"Ellen," she said gently, "I didn't say *you* had to talk, I said I would."

I looked at her.

"You don't have to say anything." She went on. "All you have to do is listen. You can hold up your hand if you want me to stop, and I will, but at least let's give it a try."

I wasn't sure how much she knew, but I'd a fair idea it was more than she let on. Liam talked to her, plus she had eyes in the back of her head — she missed nothing. Deep down I thought that probably she knew about the spiralling. Part of me was glad. And part of me wanted to hear what she'd say, but the other part couldn't bear it.

"Alright," I said at last. "But if I even begin to lift up my hand, you promise me you'll stop?"

"I promise."

"On your honour?"

She shot me a look to see was I serious. I was.

"On my honour," she said, making a face.

Then I sat waiting for her to tell me where it was she thought I was standing.

"I'd say you left home a good while ago, but you didn't know you were leaving." She spoke slowly, her voice going dreamy, unfocused. "You went strolling along through the woods, heading for open country. Things happened. You met with the talking fox, and you gave him half your sandwich. The woodcutter told you the way, and the frog with the golden ring in its mouth knew your name —"

Catherine's clever, she knows the children never have to ask twice for a story. Most of all, I like fairy tales with youngest sons and talking animals.

"Is there a raven?"

"I'm the raven," she said. I laughed. Then I realised I was laughing, so I stopped.

"Now you're walking along on the edge of the woods, and you've come to the place where the road forks and you have to choose your path —"

I shot her a look, but her voice didn't change and she kept her eyes fixed on this inner landscape.

"The road forks and you have to choose," she repeated. "It's getting dark, the fox has gone hunting, the frog's hopped off, the raven's got laryngitis and lost her voice. But there are sign-posts. One sign says God and the other says Magic. Decision time."

I got up from the chair. "That's shite," I told her. "Pure shite."

"What is?"

"Forks and roads and God and Magic."

"Ellen," she said softly, "it's not going to go away."

"It might. It did before."

"Sit down, Ellen. You don't believe that any more than I do."

I sat down.

"So, the one sign says Magic . . . the other says God —"

I shivered. I could feel the fear rising up in me, but my hand stayed flat on the table.

"Ellen," she said, leaning forward, and suddenly changing tack, "what does Presbyterianism *feel* like?"

"What does it *feel* like?" I was that surprised at the question, I nearly laughed aloud.

"That's what I asked. Don't think. Just say."

"Partly it's like being in the front room on Sunday," I said slowly. "Too much furniture, everyone on their best behaviour. At the same time you're up on this high, windy plateau with no one around except God. There's this terrible light. Apocalyptic. You can't hide."

"And Catholicism?"

"Darkness and candles and incense and graven images." That came out easily; I could get into this.

"And Magic?"

"Snakes. In a pit and it's dark."

"So it's snakes," she said softly. "Or else it's the plateau."

"What's the point of this?" I could hear my voice, sharp with fear.

"Ellen, you haven't been given this thing accidentally."

"What is it, Catherine? Why me, and why won't it go away when I don't want it?" Now it was something closer to hysteria I was hearing.

"I don't know the answer to any of those questions," Catherine said steadily, "but I think you've been given it because as a channel you may not be perfect, but you'll do."

"Given? You mean *forced* —"

"It feels like you're being forced because you won't accept it. You can change that. But if you decide to accept it, you'll need help. I don't think you have to worry about that; I think it'll come as you do the work. But it might be as well to be conscious about where you want the help to come from. As you've said yourself, you're only a channel —"

"For energy. Energy's neutral."

"Agreed. But there are other forces that aren't."

"No." I surprised myself by my own vehemence. "It's not like that, it's all the one. It's not *this way's good, that way's bad*, it's all everywhere and the same thing and there's no limits." I stopped and put my elbows on the table and rested my head in my hands. There was this weird feeling in the room. I had no idea what I was talking about or where this stuff came from, I just knew it gave me a ferocious headache, and I wished it would go away.

"You're right, Ellen," Catherine said slowly, and from right inside the weird feeling, "you're dead right." She sat back in her chair and put her hands in her lap and waited. The weirdness eased up, and I began to think I'd imagined it.

Catherine leaned forward again. "I wanted to help you to make a conscious choice because I thought it would steady you, take away some of the fear," she said. "But you're right, that's beside the point." She paused. "Ellen, did you know that healers were recognised by the early church? Not faith healers — gift healers. They weren't anything to write home about, they were just part of life, the way doctors are today. And another thing — if you had the gift you were looked on more favourably if you wanted to be ordained."

I stared at her. I didn't know what she was talking about.

She looked at me curiously. "Ellen, what have you got against God?"

"Fear," I said. My voice came out cracked, like the raven with laryngitis. "Fear God. It's in the Bible."

"God is love. That's in the Bible too."

"So they told us. I never believed it. I don't trust God, and I never will."

"That isn't the point."

"Isn't it? Why? Because He doesn't care?"

"Because God can't be anything we can recognise or imagine, or God wouldn't be God," she said quietly. "God can't be like us — to be trusted or distrusted. A God you felt you could trust would have to be quite small."

"The minister in Derry called Christ 'Our Leader.'" Not a flicker. Catherine usually relished the idiotic, but not this time. She didn't even smile.

"Christ's supposed to be tangible," she said, her voice flat, her face dead straight.

"Feel-my-wound?" I sneered. "Like for doubting Thomas?"

"No, not quite, that was a one-off thing, a proof-of-resurrection. I think Christ's really an avatar, an avatar of love."

"What's an avatar?"

"Something that represents God. Something small enough for us to get our minds around."

"You're telling me Christ's not God?"

"Love is an aspect of God."

"Only an aspect? What happened to God is love?"

She looked at me, but she didn't answer.

"I hate this sort of conversation," I told her, angry enough to forget I'd been afraid. "It just goes on and on, getting vaguer and vaguer, more and more abstract. I don't want to think about God at all."

"Then don't. God will most likely come and get you if He wants you. If He doesn't, He'll leave you alone." She said it so casually it took me a second to hear it.

"Stop." My hand shot up of its own accord, then the other one joined it and I clapped them both to my ears. It was like being ten, when Brian was teasing me and it was the only way I could defend myself. Catherine sat looking at me. I kept my hands there till the look on her face changed. Then slowly I lowered them. She got up and began to collect her things.

"It's your decision," she said. "Only you can decide."

"Liam —"

"You can stand up to Liam when you want to. I've seen you. You won't get off the hook by blaming Liam."

Chapter 15

*L*iam won a big prize a few weeks later, so for once in our lives we had money going spare.

We bought a new range for the kitchen. Well, not new, second-hand, but still about fifty years more recent than the old one. It heats the water and runs eight radiators, and it's oil so I don't have to be forever lugging in solid fuel. I love it. I used to listen to women saying they loved their kitchen appliances, and I'd be certain sure that I'd never come to that. And now, here I am, saying I love my Stanley. Comfort. How easy put to sleep we are.

But I don't love the car, though that was upgraded as well and these days it mostly starts.

Liam didn't want the range or the car; he wanted to leave the children with Connor and Kathleen and spend the lot on a trip. A long trip — China or Africa — somewhere neither of us had ever been or were ever likely to go. Which for me was everywhere outside of Ireland, but Liam had travelled in Europe when he was a student and had been to India two years later. He'd got the taste.

We argued and argued. I told him the car was a heap, we needed heating, we needed professional work on the plumbing, we might even start to pay off the loan from the bank —

He said the bank could wait. He promised he'd ask Tom for help with the plumbing, and somehow he'd get me some heating.

"You don't understand," he said. "A trip like this is worth twenty cars, it'll change who we are, and that'll change our whole lives. And anyway, we can have Connor's old car for a song when the new one's bought."

But I wouldn't shift, I kept saying the same thing over and over. I was tired of always, always making do.

Then Liam said he'd let go of the trip if I'd give the Healing a try.

I thought I hadn't heard him right, so he had to repeat it.

This time I knew I'd heard right, but I said nothing. I sat and stared, for I didn't trust myself to speak.

"I'll give up the trip, I'll change the car, I'll get you some heating and anything you else you want for the house if there's any money left over. And I'm not saying make a big deal of it. You don't have to stick up notices or charge people, or do anything else you're not happy with. All I'm asking is that you stop turning folk away when they come to the door."

Still I couldn't speak.

"Ellen? Ellen, answer me —"

"Just heating," I said at last, my voice coming out in a croak. "You go. Forget about the car. Forget about the bank. Just go and I'll stay, and we'll pay for the heating out of what we save on my not coming."

"No. We go together, or else we both stay and you give the Healing a try."

It wasn't that I hadn't thought of giving in and letting people come for my hands — I had. Not from pity for them, nor belief in myself, but from the outside chance it might bring me some peace from this awful spiralling-thing that grew harder to bear as one day followed another. I looked at Liam, but there was no softness and I knew it was all or nothing — he wasn't going to relent.

"Six months," I heard myself say through the dread that

shortened my breath and made my hands shake and clung to me like a sickness.

"A year," he said.

I nodded, unable to speak.

So I sold my soul for a mess of pottage, or rather a Stanley cooker and a car that mostly starts. I said that to Liam not long afterwards, but he didn't understand, for he didn't know the story — Catholics don't go in for the Old Testament much — so I had to explain about Jacob and Esau and soup and birthrights.

He said selling your birthright wasn't the same as selling your soul.

I said that in my case it was, for my birthright was freedom from ignorance and superstition, and now here I was, immersing myself in them both. He looked at me then, for he remembered those words, and he knew I was quoting my mother. I knew that he knew, and I meant him to. I felt bullied by him and cheated out of myself.

But for all I love the Stanley, I am sorry now I didn't let him travel when he had the chance.

Liam was right. Life was easier when I did what he wanted and started putting my hands on the people who came — which was what the thing inside me wanted as well. It had an outlet so it stopped backing up, and the feeling of having live electric cables spilling inside me began to ease off. The spiralling didn't stop, but whatever-was-causing-it flowed out through my hands and I was only a sort of a storm drain that it passed through. I suppose it had been a good while building up in me, so by the time I gave in it was a whole lot stronger than I even knew myself.

I'd nearly forgotten peace in the body, but now I remembered and so did everyone else. Liam cheered up, and the children stopped squabbling and Whiskey followed me round the place, watching me silently, swishing her tail. It was lovely, so it was. I relearned how to laugh.

There's a lean-to shed opening off the kitchen that we used as a store for fuel. The roof was sound so it was dry, and it was handy not having to go outdoors on a winter's night to fetch in logs and turf for the fire. Now Liam cleared it out, plastered the walls, laid a timber floor, put in electricity and a new door that opened straight onto the yard. He wanted to plumb in a sink as well, for I needed to wash my hands a lot with this work. I wouldn't let him. What was the point with the kitchen so close?

It was pleasant enough at the start. People knocked, the same as before, and I'd take them through and we'd sit in my room while they told me their stories. The Healing itself wasn't near as bad as I'd expected either. I only did what I'd done before, but now I allowed whatever-was-happening to happen, instead of using all my strength to block it from coming through. Which was useless anyway — like trying to stop the river's flow or the trees coming into leaf. More than that, when I didn't block it, it was kinder and easier to live with.

It was always local people back then. Country people who expected little, who'd lived a good while with whatever was bothering them, had tried the doctor without relief, and now were ready to try my hands instead of another course of tablets. They weren't all strangers either — a few of them I'd have known from the library, and there were others I'd recognise from around the town. If I eased them at all they were grateful, and if I failed them I never knew it, for they were at once too courteous and too humble in their expectations to come back to me and complain. Everything was simple still; it was always minor or chronic conditions I was dealing with — muscle strains and burns and skin problems, bed-wetting, tinitis, and cramp. Debilitating, but not life-threatening. I never saw organ failure or cancer or serious illness as I do now, I never had to reach very deep into pain or into life.

I have to admit that once I got the hang of the Healing I began to feel a wee bit excited. I thought it was partly me, you see, and though I felt shy and shamed by it, there were times I felt important as well.

I hardly spoke at all to begin with, but after a while I summoned my courage and ventured the odd remark. The odd remark was ventured back, and soon I began to enjoy the exchange. They were modest people for the most part, readier with a soft word than a hard one, more likely to belittle their distress than to blow it up with complaint. When I was done they'd fumble for their purses. I'd shake my head and turn away, but later I'd find gifts left on the step. Mostly home produce — eggs and vegetables, sometimes flowers or plants, a dressed hen or a jar of honey.

I'm making it sound as though I decided then opened the door to a whole crowd of people standing outside only waiting to come in. It wasn't like that at all — two knocks a week, and I thought myself busy; half a dozen, I said I was run off my feet. Which meant that the old life still wrapped me around, and I told myself nothing had changed, though underneath I knew different. This new life was there at the core as the heart is — secreted in flesh, yet directing the life of that flesh.

———

Liam says now that I lied to him about Andrew and wouldn't trust him. He doesn't understand, I didn't lie, Andrew *does* heal up well; all I did was stop his body from panicking so it could get to work on the cut.

Sometimes I think that's all I ever do. No, that's wrong. *I* don't do anything, something works through me, my part is only to let it.

This, as far as I can remember or work it out, is what happens when it happens. A tingling, shivery feeling begins in my head, emptying it and opening it up in a way that I can't describe. The tingling spreads over the body, then fades. Something starts in the feet, it flexes my toes so I know that it's there, it strengthens, then dies away. My hand lifts itself of its own accord. It stiffens. The fingers stretch out. It places itself onto the body or above the body. Sometimes it stays there, sometimes it moves itself on to somewhere else. It's not so much that I let my hand do this, it's more that whoever I am goes missing so it does what it wants till whatever is moving it stops. Then my hand goes limp and falls away.

That's all there is to it. Except that the place where the hand is gets hot, but I don't feel any heat in the hand, I don't feel anything at all except the stuff at the start. It's as though I'm full up with an emptiness that's completely alive but carries no feeling. I don't know what this emptiness is, and I don't know what happens when my hand's doing its thing. I don't know if whatever it's doing will heal or make things worse.

When the phone call about my mother's cancer came from Derry, I'd no premonition, no warning at all. So from where I'm sitting now, I can say that the death-seeings stopped after Robbie died and haven't resumed.

I was pregnant when I saw Jacko Brennan blown up, and I must have been just pregnant when I saw the white-faced girl who was Robbie's death. But when I was carrying Andrew and Suzanna I never saw anything at all. Then, a few months after Suzanna was born, the spiralling started, and since then a day hasn't passed without it. But no more Pierrot masks, no more deaths-before-their-time. The Healing came instead.

So this thing, whatever it is, laid off for Andrew and Suzanna. Which is strange when I think how afraid I was of pregnancy, for I'd convinced myself that seeing things was to do with Barbara Allen.

Yet all the time I knew different, for I hadn't been pregnant when I saw the dandelion flowers change into clocks, or heard about Fiona Clarke, or knew, that night in the bar, that my future was Liam. But we make up our minds to what we want to believe, and we'd rather roll a boulder up a mountain than shift away from that belief once it has set.

The change from seeing to healing was something to do with the children being born, but I don't know much more than that. I stopped thinking things, I experienced them instead. I left the realm of the mind, where I'd mostly lived, and was moved full into the stream of the incarnate world. A baby in a rush basket, that's what I was. Carried down to the river, laid in the water, pushed from its banks by an unseen hand.

I hate the Bible, yet my hidden life is formed of its images and its language, its awful light is the light of my inner world.

I wonder what would happen if I had another baby now? I wonder would it stop this energy-thing coming through my hands and destroying my peace of mind? I've never thought of that before. I wonder would it ease off as it did for Andrew and Suzanna, or get stronger like for Barbara Allen and the other one I was carrying when I saw Robbie's death? And while I'm at it, I wonder, did it know that Barbara Allen and the other one weren't going to make it anyway, so it went on pushing through? Or did it just get rid of them because they were in the way?

What is it anyway? All I can say about it is that It is as It is. I could frighten myself, thinking thoughts.

—∞—

I still had my hours at the library in the mornings, and then in the afternoons I was home with the children, so it wasn't as if I was hanging around doing nothing, only waiting. If Liam was there when somebody came, he minded the children, but if he wasn't, I had them near me while I worked. They were five and three when I started, so it's natural to them, it's always been what I do.

Suzanna thrived on it, which was no surprise, for there's nothing she loves like company. I'd tip out the bricks Liam had made for her, and she'd busy herself building castles all over the floor, knocking them down again, chatting away as she worked. It was harder for Andrew. He wouldn't stay in the kitchen when someone came, he'd go next door with a book or he'd mess in the yard and reappear when he heard the sound of a car driving off. He never liked strangers while they were strange, whatever he might think of them later on, when they'd turned into people he knew.

They were chalk and cheese, the two of them, and it made me wild the way they carried on. Andrew always insisted on differentials: on being first, on going to bed later, on getting more than Suzanna. I thought at the time he was only asserting his rights as the eldest, but it could be that he was trying to make me understand that he wasn't her.

If I gave her as much as I gave him, he worked himself into a fury, but if I gave him more, she let on not to notice, then she made it her business to get even when I wasn't looking. She might have been drawing or colouring, humming away quietly to herself, the very picture of contentment. Then she'd take a wee look at her juice or the size of the biscuit I'd given her, she'd shoot another wee look at his, and go on humming. I'd turn my back and there'd be a yell out of Andrew. She'd jog his arm so he'd spill his juice, or he'd drop a piece of his gingerbread man, and she'd stamp on it, quick as a flash. It was always over when I looked round. He would be white with rage, and she would be smiling sweetly.

I'm making her sound sly, but she isn't, she's only well able for him and very determined. Way too determined. Liam likes it that she stands up for herself; he thinks Suzanna's pure heaven, faults and all, and she is — was — especially then, when she was three going on four. She was one of those delicious children, all merriment and brown curls and little round limbs and bright eyes.

I didn't want to squash her down, yet I needed to encourage Andrew. Sometimes I ached for him, he had to try so hard, while the whole wide world responded to Suzanna. Often and often we've stood in the road watching the young calves come galloping and barging across the field, stopping dead at the gate in sudden quiet, their liquid eyes and the soft blowing sound of their breath in the rainy air. Suzanna could stand close, her round eyes on theirs, and they'd watch her and you could see they liked her, for they'd drop their heads down for a better look. Andrew would stand back a bit and a little to the side, but if he made a sudden movement they'd skitter and start away. Yet Suzanna could laugh and clap her hands together and bang with a stick on the gate, and they only drew closer again to watch her.

I don't worry about the way she is, but I worry that she makes Andrew worse than he is, that Little-Miss-Win-All-Hearts makes his heart thinner and stranger than it should be, makes it fly off up to a rafter, where it sits, hunched in on itself, like an owl. It's hard to get it right, and many's the time I didn't and don't, but I was lucky in that I had time with them while they were very young. And the gentle start to the Healing meant that I went on having time for at least another year.

When I landed in here I was moving way too fast for the country, but once I slowed down I surprised myself at how easily I settled in these fields. All those farmers in my mother's family, or maybe it was the memories of my childhood in Dunnamanagh. Whatever the way of it, there was nothing I liked better than wandering about in the meadows, and having children to teach let me out from under the weight of my own belief that the kitchen was where I should be. Spring after spring we walked up the road and I showed them the grey paired leaves of the wood-bine; the comely, red-stemmed herb robert; the ferny, singing green growth of the cow parsley. We went to the river and studied the frog spawn, the blue spears of the flags pushing up through the wetland, the strange segmented spikes of the horsetails before they opened. They saw mallard duck in the rushes, the blue flash of a kingfisher, the herons standing about in the shallows, stoic and unsociable, beings from some other realm.

They knew the cattle as well, the black-and-white Friesians, the donkey-brown Charolais crosses, the creamy gold of the pure-bred Charolais. Anything in the farm-line I wasn't sure of, I asked Liam, who knew without stopping to think. They liked hearing me asking him, liked it that he knew, that he had a place and an ease in the life around them.

All I had was Derry — and what was Derry? — all glamour of violence had long since gone from the North. The Peace Process was only a dream back then, the IRA was still planting bombs, still killing human beings on behalf of the People-of-Ireland, though the Southern People-of-Ireland had mostly lost patience with being used to justify something they wanted no part of any-more. The Protestant violence — the steady stream of sectarian assassinations — somehow didn't bother the Southern People half as much as the IRA did, for no one claimed to be killing any-one else in their name.

But though Liam knew the breeds and the crops, I was away ahead of him on the wildflowers.

"How would I know?" he'd say easily, when I showed him a flower that was strange to me. "'Twas your mother was the school-teacher, not mine. Farmers don't have the time to be messing with flowers."

Which isn't true, some would and some wouldn't, and mostly you'll find that the bigger the farm the less the farmer cares for such things.

So I asked the country people I met out walking the roads, for they knew the names and habits and where the plants grew. Often as not the name I was given for a flower was a local one, describing some feature of its growing, or a cure to be got from the root or the stem. Sometimes the name was strange altogether and came from the Irish.

That was a shock to me. When I was growing up we called it Gaelic not Irish, this funny dead language they made a big deal of down South, forcing children to learn it instead of a modern one that might have been of some use to them in the world. For the first time I saw a real language that had been everywhere once — with words from it sitting inside the English that had been spoken in most of Kilkenny now for years. And here was my own child, just starting school and bringing home little books with the words in Irish, and me sitting helping him learn and learning myself, in spite of myself.

That made me think, and the more I thought the more I fancied I understood why the language issue was being taken up so strongly by Nationalists in the North.

"It's a tool for them," I said to Liam indignantly. "They're using it — saying they were here first — Protestants are only Planters. They're taking over — in a sneaky, stealthy sort of a way from underneath."

Liam laughed. "Didn't you do that yourselves once?" he asked. "In an un-sneaky, un-stealthy sort of a way, with muskets and swords?"

"That was hundreds of years ago," I shot back. "Nothing to do with now."

"They could set you down in Iceland or in Africa, Ellen," he said. "Wherever you are it's always the same — all roads lead back to the North."

I didn't speak, I was too offended. He finished his coffee and moved his chair out from the table.

"Come over here, Ellen, my Wee Black Bigot," he said. "Come and sit on my lap while I show you some sneaky, stealthy things from underneath. Ah, don't be like that, don't clamp your mouth shut and turn it hard down at the corners. You've a pretty mouth, and it's mine now, I'll not let your ancestors take it back."

I still didn't speak.

"No? You won't come and sit on my knee? Your Mammy won't speak to me, Suzanna, or sit on my knee, she's afraid I'll make a Taig of her, and I'd never do that — even I could, which I doubt. Maybe she'll do it herself though. Or whatever it is that comes visiting her."

I turned my mouth down worse then, I don't like him speaking of that in front of the children. Why not? he asks — look at the things they come out with. Don't they still live half in some other place themselves?

But Suzanna took no notice. She was standing up on her chair, making big blue circles with a wax crayon on a sheet of paper, her brown curls bouncing with the effort she was making. She has the determination from Liam as well as the curls and the drawing.

Taig. They don't say that down here. That's his word for himself when he's sending me up. And I'd never call him that, I wasn't reared like that, when I'd used the word she'd punished me hard so I'd understand that I'd let her down.

Your children bring back your childhood in a way that I'd never have guessed at or wanted. Those walks were the walks I'd done with her before Daddy died and she moved us to Derry and went out to work to earn the money to rear us. That was the way she spoke of it. Resentful. As though she could have had the life she'd wanted if it hadn't been for us. She never liked the teaching. Maybe she'd never intended to teach, maybe she'd only trained to get herself a better class of a husband.

Whatever the way of it was, she was often in my mind outside in the fields in the spring with the children. Sometimes I'd even imagine talking with her: dialling the number, hearing the ringing tone down the line. Then I'd watch her lift the receiver in the hall in Derry.

I never got any further. The sound of her voice in my head was a cure for any softening.

Chapter 16

There began to be money left as well as produce. Coins, with notes wrapped around them, pushed in at the back of the step or set out on the windowsill. I hadn't minded the produce, but money was different — the sight of it filled me with unease so strong it was closer to fear.

The first time it happened I picked up the notes and carried them out to the workshop between my thumb and my index finger. A dead rat I had by its tail.

"I won't take payment," I told Liam. "I won't do it at all if they're going to try to pay me."

He set down his chisel. "Why ever not?"

It was so obvious to me that it hadn't occurred to me he might not see it as I did. I searched for words, but none came. I stood there, gaping at him, fish-mouthed and stupid.

"You're providing a service," he said carefully. "People come because they want that service. It's *your* time and *your* skill; if they feel they've had value they'll leave money to show their appreciation."

"My time, *not* my skill," I told him, the words shooting out hard and sure before I could think to stop them.

"If I lay a floor or light a show, I get paid for it," he said, his voice still even and reasonable. "I get paid, and I bring home the money and I never hear you telling me to hand it back —"

"I can't Liam —"

"Why not? We need the money —"

"I can't. You don't understand, it's not just a skill that you learn, like laying floors."

There was a silence.

"You're afraid that money will drive it away," he said, his voice no longer careful, but flat and angry. "That's it, isn't it, Ellen, that's what all this is about?"

I stood there, miserable, unable to look at him or answer.

"Ellen," he said more quietly, "you're never done saying you wish to Christ it would go away —"

I lifted my head and tried to stop him with my eyes. It made no difference. He went on saying the things I didn't want said.

"Why don't you just come right out and charge for it and see what happens? If it goes, it goes. You don't want it, what's there to lose?"

The question hung there, whole minutes seemed to be ticking by.

"You don't believe I want it to go," I said at last.

"That's about the height of it."

"It might turn against me." I spoke very low, for it was one of those thoughts that is like pain to speak.

"Meaning?"

"I don't know. Sometimes I do it when I shouldn't or I try too hard or I don't do it when I should. . . . It's horrible, something horrible happens —"

"What are you trying to say, Ellen?"

"It might punish me —"

"Why would it do that?"

"For misusing it —"

"So you *do* believe that it's positive."

"No, I don't," I said miserably. "You're putting words into my mouth. I only believe that it's powerful. Power makes its own laws. . . ." My voice trailed off.

"Take donations, leave out a box. If they want to leave money at least there'll be somewhere to put it."

"I'd never ask for money. Never —"

"You wouldn't be asking."

I'd hit a blank wall with Liam, so I turned to Catherine for help.

"Liam wants me to take money," I told her.

"Donations," Catherine said. "Or that's what he said to me."

"Donations, charges, what's the difference? It's all money."

"What's wrong with money?"

I looked at her, but I didn't bother to answer. No point in talking if she was going to be stupid on purpose. And I minded that Liam had got to her first. Besides, there was something else that I wanted to say, but I didn't know what it was so I couldn't say it. I rolled the dough round the bowl till it gathered all the loose flour to itself, then slapped it onto the baking tray and quartered it into farls.

"You're angry because Liam's talked to me already," Catherine said.

"Liam has plenty of people to talk to. I only have you."

"He thinks you're hung up on secrecy. He thinks that's part of the problem."

"What problem?"

She looked me straight in the face. "Ellen, Liam thinks you should talk about all this."

"All what?" Now it was my turn to be stupid on purpose.

"The Healing. What goes on behind the Healing. Not to everyone, just to the ones you trust, the ones you see every day, who are part of your life. He says that they'd understand, and your life would be easier. He could be right."

"No." I was shaking my head as I spoke. "Liam knows nothing."

"He's lived with you for eight years. You talk to him. He knows more than anyone else except you."

"No, Liam doesn't understand. It's not right for me. It's not our way."

"What's not your way?"

"Standing up. Speaking hidden things. Things aren't hidden if they're spoken. Once they're spoken, everything changes. I don't want Liam to speak, but I can't stop him. I'd never, ever speak of it myself."

"Did you know you just said *our* way?"

"Fuck away off, Catherine," I said softly. She looked at me. She saw I was serious.

There are times something old rises up in my blood, and I say things I hadn't planned or thought. I don't know where the words come from. Once they are out, I can't take them back.

But I wasn't going to say that to her. I might have done, for I thought so much of her then, but I didn't know how.

"I had a fall in the yard, but it wasn't too bad at the start. Well, I hopped about for an hour or two, but the son came round and the minute he saw it nothing would do him but the hospital. So off we went, and they tried, but it done no good. The tablets dull the pain by day but it's worse at night, I get no sleep."

"Would you put your hands on my hip? It's the old arthritis is getting to me, and I don't want them sawing me open, or not yet awhile."

People kept coming; money was left around in places I'd find it. Or rather, where the children would find it, for they'd make the rounds in the evenings, searching it out, as you'd search out eggs tucked away by a straying hen.

At first they brought the money to me, but I shook my head

and turned from them. I couldn't help it, I didn't mean to confuse them or spoil their game; I tried not to turn away, but my body moved itself round of its own accord. So they took it to Liam instead.

And Liam accepted it from them. He laughed and tousled their hair, and they sat on the ground beside him and watched while he sorted and counted. Then he gave them five pence each, but the rest he put in his pocket and deposited in an An Post savings account in my name. A few months later when nothing had changed and the energy kept coming through, he gave me the post office book. I opened it, and looked at the balance, amazed.

"Alright," I said, "I'll put a box out for donations."

Liam stood watching me very intently, letting the silence run on.

"They can leave it if they want to and not if they don't. It's all the same to me."

And it was.

Chapter 17

Liam Kiely's pieces, though attractive, show little real development' . . . blah, blah . . . 'formulaic and obvious' . . . blah, blah . . . 'the large untitled piece has a certain vigour, but most of this work lacks energy' . . . blah . . . 'disappointing and predictable' . . . blah . . . 'an artist capable of so much more.'"

It was a review of a group show in Galway. A show *to highlight the work* — so ran the blurb — *of seven midcareer artists currently living and working in Ireland.*

It was awful, I never knew a few words in a newspaper column could hold so much pain. Liam's work had drawn nothing but praise until then, not so much as a lukewarm review. And now this. Worse than lukewarm — plain bad — and the tone so easily, spitefully dismissive. I wanted to kill the reviewer.

Liam tossed the paper casually onto the table.

"You can't win them all," he said. He lifted Suzanna onto his lap and sat with his arms wrapped around her.

Catherine phoned as soon as she read the review. She said it was shite — Liam's work in that show was serious and strong — she reeled off a whole list of artists they both knew who'd said the same.

Then Dermot called round. He'd read the review, but he read

it again, shaking his head, whistling softly at the more negative phrases.

"Tom Maguire," he said when he reached the end. "Who the hell's he, anyway?"

"No idea," Liam said.

"Some pup wanting to make a name for himself. Don't take it to heart; it doesn't have to be negative. Sometimes we all need a kick in the pants."

So I thought I'd kill Dermot instead, but before I had time to gather myself, he was gone. Liam stared after him, baffled surprise on his face.

The sound of Dermot's car had hardly faded when we heard another pull into the yard. Catherine.

"Marie finally left him," Catherine said when I'd calmed down enough to tell her what Dermot had said. "Yesterday. And this time she means it, she's at her sister's with the children, she's looking for somewhere to rent."

Liam gaped at her. "Why didn't he say anything? Why didn't he tell us?"

Catherine and I stared back.

"Oh, I knew things weren't great," he said to our silence. "But it's always been stormy — right from the start — I never thought they would split." He went to the phone.

We heard him ask Dermot did he fancy meeting up for a pint. He listened, grunted, said something noncommittal, put down the receiver.

"He says Marie's away for a couple of days. He doesn't want to meet. He says he's busy."

I got up and put the kettle on. Catherine looked at the table.

"He's my closest friend," Liam said. "Why can't he tell me?"

"Maybe telling you would be like admitting to himself that it's real." Catherine spoke slowly and carefully. "And you know what Dermot's like — there may be the odd problem now, but everything's always going to work out."

"He told *you* —"

"I'm not married. Besides, he's not jealous of me. In work terms, I don't count."

The next day Liam cut out the clipping, highlighted it in orange Day-Glo, and stuck it up on the workshop wall. He had no experience of adversity; he didn't know what he was doing.

I always knew by Liam's walk when he'd finished something. He'd come out of the studio slowly, an odd, dazed look on his face; then with each step away from the workshop, the strangeness around him faded and changed. He'd been off somewhere else, a long way away, but now he was remembering that he'd lived here once, and might live here again.

When he reached the door he'd be fully back; his head would go up, he'd lep the steps, and stand in the kitchen shouting.

"Ellen, Ellen, where are you? Come out here and see what I've done."

It could be anytime; I could be anywhere.

If I'd seen from an upstairs window, I might not answer him, I might stand pressed against the wall behind the door instead, my whole being shot through with simple happiness at his need. He'd find me, then he'd grab hold of my wrist and pull me downstairs and over the yard.

"What are you waiting for, woman?" he'd say as I hung in the studio doorway. "Come here and see; I need to know what you think."

Only he didn't. We both knew it didn't matter what I thought, that what he wanted was to show me — me, his Ellen — to say, *I did this for you*, which wasn't true either, he'd done it for himself.

And I loved it, all of it. Knowing he was fully there, fully himself, and the person he most wanted to see him being like this was me. Afterwards, if the children weren't there, we'd make love.

I don't know when the way we were together started to change, but one day I caught myself remembering, so I knew then that it had gone. The realisation brought a strong, dark tide, like grief. It dawned on me that I'd lost something, and if I didn't watch out I might lose a whole lot more.

Liam is sociable by nature — warmhearted, good-natured, liking a bit of craic. He attracts attention, and attention releases something in him, like the fragrance rising out of cut hay in fine weather.

I never was comfortable in company. Then, when all this started up I wanted to stay clear of outside eyes and ears.

"Where's Ellen?" they'd ask in the pub, at an opening or a party.

"Babysitting."

I was always babysitting. The men said I was great, but the women made him feel selfish. It had made sense when the children were babies and there was no money, but later on things could have changed and they didn't. People stopped asking. It never occurred to me that it might be lonely for him or that our lives might grow apart. Robbie had liked going out with the lads, he didn't need me alongside him — mostly he didn't want it. Just as long as I was always there when he got home.

So Liam was relieved when Catherine decided to be my friend. It lessened my isolation and he had someone else to help him carry its weight.

Or that's what I tell myself when I'm feeling rational.

It's not comfortable, living the way I do, being one thing with part of myself while the rest of me's off at a distance, watching.

Some healers aren't this way at all. They're not separate within themselves; they don't know what's coming to them from the conscious level and what they're getting from another level; it's all mixed up in the one big stew, and they don't care. Not me. I don't want darkness and moil and chaos. I crave long windows filled with the clear light of day.

Presbyterians are into the rational. The first hint of the irrational and there's an audible shifting onto higher, drier ground. Catherine says the rational bit is strange when you think about Luther.

I ask her why, and she says that Luther believed salvation was always through grace, never through works, and grace isn't rational.

I think it's strange that Catherine knows about Luther when I don't.

It's even stranger when you think of the Bible. All those miracles, yet we cling to what we can see and touch. Presbyterians have services of healing. The sick line up and the minister lays on his hands, but everyone knows it's sort of token; the minister isn't Christ, and you'd need to be a bit weak in the head to believe that such things can happen now. It's not like Catholics, saving up their pennies, going off to Knock or to Lourdes or Medjugorje for a cure.

Liam says my life would be easier for me if I'd been born a Catholic: I'd let go, leave off fighting myself, just let whatever-it-is flow through me as he does when he's cutting stone.

He says this, then he stops. It's because he's an artist as well as a craftsman, and the artist in him knows that flow is only half the story. The vision comes through the fight; the work comes through the flow — that's what he's always telling me. So he looks at me and closes his mouth. Neither of us knows what I'd be like if I'd been born Catholic.

Liam is proud of what he calls "my gift." At the same time he's more than a wee bit uneasy. There's this closed, secret place, and I'm in there with only the person who's come to me to be healed. And it's not just secret in the sense of being confidential (so I can't say and he can't ask), but secret in the sense that something happens in there and neither of us knows what it is.

And secrets are powerful, so I become powerful — although it's not my power.

And the secret brings us closer because he protects it, but also it keeps us apart because it's only mine.

It's as though there's a way through the great tangled hedge of thorn that grows around Sleeping Beauty's castle. I don't *know* the way through, but sometimes it's there; sometimes it opens like the Red Sea parting. But not at will — only when I'm allowed — that's important. And I can't bring out any memory of what I did when I was there.

I'm not the prince or Moses — what happens in there has nothing to do with me, with Ellen. Yet sometimes I can come and go.

I'm a channel. There it begins and ends.

Catherine and I weren't close straightaway. First I had to get used to her, and then I had to get over the nun-thing, which was there like a door I pretended I couldn't see. A closed door, and one that we only ever glanced at in passing.

"In the convent . . ." she might say, as I would say "in Derry . . ."

When she did I would change the subject or else go on with the conversation as though I hadn't heard. After a while I thought of that convent as something that had happened once, a long time ago, like my father's death when I was no more than a child. Something regrettable and best forgotten. Something we'd never explore.

I didn't exactly stop talking to Liam because I had Catherine, but he ceased being my only outlet, and I got more selective in what I said. And Catherine was easier to talk to: she picked up on things I hardly knew I was saying; she backed off straightaway if she touched on somewhere I didn't want her to go.

It's lonely, being different. I am like the seal — a big, blubbery mammal moving deep underwater, living with all those fins and scales and gills. Then the dive up for air, the looking around at the oxygen world, the sinking back down to life with the fins and the gills.

Having a place in both worlds. Belonging in neither.

Chapter 18

*I*n the spring of '97 Liam had landed a big commission.

A good commission too — one that excited him and caught his imagination. When the letter came he'd known what it was, his shoulders had tensed, then he'd turned away and taken a long, slow breath before he'd torn it open. I'd waited.

This sort of commission doesn't fall from the sky; there's a whole long story behind it, starting with a committee and a list of names. The committee meets and looks at the list, then sends out letters to some of the artists asking them to submit a proposal for the site. Mostly the artist is given a theme or a subject, and it's a good thing, career-wise, even to be asked. So all the artists beaver away, and then the committee sits back and chooses which one it wants.

It's a bit like a competition, except it isn't because you can only enter it by invitation. Liam had spent ages on the proposal, and he'd worked knowing ten other sculptors were all doing the same. The system made me angry and always had. We'd argued it backwards and forwards for years.

"Either it's a competition and anyone can enter, or it isn't. This way they get all this work out of you for nothing."

"Not for nothing. I'm getting a fee, remember?"

"Call that a fee? You do all this work for a pittance, then they can turn round and give the job to somebody else. If they like what you do they should make up their minds and just offer you the commission."

Liam would laugh at my words and rumple my hair as though I were Suzanna. The system was the system; it didn't bother him, or it didn't back in the days when the letter mostly said that his work had been chosen.

Not always though. Sometimes the letter said they liked his idea and were glad they'd seen it, but the project was being awarded to someone else. To be fair to him, it was only ever a couple of days of gloom, and then he'd laugh at himself and move on. He had a buoyant temperament and a good attitude.

"No one's forcing me to be a stonemason," he'd say. "It's what I want to do — end of story."

I suppose the problem was mine, not his; I was defensive for him — I couldn't bear to see him rejected and hurt.

But this time there'd been good news in the letter. He'd grabbed me by the waist and whirled me around in the kitchen, then he'd made for the studio, humming under his breath.

It was a piece on emigration they wanted, but not the usual — no rags or stick-thin limbs, no desperation. It was the emigration of choice they were interested in — the people who left on account of an inner hunger, a craving for a wider experience than they could have had at home.

Liam said that in among the starving there must always have been such people, but for years so many had *had* to leave it probably felt like heresy to speak of choice.

"But now the country's booming, so it's okay," he said.

I was as pleased and excited as he was. There was stability for us both in a commission. It was good for Liam to work on something he knew would be shown and good for me to be able to budget and plan. And one thing led to another. A commission like this involved opening ceremonies and politicians and media exposure, it meant his name would be around in the public mind. And perhaps more work would come out of it; there was luck as well as talent in success, and it did no harm to dream. Anyway, it was a cheque in the bank, for they paid half the money up front and the rest would come when the piece was handed over.

But after the first elation it's a lonely business settling in to create something, and there are artists who need to talk their way all along the road and others who don't want to say a thing in case they lose sight of the path ahead. Liam always went quiet when he was planning a piece or making a piece, a strange, tense quiet shot through with excitement. He never seemed to need me to question him too much about his progress, so I just assumed he would do as he always did and I left him alone and trusted that he'd come back when he was ready.

Word spread, and more and more people came for my hands. On the way out they slid their donations into the box. I still did the library in the mornings, so life began to ease financially, but the Healing took a lot out of me, and I was always tired.

Liam said things weren't as tight as they had been. How would I feel about letting the library go?

I thought he meant I should see people mornings as well as afternoons, but he didn't.

"Keep it the way it is," he said. "That way you'll have the mornings here to yourself."

Still, I hesitated. A cheque every month is a cheque every month, no matter how small, and the only sure money we had coming in. Plus, I didn't want to lock myself into the Healing. I hesitated, but the next time he brought it up, I knew I wanted to let myself be persuaded.

So in February I went to see the senior librarian in Kilkenny and told her I'd need to stop work in the library for a bit. Only for a bit — I stressed that — I was fairly sure I would be coming back.

She was a quiet, intelligent woman, private and shy, not a woman I had any sort of a personal relationship with, though I liked and respected her from my part-time distance. She said they were pleased with me and she could keep the job open for me for a while if that's what I wanted, the same as if I'd come to tell her I needed maternity leave.

I blushed and mumbled and told her I liked the work and it suited me well, but at the moment I had other commitments. I couldn't ask her to keep the job open, but could I reapply in the future if circumstances changed?

She'd looked at me while I'd said my piece about stopping work, but she didn't look at me for the next bit, she looked at the mess of papers she held in her hands instead.

"I've heard about what you're doing now, Ellen, and I'd say you might find it very worthwhile — so much so that you might not want to come back. All the same, I think I can truthfully say that we'd always be happy to look at an application. Perhaps when the children are older? And perhaps you'd think of getting the qualification if you did? It would mean extra study, but that wouldn't be a problem to you; I think you might find you enjoyed it."

Once again I blushed like a pubescent girl, said something vague about thinking it over, and fled.

She was the first outsider who had spoken of the Healing,

however indirectly. I'd have thought a woman of her education and intelligence would view it with scepticism, even derision, but there was none in her voice. Rather, almost an honouring.

Whatever it was, the more I did it, the stronger it seemed to get. I was always careful to explain that it wasn't up to me; I didn't know what would happen; I could promise nothing. Yet underneath all this caution I could feel my confidence growing.

It was the men that moved me most, for they were so awkward and shy and apologetic. They'd go on about whatever-ailed-them being only a small thing, and not wanting to waste my time.

Then the eyes would lift up from the knees and meet mine, and there'd be a pleading hope in them and behind the hope a sort of desperate challenge. *You cured my neighbour's asthma. My sister's child fell into the fire, and there isn't a mark. An aunt of mine couldn't open her hand from arthritis, and now she's back at the knitting.*

The women could be the same, especially the countrywomen, but there were others with nothing much wrong except maybe a bit of an ache in the knee that came and went. I know that knee well — it's called Idle Curiosity. Liam said if I slapped on a good hefty charge the problem would solve itself. He's right, but I can't do it.

Around this time a trickle of folk of a different breed began turning up at the door. Perhaps that's too strong, perhaps not *a different breed* — the sick are the sick — but they weren't sick in the way I was used to. They were mostly women, younger and better dressed than my usual lot, and though the first ones were English or Dutch, there began to be Irish as well. They confused me at the start. They might be ill, but they weren't chronic, and mostly what ailed them was something that would have cleared by itself in a couple of weeks. Then it dawned on me that they were using my hands instead of the doctor's tablets.

Liam called them the Alternatives, and the name stuck.

They weren't backwards either; I never had to prompt them or listen for what lay under "a bit of a pain." From the moment they stepped through the door they were telling me all about their lives and their problems, as well as a whole lot more besides. They were very strong on what was wrong with the world, stronger still on the overuse of drugs in modern medicine, and as for their views on farming, once they started they couldn't be stopped. I came to know all their theories by heart, for they'd all passed round the same books, which they spoke of as Paisley might speak of the Bible.

I thought them a strange crew, both frightened and totally sure of themselves, very down on darkness and pain, always on about sharing and healing and light. They seemed to think it their task to be stuffed full-to-bursting with energy which they used to ensure that their lives were stuffed full of projects, and if that energy waned or wavered, it plunged them straight into fear. They saw sickness of any sort as a personal failure — it never seemed to occur to them that they might not be as much in charge as they thought they were, that there might just be other reasons for sickness besides their much-cherished emotions.

Liam laughed at me when I gave out about them. He said that they meant no harm, and there might be sense in there along with the dross. I should listen and learn.

"They think sickness is caused by a negative thought pattern, so you nip each negative thought in the bud and you'll never get cancer," he said. "They're only trying to protect themselves, Ellen. Their theories make them feel safe. Don't begrudge them."

"Or heart disease or AIDS or a stroke or Alzheimer's. So how are they going to die, tell me that? Or are they all going to live forever and ever?"

"Death's a frightening thing, Ellen. It's not everyone wants to look for the bones lurking under the flesh in the way that you go in for. And sometimes seeing something from sideways, or underneath, or hardly at all yields more than looking it slap between the eyes. Anyway, what harm to leave them a bit of comfort?"

My usual snort of derision.

He's right. I want to look straight and think straight, I'm not interested in theories spun to make things alright. And while we're at it, spare me guides and angels and crystals and all that New Age blether. Not that they matter, but they offend me. Especially guides. We are our own guides, our own responsibility; we can't wriggle out from under our lives as easily as that.

And spare me all this white magic stuff the Alternatives come out with as well. Magic is magic — the Dark Art — to be stayed away from. If you meddle with white you meddle with black, for it's stronger than we are, and who are we to decide when it's the one and when the other? We have no overview — it isn't allowed us. So how can we begin to know?

And another thing — magic requires assent.

I do not assent to the use of myself for magic, and I never will.

Over time I grew used to the Alternatives, but I never was easy with them. Maybe they were right and maybe they were wrong, but my hands wanted none of their theories, they wanted only to be placed where they directed me. And in this I was one with my hands, for I didn't like all this head talk; it wore me out and distracted my attention.

Chapter 19

That was a cold, slow spring when it came, reminding and reminding of the North. Everyone else was complaining. Not me. It was the thinness I liked, everything breathing slow and quiet and almost — so you could nearly see through into somewhere else. Sometimes down here the spring comes all in a rush. There's warmth and an ease that holds; the fields and trees are decked out overnight, and it all happens so fast you come close to forgetting the strangeness of it, the death-become-life. Not this year. This year everything was miraculous: the buds on the chestnuts fattening and opening, the new-paint plumage of the songbirds, the first swallows flicking around the cold sky. And behind it all, the rain moving over the mountains. Blue light before. Blue light after.

Andrew checked on the buds every day and wrote reports in a notebook that Catherine had given him. It was a beautiful note-book — hardbacked and ruby red in colour, a single vertical dark-yellow stripe running up beside the spine. I wished I had given it to him myself. Even more, I wished that Liam had.

Catherine had been offered three days' teaching a week at Limerick College of Art. She'd dithered around for a bit, then she'd rung them up and accepted. As soon as she'd put down the phone to them she rang to tell us.

"Why not?" she asked herself down the line. "I'm sick and

tired of the Bugs and Blooms, and I've nothing else ready to work on. Besides, if I'm stuck for time I might get an idea. If you haven't got time you *always* get an idea."

This was a good spring for Andrew because there was much to report. Everything came at the wrong times, the early things late and the late early, all muddled up and confused. He checked progress, drew diagrams and sketches, wrote detailed observations. The notebook was supposed to be a secret, so I watched but I never asked, and I was always careful that my face was blank and my eyes somewhere else when he looked up from his task. I thought he might have Liam's eye, combined with a bit of the farmer, and the two strands twisted together would strengthen over time and steady him in the world. I was like any mother — planning, dreaming, yearning. But I never could see through to the children's futures, and maybe that's as well.

Suzanna wasn't into buds, she was into starlings. Suzanna's so round-faced and pretty you'd think she'd be into round, pretty birds like wrens and tits and robins. No chance. The starling-thing had started when the autumn flocks were in the air. She knew the swishing sound of their coming, and she loved the way the air seemed to thrum and change shape with the birds as they wheeled and dived. When the flocks began to break up in the spring, two pairs made their homes in holes in the ruined out-building across the yard. One day she came rushing in, for she'd heard the steady cheep of the hungry chicks deep in the wall.

"Mammy, Mammy, the babies are hatched," she said, the awe in her voice like someone telling you the Berlin Wall had just come down. She said she liked their coloured speckles and that fluting noise they make, but I think what she really liked was their untidy shamelessness and that cocky chancer-ish air they have about them.

That was the spring the Good Friday agreement was signed

and the Troubles were formally brought to an end. Everyone here breathed a sigh of relief. *Thank God that's over and done with. Time to forget the past and move on to mobile phones and shopping malls and self-esteem.*

I sound bitter? Liam says I do. He says if he didn't know better he'd think I was an unreconstructed Republican, still moaning on about abandonment, still ready to kill and be killed for a country united and free.

It's easy for him — them — the citizens of the Republic. It's not that I don't want the peace, but thirty years don't vanish away on account of a few politicians putting their names to a bit of paper. They're there like a bit of old iron lodged deep in your gut, and the rust goes on seeping, year in and year out, till it has you stained right through.

That was the spring I began to notice that something was wrong with Liam. Liam has always been noisy about the place, if I wanted to know where he was, I'd only to stand very still and I'd hear him humming or banging or singing along with the radio. If Whiskey was with him he'd be having a whole long talk with her, and if she wasn't he'd likely as not be talking to himself.

One windy morning in April the phone rang for Liam, so I went outside as I always did and I stood in the yard and listened for where he was. Silence. I called, but there was no answer. I went back to the phone and took down the number, saying I'd get him to ring when he got back. Then I went looking.

He was in the studio alright, but the radio was off and he was sitting over by the window with some papers he wasn't reading held in his hands. He was deep in his thoughts and hadn't heard me come in. I was going to call out, but something about him stayed me. I waited a moment, then turned round and let myself out very quietly. Then I stood in the yard and thought about what I'd just seen.

The rain had stopped, and the birds were starting up again. I wondered if that was the first time Liam had gone quiet or if he'd been silent for days or weeks and I hadn't noticed. With part of my mind I thought about hanging a wash, but when I saw how blue and close the mountains were I knew not to bother, for there was more rain on the way. I tried to think about Liam, but my mind didn't want to go there. It stayed where it was, like the stopped hand of a clock. I heard a car draw up and park on the other side of the wall, and I heard the door opening and someone getting out. My mind held itself very still, and it held my eyes open so that the green world flowed into them, filling them up to the brim.

The door of the car slammed shut. Someone for my hands, I thought. But I hadn't finished thinking about Liam, I hadn't begun; I hadn't even given him the message.

But I'd started to see him again. And once I'd started I couldn't stop.

One night I went to bed and woke with an ache in the pit of my belly. I waited for it to go away, but it didn't, so I thought it must be my period coming early. My period passed, and the pain got stronger. Then it dawned on me that it might be to do with Liam.

There was something wrong in the studio, but what it was I didn't know. Liam went there, the same as before, but it wasn't the same as before, he went in earlier, and he came out later and when he did he wasn't dead tired but excited as well — he was oozing the tiredness of defeat.

I thought about talking to Catherine, but she was busy and full of her own life. She called in less, and when she did it was all the new job in Limerick.

"It's a gas, so it is," she told me. "They sit there, drinking in every word I say — I'd swear they nearly think I know what I'm doing."

But she hadn't had any ideas. She'd done loads of sketches, but nothing that really grabbed her, she said. Certainly nothing that filled her up till she couldn't stop thinking about it, couldn't focus on anything else.

"You make it sound like falling in love."

"Do I?" She looked thoughtful. "If that's what it's like, I think maybe I'll stick with the clay."

I was embarrassed; it hadn't occurred to me that she wouldn't know. For an eighth of a second I wondered, was she a virgin as well? No, she couldn't be, I decided. Not Catherine. You couldn't be the way Catherine was and never have slept with anyone at all.

The weeks passed, and Catherine got used to the job. She came more often and started to notice our world again. Sometimes she went to the studio to see Liam, but she never stayed there for long. If the evening was fine we sat outside and she smoked and watched me and waited for me to talk.

But I didn't, I couldn't, the moment had passed.

⸺◦◦◦◦⸺

About a month after this the Seeing came back, but not in a way I'd ever had before or ever want again as long as I live. I opened the door on a woman who was a stranger to me, and I knew just by looking at her that she'd heard the things people said and she'd come, without hope, for a cure. I knew, too, that she'd been ill for so long there was no point me even trying; I wouldn't get through to the sickness, there were too many layers in the way. But I brought her in, though I didn't want to, and I sat her down and listened while she found her few words and laid them out for me to look at with the front part of my mind.

But with the other part — the part that isn't mind at all but something else — I was reaching out in spite of myself and slowly moving towards her. And as I did I met with the layers that covered her sickness, and the layers changed into forms, but not ones you'd see with your eyes alone — more like those you'd half sense and half see inside a dream. Without thought I began to name them, and each time I found a name for the form, it dissolved and another walked forward to take its place.

The first form was wrapped round in filth and its arms hid its face, so I named it as Shame and it left. Next came a figure straight as a die, an awful, clear stillness about it, and I knew that suffering had made it so, and I named it as Courage. Then came Despair, turned in on itself, naked and huddled and barely human, but at the sound of its name it went scuttling away. Behind Despair was a wild-haired, demented figure, shaking with rage, and I knew I was looking at Pain. Then something came forward shuffling and weeping, not caring who saw, so I named the form as Self-Pity and it was gone. After that I could stand no more, so I closed myself down and told the woman I couldn't help her.

If I could have let myself go on seeing and naming I might have got through to her sickness, but I couldn't. To reach deep into sickness you have to know darkness yourself, like must touch like, though your darkness may not be physical. And you're vulnerable, just like the sick, and what is available to you is limited and your courage is already sorely tried. I could name and dissolve the outer forms, but each time I did I lost part of myself. I stopped because I was too afraid to go on.

She looked at me then with a weary derision and got slowly up from the chair and began to button her coat. Shame seized me, but it was drowned out by anger, though I don't think she knew what she was doing to me, I don't think she had any idea.

It shook me, that Seeing, shook me so profoundly I couldn't have told Liam or Catherine, couldn't have got the words out if I'd tried. Which I didn't, for they were too deep in their own lives just then, and besides that I wanted only to push it away and forget.

I must live with what I am, though it has driven me from the world I was reared to, a world that condemns me as surely as that woman lived condemned by hers on account of the sickness from which she had failed to recover.

At last I had the wit to ask Liam straight out how the work was going.

We were in the kitchen. I'd chased the children off to bed, which was hard enough on those long, sweet summer nights. The television was on — it was always on these days — and Liam was sitting while I was doing the ironing. I'm like my mother in that: I can't abide just watching with idle hands.

The news and weather finished. Prime Time came on, and we watched it through to the end. I lifted the last tea towel out of the basket and ironed it carefully, poking the tip into all the corners, then folding it into a rectangle, pressing the rectangle smooth. The basket was empty. I set the iron down on its stand, unplugged it, coiled up the flex, collapsed the ironing board, put it away.

"It must be near finished, by now," I said to no one in particular. The door was open onto the yard, and the summer dusk was growing. The sky was beginning to thin and glow, and the trees were darkening against it. A little wind had got up and was stirring the leaves.

Liam never took his eyes off the screen.

"It's a good feeling, finishing," I said deliberately. "Finishing what you set out to do, all the work red up and put away."

Liam glanced across at me; then his eyes went back to the screen.

"No point finishing when what's finished is only fit for scrap."

I tried to think I hadn't heard right, but I knew I had. Then I thought maybe it was finished but something of what he was trying to put in was eluding him still. There were times when this happened. He'd get almost there — seven eighths of the way — then no matter what he did he couldn't get it the way he knew it should be. So he'd struggle and struggle till something changed or gave, and after that he could always sort it more or less to his satisfaction.

Those times I had to watch what I said. Since I couldn't see what was wrong in the first place, I mostly didn't notice what he'd done to put it right.

"It's probably more nearly there than you think it is," I said carefully. "You get too close and can't see it — you tell me that over and over. Maybe you need to stand back, take a few days away from it, not let yourself even go in and look."

"You've not been listening to me, Ellen. The problem has nothing to do with being too close. The problem is that the piece is no good. I've changed it and changed it, and now I've taken it too far and I can't get it back."

I'd never heard Liam talk this way. He reached over and turned the television off.

He said he'd hit something wrong about halfway in. The thing that he wanted, the lines he'd caught in the maquette, just weren't coming through as they should in the full-scale work. He'd been pissed off but not unduly worried. This had happened before — he knew what to do — so he set about making a full-size polystyrene model. He would solve the problem on it and not mess with the stone itself till he knew exactly what he needed to do. He'd solved it — or he'd thought he had — but when he went back to the stone it still didn't work. More drawings, another model, the same thing over again. He was scared by now; he'd never gone this far without breaking through.

"You can start again," I said, hearing the panic in my voice. "Put it down to experience, order new stone, don't mind the cost, the next one will be alright."

"I could, but I'm not about to. You don't understand, Ellen — it's not about the commission at all, the commission is only coincidence. I make abstract work, which means I'm exploring a language I'm also creating and only I know the linguistics. That doesn't matter. If it works, those linguistics make an energy inside the shapes and under the surfaces. Line and shape, balance and imbalance, something glimpsed at the edge of vision. Starting again wouldn't make any difference. I can't hear the language anymore. It's as simple as that. I've stopped believing I ever heard it at all."

He went quiet, and I thought he'd finished. But he hadn't at all, it was only a pause, he collected himself, then went on telling me things I neither understood nor wanted to hear.

He'd realised the language was lost to him because his confidence had gone. He'd tried every trick he knew to restore it, but only ended up making things worse.

"I took out the photographs — photos I'd loved, that I'd used in the past when I'd hit a low. I would leaf through them, thinking, *God, this is wonderful stuff. Did I make these things, was it really me, not somebody else?*" He stopped talking, stared at the table. I waited. "Nothing," he said, without looking up. "No excitement, no elation, just a bunch of carefully angled photos of some fair-to-middling work."

I stirred myself to protest, but he was too sure of what he was saying, too steady in his negation.

He said the light had gone out of the photos. Worse than

that, he knew for sure that the light had been self-delusion. But he also knew that artists went through these things. He told himself not to bottle it up, to go to someone he trusted and talk it through till he got his courage back.

"Dermot?"

He shook his head. I remembered Dermot's words about the review.

He'd lifted the phone to a painter called Luke, a friend of his since college days who'd been through just such a crisis. "I dialled the number and waited while it rang, but when I heard Luke's voice on the other end I put it down. I couldn't talk to Luke," he said. "I was too ashamed.

"It's like up until then I'd been riding around on a monocycle. And it was always easy — so easy I couldn't understand why people like Dermot went on about it being so hard. Everyone always said I was great — that they didn't know how I did it — and it never once occurred to me that I didn't know myself. I only found that out when I fell off. When I got back on again and tried to ride it, I didn't know how."

So far, I had listened in silence, but now my head went up and my mouth opened of its own accord.

"Why didn't you come to me?" I demanded. "Why didn't you tell me; why didn't you let me try?"

He looked at me, astonishment on his face. Then he shrugged his shoulders and looked at the floor. I understood.

"It's alright for other people," I said bitterly. "Cures and superstition and such. It's alright for them, but it's not for the likes of you —"

He went on staring at nothing. Finally he shook his head as though he was trying to clear a mist from across his vision.

"It's not like that, Ellen. If this was a burn or a cut or the flu I'd have asked, I always do. But this isn't the flu — it's not knowing how to ride the monocycle. You can't teach me that with your hands."

"We don't know that I can't," I said. "The Alternatives come for all sorts of things — tiredness, depression, even because they can't stop being angry. They tell me it helps, they come back for more, at least let me try."

Still he didn't look up. Then at last he nodded.

I went to the sink and washed my hands, dried them well on the towel, and rolled up my sleeves.

And I tried, but I could do nothing, for nothing came into my hands. After a bit I stopped trying. I said we were both upset so we'd leave it for now and wait until I was calmer.

Liam was relieved, he didn't want my desperation. He got up, took his jacket from the hook, opened the door, then stopped.

"I should have told you before, Ellen, but I thought it might come right. It's hard enough for you . . . the way things are . . . what with never knowing when the money's coming in and having this thing inside you that frightens you so." He was looking at me as he spoke, and I knew then he'd reached the end and couldn't bear to be pushed.

"I wanted to look after you, Ellen," he said. "I never wanted to let you down."

I didn't move, I only stared at him. It was so unlike Liam — soft talk like this — but I saw he was speaking the truth. I should have gone to him then, but I didn't. I sat with no sign or word, and he turned from me and went out into the summer night. Sometimes now I remember that moment, but I push the memory away.

After he'd gone I sat at the kitchen table drinking tea and thinking of what he'd said. He wanted to look after me; I wanted to be looked after. More than wanted — I craved it with a hunger like starvation that I knew could never be fed enough to stop it craving more. I sipped at the tea. I'd believed he could look after me, had lived for a long time in that belief.

How can something that's built over years crumble and fall into dust in an hour?

I found I was thinking of my mother, how she'd sit at the kitchen table at night drinking tea after Daddy had died. I'd wake and come down; I'd see the line of light round the kitchen door with the faulty catch that always unlatched itself, then I'd stand in the darkness watching her through the crack. I'd watch till I couldn't feel my feet and my whole body hurt from the cold. Then I'd creep up the stairs, stepping over the one that went off like a muffled shot. I'd slide into the freezing bed, pulling the covers up tight round my ears.

At last I understood that she couldn't forgive my father for dying on her, that what she was feeling alone at the kitchen table wasn't grief but anger at his betrayal. Now I saw it had been the same for me — it was why I had watched her with that blind hostility that possessed me like love. I couldn't forgive him for dying and leaving me with her, for not being there to look after me when I needed him. And I wouldn't forgive her for being the one who stayed alive.

Yet I didn't know why I had felt like that, for it wasn't rational. He'd never defended me from the world, nor from her, nor from anything else. He'd been a gentle man, appreciative of whatever life threw at him, grateful it hadn't been worse, spitting in no one's face. After he died I must have craved his protection, even so young, even though I must have already known, deep down, that he couldn't protect me. I'd gone on hoping against hope, defying gravity. And then there'd been Liam, and I thought I had got what I needed at last.

I made a fresh cup of tea and sat there, sipping away, till I was calm again. Then I settled myself, put my hands flat on the table in front of me, and thought of Liam. Nothing. No emptiness, no energy, nothing running through them. I knew without surprise that it wouldn't be given to me to help Liam. I sat with my head in my hands feeling more alone than I'd ever felt since the time I'd lost Barbara Allen and seen Jacko Brennan die before he died. For the first time in a very long time, I remembered Catherine saying that it wasn't me and it didn't belong to me. I was only a channel — not perfect, but one that would do to be going on with.

Chapter 20

*L*iam was in the Wildwood. That's what the pain that lived like a worm in my belly was all about. And it wasn't anything distant or controllable; I was nauseated with the dread of what might come.

I knew that the dread was for me as well as for Liam. He is stronger and coarser grained than I am, saner. He'd never let me down, and he wouldn't have now if he'd had any choice. Deep down, deep as the sea, I'd believed he was safe from the Wildwood. Hadn't he comforted me when its dark trees crowded around me? Hadn't he taken me by the hand and led me through? So how could it touch him now? How could he be in the Wildwood, his hounds lying swollen and stiff at his feet?

I knew that the dread was more than it should be, but I never was one for proportion. Trees walk, the Wildwood is always there waiting, just round that turn in the road or behind the sweep of the hill. Don't turn your back on a tree, especially one in its prime, full-leafed and heavy with mystery. That's the one that moves close when you're looking away.

But life doesn't hold itself back till you're able to face it. It's inside you all the time, being lived.

I got up earlier, and I went to bed later; I made myself busier and busier. The house was spotless, the garden well tended, I didn't mind how many came for my hands. And I tried not to watch what Liam was doing, nor to think of the future; I tried just to wait, but it was hard.

Liam had always taken on extra work hanging shows in galleries and arts centres. Sometimes he'd helped with theatrical lighting and sound or with setting up before a concert or a gig. Now the economic boom worked in our favour, and when it was known that he was available the Ansaphone was busy for him as well as for me. He was competent and reliable, and he didn't mind travelling; more than that, people liked him and went out of their way to keep him in mind when work came up. In the old days he'd cursed when he'd had to abandon the workshop, but now he seemed glad to leave it behind, for he never turned anything down. But he didn't stay on after a job for a pint as he'd once have done, and when he came in he was very quiet and tired. He'd stopped going to the local pubs as well. When I asked why, he said there was no one he wanted to talk to.

When the commission's delivery date was almost upon him, he made himself write to the government office to let them know he wouldn't complete.

"What about the money?" I asked him.

"I don't know. I've never not delivered before; I suppose it's possible they'll want it back."

I couldn't believe what I was hearing. I hadn't meant the advance, I'd meant the second half of the money, the money that came at the end. "What about all your work?" I asked when I found my voice. "Months of work, not to mention the cost of the stone?"

"They've paid out for work they thought they were getting. It's not their fault this has happened."

"You tried, didn't you? Does a doctor give you your money back because he hasn't cured you? Does a dentist when he hasn't fixed your tooth? Like hell they do. They charge just for letting them try, then they charge again when you're back saying your tooth still hurts. What makes a sculptor so different? Anyway, we haven't got it."

"I know," he said. "If they want it back they can sing for it."

I had more to say, but I saw his face so I stopped. I did that a lot that summer. Bit my tongue and kept quiet. The problem was, he knew.

A week or so later the phone rang, and a woman's voice asked me for Liam. She said she was from the department that had commissioned his work, and she'd like to speak to him if he was there. I covered the mouthpiece to tell him. I thought he would shake his head and I'd have to say he was out, but he went next door and took it on the extension.

When he came out he looked angry.

"I told her I thought I was having some sort of a breakdown. I said I doubted I'd ever finish the piece, or work as a sculptor again. She didn't seem to understand English. She kept saying the project was running late anyway, and most likely I just needed a break. She said she has to consult but maybe a year's extension . . . ? She's going to write me a letter."

I went back to washing the dishes, careful not to look at him when I spoke.

"Why don't you give it to them the way it is?"

"You've been talking to Dermot —"

I opened my mouth to lie, then I changed my mind. "Dermot says public commissions are just bread and butter, no one breaks themselves over them, that's why there's so much bad public art around. He says you'd be mad not to give them the piece, they're not expecting perfection. Anyway, most of them wouldn't know what perfection was if it flew down and sat on their heads —"

Liam looked at me. "He's right."

"Then you will —?"

He shook his head. "I'm not Dermot," he said.

———

It had rained for days — you would never have guessed it was only the end of August. I had the kitchen door open in protest: at least the world outside was green through the rain.

Catherine had tucked herself in at the table, a tin of fresh gingerbread close to her hand, which dipped in and out, lifting slice after slice to her mouth. Catherine's like me, I thought — her hands do what they want. And she never puts on weight. But maybe that's because she forgets to eat when she's working.

"He told me he's very depressed," she said carefully.

"He is."

"Have you tried to do anything?"

"With my hands?"

She nodded.

"I've tried, but nothing comes through. He could be blocking it."

"Why would he do that?" She was looking at me, eyes questioning. I took a deep breath and steadied my voice. I didn't want her thinking that I was being callous when Liam was suffering.

"I think he's been working up to stopping being a stonemason for ages. I just never saw what he was at."

She looked up at me sharply. "It's his whole life, Ellen. You surely don't think he'd turn his back on it now?"

"He's been saying on and off it's a young man's game —"

"It is, but they all say that. I'd swear he had no real intention of ever laying down his tools till he hit this."

Silence again, and neither of us breaking it. Catherine licked her finger and dabbed up the crumbs on her plate. She put the finger up to her mouth, and her tongue flicked out and cleaned it, like a cat's.

"He says it was that review," I said. "Pinning it up in the studio, reading it over and over every day the way he did —"

"Sometimes you hit a wall and it feels like the end of the world, but it isn't," she said. "The wall's there because the undervoice is trying to tell you to change, but you won't, so it acts to stop you going on as you did before. I think he'll get past this block, Ellen. Maybe not in exactly the way he thinks he will, but he'll get past it. He'll get back up onto his trick cycle and pedal off into the sunset." Her voice was dry. I shot her a look, searching her face for a sign to match her tone, but it was neutral.

I was angry then, with her as well as with Liam. I should have kept my own counsel, I thought. All these things she thought she had the right to say because they both lived in this world that I couldn't enter.

I got up, picked up the gingerbread lid, put it back on the tin. "He says he has to forget trick cycles and learn to walk like everyone else," I said.

She stood up and began to collect her things. At that moment Andrew came scuttling in through the rain, dripping wet, smiling and shy at the sight of Catherine. I glanced at the clock. Usually I heard the school bus dropping him off, but I must have been too absorbed in the conversation. She sat down again.

Andrew shrugged off his anorak, dumped down his bag, and wriggled himself onto the chair beside Catherine. I threw him a towel, but he had a new book about trees that he wanted to show her, his hair got no more than a wipe. He turned its pages, pointing out leaves and twigs.

My heart confused me so that it hurt. Catherine had never tried to woo Andrew, she'd just stayed still and let him walk round her until he grew used to her. When she talked to him now it was clear that she knew that he'd show her things that would interest her, because they interested him. She took him seriously and steadily, and he loved her. I had a feeling she loved him back, but I would never have intruded on their relationship enough to discuss it with either of them. It was separate from me, and I was grateful to her.

I watched them now, the way she sat close in to Andrew, the way his face was turned up to hers, resting himself in her interest.

You trusted them, and they let you trust, I thought. Well, more fool you. They bided their time, but in the end they cleaved to their own, and turned against you.

I knew I shouldn't be thinking this, but I was. I'd gone in behind the walls, dragging the gates shut, making them fast with iron-shod bars as thick as a grown man's thigh.

She didn't stay much longer. She waited while Andrew leafed through to the end of the book; then she looked at her watch and said she should be going. He shut the book. I watched his careful, closed face as he asked her if she thought she might like to look at it again the next time she came.

She told him she'd like to. She said she would leave more time, she was sorry she had to go now.

It happens to me sometimes, this behind-the-walls-thing. Catherine calls it "race memory." She says it's those times when you find yourself doing or saying things that you'd never let yourself do or say when you're only yourself. Things that don't belong just to you, but to everyone in your tribe, to everyone who came before you. You're tapping in to race memory.

When she said that the first time, I opened my mouth to protest, then I suddenly got it. The moment I did, it felt like she'd dropped a round stone right into the heart of the pool of myself. The stone sank down, and the ripples rose up and spread and spread till they died away in my mossy fringes. Bull's-eye.

So this time I knew that it wasn't just me who'd been thinking that thought about trusting them and them turning against you; I knew I was all the settlers who'd come to this country a long time ago and struggled to settle, to make new lives on forfeit lands, knowing themselves to be hated.

"Planters," that's what they called us. A planted people, working the lands they'd lost through rebellion and confiscation.

I felt bad after Catherine had gone. I needn't have bothered; I should have trusted my instincts.

Chapter 21

I was out on the hill picking plums, for I'd no one else in the book for that day and the children were gone till the evening. I heard the car in the yard, and I knew right away it was Liam home from hanging a show in Waterford. I scrambled down from the ladder and made for the kitchen, flushed with autumn and laden with windfalls and plums.

Liam said the show looked well, he was pleased with it, and so was the woman who'd hired him.

"She said there's a permanent job coming up. She asked would I think of applying."

I was delighted; I thought he must be over the worst if he'd started to think of a proper job. After all, he could always pack it in if his confidence came back. There was the money as well, I'll not deny that — but I'd dug in my heels over charging a fee, so I didn't mention the joys of a monthly pay cheque.

"I don't want the job," Liam said. "I'm not about to apply."

I heard, but I didn't take it in; I was too carried away with the thought of a bit of security and the prospect of Liam having something to do that he might half like. Then his words hit me. I stopped and stared.

He stared back at me. Liam is so easygoing on the surface that sometimes I nearly forget what he's like underneath.

"Why not?" I said, knowing full well I was wasting my breath.

"Spend the rest of my life hanging flavour-of-the-month crap painters? Painters still wet round the ears and only getting shows because they're doing the scene?" His voice was scornful and came through from a long way away. "Thanks, Ellen. Thanks for the support."

"You're welcome," I said. "I'm sorry I spoke, but I didn't know Waterford specialised in crap painters. Somehow I sort of imagined there'd be the odd one in there who was good." I could hear the nastiness throb in my words, but I didn't care. Was it my fault that he'd lost his confidence and couldn't work? Had I reproached him even once, or told him to pull himself together?

I stood there, all defiance, waiting for what he'd hit me with in return. He didn't speak. Instead he got up and went out without looking at me, so all I got by way of response was the click of the closing door.

I sat down and was filled with a feeling so empty and strange that I hardly knew where I was. I looked around, and I couldn't understand the sugar bowl or the tea mugs or the windfalls I'd picked up from the fading grass and set on the table less than an hour before.

What had happened to us? Where was Liam, my Liam, who knew my most hidden self and forgave it, who loved me whoever I was?

I went outside in a daze and sat on the bench and leaned my head back against the old stone of the house. I stared at a dense mass of fleshy leafed sedum and then at the pure, tall, white flowers of the Japanese anemones growing around the place. The sweet wind rocked them and bounced them against the purplish-pink of the cosmos, while the raggedy yellow daisies that stood as high as my head dipped and glowed in the pale September sunlight. The thick mist of the morning had burned off hours ago, and the mountains lay in long, pale mounds against the thin blue of the sky. Above me a few swallows hunted high up in the sunny air. Watching them, I remembered I'd forgotten them all summer. They'd be gone soon, though I'd barely seen them, for the months had passed in struggle and strife and now I would have to wait through winter's emptier skies. I was filled with grief at the loss.

I sat on, watching the tree shadows stretch themselves out across the fields in the autumn sunlight. In a month or two they'd lie long like this in the middle of the day, and at four in the afternoon the night would be pressing in. Mud and water and darkness. Sometimes frosty stars in the sky at night, frosty shards in the puddles in the mornings. But mostly mud, the secret life of matter, the secret essence of life. All sentient life is dull, only the eyes shine. All sentient life is dense, warm, soft, moist, liable to decay. Perhaps I could sit like this forever, I thought. Perhaps if I stayed close enough to matter — to all that I saw, touched, tasted, smelled, heard — I would understand flesh. Perhaps I would even begin to understand why we seem to need this flesh to decay in.

So we know who it is that is dying when we die.

It wasn't a thought or a voice or a Seeing, yet there it was.

A flight of crows went over. I'd forgotten the crows as well. Great crowds of them climbed the skies in the autumn, lifting and diving and falling, swishing their strong, black, raggedy wings through the thinning air. I felt better then about losing the swallows. I thought of the centuries of autumns dying into winter here in this valley, the thousands of eyes that had watched this death all down the years. I felt I was one with them but also only myself. I was mud and the sideways shine of light on the mud.

I always thought Liam's work was only his, that it went on somewhere else that was separate from me and didn't affect the life we lived between us.

There's a painter Liam knows called Tom Gallagher, whose wife has devoted her life to her husband's work, and the end of it is that he's famous. She has the most wonderful eye — Liam reckons she could have done it herself if she'd had a mind to — plus she knows nearly more about painting than Tom does himself. She does everything: talks to the galleries; goes to the functions; sources and buys his materials; keeps the books, the house, the garden; rears the kids. She creates all this space for Tom to work in, and all he has to do is make great art.

I've never done a thing for Liam. I wouldn't know great art if it leapt out and bit me on the nose.

He says he doesn't want me to; he says he'd go crazy if he had to stare at his work every day, all day, and never an excuse for doing anything normal.

"Besides," Liam says, "Gallagher's the real thing. He works from a place I only get to visit from time to time. . . . If he wasn't the real thing, Annette could have jumped through hoops of fire — it might have given him a better start in the early days, but it wouldn't ever have put him where he is now."

But it isn't just that I've not done anything for Liam — I've hindered as well as not helped. I didn't know the first thing about art when we met, and maybe I wasn't as ready as I might have been to learn. I was awkward and shy, a fish out of water, and I never wanted to go to the parties and openings where he'd have met the right people and got his face known. He never pressed me, we never fought about it, and sometimes he went on his own, but mostly he didn't. He despised the system — the doing of the rounds, the putting in of appearances — but lots of them do at the start; then they buckle down and learn how to work it. I listened and sympathised when he ran it down, but when he showed signs of wavering I despised his change of heart aloud. I would be like that: black is black and white is white and compromise only a sniff away from corruption.

Liam calls it the No-Surrender Mentality. The first time he said it I was furious.

"That isn't fair," I protested. "Look at Gerry Adams. You'll not find him seeking out a middle way."

"Sure, why would he?" Liam asked. "Isn't he a Northerner, the same as you?"

That was a shock to me. The discovery that down here they think what the British think: that Northerners — Catholic and Protestant alike — have more in common with each other than with them. (And may plagues descend on both their houses, wiping them from the face of the earth and leaving it to more rational and deserving beings.)

But I see things now that I couldn't see then. If Liam had done the rounds a bit he might have had more opportunities, and more opportunities might have stretched him and given him confidence. Most likely more money as well, which would have made our lives easier. It was alright when he was younger. Liam never gave a toss about being broke, and he doesn't now, he's not an acquiring sort of a man. But we were living off an overdraft stretched as far as they'd let us stretch it, the children were growing and needing, and everything had to be mended and fixed, there was nothing ever just thrown away. The house was bad enough, but at least you could patch and make do. The car was much worse — the suspension going or the clutch giving up — these were major disasters.

And it's harder since the prosperity came with the Celtic Tiger. We wouldn't be the only ones left behind, but sometimes it feels that way. Sometimes when you've had a bad day then watched too many slick ads on TV, it feels like choosing not to make money your aim in life is the same as choosing failure.

Sometimes when I looked at Liam I'd see him not as my husband, with all the complicated emotions and thoughts that that brings up, but as a man nearing forty, with strengths and gains but also with losses and disappointments that would probably always be there now. I'd see him like this and I'd be swept through with such love for this vulnerable, imperfect man who was quietly folding and putting away his dreams that I'd wish from the bottom of my heart that I could have seen him this way before. If I had, I think I'd have given up all my wants and needs — I might even have given *him* up if it meant he could have been what he'd dreamed once of being.

Then only days, hours later I'd swing right round and be filled with anger at him for poisoning our lives with this endless depression. I was sick of art, I didn't understand his work or what it meant to him, I didn't care whether he was hanging other people's or making his own.

So all through that autumn and winter I argued it this way and that inside myself, the whole weary cycle over and over, the whole weary drag through the days. Sometimes I wanted to kill him, and sometimes I'd only to glance at him and the pity rose up so strong in me I nearly felt my heart would break. It was exhausting. Then, at the back end of January, a letter came with "Limerick College of Art" on the front. He opened it and read it through.

"Catherine," he said, passing it across to me.

I waited for more explanation, but it wasn't coming so I read it instead. One of the lecturers in the Sculpture Department had taken time off on account of a family crisis, and they were looking for someone who might be willing to fill a temporary vacancy at short notice. Liam's name had come up. Would he by any chance be interested in two days' teaching a week?

"Would he?" I heard myself ask.

"I expect so," Liam said. "I'll show him the letter."

Chapter 22

wo, sometimes three weeks ahead, the book was completely filled up. I was busy, too busy, you couldn't just get sick and call over, if you had an appointment with me you'd already been ill for a while.

Liam was busy too. The absentee lecturer hadn't come back, and they'd asked if he'd think of another term, this time three days a week instead of two. He said yes right away. He liked teaching and he was good at it, he began to find himself easier to live with, and so did I. He stayed over in Limerick with colleagues a couple of nights a week, then came home and took on other work as it came up, so the money situation eased as well. We needed a second car, so we bought one — not new, but newer than anything else we'd ever driven before.

I was more used to the Healing, I could feel my confidence growing, and after a while I noticed my hands no longer flew straight to the site of the pain. Sometimes they'd set themselves down somewhere different altogether; they'd rub at that place or press into it, and I wondered, was this where the problem had had its beginning? I began to want to know more about the body and its functions. I'd get books out of the library, and if I found something useful I ordered it from a bookshop in town; when it came I would scribble notes in the margins and mark off the relevant passages for myself. None of this happened overnight, you understand, but I could feel myself getting more detached from what I was doing and, oddly, more sure.

I didn't always like this. Sometimes I would stand back and listen to myself, pronouncing on this or on that, and I'd miss the shy, quiet Ellen, the dreamer of private dreams, the Ellen who stood out under the trees or walked up the road in the springtime, following in its steps.

One shining morning in May I took my coffee out into the yard and sat on the bench and watched the soft light on the stones and the running shadows laid down by the ash as the wind streamed its leafy branches. A goldfinch crammed its beak for its young, and a wren flicked in and out of the sprawling silver-grey leaves of the marguerite daisies, swift and neat as a mouse. It was there and gone, there and gone, and as I watched, it dawned on me that I lived a life now that drummed with too much sound and movement, that left no space for small, elusive thoughts like wrens, that ate up my time and negated my solitude and left me lonely among all the people.

Then I began to review this new life of mine that seemed to have overtaken me almost without my noticing. Marie had moved to Dublin after the breakup, but Dermot had stayed in the house where they'd lived and often he had the two boys with him. Sometimes he'd bring them over to us, but more and more rarely these days, and he seldom came when he was by himself. With Catherine it was different as well. I saw her because she and Liam shared lifts to Limerick, and often she sat and drank tea in the kitchen, but not in the old way, for now it wasn't just the two of us and the conversation was always general or shop.

As I was thinking this thought the door of the studio opened, and Catherine came out, talking over her shoulder to Liam, who followed hard behind. I made no movement, and they didn't see me. Catherine was speaking, then Liam was nodding; she said something else, and he threw back his head and laughed. How much better he looks, I thought, with that sudden insight that comes when you suddenly notice someone you see every day without seeing. His colour was good; the grey hardly showed in his curly brown hair; his body seemed less weighted down. Liam was coming back into himself, and I'd been so busy with living my own separate life I'd hardly even taken it in. I did now. Then I saw that his overalls were marked with paint, and that was another shock.

Catherine wore her androgynous look: she had on a man's light-grey T-shirt, with those loose, open sleeves that always made her arms look wistful, her hair was clipped back, and she wore faded jeans and sturdy brown boots on her feet. She turned her head and saw me. There was a moment when she was still off somewhere else, then her eyes accepted mine, and her mouth opened out to that wide, free smile that was the thing about Catherine I loved best of all. She said something to Liam, and he glanced at me, nodded, touched her arm, and went back inside. She came over and sat on the bench beside me.

Catherine leaned her shoulders against the wall, stretched out her legs, and we stayed like that without talking.

I don't like talking much, but most people do, they seem to want to spend as much of their lives as they can with sounds coming out of their mouths. Catherine could talk if she wanted to, but if she didn't she could stay quiet without any awkwardness or unease. Most people aren't like that — they're either talkers or they're not, and if they're suddenly caught in the opposite mode they're so unnatural you want to shift yourself off away from them as fast as ever you can. That's me. When I try to make small talk people go from relaxed to tense in about ten seconds flat, and their eyes start shooting around, looking for how to escape.

"Liam is getting better," I said, when I finally wanted to speak.

"Yes," she said. More silence. "Cancellation?" she asked, her gaze on the chestnut tree standing full-leafed by the gate, all its tall candles burning creamy white and proud.

"Didn't show up," I replied.

"So why aren't you inside?" she asked. "Why aren't you baking bread or ironing or washing the floor?" She hadn't stirred or shifted, but there was the faintest edge to her voice.

"Is that what I'm usually doing?" I asked her.

"Something like that. Something busy and useful."

"Is this criticism I'm hearing, Catherine?"

"Observation. It's not like you to be sitting around."

I didn't say anything. I was in a strange mood. Here was Catherine, whom I'd been sort of longing for, and suddenly I wasn't sure if she was enemy or friend.

"I was trying to remember who I was," I said. I didn't know why I said it, or why I was suddenly angry with her, a dense, dark anger that I thought was to do with having to carry so much while Liam got well and she laughed with him, then sat here implying that I might be less than perfect.

"You've forgotten?" she asked.

"More or less. All these people. I feel invaded."

"And you don't like it?"

"I want to remember what it's like to feel lonely again."

"You could try doing more of what you're doing now."

"And who'd do all the rest? Liam?"

"Why does it have to be done? Why does everything have to be perfect all the time? Liam is getting better, the children are well, isn't all that more important?"

"Not perfect," I said, ignoring her last question. "Only clean and tidy."

"Perfectly clean and perfectly tidy."

"You don't understand, do you?"

"No. And I don't understand why you want to be lonely. I'm lonely, and I don't much like it. Most people don't."

"I'm not most people," I told her stubbornly. "No one is. I'm me, you're you, we don't have to be the same. You used to tell me that. It was one of the reasons I could talk to you. I didn't have to be everyone else, I only had to be me."

"What is it, Ellen? What are you so angry about? Is it the Healing?"

"I'm not angry," I said furiously. "Or at least no more than I always am. And yes, of course it's the Healing, it's always the fucking Healing."

"I didn't know you still felt like that," she said quietly.

I said nothing.

"I thought you'd begun to like it," she continued, her voice soft and careful. "You seem so much more confident now. You've *grown* so much."

"You sound like a fucking Alternative."

She winced. "Don't you get any fulfillment from it at all? Even from the results? I mean, some of it's incredible —"

"For fuck's sake, Catherine, it's not incredible. Everyone wants fucking miracles, but it's their own bodies that are the miracles, most of them would get better if I never went near them at all. Rest and time — that's all they need. Let their bodies do the work."

"That's four *fucks* in as many minutes," she said.

"Well, that's too fucking bad. Maybe I'm reverting; maybe I want to stomp around and say fuck; maybe I'm sick and tired of helping people and being good. Anyway, why do we always have to talk about me? Why don't you tell me what you're doing, how *your* work's going? Why don't you get a life that isn't art or mine, Catherine, why don't you go to India or China or somewhere, why don't you fall in love?"

I stopped. I didn't know why I'd said that; I'd never thought about Catherine as someone who might fall in love, but why shouldn't she? *One is one and all alone and evermore shall be so.* The song line sang itself in my head. That was how I thought about Catherine. What was the song? I wondered. Clear as a bell it came back to me. *Green Grow the Rushes, O.* I hadn't heard it for years. I sneaked a look at Catherine. Her face was tight and even paler than anyway. Hadn't she just said she was lonely and I'd completely ignored her? Perhaps she'd really meant it. She always seemed immune to men, as though all that was grand but not something she'd ever bother with herself. Perhaps she wasn't as immune as I thought she was.

Suddenly I felt terrible about her as well as everything else. First I'd deliberately not heard her, and then I'd gone and hurt her as well and only because I was in a stew and I wanted to take it out on whoever was around. I glanced at her again. She had pulled in her feet and was getting up from the bench.

"I'm sorry you feel I'm intruding on your life, Ellen," she said formally.

"Catherine," I said, and stopped. She turned and looked at me.

"I don't," I said. "I don't feel that at all, I don't know what came over me. This is all just about the Healing." She waited. "It's not that I don't like it or that I do like it, or anything like that; it's sort of beyond all that. . . ." I paused, unable to go on. She waited again. "If it wasn't so strong I don't think I could bear it. That doesn't make any sense, does it? I mean, I do it because I've no choice. If I didn't I couldn't live with it; I wouldn't know where to put it, it's so strong. But it's wearing me out. Whatever it is. It just gets too much for me."

"It does, of course," she said gravely. "But it's what you've been given."

I never expected such a cliché from Catherine, but there was something so strange about her that I didn't point it out. It was like she was showing me a part of herself I'd never seen before: intimate and vulnerable and awkwardly sincere. I'd never thought of Catherine as being vulnerable, and it dawned on me that I'd never seen this sincerity either. She was mostly dead off-hand and matter of fact, especially when what she was saying was important. That's why I trusted her with all this weird stuff. She took the fear out of it. Or she had so far. Maybe that was about to change.

"Catherine," I said carefully, and stopped again. I wanted her to go away now, but there was something I wanted to know before she did. "Catherine — that paint on Liam's overalls. Is he painting?"

"Yes," she said, surprise in her voice. "He started after hours in the art school, just messing around to see what would happen. Did he not tell you?"

I shook my head.

"Maybe he couldn't while he was that low. Too risky. He might have fallen flat on his face all over again."

"But he hasn't?"

"No. Now he's setting up here in the workshop. He's planning to move his stuff here when college finishes for the summer." There was a lift in her voice, excitement. "And, Ellen, I think this is really going to work for him."

Chapter 23

Catherine hadn't been over for ages and ages, but when she walked in I'd this funny feeling that there was something she wanted to tell me.

I remembered how I'd messed up before and I made up my mind that this time I'd meet her halfway.

I thought it must be the nun-thing.

So I asked, but as soon as I'd opened my mouth I wished that I hadn't, for now I was getting the lot.

"After I'd left the convent," she said, "I didn't know what to think about it. Part of me was okay with it but the rest was so twisted up and ashamed that I wanted to lock the whole thing away in some press that was never used and fire the key into the river."

At first I thought she was talking about having been a nun, but then I realised she meant the shame was in leaving the convent at all.

"Keeping the press door locked was like being a teenager with a secret diary," she went on. "The more you wrote in it, the more you dreaded somebody finding it on you and reading it through. . . . So I told myself I wasn't a teenager anymore and if I let myself go down that road I'd end up in an even worse mess —"

She stared into her tea mug as though she was reading the leaves. Then she looked up and her eyes were full on me and so I dropped mine.

"I tried to slip it casually into conversation," she said, "but it didn't work because I didn't feel one bit casual about it. I was so paranoid that I always heard this silent gasp when I said the word *nun*. And I knew it was all my imagination — even back then they were leaving the orders in droves — but telling myself that made no difference, I had to *force* myself to talk about it. After a while it got easier and soon it was old news.

"It was a bit like leaving the diary lying around unlocked," she added. "In the end I'd got so used to people reading it that I stopped minding. And then the minute I stopped minding, they stopped bothering. So dull. All those closely written pages. At times I was almost offended."

I nodded to show I was following her, though I wasn't at all — she might as well have been speaking double Dutch.

"But it was different with you," she said. "You looked so frightened I tried not to mention it. But then I'd forget and out it would come. You always changed the subject."

I was trying not to show that she'd got to me when she'd said I'd looked frightened, so I made myself ask her why she'd left the convent. This seemed more tactful somehow than asking her why on earth she'd gone in in the first place.

"I didn't leave," she said.

"Well, you're sitting here now so you must have —"

"I had this cough that wouldn't respond to treatment. It meant I couldn't sing anymore, which wasn't easy because the choir was the only part of the whole way of life that I loved. But I thought I'd been stopped from singing because I loved it so much that I was using it to make all the rest bearable. I thought it was an attachment that I needed to give up."

At last I calmed down enough to hear her voice, but I still couldn't speak. "Ellen," she was saying urgently, "Ellen, tell me about tray bakes."

I gulped and spluttered. The tissue was a sodden mess in my hand. At last I could speak.

"Wise up, would you, Catherine? I just got upset. . . ."

"No, tell me," she said, sitting down again. "I want to know."

"A tray bake's what you were eating," I managed, my voice very small and shaky still. I stopped. "For Christ's sake, Catherine, this is ridiculous, I don't know why I said it, it's got nothing to do with anything —"

"Tell me."

"A tray bake's a baking tray slathered with flour and butter and eggs and stuff in different combinations. You bake it. You cut it into squares while it's hot, and when it's cooled down it goes into a tin." I was dabbing away at my nose as I spoke.

"The tray-bake tin," I added. "You'd know it right away. It has to be full all the time, that's really important — it shows you're a virtuous woman." Suddenly I heard myself, and I started to laugh and I couldn't stop. It was the other side of the crying. It was like when you're a child and you do whirlys too long, so you have to unwind in the other direction to stop yourself falling over. Catherine didn't laugh. At last I was through it. I felt flat, calm, completely exhausted.

"A virtuous woman, her price above rubies," Catherine said quietly.

"I thought Catholics didn't get to read the Old Testament?"

She shook her head, but she didn't say anything. I was glad. I didn't want to talk anymore, I was through with talking.

She smiled, an ironic self-deprecating smile. "You can make yourself believe almost anything if you want to believe it badly enough —" She picked up her empty mug and drained it. "The cough kept getting worse so they sent me to a specialist. He did tests for TB, but they came back negative, so then he wanted me in hospital for observation. I went, but they couldn't find anything, not even a chest infection, so they thought it might be psychosomatic. Then my sister came to the hospital to see me. She stood by the bed and told me enough was enough. She made me get up and get myself dressed in the clothes she'd brought, then she took me home. She left my habit laid out on the bed like someone who'd died. After that the cough went away and it never came back. So you see, I never decided to leave, I wanted to stay, it was only my body that didn't. I suppose I must have been deeply unhappy —"

I stared. "Why did you want to stay if you were unhappy?"

"For God," she said simply. "I wanted God, and I thought a convent was the quickest way. I didn't care about being unhappy."

She stopped. I knew she wanted me to say something, but I didn't because I couldn't. I was embarrassed for her. I was even more embarrassed for myself because she was my friend.

"You think I'm cracked, don't you?"

I nodded. She waited again, but still I didn't speak.

"I suppose I had what you'd call a very privileged childhood," she said quietly. "I always wanted the best, and everyone always went out of their way to try to see that I got it. I had so much, and so much was never enough. . . ." Her voice trailed off.

"It's sort of hard," I said carefully, "from where I'm coming from, to understand why you'd want God at all."

She looked at me as though I was a bit slow. "I told you, I wanted the best. God was the best, so I wanted God. That's why I wanted to be a contemplative. It was the purest, or that's what I thought at the time."

I didn't look at her. I concentrated on the apples I was peeling for a tart. In that moment it seemed as though my whole life I'd been doing the opposite. Trying to get away from God. All my life I'd been running, and God had been thundering after me. Raging from pulpits and platforms, shooting out of people's mouths in tongues of fire, *Thou Shalt Nots* falling thick and fast, like rain. I'd felt harried and persecuted and spied on. The hundred and thirty-ninth psalm had pursued me: *Thou knowest when I sit down and when I rise up; Thou discernest my thoughts from afar. . . . Whither shall I go from thy Spirit? Or whither shall I flee from thy presence?* But down here was different, down here was ignorance and super-stition. My mother's words, and here was I, thinking them. Down here was the first time in my life I'd felt even halfway safe from God. I could do what I liked, far away from those terrible psalms.

"What have you got against nuns, Ellen?" She was smiling now. "Apart from Presbyterian bigotry, that is? I bet you'd never met a nun in your life till you came here."

"Presbyterians don't consort with nuns," I said calmly, not taking my eyes off the apples. Or I hoped it was calmly, I didn't feel it — I didn't like that "Presbyterian bigotry" bit. Which was illogical as well, for I was always calling Presbyterians bigots. But that was my right, not hers.

"Were you a virgin when you joined?" I asked just to cover up.

"I was. Don't look so shocked. I wanted God, I was very deter-mined, I thought you had to be a virgin to get close to God. And you don't *join,* you *enter.*"

I didn't say anything.

"I don't blame you for thinking I'm cracked."

This time I looked at her, but still I didn't speak.

"I understand, really I do," she said. "If I wasn't me, *I'd* was cracked as well."

I didn't like that either. I felt patronised and condesc to. The anger was rising strong in me, and I didn't want to down anymore.

"No, you don't," I said quietly, "you don't understand You think you do, but you don't, you've got no idea what I inside or what I feel and you never have. How would you? Y never been to a Presbyterian church. You've never even be the North, you've never bothered your arse, you've got all assumptions you just assume that I share." I heard my voi was still quiet, but she couldn't have missed the fury.

"You think you know everything, but you don't." My was finally rising. "You know fuck-all about anything —"

I got up, carried the peeled apples across to the sink, came back and stood by the table. I couldn't stop my hands shaking. I cast around for some way to prove to her that I right and she was wrong. My eye fell on the open tin half fu the shortbread she'd just been eating. I picked it up, slammed it hard back down on the table and pushed it under nose. "You don't even know what a tray bake is," I yelled in face. "You don't even know you don't know, you don't even c you don't even *want* to know —"

It was too much. I gave up. I sat down abruptly, laid my he on my arms, and cried, though I didn't know why. Once started I couldn't stop. I cried so long and so hard that I got th funny gulpy thing I haven't had for years. When I came rou enough to want to stop I realised that Catherine was standi over me, stroking my hair. She must have been like that for age but I didn't know it. She pushed a not-very-clean tissue into n hand, and I wiped and blew.

Two weeks later I put back a shoulder, and that was a first. A neighbour came without an appointment, his young daughter held in his arms. I glanced at the child, and I saw right away what was wrong.

"Take her to Casualty, Mikey," I told him. "I think her shoulder's out."

He pushed her towards me as though he was thrusting a gift on me that I was too modest to take. "Well, put it back then," he said. "Isn't that what I brought her for?"

I told him I didn't do bones, I didn't know how, he'd be better off at the hospital.

"You can do it," he said, "I know well you can. And you might as well do it now, for I'll not take no for an answer."

So I took hold of Geraldine's arm, and before I knew it I'd given it a bit of a twist and her shoulder had clicked back in.

Mikey nodded his satisfaction; it was only what he'd expected, he'd no idea of the shock I'd just got because it had happened all in one go and without anything coming into my hands at all.

That's the way of it now with bones and disks. Nothing else. I do them because people ask, but it isn't the Healing, it's technical through and through.

It's nearly as though my hands have been taught a new skill from all the time that they've spent at the Healing.

When I'm doing the Healing now it's different from how it used to be. I get hollow, like a pipe, and it's like there's something inside the pipe, but I don't know what. It isn't like flowing water or even an electric current anymore — it's more a dynamic emptiness that has no colour or substance.

I don't feel occupied or invaded when it comes, but I feel myself being moved effortlessly to the very outside of myself so it can take up all the available space. What is this *it* that I speak of? Who knows? It's something without form or outwardness, yet it's strong — much stronger than I am.

Maybe it's life itself?

Right from the start, it came when it wanted, left when it wanted, gave me no choice or say. It would stretch out my hands and place them where it directed them — sometimes they stayed on the body itself, but sometimes they held themselves over it, on the level the Alternatives call the "aura." I didn't have to know anything, I only had to follow my hands.

I still don't know much and I don't seek out patients, they seek me out, and I promise nothing. These days if I don't feel the emptiness in my hands — if they don't uncurl and go from slack to rigid, fingers separate — then I keep them to myself. I shake my head and turn away, and they hate me and I can't stop them. They hate me because the sick will always hate those they think can return them to health but deny them.

At first I thought if the emptiness came it meant that the Healing would work and the patient would recover.

But I found that it wasn't always to be like that.

Which upset me. I couldn't think what the emptiness was coming for if it wasn't going to do its stuff and heal.

Then I noticed that sometimes people didn't just not get better — they might get much worse, and quite quickly. Twice I had people with late-stage cancer, and I felt the emptiness in me so fierce I was certain sure they'd recover. But they went home and told everyone they felt much better, then inside the week they were dead. For both of them it was the same.

For a while there I wouldn't touch cancer. I was too afraid of what might happen when I did. Afraid for myself as well. I remembered the woman whose presence had summoned those awful figures I'd seen and named.

Sometimes I think that the body pursues sickness, seeking out the truth of its own mortality. It wants to know about death, which the mind disallows and denies.

The body, knowing that truth, carries it back to show to the mind so the mind will understand its fate and begin to doubt itself. Or that truth is carried forward — entering death — abandoning body and mind. And the world is constantly readjusted by the presence of that truth. This is the sinew in the meat of incarnation, which is what we are here to eat.

Such carnivorous language. I think these things but I don't understand them.

"Decay is the beginning of all birth, the midwife of great things . . . the deepest mystery that He has revealed to mortal man." That's Paracelsus, a doctor and a mystery man of the Middle Ages. When I left the library the head librarian had given me a book about him and his writings. Catherine's always trying to give me books about psychology and healers and therapies but I don't want them. I want to know only basic bodily functions. I read that Paracelsus book because it was a gift.

Incarnation does for us — the jaw throbs with abscess, the head explodes with migraine; pain gathers the body and mind to itself, it's the only thing that brings us to heel. Without it we strut like feathered cocks, having no need of Paracelsus's mystery.

Our flesh is of the world — it is us and is not us; it's the part of us that belongs to the world. When it's time for us to get free of our flesh, we'll get free.

Carrion eaters — jackals, hyenas, vultures — haunt the nightmarish fringes of the imagination. Circling and waiting, they are the mind's blind terror at the body's inevitable dissolution. They have their uses. The body is only itself, only clay to go back to the clay, to go down the craw of a vulture, to fuel its vigil up there in the hot, high sky, to be transformed then ejected through its anal passages.

I've stopped refusing cancer now. I tell them it's their choice, it's up to them, that I don't know if what I do will make them better or make them worse. Then I see the fear in their faces and I soften. I tell them I'll try if they want but it's up to God. For some reason that I can't fathom, that reassures them.

What happens has nothing to do with me, it's between the spirit and what it wants from its fleshly incarnation. And I think that has very little to do with us, or at least with the part of us that we think of as us.

It has to do with whatever is happening between the spirit and God.

I think these things, but I don't say them, things are hidden until they want to be known. And who would understand me, when I don't believe in God, and I don't understand them myself?

Chapter 24

I heard the latch on the gate click, and I knew without turning round that it was Suzanna, left back from Roisin's by Roisin's mother.

When she saw Catherine she stopped dead, put down her schoolbag, and gave her a long, hard look.

"You haven't been here for ages and ages and *ages*," she told her indignantly. "You haven't been to see me for at *least* a year."

I laughed and put my arm round her and pulled her to me in a hug. For once she was barely exaggerating. She squirmed and wriggled herself into my side, still staring accusingly at Catherine, waiting for her to explain herself, and it had better be good.

Catherine was teaching in Cork now, she'd given up Limerick, which meant she wasn't sharing lifts with Liam anymore, nor calling in to drink tea and talk shop. She'd been in Cork since the college year started last autumn; she was travelling up and down each day instead of staying over, and that takes time. Plus she'd had her "idea," so every spare minute she had was being used on her work. I didn't mind; it hadn't occurred to me to think of her absence as desertion — I was way too busy myself. And I knew she'd come back when her life had calmed down, and maybe by then mine might have done the same. Besides, artists are like that, they disappear for months on end, it's only part of the process.

I've a show coming up in November. You'll hear someone say that in August. Already the eyes have turned inwards, the banned cigarette has reappeared in the hand.

Fine. Hope the work goes well. See you at the opening. That's the response. Then they vanish into their work, which is only what they need to be doing, and Catherine's no different from anyone else. But the children didn't know that — I should have explained.

Then Andrew came round the side of the house, saw Catherine sitting there, hesitated, made his face blank, and drew himself up just that wee bit taller. Catherine pulled out the seat beside her and offered it gravely. He smiled at her and she smiled back, and he put his togs down on the table and stood there, smiling and smiling. I told him to go inside and get himself some juice, and he went, but reluctantly, and he kept looking over his shoulder to make sure she'd still be there when he got back.

"He's pleased to see you."

She nodded. "I've missed them," she said, "and Suzanna's right, it *is* a long time. I can't get over how quickly they change at this age."

"He's been out with Eamon," I told her.

Suzanna was busy all summer, she had friends coming out of her ears, she'd go on and off them at will — it didn't matter to her, there was always another. But Eamon was Andrew's only close friend, and his mother was relieved when the friendship took, for both boys were solitary by nature. Eamon was an only child, and his mother had time on her hands and was into walks and educational expeditions and trips to the sea, which was only an hour away by car. Andrew was always invited, and mostly he went, especially in summer when the things they did were outside. Sometimes I'd ask him if he wanted to bring Eamon home, and he might say yes but more often he'd look at his feet and say that he'd see him at school the next day.

I didn't push him. Andrew liked to keep his home to himself, and Eamon's mother had made it clear that we didn't have to take turns.

Andrew came out of the house with his juice and the red notebook under his arm. That was so Catherine would see how he loves it, I thought, but he wasn't just flattering her, that notebook was *him*. He's an old-fashioned child, happy with pencils and paper, uneasy in the fast, bright world of PlayStations and mobile phones.

"How's Eamon these days?" Catherine asked. "Is he still taller or have you overtaken him?"

"I'm taller," Andrew said proudly. "But he still looks taller because his hair grows sticking up but mine grows flat." Andrew ran his hand over his hair, which was fine and smooth despite my frizz and Liam's curls. "Sometimes he puts soap in it," he added, after a moment's thought.

"What for?" she asked.

"So it'll stick up more," Andrew said.

"Does it work?"

"Yes. But then when it's raining it runs down his forehead and stings his eyes so you think he's crying."

Catherine put her head back and laughed. Andrew looked at her for a second to check it wasn't at his expense; then he grinned and looked pleased, proud of himself that he'd made her laugh.

"Good swim?" she asked.

He nodded; he'd just taken a big bite of shortbread, and his mouth was full.

"River or sea? No, don't say, let me smell you, I bet I can tell." She leaned over and pushed her nose into his hair and had a good sniff. "River," she said. "Definitely river. But was it the Nore or the Barrow?"

"Barrow," he said through a splutter of crumbs.

Catherine laughed and flicked crumbs off her sweatshirt.

"Kilberry?"

This time he only nodded furiously, his face glowing.

"Where have you been? Why didn't you come and see us?" Suzanna demanded, interrupting this love-in. She was seven years old, and she said what she wanted to say. Now her voice told Catherine she wasn't about to be charmed and bamboozled like Andrew.

"I'm sorry, Suzanna," Catherine said quietly. "It's because I've been working so hard."

"Mammy works hard and Daddy works hard and Dermot works hard and all the aunties and uncles work hard," Suzanna said flatly. "Everyone works hard; it doesn't mean they don't have time to come and see me."

"You haven't been to see *her* either," Andrew said, rushing to Catherine's defence.

We all looked at him.

"*I've* been to see her," he said, blushing furiously.

"No you haven't —"

"Have so, haven't I, Mammy? The time we both went to Catherine's house on her birthday and I saw the rats." He turned on Suzanna. "*You* went to Roisin's to play; *you* didn't want to come with us."

"Stop squabbling," I said, trying to keep the laugh out of my voice. Andrew's so serious that people often laugh at him, and it upsets him. I was trying to teach him to ignore it, and sometimes he did but sometimes it got through. I didn't know Andrew's secret, so all I could do was watch and wait and love him, which wasn't hard because we shared so much.

"She's here now, isn't she?" I asked them. "If you go on squabbling she'll go away. Don't pester Catherine, be nice to her. Then she might just come and see us again when she's finished her work." I stopped. I hadn't meant any reproach, the words had just come out that way.

She smiled at me, a no-offence-taken smile.

We were sitting outside at the white plastic table I'd bought in Dunnes Stores four years earlier, when I'd given up on the stone one that Liam kept promising to make.

"I've done the drawings," he'd said as he'd helped me undo the cords that had kept it lashed in its place upside down on the top of the car.

"Open your eyes, Liam. Take a good look all around and tell me what it is that you're seeing," I'd said. "Flowers. Leaves on the trees. Wee birds hopping about the place. It's called summer. It's here now; in two months' time it won't be. This is a table, Liam, it's for putting food on. It may not be aesthetic, but it does the job. Besides, we'd look well, wouldn't we, all of us sitting around a set of drawings, eating?"

He'd laughed. "The cobbler's children never have shoes," he'd said. I'd laughed as well. What wasn't done wasn't done, it carried no baggage, it was simply a statement of fact back then. Back then when the world was young, or that's how it seems to me now.

"How's it going anyway?" I asked Catherine. "Liam said you'd had an idea, but that was ages ago. He said he didn't know what it was, because you wouldn't tell him."

"Sometimes it's best not to say an idea out loud too soon," she said. "Sometimes you have to keep it so secret it's nearly a secret from yourself as well."

"Why?" Andrew asked.

"So you can creep up on it when it's not looking. Catch hold of it by its tail. Pull and pull till the mouse pops out of its hole."

"Can you say now?" This from Suzanna.

"I can. It's about things that live in the sea."

"No more teapots and insects?"

She laughed. "No more teapots and insects, thank God. I never want to think Bugs and Blooms again as long as I live."

"So why d'you want to make things from the sea?" Suzanna asked her.

"It's a long story," Catherine said. No one moved.

"When I was about the age you are now I had an uncle David who was a priest in Macau. He was my godfather as well as my uncle, so when it came to my birthday he always sent me a present. That year it was Chinese water flowers. Do you know about Chinese water flowers? No? Well, I didn't either, so when I tore open the packet I thought there was nothing in it at all. Then I tipped it upside down and shook it, and five little dried-up lumpy things fell out."

We waited.

"The thing about Chinese water flowers is they don't look like flowers at all, or not to begin with."

"Wasn't there a label?"

"The label was in Chinese. But there was a note."

I glanced at Suzanna and Andrew. They both looked like goldfish.

"The note said to drop them into a glass of water and wait. So I did, and nothing happened. I went out to play, then tea, then homework, and then it was time for bed. All that waiting and *still* nothing had happened. I took the glass upstairs, but I'd more or less given up hope." She took a sip from her tea.

"When I woke up next morning the first thing I saw was the glass. Inside the glass were five coloured flowers that swayed about under the water and grew out of five little stones. I thought they were magic. The most beautiful flowers I'd seen."

Catherine smiled to herself. We knew she was seeing them again.

"D'you remember when Dermot went to China last year for that show?" she asked.

We all nodded.

"Well, I'd told him the story, so he went on a search and he brought me a packet home. They're not real flowers at all; they're pretend flowers made of very thin paper that's wrapped around the stones. When they've been underwater for long enough, the paper gets wet through, then unwraps itself, and opens out into flowers. Well, that started me thinking about things that open out in water. I remembered all the treasures I'd brought home from the sea when I was small, and how they changed when they dried out. Stones that lost their colour and shells that lost their shine. Seaweed, just like the Chinese flowers, but smelly as well as dry. Then I got out my sketchbook and started to draw."

For a moment there was silence. Then Suzanna asked could she come to Catherine's house and see?

"Not yet," Catherine said. "I want you to see it properly, I want you and Andrew to come to the party I'll have at the start of the exhibition. Will you do that for me?"

They both nodded solemnly.

"And I want your mother to come all by herself and see it at my house before it all goes up to Dublin for the show."

My face must have shown what I felt.

"D'you not want to see it?" she asked.

"Certainly I want to see it," I lied, and straightaway got up and started clearing the table. Catherine never showed me her work. I *saw* her work, but I never had to walk around it saying I like this or I don't like that, making comments and suggestions the way artists do for each other. Liam did all that. I wouldn't know how.

"Come some afternoon when you're not full up," she said, watching my face. "Next week? The week after?"

I went and got the book. "Next week's completely full, but there's only one so far in the afternoon of the Thursday after. I know her, so I could ring and change the time. Is that soon enough? I could come for a couple of hours and still be back for the children . . . ?"

"We'll mind ourselves, Mammy," Andrew said. "Then you can stay for as long as you like —"

"Good idea," Catherine said. "Thursday it is, then." She got to her feet.

———

I was late. I drove to Catherine's, the first rain smattering the windscreen, the trees and fields fading off to either side. A wind had sprung up, stirring the heavy air that had weighted us down for days.

You'd think I'd have known how to get to Catherine's — I did know — but somehow I always got lost and this time the rain made it worse. It was farm country, a maze of small roads and overgrown hedges and fading signposts; no matter how hard I tried to remember I never could hold the way in my head.

I stopped at an unsigned junction and peered through the rain for clues. I took a chance and turned right, but I'd no idea where I was. The wind was getting stronger, and the rain had gone from smatter to hard drumming — I'd have turned the wipers up if the high speed had worked, but it didn't. I switched on the lights instead, and their daylight beams put a gleam on the tatters of leaves that were flying green from the trees. I checked my watch. Well after four. Two o'clock, I'd told Catherine. I glanced at my face in the mirror. My skin was flushed, and my eyes were shiny and large and my hair had a life of its own. My mouth kept grinning although I was lost and late. What would I tell Catherine? Not the truth, I was certain of that, surprised at the realisation. Time was when it wouldn't have occurred to me to tell her anything else. I cursed myself for not having had the wit to bring the mobile. Perhaps I should just wrong-foot her, I thought, breeze in and pretend I'd said four o'clock, not two. As soon as this thought crossed my mind, I surprised myself over again. Why was I thinking of lying to Catherine, who knew my most intimate secrets? Why hadn't I phoned her before I'd left home so she'd know I was going to be late?

Because I'd been in bed with Liam.

I hadn't meant to, I'd cleared the afternoon just as I'd promised, seen the morning's last patient and made a sandwich before starting out. But the door had opened, and there had been Liam, home from a job in Wexford that couldn't be finished because the parts for the lighting rig hadn't arrived.

No children, no patients, and way too often these days we both fell into bed too tired for anything but sleep. And now here was I, late and getting later, and no excuse to my name.

It was hopeless, I'd have to find someone to ask or I'd never get there at all. At least the rain had eased, and the sky, which had hung too low and too still for a week, was lifting and moving at last. The ditches were choked with July, so the water flowed in wide brown streams down the sides of the road and gushed up from under the wheels. It felt like early October.

A turn in the road saw an old man walking ahead, a stick in his hand and a dog at his side, driving a cluster of cows and their big hefty calves through the rain. It wasn't that common a sight anymore. Mostly they let the dog do the work while they sat in the car with the window down and a hand with a switch hanging out to thwack at the rump of a cow. I slowed to a crawl, wound down the window, and asked him could he direct me to Catherine Casey's?

He could. He stood in the rain that dripped off his cap and ran down his face and told me which road to take and which to pass by. Then he made me say the whole lot over as though I was slow, which I was, for I got it all the wrong way round more than once. When he was finally satisfied that I had it, he lifted his hands off the window to let me go on. The dog nipped at the heels of the cattle and kept them close to the side of the road while I eased myself past. I looked in the mirror, lifting my hand in thanks. He was still standing watching me through the rain.

When I pulled the car into Catherine's gates the house seemed somehow bigger than I remembered, and tidier and smarter as well. Ours needs repainting, I thought, the chimney leaks, the stonework could do with repointing. I got out, feeling suddenly complicated and hostile. It was partly getting so lost and partly because I'd just realised that Catherine had this cared-for-looking house when she let on not to give a toss about appearances.

I went round to the back, but she didn't bring me in, she walked me straight across to the studio through the rain. I mumbled about being lost and driving around in circles.

"I thought you'd have known the way by now."

"It's hard. One false turn puts you wrong so you can't get right, the roads turn back on themselves, and you can't see the sky for hedges. I'd be driving round yet if I hadn't found a man with some cows."

So she wanted to know who I'd asked, and she named him right away from my description. I told her he'd put his hands on the wound-down window and wouldn't let me go till I had the directions by heart.

She laughed at that. "Ah, he knew who you were of course, no flies on Peter Nolan. He probably kept you talking to see what he made of you, he'll be working out will he give you a try if ever he gets sick."

I didn't like that. It felt as though I were undressing in a room at night, thinking the curtains were closed when they weren't. I thought of him staring after me as I'd driven away. *I know who you are*, that look had said. *You're that healer woman from the North who lives over Crohane way.*

One of the things I'd liked about living down here was no one knowing anything about me. Not who my mother was nor my brother was; not what part of Derry I was from; not even where it was I went to school. I didn't come from here, wasn't one of them, was invisible for all I stuck out. Now total strangers had seen me undressed. That shook me. I gave up trying to talk my way around Catherine and lapsed into silence.

The studio had once been some sort of an outbuilding — not a barn, it wasn't high enough, but a line of stone sheds for animals and fuel and tack. She'd had a load of work done on it; all the dividing walls had been knocked except for one, and the whole space had been plumbed and floored and wired and reroofed. There were only two areas now: the studio space, which was more or less as it had been, and a long, narrow gallery running off on the other side.

It was amazing, a total transformation, I could hardly believe it had once held Catherine's store, a dark, chaotic place that smelled of earth and rats and neglect. She would disappear into it and come out carrying discarded treasures — insects and teapot-flowers and little baked tiles, their centres puddled with shiny glaze. Suzanna always begged the flowers, but Andrew wanted the insects — he liked it that they were imaginary, yet all the details were to proper insectlike specification. I loved the tiles, which weren't really tiles at all, but small squares of clay she'd been using to try out new glazes. Catherine had taken to saving them for me, she'd asked me what it was about them, but I didn't know. All I could say was I'd always liked samples. Wool cards and paint charts and those flick-through books of curtain fabrics. Scraps of bright texture and colour.

There was a picture of a monastery in Tibet I'd seen once, but I didn't tell her that. It had white walls on a clear blue sky and strings of small, bright flags that fluttered about in the wind. Prayer flags, it said on the caption. I'd looked and looked till I nearly heard their snapping and flapping, I was filled with a happiness so intense that I'd torn out the page and folded it into the back of a book. I forgot all about it for years, but I found it again and my hands trembled with eagerness as I was opening it out. Nothing. Whatever the happiness was, it had taken itself off somewhere else.

It was a lovely place now, this little gallery of hers, warm and hushed, with rough-stone walls painted white. The lights glowed and the floor was slabbed in slate and everything felt clean and quiet and safe. There were trestles and plinths with sculptures displayed on them, niches built into the walls, and not a giant teapot in sight.

I couldn't think what to say, so I said it was lovely and warm.

Catherine said she'd put the heat on early because she was expecting me. There was no edge to her voice, but she wasn't looking at me, she was fiddling with the lights, making sure she had them just so.

"Now," she said, and I knew I'd have to look.

In the end it was easy because there were lots of things I liked so much that I wanted to reach out and touch as soon as I saw them. I completely forgot about saying the right things and walked around stroking and poking and exclaiming. Catherine began to smile and then to laugh aloud at my reactions. I'd never understood those teapots of hers, they were too big and too wrong, they mocked at themselves and at me. What was the point of a teapot twenty times too big and heavy to use? And all those nasty, weird-coloured flowers, those sinister insects with long legs and longer stings. She'd reversed the symbol alright. Poisoned chalices — that's what they were — and Catherine, daring everyone to go ahead and buy them for their architect-designed dream homes. They did too. Hence all this cash for new roofs and slate floors and fancy lighting.

But this stuff was innocent, it was all the things you'd squatted to wonder at, poked with a careful finger, dropped in a plastic bucket to carry home. And it didn't fade or lose its shine or stink. It lived on, enhanced, in the way it had lived on in your child-self's imagination.

She'd used wood and glass as well as clay, and all her talent for fantasia had been let rip. Marvellous banded stones lay in pools of clear glass; herring sprats looped in figures-of-eight through vitreous water; ceramic seaweed rippled and flowed down walls. There were conger eels half emerging from sinister holes, lobsters that sported jewelled backs, wondrous jellyfish made out of clay and glass. There were rock pools full of sea anemones, fantastic fishes, little shrimps and crabs. Found objects were mixed in with Catherine-things, and lifelike replicas of fish and sea creatures swam beside fish and sea creatures from Catherine's riotous imagination. Some of the pieces were enormous, and some were miniatures; some were subtly distorted as water distorts.

Impossible not to reach and touch, shocking to stretch out your hand to glass, not the cool of water — yet each time the expectation overcame me and my fingers tried again.

At last I was done. I looked at her amazed, and she looked back, her mouth all smiling, then we fell into each other's arms and laughed and laughed.

"Stay for supper," she said at last, pushing me away to look at me but still holding tight onto my upper arms. "Ring Liam, tell him I need you, let them do without you just this once."

"Has Liam seen?" I was already crossing to the phone on the wall.

"No. Dermot's seen drawings and the first few bits and pieces coming out of the kiln. Nothing for ages though, I've gone very secretive, no one's seen it for months, and no one else has seen it like this. It's not finished yet, but it's near. This is a private view, assembled for Ms. McKinnon alone."

"What I do is pure kitsch," Catherine said, her eyes dancing over the rim of the wineglass. "That's why I get away with it. If I made 'proper' art and it sold the way I sell, every decent artist in the country would be after my blood. As it is they forgive me. They come to my openings and chat up the buyers and invite them to their own shows. I overhear them. They'll be asking a buyer which piece he's bought, and then they'll go on about what fun my work is, and *so* refreshing. But if the buyer *hasn't* bought, they'll let him know he has taste —" She laughed, and there was nothing hidden behind it.

"Don't you mind?"

She shook her head. "Why should I, don't I get to do what I want? Besides, they've a point, there are serious artists with oodles of talent who'll work their guts out all their lives and have to get by on crusts."

She reached out and helped herself to another dollop of pudding. "You sure you won't have any more?" I shook my head. She was quite drunk, and so was I. We were having a lovely time, the two of us, eating and drinking and talking away about anything that came into our heads. Well, not anything — almost exclusively ourselves. We'd clean forgotten our prickles of earlier on, we only remembered how much we liked each other, how happy we were to be together again like this.

"Of course there are millions more crap artists than good ones." She scraped out the dish and licked the creamy mess off the back of the serving spoon. "Mostly they know they're crap, but sometimes they don't, so they go on struggling long after they should have stopped. The crap-ones-who-know catch on pretty fast and do something else. Unless they're making money out of their crap, like me."

"How can you say you're crap, Catherine?" I demanded angrily. "How can you make all these beautiful things and run yourself down like this?"

"You know something, Ellen, you're making me nervous. You never liked Bugs and Blooms, and they've paid the bills for years. Would you think you could start into hating this stuff, then maybe it'll sell? I've an overdraft as long as your arm with all the work I've had done on this place."

"It'll sell," I told her, picking up the bottle and filling both our glasses. It was the second bottle. I knew I had to drive, but I didn't care. I didn't care if I hit something or got stopped by the Guards or didn't get home at all. Suddenly I was sick and tired of my life, of its discipline and relentlessness, of all those people wanting me to fix their bodies, of Liam who disappeared into the studio to paint every moment that he wasn't out working, of the smugness of this newly prosperous country that thought so much of itself. I barely stopped short of being sick and tired of the children while I was at it.

I looked across at Catherine. She was sitting with her head thrown back, watching me. I wished that I was beautiful like her. Mostly I look in the mirror and my face looks back at me, so I stick out my tongue at it but I don't really mind it — it's just the way I look.

Now here I was, longing to be beautiful like Catherine, longing hopelessly and with an intensity that I rarely felt for anything. What was happening to me? I fought my mind back to what we were talking about before I'd thought about Catherine being beautiful. Art. We'd been talking artists and art.

"Is Dermot one?" I asked. "A crap-artist-who-doesn't-know-he's-crap?"

A spasm almost like pain crossed her face. "No, Dermot's not crap," she said slowly. "Dermot's probably one of those artists who's good but will never be *really* good, no matter how hard he tries. But just for a moment — somewhere back there — he very nearly was. And art matters more to him than anything else, and trying as hard as he does is eating him alive."

"But why?"

"Why what?"

"If he's trying so hard and he has it in him —"

"Why will he never be really good?" She shrugged. "Who knows? The moment passed, and now it's too late. Perhaps if Marie hadn't left. Sometimes a shock like that can make you, but sometimes it does you in instead. . . ."

Her voice trailed off. I nearly asked her about Liam, but I was afraid of what she might say. I dragged the conversation stubbornly back to where it had started.

"But you're not crap, Catherine, you're so talented —"

"What's that got to do with anything?"

"And so accomplished. Technically, I mean. So accomplished *technically* —"

"Will you look who's talking? I thought you weren't supposed to know about art?"

A thought struck me. "Don't you *want* people to take you seriously? Don't you *want* to be famous?"

She shook her head.

"Why ever not?"

"Fame has its drawbacks. I've seen a load of people make awful eejits of themselves once they got famous. And I like my life the way it is."

Catherine was always so sure of herself, it was hard to argue with her statements. She'd set a plate on the table in front of me. Glazed tiles, arranged on it like biscuits. I moved them around with my finger.

"Let your hair down, Ellen," she said out of nowhere.

I reached behind me and undid the clips. Its red mass sprang free and floated around my shoulders.

"Now you look like a witch."

"Perhaps I am," I said, looking straight into her eyes. "Two hundred years ago I'd have been burned. A hundred, and no decent man or woman would have come to my door."

"They'd have come at night," Catherine said softly. "Times change, Ellen."

"If I'd told my mother I saw things she'd have got the Elders to pray."

"What are Elders?"

"Pillars of the Church. Righteous Men. Even the very occasional Righteous Woman."

"Maybe they've changed too."

"Maybe. Pigs may fly about on broomsticks — anything's possible." Catherine didn't move or take her eyes from my face. "You're thinking Ellen's off again, better not say anything or she'll get worse? Daniel O'Connell said Irish freedom wasn't worth a single life — that's what Liam's always saying to me when he's trying to justify not giving a damn. And you know the weirdest thing? I get so angry when he says that, I could nearly vote Sinn Féin. I can accept his not giving a damn — maybe I wouldn't either if it wasn't my home — but it's the self-righteousness that gets to me, the holier-than-thou —"

"Am I being self-righteous?"

"You're not being anything. You're sitting there and listening, the way you always do. I've drunk too much —"

"Why don't you drink some more?"

"Because the bottle's finished."

"There's another one." She got it out and opened it. She poured its redness *glug glug glug* into our glasses. She lifted hers to mine, I lifted mine to hers, and all the Northern-ness that comes upon me when I'm drunk slid away. She cut herself a wedge of cheese and pushed the board across to me. I took a big lump off the best bit of the gooey one and slathered it onto a piece of bread.

"I won't let Suzanna do this," I said, biting into it. "I make her cut from the edge, not the middle, and if she takes a lot I tell her not to be so greedy." I laughed, and a burst of crumbs flew out across the table. "And I won't let her talk with her mouth full," I said, my mouth full. "I hate putting manners on them."

"Then why do it?"

"Because my mother lives in me. Because I hate children who haven't any. It's a pain. You tell them not to do something, then you can't do it yourself. Except when they're not looking, and they almost always are."

"My mother had a way round that one. *Do what I say, not what I do.* She loved saying that; she loved turning round and doing whatever it was she'd just told us not to, right in front of our eyes. *I'm grown up, I can do whatever the hell I like.* That's what she meant. I couldn't wait to be grown up."

"But the minute you were, you went and joined a convent."

"I did," she said. "What did you want to be? A wife?"

"Catch yourself on, Catherine. Why would I want to be a wife?"

"You were only twenty when you married Robbie. Still a student — maximum independence time. That's nearly as bad as me and the convent."

"Jesus, Catherine, marrying Robbie was sex, the exact opposite to a convent. Though God knows why I imagined I had to get married for it; maybe I thought I could have it more, or better. Or maybe it was the part of me that wanted to be respectable. And Robbie was very insistent, he wanted Property, but I hadn't the wit to see that then." I put my hands behind my neck and ran them up through my hair. "I like sex," I added drunkenly, suddenly remembering the afternoon and Liam. "D'you not like it, Catherine? You don't seem to . . . ?"

"Did Liam?" Catherine asked, ignoring my question.

"Did Liam what? Like sex?"

"Did Liam want Property?"

I thought a minute. "No, Liam wasn't into Property. In those days Liam only wanted me the way I was, that's why I'm here."

241

"And what did you want?"

"Sex." Catherine's eyes rolled heavenwards, so I thought again. "And refuge as well, I suppose. It all got mixed up — Liam and sex and refuge. Then Liam stopped being a refuge, and everything changed —" I sighed. "It was complicated. I was in love with him, and I wanted him to look after me, but part of me thought he'd turn out to be Robbie underneath. I had a bag always packed that first year. Money, documents, everything. I was waiting all the time for him to change into Robbie."

"But he didn't."

"No, he didn't." I stared into my glass.

"Were you happy when you came here first?"

"Was I happy? Yes and no. Yes, on account of Liam — very. No, on account of here."

"What was wrong with here?"

"Too quiet, too different, too Catholic. That made me angry."

"Why did that make you angry?"

"So arrogant. The assumptions. The One True Church, and everyone else in the whole of the world a heathen or else a heretic. All those saint's days and feast days and masses for every-thing."

"'A Protestant parliament for a Protestant people,'" Catherine quoted softly.

I looked at her, thinking I might ignore that one. Then I suddenly sat up straight in my chair, and my eyes must have opened wide because hers dropped to the table.

"Catherine, look at me," I said.

She wouldn't.

"Catherine, you know, don't you?"

"Know what?"

As soon as she spoke I knew that she knew, but I had to go and say it anyway. "You're pregnant."

I have nothing up on the walls of my room — no crosses, saints, Madonnas, no pictures of Indian gurus or Zen masters or Tibetan Rimpoches. I don't go in for candles or incense or crystals, there are no ornaments, the walls are painted white. And you wouldn't believe how many times someone or other has looked round sadly and told me how bare and cold the place looks, how even a Bridget's cross would help.

I supposed at first it was Catholicism made them this way, but now I'm not so sure, I think it may have more to do with human nature. People *want* the miraculous, they like signs and symbols — the invisible Invisible is way too far away.

And they want to believe in clairvoyance. They want their privacy invaded, they want to believe that I'm sitting there reading their minds when I'm not. Oh, I have the odd flash — like knowing that Catherine was pregnant — but these flashes rarely come to order, and often as not I get things all mixed up and messed around. I'll know something and I'll think it's about someone sitting in front of me, when it really belongs to the man who's waiting outside.

Not so long ago I met a woman who does this clairvoyance-stuff to help her with diagnosis. She told me such mistakes are lack of experience, and if I practised more it would come clear. Healers like her never question their methods, mostly healing has been in the family for generations, so it's natural to them — they don't run round like headless chickens thinking they're witches or warlocks or maybe going mad. Everyone has their ways. Let them see or do what they want, if it works, it works — there isn't any arguing with a cure. But their ways aren't my ways,

I'd never practice to see things better, I don't do this healing-thing because I want to, I do it because it's in me and I can't escape.

Just the same, when Catherine wouldn't tell me who she was pregnant by, I went upstairs and broke my own rules and tried to see. Nothing, or almost nothing — a buzzy mishmash of blurry voices and faces, like when the reception on the television's gone on the blink. She may have been telling the truth when she'd said it was no one I knew, or the knowing may have been closed to me, or I may just have been too drunk. Whatever it was, I gave up, then turned on my side and passed out.

The phone woke me far too early, it rang and rang and rang till I finally stumbled out of bed to find that Catherine had got there first.

"Yes, she's here, she's fine. We rang you last thing last night, but you must have been asleep."

"Liam?" I sat on the stairs wishing I could die. Catherine held out the phone, I could hear Liam's voice coming out of it, and I shook my head. Which was a mistake, so I held on to it with both my hands instead.

"Certainly you woke us. Wasn't that what you meant to do? Now go and have breakfast or paint a picture and leave us in peace to get back to our beds." She put down the phone.

She was as white as a sheet and looked as though she might be about to be sick.

"What time is it?" I asked her.

"Half seven. We didn't get to bed till after three." She lifted the receiver off and laid it down beside the phone.

"I've got someone coming at nine thirty," I said.

"So you kept saying last night, which is why the alarm clock is by your bed, set for eight thirty. If you've any sense at all you'll turn it off."

"Catherine, are you all right?"

"I am, no thanks to Liam. Do what you want about the alarm; I'm away back to bed."

"Did we really ring him last night?"

"I've no idea. I'm sure we would have if we'd thought of it."

"Catherine —"

"What?"

"I love you."

She grinned a lopsided grin and turned on her heel.

Chapter 25

*L*iam had used his head and pinned a notice up on the door that said I'd been called away.

I was home by eleven, but I might as well not have bothered myself, for as I showed the next one in, I knew my hands had gone dead. I sent her home, then pinned up a new piece of paper that said I'd be gone till tomorrow.

The children were at school, and Liam was out on some job, so I put the kettle on, knocked back a pint of cold water, then sat at the kitchen table, finishing off the cure with more toast and tea. I was out of the habit of drinking these days, but even so I felt a whole lot worse than I ever remembered feeling before. It crossed what was left of my mind that Whatever-it-was didn't like alcoholic excess, but I pushed the thought away. Why shouldn't I drink too much if I wanted to? Why was I being punished like this?

Catherine had said that the pregnancy came from a one-night stand, but I didn't believe her, she was too closed off and unwavering when she met my eyes. *That's my story,* her gaze had said defiantly, *and that's the one I'm sticking to.*

I hadn't pressed her. She was anxious and humiliated behind the tight self-control, she wasn't having fun.

We'd both gone back to bed after Liam's phone call, and I'd slipped into one of those fretful dozes when you float so close to the surface of sleep that you nearly think you're awake. Then I fully woke and lay there listening to Catherine moving around downstairs, knowing she hadn't been able to go back to sleep and needed to talk. I put my palms on my temples and waited for the pain to ease, then got out of bed in my borrowed nightgown and padded downstairs, pretending I wanted tea.

I'd talked of abortion the night before. She said she'd been expecting that word to put in an appearance.

I'd waited, but nothing followed.

"Well?" I'd finally asked as gently as I could.

She'd shaken her bowed head wordlessly, so I'd left it at that.

But in the morning, sitting again at the table, I had another go. I said I knew how hard the thought was when you were Catholic (which I didn't), but perhaps she should allow herself to consider it as an option.

She looked at me this time. "I can't," she said. A long pause. "I don't disagree with abortion, though I think it's often sad. But no one can judge what another human being is able for, sometimes not even the person themselves."

Another long pause.

"I don't know if I'm even a Catholic anymore," she went on slowly. "I don't go to mass or obey the rules or agree with the doctrine, it would be like trying to squeeze myself into a favourite dress that's gone too small. Yet I don't know if I could be anything else, no matter how hard I tried. . . ."

She stopped, looked at the table, looked up again. "It's not because of the Catholic-thing that I'm saying no to abortion. It's because I want to live inside the flow of my life, I don't want to try to control it to suit myself."

I sat looking at her. She looked steadily back at me.

"What exactly do you mean by that?" I asked her

"'Wherever I am led I move.'"

247

She said it like a quotation. I asked if it was.

"Yes," she said, but that was all.

"Catherine, am I being very insensitive?"

She shook her head. "Hardly at all." She smiled, but it wasn't a real smile, it was put on for me.

We both started talking together.

"Catherine, you should eat something —"

"Look, Ellen, I'm thirty-eight, I'm on my own —"

Then we both stopped.

"I'm on my own, I know it's not going to be easy," she finished.

I got up and cut some bread and put it in the toaster. She was right. It wasn't.

Before the children got home I went up to bed and slept for a couple of hours. When I woke I felt much better.

They came flying in through the door, soaked through and bright-eyed with expectation. I made them sit down and eat while I cleaned out their lunch boxes and hung their coats up to dry. They wanted to tell me what Daddy had cooked, how late he'd let them stay up, the brilliant programme he'd let them watch that I never allowed them to see. I didn't mind, though most times I'd resent Liam playing Mister Nice Guy and leaving the discipline to me. But what did it matter? Here we were, the three of us together, beside ourselves with the pleasure of just that.

Often I go through my life forgetting what I've got, concentrating on the problems, then once in a while something happens that reminds me, and everything changes. So I didn't care what they'd watched or how late they'd stayed up, and they spotted it right away. Even Andrew stopped holding back and wriggled in close to my chair to tell me the highlights from the forbidden programme.

"You're not cross, Mammy?" he said, stopping midsentence, suddenly anxious.

"No, darlin', I'm not cross," I said, one arm round his waist, the other hand stroking the hair back from his forehead. I should throw my-mother-in-me a bone more often, I thought; let her lie there, chewing away at it, keeping herself out of mischief. I watched Suzanna take three biscuits from the tin at once, her curly head turned away from me, attention absorbed in her booty. She must have felt my eyes on her, for she sneaked a quick, nonchalant glance, saw there wasn't a threat, then laid the three biscuits side by side on the table.

"What did she give you for us?" she asked, not looking up from the biscuits.

"Who's *she*, the Cat's Grandmother?" It came out quick as a flash and sharp as a lemon. So much for throwing my mother a bone.

"Catherine, Mammy, it's Catherine she means. What did Catherine send for us?" This time it was Andrew, still snuggled into my side.

"Catherine isn't very well," I told them. I don't encourage expectations, I'd usually reprove them even for asking, but I saw Catherine so clearly, alone in her newly smart house, and I softened.

"She *might* have had something put aside for you, I don't know," I told them. "But this morning she was sick, so even if she had, I think it might have slipped her mind."

"Insects or flowers?"

"No insects or flowers anymore, remember? She's making things from the sea."

For Suzanna the sea meant ice creams and fish suppers and hurdy-gurdies.

"Not the sea like the Irish Sea," I said. "The sea in the West, the Atlantic Ocean."

Then I told them about the sea urchins and lobsters and conger eels, the long, shiny ropes of seaweed, the rock pools full of glass water.

"And d'you think the seaweed's going to be all slimy when you touch it, Mammy?"

"You do, but it isn't. And that makes you want to laugh."

"Why?"

"I don't know, it just does —"

When Liam came in we were still at it. He stood at the door, shaking the water from his jacket, and I moved to get up and put on the kettle, but he laid his hand on my shoulder, restraining me. He kept it there for longer than he needed to, and I felt his life so warm and strong in him that I remembered again about forgetting what I had.

He made himself coffee and sat with us and listened to the children chattering on about starfish and stingrays and sharks and the special invitations that Catherine was going to send them for her party.

He stretched out his hand for a biscuit. "What's it like?" he asked me.

"Have you not seen it, Daddy?"

He shook his head. "Dermot's seen sketches. I haven't seen Catherine properly for ages, she's been too busy."

"I thought it was great," I said. "I couldn't keep my hands off it."

He smiled, an amused, indulgent smile.

"What are you smiling at?"

"You. Your hands. You and Catherine are the same. You both get at life through your hands, though in different ways."

I was tired and suddenly touchy with hangover, so I didn't smile back, I opened my hands and laid them palms down on the table. I don't know what it is about setting them down flat like that, but it's like standing out under the sky with your feet planted firm on the ground, a wee bit apart, and it always helps. When I was calm again I got up and took Liam's dinner out of the oven, where it was keeping warm. I let the children sit with him till he'd finished, then chased them both next door to do their homework. I wanted to talk to him about Catherine.

"She said I was making her anxious on account of my liking it all so much," I told him. "She said I never liked the teapots, and they walked themselves out through the door."

"It'll sell," Liam said. "People come to Catherine's openings with the cheque already signed. All they have to do is fill in the amount."

"That can change."

"Anything can change. But having that sort of buzz around your work is half the battle."

"She said her work was pure kitsch. She said if she sold the way she does and it wasn't kitsch you'd all hate her."

He laughed and swung his chair back on its legs. "Seaside motifs are big-time naff — bathroom stuff, and she knows it. But if it's kitsch enough she can claim she's being ironic and it might just pass. Anyway, she's got enough money to be going on with, and we'll all forgive her everything if it doesn't sell. She can be poor but loved. See how that feels for a change."

"She needs to sell."

His eyebrows went up. "Any more than anyone else?"

"She's pregnant."

His chair came out of its swing and hit the floor with a thump. "She's what?"

"She's nineteen weeks pregnant."

"But she can't be — not Catherine."

"Try telling *her* that."

———

It was no good the next day either. It came alright, but it wouldn't move through me, it was as if all the little ducts and valves it normally uses were silted up and blocked. I sat by the phone, cancelling anyone I could get hold of. I'd never needed to cancel before, so it hadn't occurred to me to ask for people's numbers, and finding them out of the phone book took forever so in the end I just gave up and stuck another notice onto the door.

I said there was a funeral in Monaghan I had to go to. I always say I have to go to a funeral if I need an excuse in a hurry. Liam couldn't believe it the first time he heard me, he thinks saying a thing out loud is halfway to making it happen. That's stupid. It's a good excuse, and it hurts no one. Anyway, going to a funeral's a courtesy, half the people there have come out of friendship for someone they know in the family, it doesn't matter that they've never laid eyes on the deceased. And I had to say something, I wasn't about to tell them I couldn't work because I'd had a heavy night two days before.

It was horrible being me. My head still ached and ached, and the energy crackled about, trying to find a way through and failing, for every channel it normally used was still blocked. It felt hot and stingy and dirty in there, as though a great swarm of angry insects was on the loose inside me, all buzzing and crawling and biting and never for one second staying still.

I kept thinking about Catherine. I worried because she was so alone, and I'd never thought of her like that before, I always saw her as being so self-sufficient. Which she was — is — everything doesn't change completely because you're pregnant, but at the same time somehow it does. I fretted some more, then made up my mind to phone, though I hardly ever phoned her and never without a definite reason. No one answered, so I let it ring on until it switched to the answering machine, but I didn't leave a message because I couldn't think what to say. I tried her mobile as well, but it was the same.

I told myself not to be stupid, I hadn't worried before I knew, so why was I worrying now? Besides, there were loads of people in Catherine's life, which is something I often forgot, for she was my only friend. But I kept seeing her bowed head when she told me she wouldn't have an abortion. It upset me so much I almost wished I could pray for her. People round here are always praying for each other, they really believe it, they send up prayers in flocks like little grey birds flying up into heaven to say their piece to God. They should be so lucky.

Still, my mood was so strange that I thought I might give it a try. I walked up and down, searching around in my mind for a God I could trust enough to pray to. It wasn't any use. I wouldn't pray to the angry black God of my childhood, I wouldn't even say Catherine's name out loud to Him for fear He might hear it and write it down in His book. If I'd been a Catholic I could have prayed to Our Lady, which is what they call Mary here, as though she's mine as well as theirs. But I wasn't, so I couldn't.

Women down here are forever complaining about having Mary for a role model, they don't want to be virgin mothers, forever meek, forever mild, they want a bit more than that to aspire to. Well, they're right, but at least she's a female being. They should try having only a Trinity without so much as a smell of a woman about it.

Liam had been more disturbed by the news than I'd expected.

More disbelieving as well, he'd kept saying over and over that it couldn't be true, he said it so often that in the end I'd got annoyed.

"Why shouldn't Catherine be pregnant?" I'd asked him. "Sure, can't anyone get pregnant? Sometimes it seems to me that the only ones who can't are the ones who want it most."

He'd shut up about not believing it then. Instead he'd said Catherine hadn't mentioned a boyfriend, and he hadn't heard any talk.

I'd understood then, or I'd thought I had. Liam and Catherine were close; they were colleagues in a shared world, and more than that they were "mates" in that comfortable, easy, everyday way that breeds a steady affection. Perhaps he assumed a love in her life, perhaps he was hurt that she hadn't said anything? Suddenly, unaccountably, I'd been hurt for him as well.

"Maybe she was working up to telling you. You said yourself that you haven't seen her for ages —"

"Does she know you were going to tell me?"

This time it was me who was surprised. I'd not have told him if I hadn't cleared it with Catherine first, I thought he'd have known that. She'd hesitated when I'd asked her, then nodded her assent.

"She does," I'd told him.

There'd been a thud from next door and a muffled squeal, but neither of us had moved to intervene. Liam's eyes had been fixed on my face.

"Who is it?" he'd asked me, his face almost apprehensive.

"I don't know, she wouldn't tell me. She kept saying it was only a one-night stand so it didn't matter."

"It'll matter alright when she can't pay the bills and she's looking for money for maintenance."

His tone had been coarse, almost brutal, making me angry.

Why did he have to say that? Why did men always move in a dead-straight line from pregnancy to paternity to money?

"Catherine's very independent," I'd told him. "I doubt she'd take anything from anyone, whoever it was."

"Can't you see who it is?"

I'd got to my feet then and started clearing the table. I'd hoped he could read my face, I'd hoped it would tell him loud and clear that he didn't deserve a reply.

"Ellen, I asked you a question —"

"I heard, and the answer's *no*. I can't, and even if I could, I wouldn't tell you."

Very principled I'd sounded, very high and mighty, but I'd wanted to know as well, and my thoughts had kept sneaking back in that direction. I even considered trying again, and it was hard to be obedient to myself when I forbade it. And I honestly didn't like this prurience in myself; I thought it was Catherine's business, and if she wanted to keep it private then she was entitled to do exactly that.

But if I'd known what I know now, I might have let myself.

<hr/>

It was around that time that people began to turn up at night without ringing for an appointment. They'd have done a day's work then got into the car and driven someone sick a good long distance.

I had no idea there were so many people who lived, day in and day out, with pain or sickness or with someone trapped inside pain and sickness, I never thought about it at all before I started doing this. If you're healthy and everyone belonging to you is healthy, then you don't. And you don't see the sick because when they're too sick to be out they stay home, and when they're well enough to be out you see them and you take it for granted that they're well. Before I did this I thought — if I thought at all — that either sickness killed you or you got better.

Unless you were old, that is. I knew that people who were old got arthritis and angina and diabetes and stuff like that, but that was about being old and old age seems a long way off when you're under forty, it seems like another country that you'll maybe end up visiting one day, but perhaps not. And I didn't understand how much people who are old protect the young from knowledge of old age, I didn't understand their feelings of failure and shame when the body starts to wear out, I didn't have the wit to see that behind that bent knee there's most likely pain, that behind the figure stuck to the chair lies malaise and exhaustion.

A man came last spring, and he said that pain was personal. I asked him what he meant, and he said it wasn't abstract and it wasn't general. It lived there with you, inside you, and invisible, and just the two of you. No one knew it except you, and no one knew you as it did, and everything you did or said or thought was in its presence. It was more intimate than a wife, a child, a parent, or your dearest friend; it lived from your body, as mistletoe lives from a tree, yet it was contrary, for if you died it would die with you, but it used its very best energy to make you want to die.

He was speaking, and I kept looking at the tulips outside the window and I knew there was a connection but I couldn't figure it out. I still can't, I can't figure out how the beautiful and the terrible can walk side by side at the one time. When he came in the man had said he'd been sitting outside, looking at my tulips while he waited. He said he loved tulips, and his mother had loved tulips — they'd been her favourite flower. So the pain hadn't blinded him, and his joy at the tulips had existed at the same time and alongside his despair at the pain. He could hold two extreme and opposite emotions together there inside him, and he could put his dead mother in there with them and then sit quietly in the chair across from me and tell me about all three.

The people who came to the door late at night weren't local and they weren't Alternatives. They were chronics or else they were dying, and someone or other had told them, or someone who cared for them, of a woman in Kilkenny who might be worth a try.

It wasn't long before I stopped going to the door at night, and now I don't let the children answer it either. Liam goes and he talks to whoever is standing there, and if he thinks the case isn't life-threatening he'll tell them to make an appointment, but often as not he'll tell them to wait. Then he'll come in and ask will I take a look at whoever they have sitting waiting in the car.

I might be in the chair by the fire or I might be standing in the summer dusk at the window, watching and listening. I'll hear the quiet voices, and I might see part of a face where a slice of light from the other window falls across it. But wherever I am — by the fire or by the window — nine times out of ten I can tell. No more than that. Not will I do any good, will I even help them die quicker, just that the need is urgent and I should try. I was afraid when it started, these people were deeply sick, and I didn't ever want to see those Pain and Despair and Courage forms again. But they never came and the strange thing is that something in me has changed and even were they to come again, I don't think I'd fear them as I once did.

We've got so Liam only has to look at me and I'll nod or shake my head and it's done. He goes back out, and I'll go into my room and turn on the heat and make ready. Or else I'll hear the car door bang, an engine start, I'll see the taillights vanish off into the dark. I hate doing that, it seems to me the saddest thing — the car door opening, the interior light coming on then going off, those red taillights turning around and disappearing into the night. I hate it, but what else can I do? I have to live.

I don't mean to speak as though this happened every night, or even every week, because it didn't and still doesn't. If it did I think every scrap of compassion would be driven from me, I think I'd bolt the door and disconnect the bell and let them stand there hammering till their fists fell off. Yet there are healers who live like this day and night, have lived like this for years, who don't turn anyone away, no matter what the hour.

Not me, I couldn't stand it. One every two or three weeks is the most I can manage. Any more than that and I'd go mad.

Chapter 26

*T*he invitations for Catherine's Dublin opening arrived in the post. One for me and Liam together, one each for Andrew and Suzanna. I hadn't planned on taking them to the opening itself, in spite of Catherine's request; I'd thought we'd go up quietly, the three of us, later on. But once those invitations arrived, there was no way I could refuse.

Liam drove and the car behaved and we found a parking place not too far from the gallery. Liam strode in, Suzanna trotting behind him, with Andrew and I bringing up the rear. The place was stuffed, you couldn't see any of Catherine's pieces, all you could see was this big crush of people with wineglasses in their hands. I could feel Andrew tense and draw back at the sight, so I caught his hand and gave it a quick, tight squeeze. He looked up at me, but there was concern in his eyes, and not the dread I'd expected.

"Where's Catherine?" he hissed at me. "Where's her sea things?"

"They'll be in there," I told him. "Behind all the people — on plinths and up on the walls."

"But they're standing in front of them, no one can see them."

259

He wasn't whispering anymore, his voice was firm, his body was stiff with indignation.

"It's a party," I explained to him, "a celebration. First people want to talk to each other, then a woman who knows about art will come to the front and tell everyone about Catherine's work."

"Will we see Catherine?"

"Of course we'll see her, she'll be standing beside the woman when she's talking, then she'll speak a bit herself."

"Will it make her happy?"

I laughed. "Of course it will, it's her party." Andrew was up on the tips of his toes, craning to see between the people. Liam had vanished off into the crowd, and Suzanna had dropped back to join us. I felt a small hand reach out and curl itself around mine. Suzanna, looking for comfort. I was touched. Andrew pulled firmly on my other sleeve.

"Over there," he said. "There's seaweed on the wall. Come on." He squeezed and shoved his way through the crowd with me following after, Suzanna still clutching tight to my hand. When we got there a long, fluted band of beer-brown seaweed was snaking and shining from ceiling to floor. Framed drawings hung to either side of it, and further along a brace of jewelled flatfish slid over the sandy bottom of an alcove. Andrew's hand reached for the seaweed. Suzanna let go of me, ducked under someone's elbow, and quick as a flash, her fingers were on the fish.

"Please don't let the children touch the exhibits." A young woman carrying a tray of wineglasses spoke from just behind us. Her voice was harassed, but not unpleasant. Andrew's hand retracted at the speed of light.

"It's alright," another voice said, a familiar voice. "They can touch; they're friends of mine, they won't break anything, they're used to handling my work."

Beside me Andrew swelled up like a little bullfrog so I nearly thought he'd burst.

Catherine stayed with us and talked for a bit, then someone came looking for her, and she had to go off and stand in the middle of the room for the speeches, which were long and boring, one person introducing the next for what began to seem forever. At last it was Catherine's turn, but she only smiled her wide smile and told us all we'd made her night.

"Is that *all* she's going to say?" Andrew was dead disappointed, and so was Suzanna — I think they were nearly expecting a special mention.

After that we worked our way round, the two of them ducking and wriggling and using their elbows until there wasn't a piece in the show that they hadn't minutely examined. Then we went and found Liam.

"What did I tell you," he said, his arm sweeping round.

He was right, there were red stickers everywhere, you'd have to look hard for even a drawing now that still hadn't sold.

The children were dead on their feet, so I left them with him while I went for a last word with Catherine. I'd been watching out, hoping for a private word, but as one lot departed the next lot arrived — she seemed to be always caught in a throng. I hovered about, awaiting my chance; there was only this one man beside her, which was as nearly alone as she was about to get.

I went over and she hugged me happily then introduced me, but we weren't even through the first sentence when one of the gallery staff came to call her away.

"Don't move, either of you," she told us. "I'll be back before you've even noticed I've gone."

What could we do except wait for her and try our hand at a little conversation?

He was fifty or so, very smartly dressed, but kind as well, for he picked up how shy I was and he started to tell me about himself to fill up the gaps. He was into modern art, he said, and he ran off a list of artists whose pictures he'd bought, then explained which period in a career each painting belonged to and what he thought was the artist's strongest phase. He was showing off as well as helping me out, I could see that, but he loved the whole world of paintings and artists, there was an innocence and an enthusiasm about him that I completely fell for. If I'd been Liam I could have lobbed the ball back, discussed his views, argued the toss on who had peaked and who was going to go on getting better, and he'd have loved that too. But I wasn't, so I couldn't. Instead I just smiled and nodded and searched around in my head for something to ask him to keep the conversation going and not let Catherine down. I was working up to some idiot question about what he did if his wife didn't like a picture he'd bought, but at that moment Catherine came back and saved us both from each other.

He switched to her right away, but he didn't dump me, he went on including me with his eyes as he spoke. It seemed he'd just bought Catherine's best rock pool, and he was as pleased with it and with Catherine and with himself as any child. He was even pleased with me as well, while he was at it.

I managed a few more sentences, then mumbled about going home. Catherine said something effortlessly courteous, then slid an arm into mine and walked me away.

———

Two days later Catherine was sitting in my little room with my hands moving themselves across her head. Sometimes my fingers found a place and pressed hard; sometimes they dragged and rubbed across the bone. Standing there, looking down on her, I could see her belly's swell beneath her loose sweater. When she stood you'd hardly notice, but it wouldn't be long before you couldn't not.

She was as high as a kite still from the success of her exhibition, she couldn't believe her luck.

"Imagine it, Ellen. People paying out money like that for bits of glass and clay! My bits of glass and clay. Gas, isn't it? Who'd have thought there'd be so many people around with all that cash going spare? Would you like some, Ellen? I'd love you to buy something you've been hankering after, I wouldn't mind how boring it was. What about a tumble dryer? A fridge freezer? A smart new cooker?"

I told her I liked hanging washing, and what was wrong with the fridge and the cooker I had? I said she should take herself down to the bank to pay off some of those loans.

"To hell with the bank and the loans," she said, "why won't you take my money? From the look on your face you'd think I'd been running guns."

So I asked if her gynaecologist had said anything to her about blood pressure.

That stopped her short. She asked was there anything wrong.

"I don't know," I said. "The question popped out of its own accord, I didn't feel it coming on."

"He hasn't mentioned blood pressure. But he thinks I might need a section on account of my age." She sat there, the lines of her face all dragged down with unhappiness.

I stared at her, not knowing what to say. I make a point of never going against a doctor's advice to a patient, no matter what they tell me their doctor has said. What do I know? Nothing at all — beside a doctor I'm barely literate. And I'm not in for the long haul: I don't write prescriptions, I don't have to deal with side effects or recriminations, no one sues me, I don't have to watch my patients die. At worst I'm a last resort, a shot in the dark when there's nothing left to lose. If I fail, I fail. The people who come here have no expectations. Everyone else has failed, all they're asking me to do is try.

But I hated seeing Catherine like that, head bowed, all the excitement gone out of her like a doused light.

"Did he give you any more reason than that?" I asked carefully. "Did he say what he was afraid of?"

She shook her head. "Just my age. He said it would be safer — for *both* of us." She stroked the palm of her hand slowly down the curve of her belly. "It knocked all the fight out of me. When he said it like that he made me feel it was selfish to object."

"You've a bit more time yet," I said as gently as I could. "And since you're so rich, you might even think of getting a second opinion . . . ?"

She looked up, the light back in her face. "I never thought of that. I don't know why I'm being like this — so passive, so accepting. It's not like me at all —"

"Partly it's the process. You're supposed to be passive; you're a vessel for carrying and growing a baby. And you've never done it before — it's scary."

"It is, isn't it?" The light was still in her face, but the tears were running down it as well. "I cry a lot. It's not like me. I keep saying that, don't I? Were you like this, Ellen?"

"Almost everyone is." And as far as I knew that was true, but I wished she wasn't so alone. I tried to remember my way back to carrying Barbara Allen. Robbie had wanted that baby, but for all the use he actually was I might as well have been alone. I'd survived. The same could not be said of Barbara Allen.

She was the last appointment, so I asked her to stay and eat with us, but she shook her head. She was off to visit a sister who lived in Kildare, she said, her favourite sister — one with a husband and children and ponies and rabbits and dogs.

"Everything perfect," Catherine added. "And a perfectly plain gold ring on her wedding finger. White gold, very understated. I've dropped a few hints to prepare the way, but tonight's the night."

"Will it be alright?"

"It will. She'll tell me I can't, she may even cry, but Tom will be there, he'll fill her with drink, then she'll cry again and give me her blessing. She thinks babies need daddies and fluffy pet rabbits and stable lifestyles. So do I, but there you go — things don't always work out the way you intended. All I need her to do is tell the parents. God knows, it's no big deal anymore, but there's no saying which way they'll jump and Fran's much better at all that than I am. Better at everything. She's solid gold — like her ring."

"Not better at rock pools."

She grinned, her pleasure at the opening resurfacing. I walked her out, then waited on the step, watching while she stood by the car searching her pockets for keys. She found them, held them up to me, smiled, and signalled for me to go in. I waved and headed for the kitchen, my thoughts already moving ahead to the dinner.

I don't know what made me turn back when I reached the steps, but I did. Dermot was there, opening the passenger door, about to get in. I was surprised, for I hadn't known he'd come with her and she hadn't said. He must have been round in the studio with Liam, I thought, and at that moment he'd lifted his head, looked me full in the face, and smiled. He looked well, better than I'd seen him looking for ages. I waved again and went in.

The next morning Marie phoned from Dublin. Dermot was in hospital in Kilkenny — flat on his back, drips and a catheter — a neglected kidney infection. He'd been there three days without telling anyone; she'd only found out herself because she'd been trying to change the weekend arrangement for the kids. Would we go and see him, find out the story?

I said I'd send Liam right away, and I'd go myself when I could, then I'd ring her.

I put down the phone. Dermot had been here, flesh-and-blood Dermot, not something vague that I nearly saw, some intuition or flash of knowing. He'd stood there, not twenty yards away. He'd turned his head and looked me straight in the eye. And all the time he'd been flat on his back in a hospital bed.

Catherine had been going off to her sister's house to break the news to her family that she was pregnant. I'd watched Dermot get into the car with her and drive away.

So that was it. Catherine's one-night stand that had been a mistake.

Catherine came back every week, she said she felt better after I'd had my hands on her, and safer as well, for they gave her the courage she needed for what lay ahead. From time to time I'd slip Dermot's name in, testing to see had things changed for her, but they never had.

Dermot was over his kidney infection, and for once he had luck on his side and there weren't any complications. At first the scare sobered him up, but that soon wore off and he went back to his old ways. Liam said Dermot's studio was littered with half-realised paintings, hardly touched for months, and the shake in his hands was getting worse.

"Can't you do anything?" Liam had asked me when Dermot had been in the studio, talking, and then had stayed on to eat. *Eat* did I say? He'd pushed the food around the plate, then left looking white-faced and sick. I'd shaken my head, surprised at the request, though I knew how hard it was for Liam, watching his best friend self-destruct.

I'd told Liam addictions were outside my field, which might have been true — I didn't know, for I'd never been asked before. But Dermot's was — I was certain of that, I'd never felt anything in my hands at all when he was near me. I came close then to telling Liam about Dermot and Catherine, I thought if he knew he might talk to them both, and that might ease some of the pain, or it might for Dermot. Not for Catherine though, which is what stopped me. Catherine was going for the virgin birth; if she'd wanted Liam to know the truth she'd have told him herself.

I kept wondering how she'd got Dermot to keep his mouth shut, even in drink, but as well as that I wondered how she'd landed herself with him at all. From her dates it must have been sometime around the back end of February, the four-o'clock-in-the-morning month, the hour before dawn when the knock comes at the door. Perhaps it was as simple as that, perhaps she'd just been lonely for too long.

When I'd first come here I thought I liked everyone Liam liked, especially Dermot, who was always good craic and easy to have around. But when Liam asked me to help him, I realised that deep down I didn't — perhaps never had — and that was disturbing, and a shock as well.

And he wasn't good craic anymore, he was alcoholic, which meant that a whole lot more of him was visible than ever had been before. He was a beached ship hauled up onto the sands, the hull exposed, its burden of rust and barnacles laid clean to the morning sky. I realised then that Dermot was noisy around women because he was afraid of us. More than that, he didn't much like us except when it came to sex. But he liked Catherine. It wasn't only that she was a mate, an honorary man, it was because she'd always seen under his act and she'd liked him, rust and barnacles and all. He must have sensed that and found it soothing, so he'd relaxed with her in a way he couldn't with most women. She didn't put him down or make him feel clumsy and stupid, so he wasn't.

But now he wanted to be with her both sexually and as a partner, and she didn't want that, though she must have tried the sexual bit because there was a baby, getting nearer all the time to being born. The end of November seemed suddenly way too close. Maybe Dermot was staying quiet because he loved her, or maybe he couldn't bear the thought of her contempt if he spoke out. Whichever it was, once you knew, it was plain as the nose on your face that Catherine was his obsession. What had been simple between them had gone all twisted and wrong.

So I didn't say anything to Liam, and he didn't seem to notice, or maybe he just didn't want to see. But it was awful, all this pain, and in an odd way I felt worse about Dermot since I'd discovered that I didn't much like him, for I couldn't pretend to myself that I wanted things between him and Catherine to work out.

Chapter 27

There was a ring at the doorbell, and Liam got up from watching the news. He was gone for longer than usual, but I knew I'd not have to rouse myself, for whoever was out there wasn't in need.

Liam came in, closing the door behind him.

"You'll never believe who's there," he said, an odd look on his face.

I rested my head on the back of the chair and waited to be told.

"It's the buyer you were talking to at Catherine's opening —"

"Buyer?" I was puzzled. "I wasn't talking to any buyer —"

"The businessman. The rich one who bought that big rock pool of Catherine's for his third-best bathroom —"

"His daughter's bedroom."

"His daughter's bedroom. Well, he's out there waiting, he's driven all the way down from Dublin to see you."

"He's not sick."

"I never said he was. He wants you to look at some plans, some property he's thinking of buying. He says the deal looks sound, but there are glitches, it could seriously backfire." Liam paused, and it dawned on me that he was trying to keep a straight face. "It's a gamble, he says. Could go either way. He wants you to tell him if he should go ahead —"

"He wants *what?*"

"Someone told him you were clairvoyant. So he wants you to look at the plans and tell him if he should buy. He's got his business partner with him and a wad of money he keeps waving under my nose —"

I stared at Liam. He stared back, completely po-faced, then all at once we were laughing so hard we couldn't stop. It was the unlikeliness of it, the sheer silliness. I laughed till my stomach hurt. I tried not to look at Liam, but then I did and I was off again.

"What'll we do?" I asked Liam when I could speak.

"Tell him you can't read plans." We both cracked up again, though it wasn't that funny. Then I straightened up, wiped the laughter tears from my eyes, and went to the door. There on the step was the man who'd been kind to me at the show.

"I'm not clairvoyant," I said. "Whoever told you that, told you wrong."

He didn't believe me, he kept saying he'd come a long way, and all he wanted me to do was take a look.

I told him I didn't care how far he'd driven. I wouldn't because I couldn't, and that was flat. I was very firm and determined. The business partner kept nodding encouragingly at me as I spoke. It was clear that he thought your man had lost the run of himself altogether.

I went on saying no, but I must have been smiling as well because Mr. Rich-Man started in about being sent home empty-handed and without so much as a sup of tea before setting off —

So we brought them in and he set the roll of plans down on the table, and I thought if he mentioned them even the once he'd be out on his ear. Liam's hand reached for the press where the whiskey lived, but I vetoed it with a look. They'd asked for tea, so tea they would get.

I made a pot and down we all sat. Mr. Rich-Man was in no hurry, though it was clear as the moon in the sky that the sidekick just wanted them both to get back in the car and drive home. We talked about art, about Catherine, about her show; he even had me describing the baby's stage entrance en route to the hospital in Catherine's sister's borrowed four-wheel drive.

"She was staying here?"

"No, Ellen was over with her," Liam said. "Only visiting, keeping an eye. It wasn't supposed to happen like that, she wasn't due for another eight days."

"Daniel Conor," I told him. "Eight pounds, seven ounces. And they were both fine — he was early because he was ready, so what was the point in hanging around?"

Mr. Rich-Man took it all in, and he never so much as glanced at the plans. Instead he asked about Liam's work, and nothing would do but he had to go out to the studio to see for himself.

When they came back Mr. Rich-Man's attitude to Liam was different, so I knew he'd liked the work. He told me my husband was going to be a better painter than he'd ever been a sculptor, but both were there in the new work, there was no such thing as wasted time. Then he picked up the roll of plans and tossed them across the table, and before I had time to think, my hands had lifted and caught them. At once they began to vibrate.

At first it was just a small vibration, but it didn't stay small for long. I wanted to let them go, but I couldn't; my fingers were glued to them, my hands were rocking and bucking like a dowser's when he's close to water. The others stood and stared as well — it was that peculiar. Then Mr. Rich-Man walked across and lifted his plans from my hands, and my hands let them go.

He smiled and smiled, a cat with cream. Then with a flick of his eyes he summoned the sidekick, thanked us for our hospitality, and made for the door. Just as he got there he turned, and his left hand came out of his pocket and tossed a bundle of rolled-up bank notes in my direction. I was wise to him this time. I kept my hands fisted tight at my sides, and the money rolled onto the floor. We all looked at it. Mr. Rich-Man said he'd got what he wanted, let someone else do the clearing up, he was away back to Dublin to pin down his deal.

"You've not seen the last of me," he said. "I'll be back down to look at the work when it gets to where it's going."

He didn't take his eyes off mine all the time he was speaking, and I didn't drop mine or look away. It's strange when something deep inside you connects like that with someone else, though there isn't any connection at all on the surface. Strange and strong.

"Look after her," he said like an afterthought to Liam. "She's a rare one." Then the door closed behind them, and they were gone.

Chapter 28

What was she doing here? I didn't know. All that was wrong with the child was a head cold — no need for panic. Marie would know that, she's a capable woman — that's why she'd extracted her life from under the weight of Dermot's.

The only puzzle for me was her marrying him in the first place.

"She was pregnant, glad enough of a ring on her finger. It wasn't like it is now." That's what Liam had said when I'd asked.

You share the same bed year in and year out, but if you think you know each other's thoughts then think again. This was my latest discovery — the way that I felt about Dermot was how Liam had always felt about Marie.

And now here she was, two days after Christmas, and she'd brought a child for my hands who should have been home in his bed.

"You're staying with Dermot?" I asked when I'd finished on James.

She shook her head. "No, not with Dermot. We're in Callan for Christmas with their gran."

I nodded. I'd forgotten that Marie was almost local.

"I'll leave them over with Dermot for the New Year," she said.

"Or that's the plan for the moment." The child looked up at her quickly, anxiety like a flickering light through his snuffles.

"Now away off next door and watch the TV with Andrew and Suzanna," she told him, dumping any lingering pretence that they were here for him. "I need to have a word or two with Ellen before we go." She stroked his hair briefly with one hand, then propelled him off through the kitchen door with the other. For a moment I nearly felt sorry for Dermot; he wouldn't have stood much chance against Marie.

"Could we go into your room? I want to talk to you in private." Her eyes roamed the kitchen as though there were microphones hidden away in the walls.

"It's freezing in there," I said shortly. I was annoyed, we'd never exactly been friends, but there hadn't been any bad feeling either. If she wanted to talk why hadn't she said it straight out when she'd phoned?

"I don't mind the cold so long as it's private," she said, her hand on the door.

So I gave in and fetched the blow heater and followed her through. She got straight to the point, which was Dermot — the state he was in, how good Liam had been — and how it was time now for Catherine to come onboard.

It all came out fast, with behind it this relentless determination. I'd no time to figure out her agenda: all I could do was stall and try to deflect her from Catherine and little Dan.

"Catherine?" I asked, hearing a feeble surprise in my voice. "What makes you think Catherine can help? Liam's every bit as close to Dermot as Catherine is, and he's been trying for months and getting exactly nowhere."

"Dermot's not in love with Liam."

Drinkers. Sooner or later they talk in their cups.

"What Dermot feels about Catherine is Dermot's problem. Catherine doesn't feel the same way."

She stared at me. "I know that," she said. Her face was calm and expressionless, but her eyes never once left mine.

"What exactly is it you think that Catherine can do?" I asked cautiously.

"Get him signed up for a programme to dry him out," she said. "Then, when he's off the drink, get him back to his work."

Marie was wearing a dark-red sweater that showed off her figure. Her face was made up, she looked pretty and sexy, and she wasn't asking, she was stating. It was weird. Her calm, and the way she looked, and the words coming out of her mouth. "Catherine thinks she can do it alone, but she doesn't know her arse from her elbow. Children need a father. Dan's no different from my two."

That stopped me short, which was exactly what it was meant to do. I got up and walked across the room, furious with her, though I wasn't sure why.

"Are you trying to tell me that Dermot's Danny's father?"

"You know I am."

"Why would you think a thing like that?"

"Dermot. He told me himself on the night of Catherine's show."

"Lies and wishful thinking. You said it yourself, he's in love with her. As well as that there's the drink."

"It could be, but it isn't. And there's plenty of talk to back it up — ask anyone who saw that baby before she hid him away at her sister's."

"If there's talk it's all coming from Dermot. Catherine's not telling anyone who Danny's father is. Ask her. She looks you smack in the eye and says it's someone we none of us know."

"She's told you."

"She has not."

"You weren't one bit surprised just now when I said it was Dermot —"

I opened my mouth to argue, but what was the use? Marie's nobody's fool, she had read me right, and more than that, I could see from her face that she'd guessed how it was that I knew.

"Dermot's besotted about her, and she hasn't seen him for months. Now she won't let him see that baby at all, and it's making him worse."

"She's gone to her sister's."

"I *know* she's gone to her fucking sister's, you'd think her sister lives in Africa to hear you all talk. Well she doesn't, she lives in Kildare, about an hour's drive up the road." She stopped and steadied her voice with an effort. When she continued it was even and expressionless, like her face. "He phones, and whoever answers says she's not there. He's been over four times, but she doesn't come out and they won't let him through the door. They've told him they'll call the Guards if he comes again."

That was cold alright; it shocked me in spite of myself. I stopped pacing about and sat down again across from her. I would hear her out, I decided. That wouldn't hurt me, or Catherine either.

"What is it you want me to do, Marie?"

"You're her friend, persuade her to see him." She was urgent now, the unnatural calm finally slipping. "He needs to see her — not seeing her's making him worse. That's why I'm sitting here dumping this shit in your lap."

"It won't solve anything. She doesn't want to be with him."

"I know that, but it might calm him down and she might be able to talk him into getting help —" She got up, stared at the black uncurtained window, sat down again. "Ellen, in two days' time I'm supposed to leave the boys with him for the week, and they need to go. They're dying about him — you saw James when I even hinted it might not happen. But I *can't* when he's the way he is, I can't. And that makes him worse as well. What would *you* do if it was Andrew and Suzanna?"

"Cancel," I said, no hesitation. "He's in no state to mind children. He's in no state to mind himself."

"I've cancelled the last two visits." She slumped back in her chair, defeated. I sat watching her, saying nothing.

"And what about *my* life?" she suddenly said, and she might have been asking herself, for her face was moody, withdrawn, her eyes avoiding mine. "I'll have to put it on hold again — yet again — and people don't just wait around, you know, they run out of patience, take themselves off, find someone else without all these problems —"

I realised she was talking about a lover. I don't know what my face was doing, but it must have been doing something because all of a sudden the apathy went. She stood up, took out a cigarette, lit it, the lighter trembling in her hand.

"Saint fucking Catherine." She inhaled, then blew the smoke out in my face. "I don't understand you, Ellen," she said. "You judge me for wanting a life after Dermot, yet Catherine sleeps with your husband and that's all grand by you."

I didn't hear her at first, or rather I heard her words perfectly, but they didn't go in. Even when they did I understood only that she was telling me something important. I didn't understand how it related to me.

I suppose she must have been standing there watching this happening on my face, at the same time as I was watching what was happening on hers.

I saw her slowly realise that this was all news to me.

"Oh, Jesus, Ellen," she said. She put her hand over her mouth, and her eyes looked at mine with a sort of despair.

"I'm sorry," she said. "I'm sorry, so sorry, I thought —"

She broke off, then she started again.

"I thought you'd have *seen* it. I didn't know you didn't know —"

If she hadn't said that I might have doubted. But she did, so there was nowhere left for me to go.

And I'm certain that she was as horrified as she looked. Marie's a strange woman — self-contained, set on some goal of her own that's away beyond me — but she isn't malicious. She'd assumed that I'd know through the Seeing. She'd assumed there'd been some sort of reconciliation that meant that Catherine and Liam and I could go on being friends. She wouldn't ever have said it otherwise.

But I've never had the Seeing for my own. Neither for Liam, nor for the children. I had it for Robbie when he died, but that was a long time after he'd ceased being one of my own.

—⚬—

A beast came and sat in my entrails and devoured them. Its teeth gnawed my bowels, its claws gouged my heart, its foul breath breathed in my face when I lay down at night and when I awoke in the morning. It lived inside me and gave me no peace.

No peace for Liam either. All I could think of was what he had done with Catherine. I couldn't eat, I couldn't rest, I followed him round, spitting bile. It was a living nightmare. A thousand times worse than the pain of the first discovery.

"How many times?"

"Ellen, what are you doing this for, why do you have to know?"

"How many times?"

"In all? About four."

"Liar."

"What's the point of this? Whatever I say you don't believe me. What's the point of me telling the truth if you turn it into a lie?"

"Liar, liar, liar. Four means eight, eight means sixteen. I know you Liam — tell me a figure, I know to double it. If you say four, it's eight at the very least."

Silence. He tries to not answer back, to end the exchange, to go on doing what he's doing.

I'm not having any of that.

"How *dare* you talk about truth. You don't know the meaning of truth, you wouldn't know truth if it sat on your head and beat its heels in your face."

Who is this woman, this crazed egomaniac, this foul wee tyrant who thinks the whole world revolves around her betrayal?

When she wasn't shouting she wept; she wept so her heart would break from self-righteousness and self-pity.

The children were stunned, they didn't know what was happening. But something was, they were certain of that — they'd never seen me like this. I'd never seen it myself. I was possessed — all that other stuff that I'd casually called possession was nothing at all to this.

Catherine came. I stood at the door, screaming insults till she finally turned and got into the car and drove away. She phoned, but I slammed the receiver down and hurled the phone at the wall. When she tried again I said things I didn't know were in me to say, things that stank with the breath of the beast.

Liam tried too. He waited till I was running down, then he stood in the kitchen and tried to make me understand.

"Ellen, I know you're hurt and betrayed, but you have to forgive me, there isn't any other way. If we go on living together it has to be because we want it — both of us — regardless of whose fault this is, and I'm not saying it isn't mine. But if you *can't* forgive me, if you *keep* going on like this, then I don't want to stay because I can't stand it and that's the truth."

I couldn't believe what I was hearing. "Truth?" I sneered at him. "What would *you* know about truth? And what can't you stand, Liam, ask yourself that? Is it me? Or is it what you've done to me and the children?"

He didn't answer.

"And I don't *have* to forgive you, Liam. I don't *have* to do anything. *You* have to *earn* my forgiveness."

He sighed and turned away. I went back to chopping the carrots, hot tears splashing down onto my hands.

Dermot came and saved me. He was drunk or hungover, I don't know which, he was unshaven, red in the face, and he smelled.

I told him to go away.

He took hold of me by the upper arms and pushed me down into a chair.

"Sit down there, you stupid bitch," he said. "Sit there while I talk some sense into you. After that I'll be more than happy to take myself out of your sight."

I sat. I was too worn out to take him on as well.

Dermot got straight to the point.

"What is it, Ellen? Your husband's cock in another woman, is that what all this is about? Is that why you're wrecking your marriage and hurting Catherine and frightening your children silly?"

Hurting Catherine. I heard that through the exhaustion, but I couldn't believe my ears. "You have it the wrong way round, Dermot," I said. "Drink has pickled what's left of your brain, Catherine's the one who's hurt *me*."

He lit up a cigarette.

"That's how you see it, is it? Well, listen carefully, Ms. Wronged-Wife, while I tell you a thing or two." He paused, took a drag at his cigarette, and gave me a look that kept me sitting where I was. "Catherine's in love with Liam. Has been for ages, most likely still is, I can't say for sure, she isn't speaking to me at the moment." I opened my mouth to protest, but he silenced me with a gesture. "*Listen*, Ellen. I'm telling you what really happened, so fucking sit there and *listen*. You and Liam were going through a bad patch, remember? Liam lost his way over that commission, he was very depressed, then Catherine got him the job in Limerick, trying to help you both out." He looked round for an ashtray, found none, used a plate. "So they're working together, travelling together, the proximity gets too much, they have it off a few times. So? *It doesn't matter, Ellen.* What matters is that they both pulled back. Liam came home to you. Catherine walked away."

I opened my mouth again, but he held up his hand. "I haven't finished. You might as well know the truth, and you might as well hear it from me. The two of them did that — they walked away from something they both of them wanted — they did that for you because they both love you, though sometimes I swear to God I wonder why. Catherine took a job in Cork that she didn't want just to keep herself clear of Limerick. She stopped coming here, though you hardly even noticed. Liam fought his way back up from the pit and turned himself into a painter. And then you find out and what do you do? You carry on like a five-year-old, kicking and screaming because someone borrowed your best toy then put it back before you'd even noticed it was gone. Liam's not a toy, Ellen, he's flesh and blood and so is Catherine, and you'll have to decide if you love him or if he's just there while it suits you. And I'll tell you something for nothing while I'm at it. If you don't wise up and rein yourself in, you'll lose them both for good."

I couldn't speak. A sort of enormous numbness was on me. An enormous weariness too. All I could do was stare, and I never felt the tears come into my eyes, I only knew they were there when they ran down my face.

"You know something else, Ellen? Catherine only slept with me because she couldn't sleep with Liam. And she only did it the once because try as I might I couldn't convince her I'd do instead."

It wasn't all suddenly grand on account of what Dermot had told me. I wasn't able to turn myself round and forgive them, and nor did I even want to. But the beast let go of my entrails; it slunk away off and found someone else's guts to lodge in and eat up instead.

I cried a lot, I wouldn't hear Catherine's name, and for Liam there was this icy and unrelenting distance. But I didn't follow him round and scream abuse, and somewhere I knew that when he'd been punished enough I didn't quite want him to go.

*I*t's half past six and the light's coming grey to the window, but it's not as cold and clear as it promised last night. Sometime around four a little wind got up and the moon clouded over, and that was the end of the frost and the cold, bright stillness. The house is waking — I hear the small ticks and creaks that it makes when it's stretching and changing — it'll not be long now before there's the sound of the heating kicking in. Wumph.

Sometimes I feel that it's hopeless, we're different, too different, Liam and I. I look back and think it was hopeless even before the Catherine-thing blew the roof off the house we had built together.

Then other times it seems that there's a road through and we're finding it, though every inch of the way is hard won. Maybe it's like that for everyone, I don't know; I don't know about anyone else, only us.

It would be easier if I wasn't who I am.

The children will wake soon. Suzanna will be alright while I'm gone, tomorrow she'll open her eyes and most likely head straight for our bed. I never let them in unless they're sick, I wasn't let myself and neither was Brian, it gets to be a habit that's hard to break. They're gone too old for our bed now, but that won't stop her. And Liam is soft, they know that. When they were little they'd come to his side the minute I was up, and he'd always lift them in.

It won't be so easy for Andrew, but then nothing is.

I've learned to stop calling them "weans" the way we do in Derry, but I can't take to "lads," which is what they say in Kilkenny regardless of sex. Liam says "lads," and I tell him there's no way Suzanna's a lad, and he laughs and says time enough for her to be finding that out for herself. I don't like the word "kids" either, so I always end up saying "children," which is a bit formal even for my taste. There are times you frighten yourself how like your mother you're growing.

I'll have a bath now and dress in the warm clothes I've put out for the journey. Maybe I'll sleep on the bus. Maybe I won't.

Chapter 29

After the first phone call comes from Derry I hold out for seven whole days.

Suzanna stands in the kitchen door announcing that people should visit their dying mammies, even mammies they don't much like. Andrew slips his hand into mine and tells me he thinks I'll start crying again if I don't go.

Then Anne's on the phone, saying she's failing much faster than anyone expected.

Anne says she's asking for me.

I stand stock still with the phone to my ear, hardly daring even to breathe. Anne is truthful, I know she hasn't made this up. I wait, and the silence runs on and then there's Anne's voice, a little girl's voice that's told me *almost* the truth, but not quite.

"I asked was there anyone she wanted to see," Anne blurts out. "She closed her eyes and didn't answer. I thought she might not have heard, so I asked did she want you to come? She opened her eyes, and she looked straight at me. She nodded her head."

I see her when Anne says that. She's propped up in the bed, her white hair against the snow white of the pillow, Anne fussing her with questions.

If she'd asked for me, I'd have refused her. But she hasn't asked — she has bent her stiff neck in assent.

So I will bend mine.

Liam wants to drive me up, but I won't let him. Brian and Anne want me to stay with them, but I won't do that either. I've booked a room in a bed-and-breakfast. I'll let no one help, I'll do it alone.

Brian is angry when Liam tells him about the B and B on the phone, and Liam says he gets worse when he hears the address. But it's Liam he's talking to, not me, so he has to mind his tongue.

"He says that address is the Cityside, but the hospital's on the Waterside, the other side of the river," Liam tells me. "So I said it's only a step to the bus station, you've told me so, and doing it this way you won't be after him to drive you about."

"It's not driving me about that's bothering Brian. It's because the Cityside's Catholic now, he wants me to stay with my own." I'm sorting and folding a heap of dried washing as I speak; I have one of Andrew's vests flat on the table, and the way I'm smoothing it out, my hand could pass for an iron.

"He thinks I'm making a statement," I explain to Liam. "He thinks I'm telling him I've gone over to your lot and to hell with mine —"

"And have you?"

I snort. "Jesus Christ, Liam, don't you know me better than that? I don't want my lot, your lot, nor anybody else's lot either. I was reared on the Cityside, I won't be hounded across the bridge because Brian thinks it's safer. And I live down here now, I'm married to a Catholic — you could nearly say I'm entitled. Besides, I don't like the Waterside, it's a dreary hole."

"Ellen, I'm driving you. I'll turn round and come straight home if that's what you want, but I'm going to take you —"

I won't let him. You can do what you like when you're the

injured party. I've become a wee Napoleon, standing firm on the moral high ground.

I rest my face on the cool of the window and watch the winter fields.

I'd caught the Dublin bus in Kilkenny, but it was running late. I'd made up my mind if I missed the Dublin to Derry connecting bus then I'd turn straight round and come home.

But I didn't miss it. We'd made good time on the road.

Once onto the Derry bus I lean back and close my eyes, a partition against the voices filling the air around me. A group from Derry on a two-day jaunt to Dublin. A bit of sightseeing, a lot of shopping. The exchange rate's strong in their favour — they have the Dublin shops bought out.

A soft gold light spreads over the fields and the hedges, it catches the empty branches of ash and chestnut, and lights the red of the sally-stems to fire. Horses and cattle stand about in their pastures, casting long shadows that lie beside the longer shadows of the empty trees. Farms and yards and barns. The straggled roadside dwellings glow through the February afternoon, and in that mythic light every house is become a home.

Brian phoned last night — he said she was half delirious, he said she was saying my name.

I didn't believe him. I know Brian — he said it to stop me changing my mind.

If she'd asked for me I wouldn't be on this bus now, I'd be safe at home with my hands on someone and the next one waiting outside the door. I don't want these two worlds of mine coming visiting each other. I might have once — before the Healing began — but not now, I know what they'd think of the Healing in the North.

My head aches and aches. My belly is knotted tight with fear.

The bus runs on up through Meath and then Louth. The sun has dropped low, it disappears and appears again between the little hummocky hills of Monaghan; the twilight's a river of shadow that flows. We pass a white farmhouse that stands among trees and barns, lights shine in the ground-floor windows, the curtains are still undrawn. Everything tidied and tended — trim flower beds in front of the house, hedges cut tight and round. The closer we come to the border, the neater and straighter things get.

In Monaghan town the bus pulls in at the depot. There's a corridor with signs for the ladies and gents, and a snack bar that smells of steam and frying rashers. I find a smeary tray and stand in the queue to buy a sandwich that I don't want and a cup of tea I'd nearly sell my soul for. There are tables in the snack bar, but I can't seat myself in that yellow world of electric light, I need a private no-place refuge, the patch of glass that the world has slid past all afternoon and soon will slide past again. I carry the tea across the yard to the shadowy bus, settle back into my seat, and nestle the cardboard cup in my two cold hands the way Catherine does.

Catherine. Best not go there.

People are trickling back onto the bus, the driver shuffles around in his seat, switches the lights on, starts up the engine, and pumps the horn a couple of times in a final warning. A man standing propped against the wall takes a last hard drag at his cigarette, knocks it out, slides the butt back into the packet. A small bright trail of red sparks falls and is gone. He climbs back on the bus, it moves off over the tarmac, swings out onto the road.

The women have talked themselves dry, the driver has turned off the radio, the bus has gone quiet. He turns off the lights as well, and folk settle themselves to sleep. Here and there hands reach up for the overhead switches. Thin pencils of light score the shadows.

I lean my cheek against the glass and follow every tree and field and roadside petrol station. The winter sun has slid down behind the rim of the world, leaving only a red-gold burn on the horizon. Above the burn is a stretch of light so pure and colourless and cold that I am emptied of myself, transformed into a being ancient and unfleshed. All I know is loneliness and longing for this cold, dark land I live my life in. I reach up my hand to my face and feel the salt tears.

It's dark, but I'm watching still, watching the signs for the names that I only see now in newspapers or in books. Enniskillen comes up, but it seems far too close. We pass a warning sign for children crossing — a triangle of black and red on white — and that's how I know. We're over the border, and I haven't noticed, we haven't even been stopped.

I can't believe it. Where are the watchtowers and searchlights, the British soldiers shouting and pointing ArmaLites in your face? That's how it always was and it always would be. Oh, it hadn't been once, I knew that. But that was a million years ago — nearly before I was born.

Brian said Daddy used to talk of the old days of small-time smuggling. He'd said the biggest part of an excise man's job was knowing when to take your glasses off and when to put them back on. Brian remembers more about Daddy than I do. Daddy was shortsighted, Brian is too. She has eyes as keen as a razor, and I have them from her, along with all the rest.

And now the border is only a country road in the dark. I'm not so innocent that I don't know it won't be that innocent — there'll be night-sight cameras and telescopic lenses and eyes behind gun sights, just as it was before, only hidden. All the same it's a shock. This must be Normalisation, I think, and here am I, hankering after the good old days of ArmaLites and torches and north-of-England accents coming at you from behind a blind of light. Normalisation seems wrong somehow, I feel the panic rise in my throat.

Hard on the panic comes the excitement. The road signs are floating up at me out of the dark like songs that have lodged themselves deep in my heart but I haven't heard in years. Dromore and Irvinestown and Pomeroy; Newtownstewart and Gortin and Strabane, the headlights throwing up names of places I thought I'd lost forever. I sit very still and upright in the sleeping bus, my hands loosely clasped, the tears running down my face and dripping off my jawbone into my lap. I feel like an open wound. I wonder who I was when I left and who I am now, and will I ever find my way back to anywhere at all?

The bus stops at Omagh, and everyone wakes up and stands up and pulls things down from the luggage racks and struggles into their coats. All change. Some people get into cars or disappear into the dark, but the shopping-spree women don't, they're all heading home to Derry. Our bus is late in, we've missed the connecting bus, and our driver looks at his watch as though the position of its hands is news to him.

"There'd be another along for yous any time now," he says. He waves his hand at the waiting room and makes himself scarce.

I can see why when we get inside and the Derry ones find out that "any time" means they'll have to hang around for more than an hour. *It's a disgrace, so it is; he knew rightly; he should have phoned on ahead and made the other bus wait* — They all begin to kick up and give out, they're all going to write and complain and demand that their fares be refunded.

I look around me. The place is brand-new, it's warm and clean, there are upholstered seats and toilets that work and phones lined up along the wall. I think of the quiet people I live among now and how glad they'd be of a waiting room that's kitted and fitted out like this one is.

Not this lot. When they finish giving out they start into phoning up whoever is meeting them and giving out all over again because they'll be late. This is all new to me — Derry, het up about lateness? — I begin to wonder should I ring the B and B? I cross to the phone, but I only have Southern coins on me so I open my mouth and ask can anyone change them?

They won't hear of changing anything, I'm showered with twenty pence pieces, advice on the new dialling code, and have I far to go when we get there, and do I know the city, and do I need a lift?

I thank them and make the call. Then I sit myself down on a comfortable new seat in this comfortable new waiting room and look around me again. I decide that someone believes in this Peace-Process-thing because ten years ago when a place got blown up they erected a makeshift shelter against the next time there might be a bomb going spare. Or else they built giant bunkers — narrow entrances, reinforced concrete, slit windows fitted with shatterproof glass. But this place is no bomb shelter, and there's nothing temporary about it either.

Chapter 30

*I*t's dark still, but I can make out the rectangle of the window, filled with a faint orange light. Street light. I stretch out my arm, fumble around for the light switch, lift my watch. Seven thirty. I've woken over and over all night, looked at the time, fallen back down into dream. Now I throw back the covers and swing my feet to the floor, glad to be giving up trying to be asleep. I'd planned on an easy start this morning, but that was eons ago — there's no way I want to put my head back down on that pillow now. I make tea from the kettle on the dresser and take the mug back to bed.

It's a nice room, small, simply furnished, and clean, with a single bed and its own shower and toilet. The floor has been stripped and sanded; the walls are white; an ocher-and-red-striped rug lies beside the bed for my feet. An old house, carefully refurbished. Tasteful. About a million miles from the Derry I thought I knew.

The same goes for everything else I've seen so far. I walked around last night to get the bus out of my legs, and nothing is as it had been when I left. The Strand Road isn't itself anymore — it's all new shops and arcades, big fancy supermarkets, smart bars with see-through windows and a clientele happy to lounge about in low designer chairs. I wondered who they were, these folk who liked to be visible when they were out enjoying themselves, and what had happened to getting drunk in privacy and semi-darkness? It was odd, this turning-around of the old ways — the citizens hanging about in the streets didn't seem to be that much changed.

Now I hear the small clickings and gurglings in the pipes as the heating comes on and the house wakes itself to the day. The orange light in the window changes to grey, it catches the cold shine of rain on the glass. I sip at the tea. I try to step clear of the night, of its dreams, but the shame of them clings about me like cobwebs I can't shake off. I'm standing on a wooden chair in the scullery. It's cold and I'm crying. She's pulling my head back by the hair and forcing a glass of soapy water hard against my shut lips so I feel them bruise on my teeth. I must take a gulp, swill it around, hold it, then spit it out. Then the next and the next and the next till the glass is empty. I'm crying, her hand grips my hair, I try to swill but I swallow instead and I retch. Then a wet warmth, flooding my knickers and trickling down my legs.

I had woken and reached my hand down. No wetness. Just the cotton cloth of my nightgown, soft and intimate with sleep.

The bus station's new and the library's new and so are a fair few buildings around it. But it isn't as new and smart as it looked last night in the dark. Some of it's new and smart, but a whole lot more is new and tacky and rapidly getting tackier. There are still some old faithfuls hanging about, but not for long — they're too shaken and battered about by the years of bomb blasts. Knocking them down will be cheaper than shoring them up, and that's what they'll surely do, making space for a whole load of brand-new sharp-edged tat to rise in their place. But behind all the new-ness the old face of the city still shows, and it's not that much changed. An aging woman, after a long night out on the town, her mascara smudged, blotches and wrinkles showing through caked foundation, only the faintest traces of lipstick left in the corners of the mouth.

I ask for a bus that goes all the way to the hospital, and they point to the one that's waiting. I climb on and sit there, sure that I've only closed my eyes, that all the years down South are no more than a doze by the fire and it's here I've been all the time. But inside those sleeping years live Liam and Andrew and Suzanna, live all the people who fill up my life so I hardly think of Derry from one month to the next.

The driver is running the engine to give us a bit of heat while we wait. Already the shock of the newness has gone — already it feels as familiar as the toothbrush I take in my hand every morning to clean my teeth. I wonder if she's waiting for me, or if that stiff-necked bend was a whim, at once forgotten or regretted. Suddenly I can hardly bear it that the bus is sitting here, waiting. If this has to be done I want it done now and over.

I never forgave her for the soapy water. I suppose I could want to forgive her with my mind, but I couldn't with the rest of me, it wouldn't let me, it would rise in revolt as my child's gorge rose at the taste of the soap. Catherine says you carry memory in your body. As far as I'm concerned memory lives in your mind and a bit in your nose as well, for we all know those smells that pick you up by the scruff of your neck and lift you back into times and places you thought were long gone. But after the dream I had last night I'm not so sure.

Taig. That was the word she hated the most, but everyone said it, their mas didn't wash out their mouths with soap. Walk down the street any day and you heard far worse.

No one else had her for a mother. No one else had her breathing down their necks.

She cut our hair with the black steel scissors she used for cutting cloth. We both got the same — a fringe, then the rest in a pudding-bowl curve so it fitted your head like a helmet, though Brian's was shorter at the back and sides than mine. It hadn't mattered in Dunnamanagh, but it mattered when we moved to Derry, for we were growing into self-consciousness and needing to look the same as everyone else. My hair shot into frizz the minute it dried. I looked like a red-haired goblin after a bad electric shock.

"Scaldy, Scaldy," they called when they saw.

"Don't mind them, Ellen," Brian would whisper under his breath. "Don't mind them, it'll grow again, minding them only makes them worse."

But I cried, I couldn't help it — it was back in the days before I'd discovered anger. Sometimes Brian protected me, mostly he didn't. Too many, and he'd join in with them, and that always made them fiercer.

Everyone was afraid; there was no one who wasn't afraid of the rest when the rest held together and stood against them.

I sit very still in my seat, amazed that I've never seen this before.

All the times Brian hadn't protected me.

Now I see that he couldn't have — not even Buster Rice protected his sister, they would have killed him for being soft if he had. Hard men aren't allowed to be soft. Man-big or boy-small, it's the same script.

And Brian wasn't hard. If there was a hard-man in our house it was my mother.

And it was a hard road she made us walk, and she neither thought nor cared what it was like for us. She had her principles, which would be ours — that was enough for her.

I swallow to rid myself of the taste of soap that clings like a film of fat to the back of my throat.

There's a throbbing roar as the driver revs the engine. I come back from wherever it is I've been. I look about me — the bus is near filled, and I never saw them getting on, nor buying their tickets, nor arranging themselves on the seats. The bus swings out into the street. All the impatience drains from me. I know myself naked and unprepared.

They've warned me that she's not great today, that she may be too tired to talk. I don't mind, I've nothing to say to her, but I open the door and I think I'm in the wrong room. Then I realise I'm not.

I sit down in the visitor's chair and I stare at a face that's so changed by drugs and sickness I'd have passed it in the street without a glance. I don't know what to do, I've never done this before, I wish she'd open her eyes then she'd know that I'm here without me having to tell her. I try to make the words come out of my mouth, but I can't. I feel panicky and trapped, and nothing useful is coming through from anywhere else. I don't want to be where I am, but it's what I'm here for, and where else is there in all this city for me to go? I feel empty and uninhabited — a build-ing gutted by fire, the inside all blackened and charred. I sit for a long time watching and waiting.

At last she opens her eyes, but she doesn't see me. I don't think she's seeing anything at all, although her eyes stay open. I shift noisily on the chair, and she moves her head very slowly and looks in my direction. Her eyes don't change when she sees me. I'm still trying to speak, but then she does.

Anne appears in the doorway. She draws back a step, surprise on her face, yet I phoned last night from the B and B and this morn-ing she's stayed clear deliberately, to give me the first hour alone with my mother.

I mustn't be the Ellen she expected.

When she's through greeting me she goes to the bed, bends, kisses my mother lightly on the forehead. Then she asks her how she is and how her night has been.

Nothing. The old woman who lies on the bed has gone away off somewhere else. The eyes don't open, the face doesn't change.

Anne goes on talking.

"Isn't it great to see Ellen, and her looking so well?" she asks the comatose form on the bed. "I thought she'd be tired out after all that travelling, but here she is, fresh as a daisy, not a bother on her at all. The girls said to tell you they're coming here straight from school but you needn't be getting ideas — it's not you they're wanting, it's their Aunty Ellen. They can't wait to get a wee look at her after so long."

She puts her shopping bag on the bed as she talks and takes things out of it and puts them on the bedside locker or in its drawer. There isn't much: eau de cologne, two clean nightdresses, a straggly posy of winter jasmine, a bottle of orange squash.

"Linda wasn't herself this morning; she's anxious about that French test they're having in class. . . . A wee bit of anxiety's no bad thing — she's inclined to be overconfident. And Brian said to remind you he has a meeting tonight, but it's straight after school so he'll be in directly it's over."

Then she sits herself down across the bed from me and asks me about my journey. We discuss the B and B, the new bus station in Omagh, the changes I've noticed in my short time in the city. Somehow she manages to include my mother in the conversation. I can't work out quite how she does this, for the non-participation of the body in the bed is total and unyielding. It's like one of those plastic maze games Brian and I used to fight over at Christmas when we were children. You tipped it this way and that, and the silver ball ran around, backwards and forwards, in and out of dead ends, almost but never quite reaching the centre.

It's no good, I can't do it, can't find my way into this maze of a game that Anne's so adroit at playing.

She sees my helplessness and gets to her feet.

"You'll be wanting a wee cup of coffee and maybe a sandwich, Ellen. There's a snack bar we can go to down the stairs." She turns to my mother. "We'll not be away long now, Edith. Just you relax and have a wee doze while we're gone."

The snack bar's an unenclosed area at the hospital entrance, tables and chairs in a row, a shop full of pastel teddies and fluffy rabbits and those flowers that look so fake they might as well be. All the tables are occupied except one, so we put our things down and go to the counter and Anne asks for two cups of coffee and two Club bars. The woman behind the counter calls her by her Christian name.

It's strange, I think. Here am I, reared by my mother's people, not knowing my father's, but my children have never set eyes on this aunt of theirs, for they're reared to their father's side alone.

Anne sits across from me at the table, stirring her coffee slowly and carefully. She has fine skin, a bony nose, and a wide mouth that's stretched across over-large teeth. As well as that she is tall and long-waisted, and her wavy brown hair is tucked in behind her ears. Nothing to write home about. She's wearing a dark tweed skirt that shows up her heavy hips, and a grey polo-neck jumper in an easy-care wool blend. I wonder what I think of her. Then I wonder if I've ever really thought of her, or if she's always just been Brian's wife.

I try to remember what she was like when I first met her.

"Dull. Smug. Boring. Perfect for Brian," I'd said to my mother, who'd looked at me with tight lips and cold eyes, so I'd gone upstairs and wept, though I didn't know why, for looks don't kill and where was the sting of words that I'd expected?

It was the loss of Brian that had me stretched on the bed, sobbing into the quilt. Anne hadn't taken him away from me, we hadn't been close since my early teens, but I hadn't ever entirely given up hope. Not until he married Anne, that is, and I saw what it was that he wanted: domesticity, respectability, a quiet life. I suppose then I finally realised I was on my own.

Anne had been kind to me in her way, she had tried to water me down and tidy me up and make me generally more acceptable to the world and to myself. She hadn't liked Robbie any more than Brian had, but she'd found in herself the self-restraint not to say so. She'd softened Brian when she could, tried to stand back when she couldn't, and taken my side against my mother in the days before I upped and walked out.

And the linen from the Ulster Weavers? That might have been innocent, I think. A woman who'd buy that skirt might well think a tablecloth the thing to send — might even think it signalled acceptance of what she'd have seen as another dubious Ellen-liaison. But I still can't believe she'd thought I'd like it.

But none of that matters now, for here she is, day in, day out, the dutiful daughter-in-law, keeping our vigil. The nurses call her Anne too.

She looks tired, and why wouldn't she? For there's little as exhausting as a death watch, few places as disinfected and over-heated and generally draining as a big, busy hospital in the middle of winter and not a window open anywhere and most folk worn out with staring fear and mortality straight in the face.

I've been here three hours, and already I'm climbing the walls. All I can think of is going through those doors, getting onto the bus, and never, ever coming back here again.

At last Anne stops stirring her coffee, lifts her head, and looks me in the eye. I don't know what she sees there, but what I see are the purpley-black stains at the insides of the eyes where the skin is thinnest, and the distant look that says that the person inside is stretched to the limit and neither knows it nor cares, for there's a good way still to be travelled.

"How do you find her?"

I lift my shoulders, then drop them and shut my eyes briefly. What is there to say?

"Did she open her eyes?"

I nod.

"Did she speak to you?"

"She did."

"Ellen, I'm so glad. I'm so glad you came —"

I nod, ashamed that I'm not. I hope Anne won't ask me anything else, I don't want to say what my mother said, but I know well I can't just sit here and hand her a pack of old lies.

Why can't I? I don't know, I've no problem with lies in the usual run of things; it must be the way she's been with my mother all these days.

But instead of asking she touches my hand.

"You must be worn out," I say.

She shrugs and reaches into her shopping bag. She brings out a package wrapped in greaseproof paper, opens it, and pushes it across the table.

"Ham sandwiches. The wheaten bread's homemade. One of the neighbours makes them for me every day."

I take one, though I don't really want it.

"The food in here's sort of dead," she adds. She sounds apologetic, as though she doesn't like to be criticising the hospital in any way. But she's right — all around us are opened plastic cartons and people lifting dead food to their faces.

"There's no call for the two of us to be in here," I tell her. "I'll do this afternoon, give you a bit of a break."

She looks at me as though I'm speaking Chinese.

"You go on home, Anne," I say carefully. "I'll stay with her. It's what I'm here for, isn't it? I didn't come all this way to go shopping."

Anne opens her mouth to speak then she closes it. She goes on looking at me. Her greeny-brown eyes fill with tears that well over the rims, roll down her cheeks, and splash on the table.

"You're tired," I say as gently as I can.

She nods, reaches for her bag, extracts a tissue, dabs at the wet places on her face.

"I suppose I must be," she says after a while. "It was you saying go home that did it. . . . What'll I do at home? I thought. The girls won't be back yet, there's no one to feed, I get up at five so's to have all the housework done before I come out —"

"You could lie on the bed."

Her eyes fill again. She nods wordlessly, then her shoulders start to heave. Her hand closes round the tissue, and she lifts it to her eyes. I sit on, watching, saying nothing. More tissues. I get up and go to the counter and come back with two more cups of coffee.

She's finishing her mopping and blowing. I set the coffee down on the table. She pulls the cup to her, picks it up, sips, tries out a shaky smile.

"Look what you're after doing to me," she says. "You're only home, and you have me cryin' like a wean."

I smile back. "Same old fiddle, same old tune," I say. "I'm only home and look at you, blaming all your troubles on Ellen."

"Are you calling me an auld fiddle, Ellen McKinnon?"

"I am," I say. "Now away home and lie down on that bed before the varnish falls off you altogether."

She nods and gathers up her things. She folds the greaseproof paper over what's left of the sandwiches and pushes them across the table at me. I don't want them, but I take them to please her. It's weird, I can't stop smiling, I'm trying as hard as I can to encourage her, though I can't imagine why.

Now we're both standing up. She makes a wee lurch towards me, I put out my arms and straightaway hers are around me, holding on tight. Only for a moment. Then she pulls away.

"The girls'll be in around five," she says. She goes out through the doors without looking back.

So there I am, back by her bedside, nothing to do but stare at her closed face or walk across to the window and look at the monochrome world beyond it, all smudged and smeared in the rain. Through the grey light I can see the Sperrin Mountains, their mounded slopes like a school of whales rising out of the sea. I think of the loose blue chain of the Blackstairs that I look for first thing every morning from the kitchen door. I think of Liam, the smell of his warm, drowsy, waking-up body beside me. Everything seems such a long way away, such a long time ago.

Was the bus only yesterday? Was this morning only this morning?

I look at the figure in the bed. The skin is puffy and yellow, the belly grossly swollen, that wonderful head of white hair has thinned and gone sparse. The hands — half opened, half closed — lie awkward and motionless on the folded sheet.

I hadn't thought she'd have a room to herself. I hadn't thought, that's the truth. I've been so wrapped up in myself and the misery of Liam and Catherine, so intent on refusing to go, that I've hardly considered her at all —

But it makes me wild that I've come all this way and she's spoken to me, and that's it — no more. She won't come out again for a second look.

If she hadn't at all I wouldn't have minded. But she has, so I know now she can if it suits her.

I turn my back and stand very still so she'll take a quick wee peek while she thinks I'm not looking. I turn back fast to catch her peeking, only she isn't. She's lying there, the same as before, that awful slack-jawed look on her face, the breathing heavy and noisy through her open mouth.

For a moment I'm almost stricken. She thought bed-in-the-day a disgrace. Others might do it — not her — she stayed on her feet till she couldn't stand up, and it was all worse after Daddy had died because she only had us to mind her. We entered her room on sufferance. It was in the door with us and away back out again the minute the tray was set down. And no hanging around or asking her how she was. In the whole of my childhood I only remember her being bed-sick three or four times.

I look away in a moment of decency. It doesn't last, and the next thing I'm back at the staring. Anyone can look at her, anyone can come in anytime they want to — where is there left for her to go but behind her closed lids? She could die now, with me standing watching her own death take her. Yet I'm still on the outside: as long as her eyes are shut she's safe from me.

A nurse sticks her head round the door, but when she sees me the smile she wears fades down to neutral. She rearranges her face and comes in. She nods at me, then crosses to the bed and starts checking tubes and drips. She's very thin, and she looks far too young. She has straight light-brown hair clipped back behind her ears and grey eyes set into a scrape of pale skin that barely covers her bones. I watch her. Her thin arms poke out from the short pink sleeves of her uniform, her hands on the tubes and machines are raw-looking, knobbly with bones.

"Where's Anne?" she asks me, a quick glance thrown in my direction.

"Away home for a rest."

She nods, tight-lipped.

"Are you the one lives down South?" She doesn't look up from the monitor.

"I am."

"She was askin' for you."

I'm startled. "She was?"

"She was, aye. Yesterday and the day before, over and over. *Ellen, Ellen, where's Ellen?* 'Twas all you'd hear out of her. Anne told her you were on your way, and she quietened down. She looked for you when she woke, so she did, but you hadn't come. Then she told Anne you were takin' your time, bein' on your way. Then she stopped askin'."

She's at the pulse now, my mother's limp wrist between her long, chapped fingers, her pale eyes veiled behind deep lids. The lids flick open, the eyes look straight into mine. I stare back, my hostility out around me like an unsheathed knife. Her eyes drop.

"Well I'm here now," I say.

So Brian was telling the truth after all.

Chapter 31

I phone home using a phone card. I ring from the public phone in the hospital or else from the hall of the B and B. I don't use the mobile. I've run the battery flat and told them it doesn't work from the North to the South. I can't risk them phoning me, unprepared.

I speak to Liam, and then I speak to Suzanna. Last of all Andrew comes on the line. I listen to his silence. I can see him as though he's standing beside me, the squirm of his body, his desperate, tongue-tied need. I can't manage the phone, nor the longing in me, can't find the words to reach him, though my need's near as desperate as his. So I tell him to put his father back on, and when Liam speaks I try using anger to push him away but it isn't any good, so I tell him I have to go. I put down the phone, then stand there and stare down the lighted corridor, seeing nothing.

"She said it won't be that long now, but they don't think today or tomorrow. She said we might think of a rota to stop us from getting too worn out."

Anne has been talking to the ward sister. Now she's talking to me. We walk the corridor, the night pressing black at the window.

305

A girl has just passed us, head down, her face stained with tears. I recognise her, she's the daughter from the room next door. We've watched them — the long, draining hours, the pain of the vigil, the sudden flurry when death finally comes. And now this bewildered departure.

Our turn next.

Brian and the girls are in with her. Soon Anne will take the girls home, and Brian and I will wait on.

"Brian doesn't want her left at all," Anne says. "He says he'll stay here all night, every night; he doesn't care what they say about it not being today or tomorrow, he won't have her die alone."

I look at Anne. She's near that place that's too tired to judge or argue, the place where you no longer try to change anything, you simply accept what someone says as fact and work from there. Yet she looks better than she looked when I came. Her hair has been washed, and she has on a skim of makeup; the shadows under her eyes are less black. I take her arm and turn her around, and we pace back the way we've come.

She likes being with me. It's strange, for she didn't before. I was Brian's wee sister, to be relied on to say the wrong things and do the wrong things, to upset Brian. I'm still Brian's wee sister, I still upset Brian, but it's different now, she's stripped down by exhaustion and vigil, and I am stripped down by this journey back through the years. And all in the space of thirty-six hours.

I like being with her too, which is even stranger. Brian I can do without, though I fell on his neck when I saw him last night. Two hours — that's all it took — by the end of two hours I'd forgotten the rush of joy at the sight of his face, at the sound of his voice, at the feel of his arms about me. Now we're thirteen and eighteen again. Implacable. If he says the corridor's white I'll swear on the Bible it's painted brilliant scarlet.

"I'll stay," I tell Anne, "if he's made up his mind he won't shift. You go with the girls, I'll bed down here in that room the nurses use, get a few hours' sleep on the floor, then send Brian home to his bed and sit with her till the morning. He can come back in before his work if he wants to. If he goes to his work at all, that is."

So I call Brian out and tell him the plan, and surprise, surprise, he agrees. The daughters are summoned. They stand looking down at the grey vinyl tiles and listen to their mother. Sometimes they shoot out a look to check on this half-new aunt of theirs, and see does she match with the story. They're good-looking girls, though it's too soon to say if the looks will last. Linda and Carol — fifteen and thirteen — they both have their mother's fine skin and Brian's brown eyes and that bloom that makes the young beautiful whatever may change later on. They wear school uniforms and carry their school bags. They've come straight from school for the second day in a row.

I can't read them at all. They're closed off from the adult world, deep in their good-girl acts, which they wear like cloaks around themselves, buying time inside to become whatever it is they're becoming. I feel no bond with them — they are snails, not yet ready to venture their little soft horns out to check on the air.

Yet I am sorry to watch them go off down the corridor, one on each side of their mother. They take with them the sweet everydayness of life and leave us here in mortality and sickness. I feel the lonely night world of the hospital closing around me.

"What did she say to you?" Brian asks.

We're banished to the corridor — the nurses are checking and measuring, going about their cool, arcane duties. It's three in the morning. I've slept fitfully for an hour or two in the nurse's room, then I've come to find Brian to send him home to Anne as I've promised.

He won't go. Or not now, not when I tell him to. Instead he is hanging about, unable to leave, and I'm cross, for I'm headachey and tired and I could be safe in my little room, sleeping.

"What did she say?" he asks again. "Anne said you told her she spoke to you."

"She did."

"Well?" He waits.

"She asked me did I still catch birds."

"What?"

"She asked me did I still catch birds." I say it again, though I know he heard me the first time. He's looking at me, but the eyes behind his heavy glasses are odd in their distance. I feel suddenly dizzy. It's as though I'm on this escalator that keeps changing direction; I try to step off, but I've forgotten where it was I wanted to go.

"D'you not remember?" I ask him. I can hear my own voice, supplicating.

"I do surely." He sounds short-tempered, almost annoyed. "What did you say?"

"I told her I did."

"And after?"

I wait. I don't want to tell him the next bit, but I have to. It's on account of the hospital and the death watch. And all the distant years coming crowding in.

"She said, *You have it off your father. Your father always had good hands.*"

"She said that?"

I nod. "Will you go on home now, Brian? I promised Anne I'd send you home."

"Did she say anything else?"

"Not a word. If you're not going, then I am. No point the two of us killing ourselves."

"You're only here and you're crying to be gone. Could you not watch with her a wee bit longer? She'll not be here next week to watch with."

"Neither will I, thank God."

"You were always the hard one, Ellen."

"What choice had I? When did I ever get any help from her?"

"She never had any help from anyone."

"There was help there if she'd wanted it." Suddenly I'm furious, shaking with rage, my whole being clenched in a knot of anger. I've no idea what's happening. "But she wouldn't take it, she couldn't stand to be beholden to anyone. And she didn't care how we suffered, so long as she had her pride."

"We didn't suffer."

"What?"

"You heard. We were well fed, well clothed, well minded. What more did you want? We didn't suffer."

I look at him, without seeing him. He is right. Whatever else it was that I'd wanted, it didn't have a name, or didn't exist, or couldn't be given. Had I ached for something from her that wasn't there? I see the dark, frantic wings of the trapped birds against the pane, their dive for shelter behind the flowerpots that stood on the sill, the storm of light pouring in through the sealed window. I feel their small lives beat in the cup of my hand, the softness of feathers, the way they struggled and fought, then suddenly stilled. They would raise up their heads from my hand and look round, their eyes bright, curious. I would carry them to the door and throw them into the air. I talked to them all the time — I never stopped speaking — and often I didn't catch them at all, I'd put my hand close and they'd hop themselves on, their small claws clinging onto my finger, their eyes alert and amazed. She was a great one for windows open and the virtues of fresh air. She always called for me when a bird had got into the room.

I am still now, the anger all gone. I am stilled in some hand that is holding me as I held a finch or a swallow all those years ago. I look at Brian, and this time I see him, I see the tears stand in his eyes. I feel the fall of tears down my cheek.

The days are harder than the nights, yet the nights are harder than the days. By day I feel empty and cold; somehow the con-stant people and noise and hospital clatter push me further into a place of alienation. All day I long for the night, but night comes bringing no relief. I'm alone with her, silence and darkness for company. The empty, cold feeling falls away, and a maelstrom of furious emotion rushes to take its place.

Even as I'm experiencing this, I'm amazed by it. My child-hood may not have been a bed of roses, but Brian's right, there hadn't been hardship, nor anything obvious to account for the chaos of feeling that kidnaps me now. And I've no one to turn to, no Catherine to phone, no Liam by my side, no safe ground any-where anymore.

So I stand with my back to her, watching myself in the great dark sheet of the window, the lit room behind me shimmered by rain that runs down the glass. Reflected, my mother lies propped on the pillows, her head drooping forward and lolling a bit to one side.

"After the first chemo most of her hair fell out, but it seemed to regrow overnight. This time they started the chemo then stopped," Anne had said. "It was doing no good, she's already too far gone."

Her hair had turned white after Daddy died, but if anyone asked her she claimed she'd been raven's-wing black, like her sisters. Years ago Brian had told me different; he'd said she'd been flame red like me. I'd called him a liar, for why would anyone say their hair had been black if it hadn't? He'd taken me up to his room, lifted his school *Macbeth* off the shelf, showed me the fading photo he kept between its pages. There she was, a young woman seated on a wall, swinging her feet, her hair a red flag on the green of the trees.

We had stared at it, the two of us, and then he'd put it back between the pages and closed the book. I'd asked why she claimed it was black, and he'd shaken his head, for he didn't know. He'd made me promise never to tell, and I never did, not even Liam. I'd understood why I had to promise. Somehow it was shameful to both of us, catching her out in that lie.

The funny thing is I was eight years old when he died, which is old enough, yet I've no memory of her hair being red at all. And now it's only the ruins of that hair that make me know for certain sure it's her.

By the second night the chaos inside me's so bad I start talking to her reflection. Or rather I talk to her hair, reflected. The bloated yellow face beneath it belongs to someone else.

But I don't talk as Anne talks, this isn't inclusion, it isn't a gentle mulling over of the day's events.

I'm calling her to account.

"I'm not here by choice," I tell her. "You needn't think I've wasted a thought on you in years —"

She doesn't stir.

I get braver, my words get harder and wilder. I'm trying to wake her up, to force her out from her stupor.

Nothing. I stand there addressing the bed-ridden figure that floats behind my other-self in the glass.

A strange feeling grows in me that there's no need to waken her, that if I speak to her in the black window, she'll hear me as she never heard when I spoke to her face to face. I get excited. I wonder why I haven't thought of this before. She's mine, I finally have her captive, she can't escape into silence or tasks-that-have-to-be-done, can't turn away, can't even answer me back. I drag the chair over to face the window, careful not to look at her form in the bed. I sit myself down and tell her about my life.

To start with it's like a first meeting, a sketching in of the principal figures and details, I'm not yet ready to trust her with more.

When I've done the outline I tell her about the journey up, I tell her about the B and B, making sure to include how much it costs because she always wants to know prices. I'm working up to my dream, which was really a memory. I tell her about it. I say she was wrong to punish us for using words she didn't like.

"If there's a word there's a reason for it. Words don't just come out of nowhere. An ugly word means an ugly feeling, you can't just ban the word and expect the feeling to go away. Or you can, but it's called repression. Did they not teach you that at school? Oh, pardon me, my mistake, you were the teacher —"

Still no reaction. I take a breath and forge on. "Ugly words are a form of bullying. So is banning them. You can banish a word, but not the feeling behind the word. It just stays down there, festering, getting stronger, turning into a hate that's worse than it was at the start —

"Did you not know that?" I demand of her slack-jawed face in the window. "Did you not know you were fostering hate? And did it not once cross your mind that some of that hatred might splash over onto you?"

After that there's no stopping me. I'm off in full flight when the door on the far side of the bed opens in the window, and that nurse is there, the undernourished one with the light-grey eyes.

She stares at the back of my head, but I don't move. Let her think what she likes, what's she to me, why should I care?

She comes in and goes to my mother. She's on the door side of the bed, so I watch her reflection in the window.

She can't stand me — a babe in arms could see that. Well, I've no great grah for her either.

"What's your name?" I ask her window-face as she takes my mother's wrist in her hand and checks her pulse. She doesn't reply till she's finished counting.

"Joanne," she says, replacing the wrist on the cover. "Joanne Doherty."

"You like her, don't you?"

She looks startled. "She came in for the chemo the last time," she says slowly. "Just for the day, like — the chemo's all out-patients here. I got to know her then. We all liked her, so we did, she had a word for everyone and she never complained —. But she always looked for me first when she came in."

"What have you got against me?"

She drops her eyes, and the colour beats in her pinched skin. She knows I'm way out of line to ask, but she's out of line herself, she shouldn't have got involved like this, and once she had she shouldn't have let it show. She lifts her face, and for what suddenly seems a long time the blue-grey eyes in the window look straight into mine.

"You didn't come," she says at last, the words so low that I only just catch them. "She was askin' for you and askin' for you, and you didn't come."

"I'm here now."

"Now's too late. She wanted to talk to you, so she did."

"She should have thought of that before," I say to the window.

"Before what?"

"Before she got herself into this state."

She doesn't speak. She walks round to the other side of the bed to check on the liquid in the drip. She has her back to the window now, so her face is hidden.

"What did she ever do on you?" she asks without looking round. Her voice comes from just behind me.

"Nothing," I tell her narrow back in the window. "Not a thing, that's the point; she only ever gave us what she had to. And that was only to stop the neighbours talking." It sounds weak and self-pitying, even to my ears. I know I need more.

"My husband's a Catholic," I say, knowing that this Joanne is one as well. "She never met my husband; she never forgave me; she never even came to see her grandchildren."

She stands for a moment, motionless.

"She told me you didn't want her to, and you never came home. She said you felt shamed by your husband. She said it was you as couldn't forgive yourself."

Then she's out the door and away off down the corridor and I'm left with all the air knocked from me.

Chapter 32

The third day, but it might as well be weeks, the intensity of this waiting swallows us all. I sit by her bed, take the odd walk round outside, sleep fitfully in the B and B or stretched on a padded seat in the nurse's room. Anne has brought in a sleeping bag, and the nurses give us blankets. They offer to put up a folding bed in the room with my mother, but I refuse it, there's no way I could sleep in there beside her. Brian is the same. He knows she wouldn't allow it.

Sometimes Brian and I take shifts with the sleeping bag, and it's like being back in childhood again — creeping in, smelling his intimate Brian-smell on the padded cloth.

Love is strange. You can't make yourself feel it, can't command it at will from anyone else; it just comes when it comes and that's it — the whole story — except that its coming is always, always grace. Well, there isn't much grace in me now — for Brian or anyone else — but the sleeping bag helps, and the dead exhaustion in his face makes me softer with him, less inclined to snap and contradict.

For the first two days I was here, Brian went into work, though he must have been about as much use as a zombie. Maybe

315

he needed somewhere to go — like me with my little room in the B and B — or maybe he thought the school would grind to a halt without him.

The consultant says anytime now, so Brian has stopped going to work. Anne stays for most of the night, and the three of us live locked together, taking turns to go off to eat or to catch a few hours' sleep and a wash. Carol and Linda are mostly here, but they're still going to school in the day so Anne won't let them stay after midnight. She drives them home and comes back, or else Brian does.

Nothing is coming through to me here. I send my mind down to my hands to feel around for it, but nothing stirs.

Time was when I thought I'd have bartered my own child to be rid of it. But now when I need some help for myself it has fucked away off and left me to do it alone.

And now that it's gone I am nothing. It must be all those years of folk being grateful right down to the depths of their beings that has me this way. Gratitude makes for respect. I must have begun to think that it's me they're respectful of, that I'm somehow worthy of this respect. It makes up for so much. The long hours and loss of privacy. The distance from Liam. The time not spent with the children. The secrets that have to be kept.

So I've let myself think it was me, but it isn't. I've let myself forget I was only ever a channel for Whatever-it-is to pass through.

If you think it's you then you separate yourself somehow from humanity, and if there's one thing in the world I'm certain sure of it's that we're all the same. That's not the same as saying we're all born equal — you'd have to be blind and deaf to swallow that one — but we're all born into flesh, flesh that is mortal and suffers.

So all the time it was Itself, not me. I was only ever the glass that held the wine.

And it was the wine that was wanted, for who in their senses cares for the glass when they need to drink?

On the journey up in the bus, I'd thought about telling Brian. I'd even chosen the words I'd use, I'd answered questions with that fluency that's never mine outside of these conversations I have with myself inside my head. Now I think I must have been mad to have entertained the idea at all. Or maybe I've just been living too long amongst Catholics.

But it's hard being stripped of your trappings. It's been with me so long I don't know who I am now it's gone.

Visitors come every evening, some in the day as well. Men and women out of my childhood, uncles and aunts, cousins I haven't seen for years, towing shy country weans by the hand. A steady procession. Anne laughs and says that it's me that they're after.

"They want a *wee juke* at you, see have you grown two heads and webbed hands from living so far down South."

But Brian scowls and looks serious when we joke, and we learn to keep our chat for when he's out of the room.

She says his first loyalty went to his mother, that he tried to make up to her for the husband she'd lost, that he's always been baffled and hurt by his failure.

I look at her hard when she says this. She looks steadily back, then drops her soft, tired eyes.

"There were times in the early years I was jealous enough," she says. "I felt I had but half a husband."

She's right, I think, though I hadn't seen it before. Brian beside my mother's chair: a teenage boy, standing guard for his dead father.

Anne is generous, as I never have been. I think of Liam and Catherine, and something has changed but I don't know what. I stop because there is suddenly loss in my thoughts, and pain.

My aunts and uncles come into the room with us. The rest stand about in the corridors, country people from Dunnamanagh, chatting softly together. Before they leave, the cousins come briefly in to see her, their faces grave, their few words quiet and kind. Then they go back outside, collect up their children, make their farewells.

"They don't want to intrude," Anne says. "They're here to support us, not get in the way."

Anne's sisters come, and she goes out into the corridor to talk to them. Anne's neighbours come, never staying long, always leaving a basket or a covered plate behind them. I see that she's loved.

By midnight even the last of the old ones have gone, and we're left to ourselves. I miss them, their white hairs, their stooped, rheumaticky limbs, their steady acceptance of dying. And the fact that they claim her relieves me of some burden. She is Edith again — their sister as much as my mother — had been Edith before ever Brian and Anne and I had known her, is not entirely ours, nor her life entirely our fault.

Liam wants to come. We've argued over the phone. I tell him he's more use at home with the children.

I don't know what'll happen if Liam comes, and that's the truth. It's like being married to Robbie again — threatened on every side and only myself to rely on.

If he comes I'll be more vulnerable, everything could fall apart. If I do it alone I've a better chance of getting out intact.

I was drawn too far out of myself by that blowy black night

and the window. I went too far down a road I've no wish to travel, and now I'm afraid. It was that Joanne who called me back — the shock of what she said, the injustice.

I hate her now, and I want her to know it. If I meet her along the corridor I drop my eyes and move to the other side, and when she comes into the room I turn my back. She doesn't try to speak to me. She goes about her duties and then leaves.

I see Anne watch, then look at me, eyebrows raised, her eyes enquiring, trusting. *What's going on?* they ask.

I look at her and I make my gaze run through her to beyond. I think Anne remembers the old Ellen then — the hard young sister-in-law, foul-mouthed, eyes full of angry contempt.

I'll close myself up and hold on, get through this as quick and as whole as I can. Beyond that I dare not think.

They sent me off, my husband and my children, but I don't know what I'm doing or why I'm sitting here waiting for her to die. Brian is right, I grudge her even this. But she never softened herself to me nor helped me when I needed it, she judged me by her own relentless standards. I think this, yet I know I'm the same, and if she'd tried to help me I'd have done what I'm doing to Liam now and not have allowed her near me. Maybe it's pride, or maybe I don't know how.

Anne's on at me to move out of the B and B and stay in their house. It makes no sense, paying out all that money, she says, and not knowing how long it will be to the end. But the little room's a lifeline for me; sometimes it feels like the only anchor I have left.

When I was home, living my life, I thought that the Ellen who lived it was who I truly was. But now that I'm back in my-own-place-that-isn't-my-own-place I'm not so sure. Sometimes I feel there's a self that's behind the self I had thought of as me.

And sometimes when the self-that-I-thought-was-myself loosens its moorings I grow more aware of this other self, and I am afraid.

The odd thing is that this other self — this deeper, stranger self — increases my sense of disintegration. It has no name, you see, no identity nor personality nor any need of either. It makes no claims and is deeply, endlessly itself.

Chapter 33

Anne says she could have gone to the hospice to die, but she asked to stay here, where she knew the staff from the time before.

Anne says Brian wanted the hospice. He thought it would be easier and quieter for her there, but she wouldn't shift so he'd bowed to her choice.

I look at my watch. It's half past seven in the morning. Anne has sent Brian off for air and some breakfast. He didn't want either, but she told him he needed to keep up his strength so he went like a biddable child. I think of Anne as a passive wife, but I see now that she is for Brian what Liam once was for me: a safe anchorage from the turbulence and storms of my own nature. It's an authority right at the heart of their marriage, though mostly it stays well concealed.

Vigils are hard journeys into rocky and comfortless terrain, with no one knowing how they'll measure up till they've measured up or failed. You get so strange yourself that you hardly notice another's strangeness, and it's only after Brian has gone that I know the relief of his absence. I look at Anne, and I see that her shoulders have slackened, her hands lie loose in her lap, the room feels bigger, quieter, more at ease. Even my mother sinks deeper into unconsciousness, the sag of her form minutely more pronounced. So Brian's relentless concentration has reached her. His overwhelming will that she should live has stiffened her.

I go to the nurses' kitchen to make tea.

Joanne's in the kitchen. She's doing something at the work-top with her back turned to me. Her bony elbows stick out, her long, fairish hair hangs lank; her neck above the pink uniform looks stalklike and frail as a child's. I hesitate in the doorway when I see her, half turn, then turn back and make myself go in. She's seen my reflection in the window. She doesn't look round.

I go to the press for the delph, find a tray, drop tea bags into both cups, am busy being indifferent to her presence.

There's a yelp of pain to my left and a sudden clatter. A knife skids across the floor.

I don't know what happens next or where all the blood is coming from. I'm so tired that time seems to break into pieces that move themselves round and won't join up or make sense.

I don't know what happens except that I'm lifting my hand from her wrist, and the long open gash that I'm certain was there is a line of pink, puckered skin. There's blood on her hand, on the pad of her thumb, on the upper part of her wrist, but it's drying and smearing. And my hands are alive, though not in the old way, the emptiness is there, but they haven't stiffened and splayed.

Her eyes are like saucers.

Yet she accepts it, despite all that training, despite the high-tech machines she operates every day with such effortless skill.

I know this because of the look on her face. I know that she understands what's been done.

She brings her face close to mine.

"For Jesus' sake, would you not help her? Would you not help your own mother?"

"She's away beyond help." I can hear my voice, cold and hard. "There isn't a thing I can do —"

"Not help her to live, that's not what I'm sayin' at all. Help her to die —"

Her words are in my head, and I can't get them out.

I try to forget this vigil, to forget that the woman in the bed is my mother, to sense her as I'd sense someone anonymous and deeply sick and striving for release.

I stand by the window, staring out at the growing daylight. I've never done this before. I've never done anything before, it's all been done for me, I'm only even beginning to understand that now.

Suddenly I am flooded with an enormous pity. Pity for her, pity for us all. I see us standing, tiny figures viewed from low down, black against a vast and darkening sky. I see our immense mortality. I am filled with tenderness like awe.

I turn from the window and close my eyes. I'm like an egg that's being separated — the outer myself falls away like the gluey mass of the white slipping over the edge of the shell.

With the white gone, my being lies open and still and ready. That's the only way I can describe it. I feel nothing I can name or identify, but my spine undoes itself from its drooping wilt and straightens out. My shoulders drop and my breathing stills, and I feel both drunken and alert.

Then I see a bird, scrabbling frantic and dark against glass. I try to open my eyes, but I can't. I've gone too deep in, I can't bring myself far enough out to give my eyes the order, I have to stay inside with the bird. And I know not to coax or catch this bird, I know it can fly out itself — the window's open, it's trapped by its fear alone.

Inside myself, I lean forward, clap my hands loud and sudden. It shoots from the glass and is out through the window, a couple of little swooping dips, then it's gone into a darkness that's the same as light. My eyes fly open. I look at my mother in the bed, and I know she's gone too. As soon as I see her dead I know that I want her here, I haven't finished, there's so much still to be questioned and tested and understood.

But it's done, she isn't about to turn back, any more than a stranded seal will heave itself back up the beach once it's found the first wave of the sea.

Then the door opens and Brian is there. He makes a small, quick noise in his throat and is out again, yelling for a nurse. The nurse comes, puts a hand on the wrist for the pulse. Brian watches, white-faced and stunned. For a moment his eyes stare into mine, but there's no recognition. No tears either — he's somewhere too deep for tears.

Anne goes to him. Very gently her hands go up, one to each side of his face, and she stands there looking quietly into his eyes. A long, deep shudder runs through him, but still he can't weep. He puts his arms round her, buries his face in her shoulder, hides himself from my eyes. I feel as though I'm afloat in the room, no one to hold, no Liam to drop anchor in, no one to tell me what to do. That's a shock — the raw need I have for Liam when all through these days I've been trying so hard to push him away.

The room has filled up, the ward sister and a doctor and another of the nurses on duty. I hear Anne asking the sister if we can stay with her. The medical people dissolve away, and we're left as before. Anne goes to the bed, bends to kiss her dead mother-in-law, then looks up at Brian and asks will he phone the school.

"Ask them to put the girls into a taxi. They'll want to be here." She's stripping the drips from my mother's arms as she speaks, ravelling the tubes and hooking them loosely over the machines. I open my mouth to protest, then understand there's no need anymore, and the next thing I know I am helping. We pull down the sheets, then bend to her, one on each side; we lift and straighten her out, her body still warm and yielding under our hands.

"What are we doing?" I ask.

"Laying her out," she answers without looking up. "Making a start on it anyway. The undertaker will do the full job later on, but we'll do what we can for her while we still have her. Brian will be back here in a minute and the girls won't be long after. Then we can sit with her."

I move down to her feet and begin to strip away the tubes from her legs, careful to pull off the plasters in one swift motion so that it doesn't hurt. We push the machines away. Anne has taken a long grey silk scarf from her handbag. She places it gently under my mother's jaw and ties it on top of her head, the ends sticking out on either side, waggish and irreverent. She sees the effect and tucks the ends neatly in under the scarf, as she'd have liked. Together we pull up the bedclothes. Anne lifts the old, limp hands from under the sheet and places them on the breast. Her every movement is tender.

Some women have death built into them as surely as they have life. They know what to do, and they know how to do it, though no one has told them or shown them or taught them. I live my life with the sick, but I've rarely seen death, for I always refuse all requests to help with someone's passing. Now I feel neither fear nor distaste, yet I know that I've none of Anne's sure instinct. I watch her drawing the chairs to the bed, amazed that so plain and tired a face can hold such grace.

The minister comes, his face careful and solemn. The girls stand, their young faces open and damp. I'll have to wait to find out my emotions.

The minister finishes his prayers, takes up his hat, says he'll call up to arrange the funeral details later on. He summons Brian over on his way out and says something into his ear.

The door shuts behind him. Anne raises her eyebrows in question.

"He said not to forget they'll be needing the bed."

Which is true, but the hospital is graceful to the last. No one hurries us, they say we can sit for as long as we like.

So we do, or rather the others do. Not me. I light out — there's no way round it — I manage about half an hour, and then I can stand it no longer. When the dying's done, everything's done, that's the truth. All the wakes and the funerals in the world can't change that.

It's black dark when Brian's car pulls up alongside me. I've been wandering round the Glen for I don't know how long, looking for her in this place we once lived.

I haven't found her yet. Maybe she's travelling so close beside me I can't see her.

Brian's headlights slide over the pavement in front of me, and I step into the shadow. Funny how deeply reflex is printed inside you. It's years and years since I'd lived in a place where a cruising car might mean something best avoided.

Brian stops the car, reaches over, opens the passenger door, and calls my name. I glance back, but I'm so cold and numbed that I don't hear him. He calls again, and I hear him, though his voice seems a long way off.

"Get in, Ellen," he says.

She looked at me only the once, spoke to me only the once, for days and days she'd barely been there in her body at all. I've watched her die, pulled the tubes from her wrists and ankles, helped Anne straighten her limbs and tie up her jaw. Yet the minute the life left her flesh she was here like an overhead light switched on in a darkened room.

I get in.

I ran down the stairs and out of the hospital; I've tramped through the Waterside, over the bridge, all the long length of the Northlands Road, and she's been with me all the way, every step. And she stayed there in the hospital room with Anne and Brian and the girls. And she's in the car with us now. She was on the pavement beside me before I got in.

I try to do the seat belt up, but my hands shake so hard from the cold that I can't get the click-bit to click. Brian watches me for a moment, then leans across and does it for me. He turns the car round.

"How did you know I was here?"

He doesn't answer. I take a quick peek, and there's that muscle, jumping beside his jaw. Brian thinks people should do what they ought to do, he doesn't like it when they do what they want or need to do instead.

He turns the fan up to full, then switches it from windscreen to feet. If I'm grateful for the blast of heat I don't say so, I sit there staring ahead, not opening my mouth. If Brian won't talk then neither will I.

I'm not being difficult on purpose — that's what he won't understand. I'm all twisted up inside, exactly the same as he is. I'm doing the best I can in my way.

Yet I'm glad enough to be rescued from the pavements. There were lights behind the curtained windows of the house we'd once lived in, there were lights on in the houses where our neighbours had lived.

I watched people coming home, doors opening onto hallways where I'd once been welcome, light spilling onto pavements where I'd played. I found myself putting names on every family along the road, and that surprised me, for I never cared for such things, I'd always been too busy with itching to get away. Everything looked much as I remembered it looking, though the people I'd known didn't live here now, and the graffiti on the walls belonged to the other side.

"Who made the Prods leave?" I ask Brian now.

"It's Prods that force out Taigs, not the other way round," he says wearily. He sighs as though I'm an irredeemable irritation, yet one he's forced to tolerate through accident of blood. "No one 'made the Prods leave,' no drama, no mobs in the night. We went of our own accord."

I wait. Brian sighs again, but I know he'll be drawn. Never one to miss out on delivering a lecture is Brian. You'd know from half a mile away that he's head man in some school.

"A lot of police lived there in our day. Soft targets. Even the RUC came home to their beds —"

I go on waiting.

"The IRA took to shooting them on their doorsteps. A minor fucking detail that seems to have slipped your mind —"

"I remember," I say.

"So the ones who were still alive took it into their heads to move," he says. "A senseless notion, I grant you, but it avoided the inconvenience of being shot."

"And the rest?" I'm fed up with all this sarcasm and portentousness.

"The City Council built new houses on the Waterside. New houses, all mod cons, *a safe estate*. They moved. Now they're paying protection money to their own."

He glances over. *Do I need that spelled out as well?* the look says. But I haven't been gone that long, I know what he's saying.

"What does it matter, anyway? We're just bigots who want to keep Catholics under the heel."

"Well, it's true, isn't it?" I'm angry now. Back four days after twelve years, everything different, everything still the same. "No jobs, no votes, no housing. When they tried to change things peacefully they were attacked."

"It *was* true, Ellen. It's not true now. It's not about that anymore."

"What is it about then?"

Brian stares ahead. We've swung left off the Northlands Road, and we're dropping down past the big, smug houses of the Rock Road. His silence goes on so long I think he's not going to answer me, but he does. "Hatred," he says slowly. "That's what it's always been about. Three hundred years that was yesterday. We got their land, they want it back, and they want us away to hell. And they want to walk on our faces just like we walked on theirs." He stops, and I think he's finished but he hasn't. "You can add in fear to that. They were afraid, living under us, and now we're afraid of living under them. They say if we can't take what's coming we should go back where we came from. But it's not as simple as that, Ellen. No one wants us, we've been here too long, there's nowhere to go back to."

I don't speak. It's true, but it's his problem, not mine. I can't get my head back into the mind-set that thinks a country not governed from Britain's unsafe. We turn right onto the Strand Road at the bottom. It's desolate down here, the wide street all but empty, the half-derelict buildings like stage sets for a film. A long wall of corrugated sheeting lifts and bangs in a bitter wind straight off the Foyle.

Further on it doesn't look so bad. There are lights and new bars and aging new supermarkets. A few passersby walk fast, heads down, collars up, a hand at the neck to clutch the coat tighter in round them.

"You can let me off here," I say. Brian slows for the lights, but they change to green as we reach them. Brian puts his foot down and accelerates round the corner.

"Brian, let me out. I need to go back to Great James Street."

"What for? I've been there. Your things are in the back. You're staying at the house."

"I've not paid —"

"I've paid. And no more runners. I haven't the time to be driving round looking for you."

"I don't want to stay at your house —"

"I don't give a shit what you want, Ellen. Your mother just died, the house is filling up, Liam's coming tomorrow —"

"Liam? You rang Liam?"

"You heard."

"Let me out —"

He doesn't even slow down.

"Brian, let me out, you've no right to do this, you'd no right to ring Liam —"

"Says who?" His voice is angry and hard. "Liam's mother-in-law just died — his children's grandmother — he's a right to be told. Anyway, it was Anne who phoned, she thought you might have gone back on the bus, she wanted to know if you'd rung for him to meet you. When he said you hadn't she sent me out looking —"

"How did you know I'd be in the Glen?"

"A wee bird told me."

There's no one like a brother to press all your buttons and

take you straight from flat calm to blind rage. I'm twelve years old again, and my hand flies up to smack him one hard on the nose. I catch myself on just in time, force my hand down, then sit on it to stop it from doing a repeat performance.

"I knew because I knew," Brian says. "You're not the only one that's psychic around here."

I hear him, but it takes a minute for the words to sink in. I sit staring ahead at the buildings flicking past, the car lights flicking past. He doesn't speak again till we're over the bridge and back in the Waterside.

"I wouldn't have your other gifts, but." His voice is heavy and sneering. "They must come with the red hair. Liam tells us you're doing great business, can't keep up with the demand. He says you've always had your wee gift, though it's stronger these last years." There's a longish pause, so I know there's more coming. "Funny you never let on about it up here. But then I'd say you're well used to keeping things to yourself. I'd say you don't talk much about your wee visit to the mental hospital now that you're living down South."

The shock of what he says runs through me. I sit rigid, trying not to show that he's scored a hit. I glance at his hands on the wheel, the set of his face in the passing headlights. The strangeness of this day is strong upon me: the vigil and our mother's death; this intertwining of our lives when I'd thought the threads long cut.

They had never been cut, nor ever would be, not in life nor in death. Brian dwells inside me. Our ancestors dwell inside me. Their furious unbelief is mine as much as Brian's.

But the longer I sit in this car, hands now quiet in my lap, looking ahead, the less there is in me of hurt or rage at either Brian or Liam. This sudden gift of an inner peace is something I'm coming to know, though I have no understanding of it.

There is nothing to say. I'm filled with an emptiness that watches from a long way off.

I walk through her kitchen door, and Anne's cutting sandwiches. She looks up, smiles, then sees the expression on Brian's face behind me. She puts down the knife and takes me upstairs. She draws the curtains across the spare-room windows, assures me the bed is aired and comfortable, smoothes a pillow with her hand. I ask was it her or Brian that Liam had told about the Healing?

"Brian."

"When you were phoning to get me to come?"

She shakes her head. "A couple of years ago. They'd told your mother she needed a mastectomy, so Brian was ringing to let you know. Liam answered the phone. He said you were working, and he didn't know when you'd be finished; it was someone who'd come without an appointment. Then Brian asked him what it was you were working at, and Liam told him." She picks up the towel she has laid on the dressing table, refolds it, hangs it over her arm. "And then your mother decided she didn't want us to tell you, so Brian never rang back. But Brian said they had quite a wee chat. . . . Did Liam not mention it at all?"

"Not a word."

"Men are funny sometimes."

"What did Brian say?"

"About the people coming to you?"

I nod. She can't say *healer*.

"He was a wee bit upset to begin with, but then he calmed down. He didn't talk about it after that, but I think deep down it made a sort of a sense to him." She pauses, looks down at the towel, takes courage. "He'll sometimes know things ahead himself. . . . Sort of premonitions."

"What kind of things?"

"There was a Saturday there, a few years back, and Carol was heading off into the town. He lost his temper with her over nothing and wouldn't let her go. Later there was a bomb in the town — the very street that Carol would have been in, and at the exact same time. A wee girl in Linda's class lost her leg, but no one was killed. Later he told me he knew not to let her go, but he didn't know why. He picked the fight because he couldn't help himself — it was on account of the strange tight feeling he had inside him. It frightened him, knowing like that. Is that the way it is for you?"

I shook my head. "I never know anything about the children or Liam. Mostly it's only about the people who come to me. Sometimes I'll know what's wrong with them before they've anything said. If it's an injury then I might know how they got it. Things like that."

"Brian said he was on a long time with your Liam, I think he surprised himself. He said Liam had his feet on the ground, yet he sounded as though he believed in what you were doing. . . . And he didn't think Liam was looking for money. I'd say that surprised him as well."

"Healers are all quacks and charlatans?"

She blushes and smoothes the towel on her arm. "Something like that. Does it work, Ellen?"

"Sometimes it does and sometimes it doesn't. It works enough for people to talk, then others come because of what they've heard."

Anne nods. She's backing slowly out of the room, but she turns when she gets to the door.

"It's good she died, Ellen. She held off the morphine as long as she could, but the pain got too bad. I know it's hard when you hadn't talked, but at least you got to see her."

What is there to say? And besides, I'm not angry with anyone anymore, and the curious, empty calm I felt in the car is still with me.

I unpack my things then there's a knock on the door, and Linda comes in with that towel again and a pot of tea and a sandwich. I'm glad of the tea, but I wave the food away. Linda looks at the sandwich and says that her mother's told her not to come back till she's seen me eat the lot.

I make myself take a bite. Chicken. I'm surprised at the surge of appetite rising to meet it.

After she's gone I wash my face and sit on the bed, but the doorbell keeps ringing. There are footsteps and voices, doors being opened and closed.

I get up from the bed and go cautiously out to the kitchen. Anne's face is soft and bright when she sees me. I hold the tea tray in my hands, and she smiles and asks if I want more.

I shake my head.

She says Aunty Doreen and Uncle Tom and Aunty Hazel are in the front room along with some cousins and neighbours. She says she thinks Brian will like it a lot if I go in and sit with them. If I don't mind too much, that is?

So I go into the front room, and Brian looks up and smiles for all the world as though he's pleased to see me. He shows me into an armchair, and I sit there like Lady Muck, doing nothing to help at all.

People come and go. There are colleagues from school, as well as relations and neighbours. They come with quiet faces to say that they're sorry, they sit for a while then they leave.

I see that Brian and Anne have no friends that are only friends. There are people they're close to, and some of their colleagues and neighbours they love as friends, but there's no one like Catherine has been for me.

What had Catherine been to me before she turned into the woman who'd slept with my husband?

Someone who sought me out and spent time with me when she didn't have to. Who liked me enough to keep coming round until something alive and wholly itself had grown up between us. And all this without much response from me and before she fell for Liam. Of that I was certain now.

These jolts we get that open a crevasse right behind the place where our feet are planted. A crevasse so wide and deep that everything that went before lies now on the other side forever. Her death had opened this crevasse, and I couldn't cross back over.

So I sit in Anne's cream-coloured armchair making conversation. Sometimes the aunts shoot quick, shrewd looks at me, but the uncles' eyes are kinder.

Chapter 34

The kitchen is swept, the dishes are done, the girls are away up the stairs to their beds.

Brian and I are drinking whiskey. Anne has a pot of tea set down on the hearth beside her. Linda made it. Those girls are minding their mother as though she's next on the list. We're all so tired we aren't tired anymore, we're in that odd, lucid drifting state that is way past tiredness.

Brian's talking about Daddy's funeral. Anne's listening. All this was away before her time, she hadn't any place in it. Neither had I, or not that I remember, but Brian keeps telling me I had.

"It was June — hot, but a stiff wee breeze blowing, the chestnuts tossing about. He was buried from Doreen and Tom's — Gran's house, the house where she was reared. When I think of that house it's always the chestnuts I see. People came from all over, they were that shocked — he was young, he'd never been sick, no one had thought of his heart. Sometimes I think it might have been easier for her if he'd been shot or blown to bits at a customs post, which was happening a lot at that time. Compensation money and special status. Someone to blame when the going was tough."

Brian bends and refills his glass. He waves the bottle at me, but I shake my head.

"There were benches and chairs set out in the yard for the overspill. But the minister looked at the day and he looked at the crowd and he told us he'd say the service outside. D'you not remember that at all?"

I shake my head again. I don't remember.

"She never wanted you there, she said you were too young, but you had her tormented. Then Doreen took your side, and the end of it was she gave in. She was sorry, but. You started roaring and crying the minute he talked about Daddy. Doreen had to take you inside and away up the stairs to put a stop to your noise." His eyes have that inward look people get when they're remembering.

"I stood beside her all through the service. I wanted to stay with her afterwards, but Gran sent me off with the men, to walk behind the coffin. I remember turning my head to look back, I remember big splashes of sun and shade on the road, and the trees, a green tunnel. . . . She was there, away off at the end of the tunnel, standing stiff as a ramrod in front of the women. She never cried, not once, and her hair blazed red in the sun. It wasn't as red as yours is, Ellen, but it fairly blazed that day — I'll never forget it. The next morning she had Hazel cut it all off, and she never grew it again. Inside six months it was white. When I try to place things that happened round then I call up her face, and if her hair was red it was before and if it was white it was after. But I can't ever see *him,* no matter how hard I try. All I see is that framed photo of him she had in her room in the house in the Glen. Can you see him, Ellen? Or is it the photo for you as well?"

I suppose there is always someone who wants to remember everything, because overwhelmingly they have loved whoever it is that has died and they've long since passed into that love all that was hard for them at the time. So the hard things aren't hard anymore, they are changed for them by this love, and it doesn't seem to occur to them that it's not like this for us all.

And I suppose there's also always someone like me — caught up in a chaos of feeling, so that every memory's a touch that falls sometimes on scars and sometimes on opened flesh.

It's painful for me, this remembering. But there's something between us now that's never been here before, and might not be again. So I shut my eyes tight and I try.

It's no good, my mind won't go back there, it's stubbornly parked in this room.

"I don't remember a thing, Brian. You're telling me I was there so I believe you, but I don't remember him even dying, only that he was dead. And I only remember that because we moved. For years I thought that's what happened, that everyone got to live in a new house after their Daddy had died. I was only eight years old."

"Eight's not so young. There's plenty I remember from when I was eight."

"Well I don't. And I don't remember feeling anything either. Only that he went off and left us with *her*."

Brian gives me one of his looks. *Only ever thinks of herself*, the look says.

"Why was he buried from Gran's house?" I ask him, changing the subject. "Why not from our house, where he'd lived?"

Brian shrugs. "I don't know. He wasn't from here, remember, he was from Glasgow, and our house was small and only rented. I suppose it seemed natural to her to bury him from her first home."

"But she owned that house we moved to in Derry?"

"She did. She paid the deposit from his insurance money. The mortgage came out of what she earned."

I nod, satisfied at hearing him reiterate what I already knew. "She always thought we were better than other folk because our house wasn't rented," I tell Anne. "She tormented the life out of us with her standards."

"She wanted to do the best she could by us," Brian says. "To make up for us having no father."

"She could have given us one, easy enough. No one was stopping her marrying again."

Brian looks shocked, and even I think I'm out of order. I don't know what made me say it except the old habit of getting a rise out of Brian. Besides, it's a stupid remark, she wasn't the type to go courting a second time.

"I don't think she could have done that," he says slowly, from out of a small pool of silence.

"Because of the way she felt about him?" Anne asks.

He shakes his head. "Not even that, though he was the world to her, and his death must have been some shock. No, I think it was more that in marrying him she'd gone against all she'd been reared to. Then there she was, a widow, still only in her thirties. About the age you are now, Ellen."

Even through the exhaustion and whiskey I feel something stir in me. Some knowledge I don't want.

He looks at me then, but his gaze is still turned in.

"I think she was strange about it," he goes on, his voice hesitant, as though he's feeling his way over rocks. I see his small-boy self now — his blue T-shirt and his bare legs. Seawater, rainy white light.

"She told me once she thought she'd been punished for marrying out," he says. "Punished by God. I don't think she ever trusted life after that."

"Marrying out?"

Brian looks at me, his face neutral.

"Daddy being a Catholic," he said evenly. "Did you not know?"

Of course I didn't know. Why else would I be sitting here, mouth open like a fish?

And he knows I didn't know. I'm wise to Brian — look at the cunning way he's slipped it in.

I catch myself on and close my mouth. I'm not about to give him the satisfaction of seeing the shock he's given me. Or at least of him seeing any more of it than he's already seen.

"You mean he turned?"

Alright, he might have been Catholic once, years ago, before ever he was my father. That was possible. Just.

"It was a mixed marriage, Ellen. Exactly like you and Liam. He never turned, he was always a Catholic." Brian is speaking slowly, spelling it out. "He just didn't go to chapel."

"I don't believe it," I say furiously, yet I do. Somewhere, I don't know where, the missing piece of some arcane mechanism has been reinserted into the place where it belongs. I hear the interlocking of tiny cogs and wheels, feel the mechanism beginning slowly, slowly to revolve.

But still I protest. "It isn't true," I say. "It can't be, it just can't —"

"Why not?"

I search around desperately. "He used to say *our church*. He used to say, *one of our own —*"

"I thought you'd forgotten it all?" he says, a sneer in his voice.

"Not all," I tell him. "Only the things you're trying to bully me into remembering." I turn to Anne. "I'm right, he knows I'm right. Daddy said those things, so he did. He talked of Protestants as *our own.*"

Anne's head rests on the back of her chair, she looks too tired to speak. But her eyes are on me, full of unspilled tears. I turn away. If Anne's looking at me like this then it must be true.

"Think about it, Ellen, think about it a wee minute." Brian is leaning forward now, persuading. "You're right, he did say *our church*, but that was for her, he never went inside that church. And the same with the other side — his own side. He never went to any church at all."

"But why would he have pretended like that? I'm married to Liam, I haven't turned, I've never pretended to be a Catholic, and I never will."

"But you might have thirty years ago," Anne says. "You might have if you'd lived in the North."

I shake my head furiously.

"I think maybe he started it to make life easier for her," Brian says slowly. "He was from Glasgow, remember. It's the same there, he'd have known the score. And this was a temporary posting. They thought they were going to England, they never thought he'd be made permanent *here*."

He pauses, sighs. "Maybe once they'd started it the moment never came to stop. . . . Think of it, Ellen. *Hold on now, I'm not one of yous at all, I'm a Taig.* Maybe the secret closed around them. Her mother was strict, remember. She had no time for mixed marriages, and Grandda was the same. He wasn't long dead when she married Daddy. She was awful fond of him; it must have been hard flying in the face of his beliefs."

"Where were they married?" I try to call up a wedding picture and fail.

"Glasgow. Nobody went. When I was fifteen I got it into my head that she must have been pregnant. I went through her things, found the certificate. It was a Registry Office, but she wasn't pregnant. I know they told Doreen and Tom the truth, and they helped her keep it from Gran, but I don't know if she ever said a word to Hazel or Elizabeth. For all I know they may both be in the dark to this day." Brian stops abruptly, sits back from his leaning pose, sighs deep into himself. He looks straight at me, his eyes intense. "And, Ellen — don't you remember? He always said that there wasn't a choice, you were born into one or the other, and no one should ever be blamed for what they were —"

I nod. I can't speak, but I remember those words. The grandfather clock draws itself up and begins to whirr. It came from Gran's house, and it chimes every quarter, I know it from the front room of our house in the Glen, and I never liked it. I look at my watch. One in the morning. It chimes all the quarters, then strikes the hour. When it's through I wish it would start again.

"How do you know all this?" I ask into the silence.

"She told me. Years ago — I was about seventeen. She didn't like the company I was keeping, she thought I was getting involved. She wanted to shock me into staying well clear of the paramilitaries, and it worked. She made me promise I wouldn't ever tell you."

"You're telling me now."

"I am. But she's gone now, I've kept my word."

"She's here in this room."

"I know that, Ellen, but she doesn't mind anymore and it's your story too. Perhaps I should have told you a good while back."

"She gave me a hard time about Liam. . . . Yet she'd done the very same herself —"

"She never said a word against Liam, not once, not in all these years. Not even when you were living with him and still married to Robbie."

"She said nothing at all, not a bloody word, and you know what that meant." I am angry now, the pain of these old, fierce, worn-out secrets makes me suddenly savage. "It meant what you'd done was so bad she wouldn't soil herself even mentioning it."

Brian sighs and leans forward again in his chair. "She was a Presbyterian, Ellen, and she believed it. She had nothing against Catholics — nothing at all — but she didn't like Rome and she didn't like graven images and she didn't think priests should stand between God and the people. She didn't want your children raised Catholics — not because she didn't like Catholics, but because she didn't want them taught idolatry by priests. Don't blow out your breath like that — that's how she saw it, and you know it. She had nothing against you marrying Liam, but she thought if she'd taught you right then your children wouldn't be Catholics now."

"They're not Catholics."

"Their father's a Catholic, they live in the South, they go to Catholic schools. Are you seriously trying to tell me they're Presbyterians?"

I look him straight in the eye. "They have minds of their own," I say stubbornly. "And what about truth? *Tell the truth and shame the devil.* She was never done telling us that. And right at the heart of her life she's nursing this lie."

"I know," he admits. "You're only hearing it now, but I've been over and over it in my mind all these years and still I can't reconcile it. The first lie I can understand, but why keep it secret once he was dead and buried? So as not to upset her mother? To make our lives easier? Because she was ashamed of what he was?"

That's what that nurse said she said about me, I think. Is it true? Was it true for her? And if it's true for me — though I'm not saying it is — is that how she knew?

"Perhaps she was afraid they'd dig him up," Anne says quietly.

"*What?*" It sounds so weird, I think it some strange kind of joke, but Anne's voice has been matter of fact.

"He was a Catholic lying in Presbyterian ground," she says. "Maybe she thought they'd make her move him if they knew. She

343

couldn't exactly have gone round making enquiries, however discreet. Maybe she wanted to lie beside him when her turn came. "

Brian looks at her. "That might be it, but still she could have told her own family, especially once her mother had died. . . . And she might have told Ellen about her own father."

"Maybe she didn't know how," Anne says.

Brian goes on looking at her, but as though he hardly sees her.

"What about his family, why didn't they come to the funeral?" I ask.

He turns back to me.

"He was an only child, his parents were dead — or that was his story. But there must have been someone. Cousins. Uncles and aunts. It could be she never told them."

It's my turn to stare.

"She'd never met them, she told me that. She said she'd never wanted to." Brian tosses back the rest of his whiskey and sets down the glass. "And it wasn't only her that was head over heels in love. *He thought the flowers sprang up where I trod* — that's what she said to me. Imagine it, Ellen, a woman like her coming out with something like that. But those were the very words that she used, I'm not about to forget them."

After that, we go up to our beds. What is there left to say?

I hit the mattress thinking I'll sleep like the dead, but I've reckoned without the thing-that-comes-visiting. When I lie down the part of me that I think is myself falls away, and some other self comes up from a place so deep underwater that light doesn't penetrate that far.

I'm filled with the same strange emptiness I felt in the car. I'm completely here and not here at all; I can't think, yet there are thoughts drifting across, touching down, lifting off, like thistledown in a wandering breeze.

I no longer doubt Brian's story, but the world has changed colour and shape. Soon I'll forget this time, but for now I still know both before and after: before her death and after it; before the secret and after it.

I don't hold with those who want to uncover all secrets, yet here is a secret that gathers harm to itself, of this I am sure.

I neither judge my mother nor understand her. I judge no one, understand no one, not even myself, especially not myself, for there seems to be no one in residence to be judged. There are times in the past when I've sensed this someone who lives behind the *me* that thinks and loves and hates and fears and wants, and I've wondered who this someone might be and what is her name? Now I know that she has no name and wants nothing. She's stronger than me, unconcerned with me, yet she has no mortal existence without my being.

I pull back the covers and swing my legs over the side of the bed and feel my way to the door. I switch on no light, for I need the dark. I open the door and make my way down the stairs, my feet in the soft deep pile of Anne's carpets. In the kitchen I find the phone without remembering where it lives, and the orange light that the streetlamps cast is enough.

I have a terrible need to smell Liam and touch him and hear his voice. My mother is beside me, and her longing for Daddy after he'd gone flows into me, engorging my longing for Liam. The phone rings and rings, but I know that he'll come. Then he picks it up and I hear his voice.

I can't speak. I see him as though he's standing before me, but this is no Seeing, it's the breathing, unreal reality of the imagination.

"Ellen? Is that you?"

I can't answer.

"Ellen?"

"Yes." A whisper.

Suddenly all my hurt and rage and my distance from Liam collapse like a building scheduled for destruction after the fuse has carried the spark and the dynamite has blown. Liam is Liam — himself, and not me. His is the life that I live alongside.

"Ellen," he says. "Ellen, it's alright."

"Yes," I say, and I put the phone down very gently.

I have one more call to make, and I know the number by heart.

When Catherine answers her voice is alert, only tinged at the edges with sleep.

"Catherine?"

"Ellen. Dermot told me. I'm sorry. So sorry. Was it hard?"

"No. Not hard." I see the bird fly to the light. "You're seeing Dermot . . . ?"

"I am. I lost the run of myself back there, but I've calmed down now, I'm starting to see things a bit straighter." A pause, then an intake of breath. "Can I see you? Can I come up with them tomorrow?" Her voice is eager, almost joyful.

"What about Danny?"

"He's on a bottle now, I can leave him with Fran for a couple of days. Sure he thinks she's his Mammy anyway, he'll be delighted —"

I feel the gladness rise up in me at her tone.

"Not yet," I say. "Stay with Danny. But soon."

"Alright, whatever you say. As long as it's not too long. I'll pray for her while I'm waiting." A low, mocking laugh. "In my own peculiar way." A pause. "How's Brian?"

"Anne's a very humbling woman."

"Is she now? So is Fran. I've decided I like humbling women."

"We're not."

"No, definitely not. How's your Dark God? Did He come for you yet?"

"He did. He picked me up, then He set me back down. I wasn't to His liking."

"I told you. Even God needs permission."

"Who from?"

"You, of course — the you that is God. It's all inside God or He wouldn't be God." She sounds surprised that I've asked.

"Catherine . . ."

"Yes, Ellen."

"My father wasn't a Presbyterian."

"We all have our problems."

"I'm serious. He was a Catholic."

A small silence. "You just found out?"

"Brian told me."

She starts to laugh. An infectious laugh, and I feel myself joining in, which is strange, for I want to weep. She stops.

"Ellen," she says seriously, "when you get to the border, don't let that Dark Fella across. Send Him back up there, where He belongs."

"It isn't only up here He comes visiting. Your lot down there know all about Him as well."

"You're right, but the Old Fecker's losing ground at last, thank God. We're learning to live in life."

I put down the phone again, equally gently.

Upstairs, I get back into bed. The emptiness has left me, and I am myself again, even my body is normal. Thoughts fly about. It matters that Liam and Catherine have fucked, and it doesn't at all. Liam's still my husband, Catherine's still my friend.

Then I am small, and I'm looking out through an upstairs window. There's a column of men and boys wearing stiff, dark clothes, and they're moving off down a road splashed with sunlight and shadow. They walk down the leafy green road, and the young ones look like the old ones look, and it could be another century.

She had held him too tight to let him go back to his own, even in death. But maybe she'd craved lying beside him when her turn came.

I slide into sleep.

Chapter 35

I stop by the rail and stand watching a shag afloat on the river. One minute it's there, then it makes a quick lep and vanishes under the swirling brown water. A wrinkle furrows the surface, then that, too, smoothes out. All trace of it's gone — like my father's secret.

I watch for what seems a long time. It pops up again a good bit further on, then cruises along, its knavish black head in the air. Big and solid and real. Then lep, it's away down under the water. The secret — surfacing, disappearing.

Cormorants and shags — she'd made us learn the difference. The teacher in her, holding us to species and identification. I always liked shags, blacker and wickeder-looking than cormorants.

Now I think of the starling flocks that move across the stripped winter landscape at home; how you'll hear and look up to this great rush of birds, lifting and diving and turning. I think of the ravens, afloat on the airstreams. Of the crows, going home at the fade of the light, hundreds on hundreds, flowing and flowing, the winter sky filled with their tide.

Dark birds, ruffianly dark birds, stronger than birds of light and better survivors. They are the undervoice, scavenging life, living off gleanings. Uncivilised. Shameless. Outside all law. They allow the return of the soul.

It's early still, the morning rush hour not yet over, the cars still piling fast down the big road behind me. This river walk's new since my time, a neat railed path replacing the jumble of warehouse and shed and empty lot. The shag's through with fishing; it's heaving up into the air, wings hitting strong off the water. For a moment its flight path shines on the river then fades in the cloudy light.

Lies breed more lies, that's what she'd taught us. She should know. There could be Catholic second cousins in Glasgow.

I'd woken early to a sleeping house, was out of the bed and into my clothes before I rightly knew what I was doing. I hadn't run a tap nor boiled a kettle for fear it might wake them, but this time I'd left a note. It said why I'd gone and told them not to come looking.

It's freezing cold by the river; I head up into the town. Breakfast. My stomach sounds like a practice session with a Lambeg drum. I sit at a table in a café on the Strand Road, getting myself onto the outside of a pot of tea and a fry. I can't stay, though I want to: I'm too restless, it's too warm and safe. I pay and go outside, but I don't know where it is I need to be.

In front of me is Shipquay Street and the girdle of Derry's Walls. On a whim, I'm through the city gate and climbing the steps.

I've never walked the Walls before because you couldn't before — they're strategic. The British Army lived up here — guns and barbed wire and big steel gates kept firmly locked and guarded. Now the metal gates stand open, and the barbed wire's all but gone. The fort's here still — an unlovely place of high metal walls — and above are the look-out posts, and higher still are the masts. Her Majesty's forces, surveying the citizens of Derry.

It's snowing now, that fine, blithery snow that wanders about, sometimes descending, sometimes meandering back up where it came from. The walkway along the Walls is lethal with frozen sludge. I inch my way up the steep bit, holding on tight, like an old one afraid for her life of a fall.

She'd loved the snow, would come bursting into our bedroom throwing the window wide, letting the warmth stream out, pound notes floating up to the frosty sky. She must have been young then, out there throwing snowballs in the snowy garden of my childhood. Younger than I am now. As young as she'd ever let herself be in her life.

She'd never been young again after he'd died.

Fires laid but not lit. Clothes darned. Shoes patched. Leftover food for tomorrow's dinner. Making ends meet — a widow's lot. Not that she'd ever been anything but careful: thrifty and frugal and clean in the Scots-Presbyterian tradition. But he'd eased her. His presence had opened her out. She had laughed. Suddenly I remember that, though I haven't before. Later her laughter was never more than a social activity, signifying tolerance of such things in others. A polite wee sound.

I love the snow — I have that from her — though my feet are wet through and my hands are so cold I can't feel them. I want to see it on the ruffed fur of the cattle and horses at home, dusting the slopes of the mountains, shining their crests. *Want* is too weak a word. I *long* for it — that's the truth. For snow is precious, and beasts and mountains are home now, and precious and home belong together. Thinking this makes me long for Liam again. I want the children as well, though there's pain in the thought of them here, the place I've denied them.

Home. Down South. Only days away now. Days that might as well be years, for they seem that far off.

They'll have set off by now. I'm glad they're on their way, glad to be glad, for I'm sick and tired of the passions of my own nature. Yet I'm panicked as well, for once they're here I'll be part of them, and I need to find out what the secret means while I'm only me, and alone.

The snow steadies and thickens. I lean on a rampart and watch a schoolgirl who stands in the street down below me. She's still, her eyes are shut tight, her tongue is out catching the snow, her hands are thrust deep in the pockets of her dark-green blazer. A hot, red, healthy tongue — the snowflakes melt the instant they touch down. She opens her eyes and sees me watching, grins joyously, strolls off like a young one walking a meadow in early summer, the air warm, the sky a stretch of mild blue.

I walk on, stop again, look down on the houses and streets that wash round the sloping skirts of the old walled city. I can see the Free Derry Corner and the murals on the gable ends. The dead schoolgirl stands there, dressed forever in the innocence of childhood. Further down Bishop Daly goes on waving his white handkerchief on Bloody Sunday. Murals of martyrdom and grief. The moral high ground. Different altogether from the gable ends of the Waterside. There it's ArmaLites and flags and *No Surrenders*.

All the political changes, yet the bottom line is still the same word, which is *careful*. Careful who you speak to, careful what you say, careful who you choose to look in the eye. And no identification marks outside your own territory. No badges, tattoos, uniforms, no talk that might give you away. Peace it may be on paper, but on the streets and in the houses it's an armed and arm's-length peace.

I'll tell Liam Daddy's secret, and he'll think it surprising and strange. But that will be the end of it — no big deal.

It's their lives, Ellen, not ours. Let it alone. It doesn't matter. It all belongs in the past. I am hearing him speak.

And he'll be right, but he'll be wrong, and his words will make me lonely. But I'll say nothing, for I'm sick of defending what I've no will to defend anymore.

Below me the snow is falling on the Bogside. Smoke slides out from the chimneys and wanders up into the snowy air. Coal, the acrid sharpness of it, mixed in with the damp, frosty smell of the snow. These smells, coming out of my childhood. They dissolve me somewhere a long way down.

The longer you live away from it, the more Liam's words make sense. But when you're here, inside it, he is wrong because it's real. And so many dead, so many lives eaten by prisons, so many families distorted and maimed.

The hills rise slate blue and snowy behind the city. Above, the thick sky broods, heavy with snow cloud. Whatever I'm looking for, I'm not going to find it here, and my feet might fall off with the cold.

I only go in to get warm.

I'm down from the Walls, and there's the Guildhall ahead of me with BLOODY SUNDAY ENQUIRY on a banner across the front of it. I go in through the entrance, and the man in the glass cubbyhole looks me over and nods me into the hall.

Inside the big doors, there's that table that used to be everywhere — the one you put your handbag on while they went through its contents, the one you dumped your shopping on for them to search. The usual uniformed searcher stands beside it.

"The Enquiry?" she asks me, waving that metal thing with the hoop on the end that screeches if you've a gun or a bomb stuck down your knickers.

I nod, but I'm not at all sure. She smiles a smile so sudden and warm that I feel I can't let her down by changing my mind. She runs the hoop-thing over me and it doesn't shriek, so she says to go on up the stairs and someone at the top will direct me.

I go up the carved and polished staircase, feeling way too damp and scruffy to be in here at all. The man at the top agrees, for he takes one look and he knows right away I'm no lawyer.

"Up those stairs," he says, waving his hand at a door that's marked PUBLIC GALLERY.

There's a heavy old wooden door, and I pull on it and it creaks slowly open. There are more stairs ahead, only these are narrow and steep, not at all like the wide, gracious staircase I've just ascended. I want to turn then and run, but some stubbornness comes upon me so I don't. They open onto a scatter of people sitting in steeply raked rows in the shadows. It's a gallery, high up under the roof, and away down below is the Guildhall and the Enquiry. I stand till my eyes have adjusted, and then I slide in and sit down.

Two big screens are suspended in front of me. On the first you can see the witness close up, while the other one shows the photos and papers the lawyers are discussing. I peer over the balustrade. They've cleared out the whole of the floor of the Guildhall and set it up so it looks like a courtroom or maybe a stock exchange.

I concentrate and begin to get the hang of it. The witness giving evidence is finishing what he's been saying, and the man who seems to be in charge of the show is asking the lawyers if they've any more questions for him. No one does. The head man tells the witness he can go. He goes. The next one comes in and sits in the witness seat, and I see him away down below but also up on the screen there in front of my nose.

This next man is called Sheehan, and he looks about sixty — maybe even seventy — and he takes his time about sitting down.

The head man waits till he's settled, then says in this gentle, dead-polite voice that he thinks perhaps Mr. Sheehan may have some objection to taking the oath?

Mr. Sheehan looks surprised. "No," he says, "I've no objection." Then he gives out the oath in a ringing voice that is unafraid. It seems he's a farmer and he's only been on two marches in his whole life, but one of them was the civil rights march on Bloody Sunday.

I sneak a look round. The public gallery is half empty. I feel stubborn and awkward, I know that my tribe didn't suffer, I haven't the right to be here, sitting with those who did.

I don't care, I decide. I'll sit it out. I won't connive as my father did. I want no more secrets and exclusions.

Then I look up at the carved wooden ceiling with its long hanging lights and I look across at the tall stained-glass windows and I look down into the body of the hall stuffed with lawyers and computers and I feel a sort of hatred for it all. For the new world of technology and suave privilege and for the old grandiose world of stubborn, entrenched possession, a world that looked after its own but only just; and only in return for their violent loyalty, for their ongoing savage willingness to make the Croppies lie down.

And there in the middle of it all is this stubborn old man, this farmer who might be a neighbour of mine at home.

He begins his story, tells how he ran with the crowd from the Saracens, tells about fear and crouching and waiting and not knowing where to run to next that's away from the shooting.

Then he tells how he runs doubled over and gets to this place and hunkers down in fear of his life and beside him's this man that he knows.

"My son Willie's lying down there," the man says to him. "He's dead as a maggot, they shot him."

When they call a five-minute break for the stenographers, I take up my coat and walk out. I head back over the ring road, for I want the new walkway again, though the river's running dark and choppy with waves. And there are the black shags, still fishing away, and the rain comes, stinging my face with half-formed sleet, and I feel about as homeless as ever I've felt and belonging nowhere, nor in either tribe, and knowing there's no one I can speak to, neither in the North nor in the South, for everyone here has ground to defend and everyone there is too angered and shamed by this long, grim drag back into the past.

I think of the man who said that about his son being dead as a maggot, and I wonder where he is now and what state his heart's in.

I think of the squirm of maggots, their undeadness, yet they are death itself, they are all that is mortal of us exploding into maggot, consuming itself with itself. The man was right, his words exact, his poor son dead as a maggot.

I think of myself, seven years old at the time. Something had happened, I'd known that, but it happened to them, not to us, I remembered low voices around me speaking of "just deserts." Then I think how I was neither an adult when these Troubles began, nor a child born into them and knowing nothing else. All I knew was this blurred thing — a time of peace bleeding into a time of violence, a homelessness even within time.

They say home is where the heart is, but surely to God the heart can be where the home is, the heart can be at home in homelessness?

And I know I am back here now, not just for my mother as I'd told myself, but because of this terrible need in me to join up the island, to know oneness instead of division, for only then can I live somewhere — North or South — and call it home.

And maybe there's Liam in there too. Maybe that nurse and my mother were right, and I haven't quite won through yet.

But I know now what Mr. Sheehan has seen and heard, so I know that my only way forward is further forward into homelessness, for only in homelessness can we dwell on this island on a deeper level than the political, on the level of life and of the heart.

To live without identity, except as a human being.

Because life, the birth-and-death essence of life, is flow, not security. It cuts all ground from beneath our feet, it picks us up and carries us where it will until at the last it dumps us down into death. And only in living beyond the tribe, in identifying beyond the nation-state — its ruthless, proud identity — is there room for the heart, where lies freedom.

———— ∞ ————

And that's that, once I've felt all that there's nothing left to feel, I'm emptied out and near dead with exhaustion. I have to get something to eat, I think, I can't even look for a bus or a taxi, much less walk back to Brian and Anne's in the freezing cold.

The dusk is seeping up out of the pavements, the cars stream past with their headlights on, the traffic lights up ahead are an orange stain. I lean myself on the wall at the entrance to Tesco's. I don't remember leaving the river or crossing the ring road, I don't know how I've got here or how I'm going to get myself back all that way over the bridge to the Waterside. I look through the windows at the lit shop. I can't go in, and I can't go on.

All I can think of is Anne's spotless kitchen and Anne making tea for me, telling me everything will be alright.

I go on standing there, blankly watching. The day is changing to four-o'-clock night, the shoppers are losing heart, the old ones are scuttling off home to their hearths, heads down, collars held tight.

Then a hand is pulling the sleeve of my coat, and someone is saying my name. I turn and look into the face of a stranger. A woman, no older than I am, her face white, the dye growing out of her hair, the reek of cigarette smoke on her coat.

"Joanne sez you're a Derry woman. She sez yer ma is only after dying yesterday, God rest her. Joanne's over there, she sez not to bother you, but it's not for myself I'm askin'; I wouldn't ever ask for myself, it's for the wean —"

I stare at her. She wants something, but I don't know what.

"Joanne sez to leave you be, but I know well you'll not refuse me. The poor wee wean's tormented."

I don't know what to do, so I look away. Joanne is standing on the pavement on the other side of the road. She has on a heavy dark coat, and her eyes are upon me, begging me not to mind.

I understand. Joanne has talked about her cut wrist, and now this woman wants a cure for a child. I turn back to face her. She's still holding tight to my sleeve.

"Joanne's my sister-in-law, so she is. She told us about what you did in the hospital. The doctors have give up, so they have, but the poor wee wean cries day and night, it has him tormented. . . ." She drags with her free arm, pulling a child out from where he's hiding behind her coat. She lets go of my sleeve, puts her hand under his chin, and lifts up the face for me to see. The child wears a cotton hat pulled down low, a woolly hat over it, a cotton scarf loose at his neck. He's about two years old, and his face is scaly and red, the skin all broken and flaking.

As soon as she lets go my sleeve I have to stop myself running. I feel the panic rise up, a black wave of fear of herself and the child, and she senses it, for she grabs me tight by the arm again. Joanne has crossed over the road and stands only yards away on the pavement, not knowing what to do. The child starts to cry, not a roar but a whinge, an awful dragging whinge that tears at your nerves. The mother lifts him. He squirms and fights in her arms, the whinge growing louder. There's no way out.

"Give me the wean." I speak without knowing I'm going to. The woman gives me the child, and he struggles and kicks. I hold on. He quietens. I wait till he's still then put one hand onto his forehead. I don't want to do this; I want them to go away and leave me alone, but the emptiness is there.

I hand the child back to his mother. He snuggles down into her arms, puts his head on her shoulder, closes his eyes, and sleeps. Gently, her hand just touches his hair, then she fumbles around for her bag, very careful not to disturb him. I shake my head and walk away.

Joanne's quick steps run behind me. I want to run myself, but I can't.

"Where are you for?" she asks when she catches me up.

I tell her.

She walks me to William Street, finds a taxi who'll take me, pays my fare in advance, and hands me in.

Epilogue

here's a stand of tulips in the corner of the yard that blooms every year. You'd think they were planned — their colour against the old wall — but it wasn't so, it was only a stray bulb that Liam let fall on his way to somewhere else.

It lay on its side in the rain then it put out some roots, and they clamped themselves into the earth. I found it like that, and its sorry tenacity pulled from me some instinct of sympathy or recognition. I scooped out a hole, circled the planting with stones, left it alone.

This spring there were thirteen heads, red and gold like a carousel, all out at the one time, bumping softly against one another whenever the wind blew. Sometimes I squatted down beside them. I listened till I nearly thought I heard them chime.

My mother died more than a year ago now, but somehow it doesn't seem that long, for so much has happened since.

Liam had left for Derry as soon as I'd put the phone down. He'd lifted the children out of their beds, bundled them into their clothes, thrown some blankets into the car, and set off. They'd arrived the next morning, but I wasn't there, I'd already gone looking for whatever it was that my father's secret might mean for me.

Liam said that they'd walked in on Brian, giving out about me, but

360

Anne had cooked breakfast and Brian had made an effort and calmed himself down. He'd managed a civil welcome, and after that everything sort of fell into place.

Anne phones every other week or I phone her. She's back at work teaching now. It seems she'd had a sabbatical when my mother took sick, but she used it all up on minding her till she died.

They're coming down in July, all four of them. Anne says the girls aren't saying much to their friends, but they're dead excited inside. She is as well, she tells me. She looks at the map and she can't believe that she's coming this far South.

We're alright, Liam and I. We're more careful with each other but also more tender. Some of the joy has gone, but there's a respect and a trust that wasn't there before.

Dermot hanged himself a bare six months after Derry. He'd worked it all out, waited till Liam was off at an opening in Dublin, then phoned his mobile and left a message telling Liam to call at the studio when he got home. He said to bring his spare keys and the Guards but on no account to come in.

The note he left said he'd never be good enough as a painter. And he couldn't kick the drink, so he'd never be any good as a father either. And he knew he was copping out, but he couldn't go on.

I phoned Catherine with the news then got into the car right away and went to see her. I didn't get lost this time, I knew the way, for I went there often. Liam had made it clear that he didn't want her around, and I'd made it equally clear that I'd found her again and I wasn't prepared to lose her. If he wanted to go on feeling guilty, I said, that was his affair.

When I drove through the gates she was standing there waiting. I got out of the car, and her face went from blank to broken. Then she clung to me and wept, just as Liam had done.

"Where's Danny?" I asked her when she was calmer.

"Sleeping."

"Go and get him and pack a few things. You're coming home with me."

"Liam . . . ?"

"Liam will want to see you. You and Liam were Dermot's closest friends —"

She started to heave again, so I put my arm round her shoulders and steered her in.

Marie fell to bits after that, so Catherine and Liam had to pull together for Dermot's sake, and to everyone's surprise things are working out well.

It's helped Liam's guilt about Dermot. And overnight Catherine began to take Danny seriously, which meant making space for his half-brothers as well.

Catherine and Danny come often now, as do Marie's two sons; many's the time I've five children sleeping under my roof and that's alright by me. People talk, but I take no notice. What do I care? They're still there in the morning, awaiting my hands when I open the door.

When first I came here I looked but I hardly saw, I was too far away still, I had to wait for the pictures I carried inside me to fade so the ones that I saw all around me could colour and glow in their place. In those early days I must have been like the tulip before it got planted — hanging in there, but only just.

When you lose your home the first time you don't lose your yearning or your belonging, but when you go back and it won't take you in, there's the loss of all those feelings you've cherished for years.

It can't take you in, for you're not who you were anymore — you're of somewhere else. Then you go back to your "somewhere else" and you find that you don't belong there either. It's where you live —

perhaps where you love — but you don't belong the way you belonged to your first place, you don't belong the way that the folk who have never left belong. So then you don't know who you are or how you should be.

I'm thinking now that maybe when you reach that point you can't be anyone else but yourself, just as the tulips flower red and gold, year after year, and they'd still flower red and gold in another place, though they might not look so well nor bloom so free.

Glossary

baby grow   All-in-one garment for small babies

boreen   Small road

Celtic Tiger   Name given to the economic boom that has transformed Ireland in recent years

chancer   Man or woman who lives out of the fluff in his or her pocket

City and Guilds   Certificate of competence issued to those practising trade or craft skills

Club bar   Wrapped chocolate biscuit-bar

craic   Informal entertainment, jokes, wit

Croppies   Rebels; refers to the short, cropped hair favoured by the 1798 insurgents; and in Northern Ireland, a general derogatory term for Catholics. "We'll fight for our country, our king and our crown / And make all the traitors and croppies lie down" (popular ballad, c. 1798)

delph   Dishes, china

eejit   Idiot

farl   Portion of a circular griddle scone

fecker   A euphemism for *fucker*, but the original meaning was thief or "one who stole," from the verb *to feck*; can be used in polite company

flex   Length of insulated electrical cable used to connect an electrical appliance to a socket

Foyle   The river that enters Lough Foyle at Derry

foundered   Frozen

Glen   A housing estate on the Cityside of Derry

Guards   Police, from *Garda Síochána*

grafter   Hard worker

grah   Attraction to, affection for, love of

het up   Upset, in a state

juke   Look

kitted   Dressed

Lambeg drum   Enormous drum, used on Orange Marches

Lady Muck   An expression meaning someone who thinks a lot of herself

lep/lepping   Words commonly used in Ireland meaning leap or leaping

Macmillan nurse   Nurse specially trained in care of the dying

naff   Lacking sophistication, coolness, or style

nixer   Work undertaken outside of normal paid employment and usually clandestinely

optics   Spirit measures behind the bar in a pub

press   Cupboard

rashers   Slices of fried bacon

red up   Finished, done

ring road   Road that goes round or bypasses a town

rota   List of people who will take turns at some task

RUC Royal Ulster Constabulary; now called the PSNI (Police Service of Northern Ireland)

Saracens Armoured personnel carriers used by the British Army

scaldy Bald-head

squash Sugary drink, e.g., lemonade

Taig/Tague/Teig/Teague From the Irish word *Tadhg*, meaning "poet" or "fool"; in Ulster, a term of disparagement for Roman Catholics

tat Low-quality or tasteless material or goods

thole Put up with, endure

toe rag An insult, meaning a bit of cloth only good enough to bind your feet with

togs Swimsuit

tray bake Sweet confection cooked on a baking tray and then cut into slices or squares

Twelfth Holiday Fortnight's holiday taken after the twelfth of July commemorating the Protestant victory at the Battle of the Boyne in 1690

UDA Ulster Defence Association, a Protestant paramilitary organisation

Ulster fry Eggs, rashers, potato bread, sausages, black and white puddings

ward sister Nurse in charge of a ward in a hospital

wean Derry word for child

wrong-foot To make out someone else is in the wrong when you know all the time that the fault is yours

Acknowledgments

I would like to thank the Château de Lavigny, Switzerland, the Hawthornden International Writers Retreat, Scotland, and the Heinrich Böll Cottage, Achill Island, for awarding me residencies which were invaluable to me in the writing of this novel.

The Tyrone Guthrie Centre at Annaghmakerrig provided sure refuge when I needed an uninterrupted space to work in. My deep thanks to the director, Sheila Pratschke, and to all her staff for their unfailing kindness and empathy.

In 2001 I was awarded a writing residency at the Verbal Arts Centre, Derry, which was funded by the Arts Council of Northern Ireland and by the Arts Council of Ireland. Without this residency I could not have written this novel, and I wish to thank both arts councils and all the staff of the centre itself. Also Dick Sinclair, who gave me invaluable gifts of friendship, information, and insight, as did Frances McEvoy. Margaret Fleming and Liz England of the oncology unit at Altnagelvin Hospital answered my questions with care and humanity, and Stella Burnside made it possible for me to spend time in the unit.

The Bird Woman had many readers at draft stage, to all of whom I am greatly indebted. These include my mother, Dorothy Jolley, who read and reread with unfailing patience and encouragement. Colette Bryce and Sinéad Morrissey — both outstandingly talented poets — read and advised and helped me to keep my nerve, while Ellen Hinsey (another outstandingly talented poet) always seemed to phone from Paris at exactly the right moment. To Yvonne Boyle, Carmel Cummins, Paddy Jolley, Olivia O'Leary, Dorothea Linder, Harvey Stahl, Katie Hardie, and Dr. Rosaleen Jolley, my thanks for their reading and overview.

Thanks to all at Little, Brown, and more thanks to Shannon Langone for her meticulous and insightful copyedit. Thanks also to the following, all of whom helped me in ways great and small and not always explicitly with the text: Joan Ryan, Carolyn Vernon, Frances Barco, Fintan Ryan, Val and Marian Lonergan, Olivia Goodwillie, Brenda Ward, Helen Parry-Jones, Richard Bull, and Claire Fletcher. And last but not least, my thanks go to Lowry Wasson, who once made the most wonderful giant teapots.

The section on the death of Ellen's mother is dedicated to the memory of Maura McNally.

About the Author

Kerry Hardie was born in 1951, went to school in Bangor, Northern Ireland, and read English literature at York University. In the seventies she worked for the BBC in Belfast and for the Arts Council of Northern Ireland. She is the author of one previous novel, *A Winter Marriage*, and four books of poetry. She lives in County Kilkenny with her husband, Sean.